The LAST
PARADISE

Di
MORRISSEY

The LAST
PARADISE

PAN
Pan Macmillan Australia

First published 2019 in Macmillan by Pan Macmillan Australia Pty Ltd
This Pan edition published 2020 by Pan Macmillan Australia Pty Ltd
1 Market Street, Sydney, New South Wales, Australia, 2000

Reprinted 2021, 2022

A catalogue record for this
book is available from the
National Library of Australia

Typeset in Sabon by Post Pre-press Group
Printed by IVE

Image in Prologue by Albert Falzon, courtesy of photographer.
Images in Chapters 1, 2, 4, 6, 7, 8, 9, 10, 11 and Epilogue from Shutterstock.
Image in Chapter 3 courtesy of author.
Image in Chapter 5 by George Muskens, courtesy of photographer.
Wayang puppet dinkus: Berkah Icon/Shutterstock.

To K'tut Tantri.

*And to her friends, (the late) Sandra Paul,
Michael Paul and Professor Tim Lindsey.*

*And to my dear friends of long standing,
George Muskens, Gary Elton and Adi
Putra, for their friendship and help.*

Acknowledgements

My love and thanks to stalwart, loving Boris, whose care, loyalty and thoughtful support make each day easier and happier!

My wonderful family, Gabrielle, Nick, Mimi and the grandchildren who delight my days – Sonoma, Everton, Bodhi and Ulani.

So many wonderful friends, old and new, who have Been There (through a miserable marriage and proved we can survive!), and those who knew Bali in the early days.

Thanks Albe Falzon, Peter Thomas, Pam Spicer.

Thanks to friends Sarah Hawthorne and Joan Frare, for sharing.

Also, thanks to lawyers Anna Kerr and Wendy Broun.

At Pan Macmillan thanks to my publisher, Ross Gibb, also Tracey Cheetham, Georgia Douglas, Katie Crawford, Danielle Walker and Hannah Membrey.

Hugs to my friend and editor, Bernadette Foley. Brianne Collins, thank you for your friendship and attention to detail! Also hugs to long-time friend, Jane Novak. Best buddy award goes to Jeff Balsmeyer (with the last hug)!

Suggested reading and extracts

- *The Romance of K'tut Tantri and Indonesia* by Prof. Timothy Lindsey, Oxford University Press, 1997.
- *Bali – A Paradise Created* by Prof. Adrian Vickers, first published by Penguin Australia, 1989; updated by Tuttle Publishing, 2012.

Thank you, Tim and Adrian, for answering my questions!

There are numerous fascinating books on old Bali that fill in more background of the post-colonial era BT (before tourism). Some include *Island of Bali* by Miguel Covarrubias; *Dancing Out of Bali* by John Coast; *The Last Paradise* by Hickman Powell; *A House in Bali* by Colin McPhee; and *Bali, Heaven and Hell* by Phil Jarratt.

Abridged extracts from *Revolt in Paradise* by K'tut Tantri (originally published by Harper, New York, 1960) are used by kind permission of Michael Paul and the Estate of the Late K'tut Tantri:

- Extract on pages 124–125: from Part 1, Chapter 1, 'The Tree', abridged.
- Extract on pages 160–165: from Part 1, Chapter 2, 'Pito', abridged.
- Extract on pages 172–179: from Part 1, Chapter 5, 'The Palace, the Rajah and the Prince', Chapter 6, 'Fourth Born', Chapter 12, 'Among the People of the Kampongs', Chapter 13, 'A Dream Takes Shape' and Chapter 14, 'Sound of the Sea', abridged.

- Extract on pages 225–232: from Part 2, Chapter 1, 'The Japanese Take Over' and Chapter 2, 'I Join the Resistance', abridged.
- Extract on pages 275–280: from Part 2, Chapter 3, 'A Prisoner of the Japanese', Chapter 4, 'Some Refinements of Torture' and Chapter 6, 'The Sight of Freedom', abridged.
- Extract on page 289–293: from Part 3, Chapter 2, 'I Cast My Lot In with the Revolution' and Chapter 3, 'The British Are Surprised – And So Am I', abridged.

The extracts are reproduced with the original American spelling. Small corrections of typographical errors or to make allowances for changes in language have been made.

Prologue

GRACE STOOD AT THE window staring into the late summer garden of neat lawns and beds of heavy headed roses about to rain petals. The roses would need pruning soon.

She almost smiled. Since when did she care, or even know anything about pruning roses?

Since she'd married a successful businessman, moved into an elegant house with a sprawling garden, and become mummy to adorable Daisy, that's when.

Their home in Dural was the last house in the street, next to an empty field that had become an informal local park. The area had once been the end of the line, on the rural fringes of Sydney. It was where homes were estates, and locals kept horses; the remnants of pastoral wealth still on display.

What was it her mother had said when she'd first seen this house? 'You've done well, Gracie. I'm happy for you.'

But sometimes Grace missed the buzz of the city. Her favourite café on the corner, a quick meal with friends and colleagues, recognising familiar faces and eccentric locals from the urban neighbourhood. Entertaining in her small Paddington apartment.

Now she lived in a quiet street of nice neighbours, where groomed dogs with expensive accessories were walked on fancy leashes. Voices were never raised and children were rarely heard, unless they were splashing in a pool. On the weekend you might catch the *thwack* of tennis ball meeting racquet, and occasional laughter and the clink of glasses from a patio in the late afternoon.

Grace poured herself a glass of mineral water and debated whether she should call her mother to see how Daisy was, but resisted the urge. After all, Daisy was only away overnight. If Grace called too often her mother thought she was checking up on her.

She heard the car in the driveway, then the sound of the door opening and closing as Lawrence came in and went straight to his office.

'Hey, Lawrence, you're not working, are you?' She poked her head around the door. 'Don't forget we're going to dinner tonight at the Robinsons'.'

He didn't look up straight away, and it struck her that his hair was thinning on top. She knew he had the hairdresser put a colour rinse through it regularly to hide his greying temples, although she wondered why he bothered now he was only a few years away from fifty. He was also looking a bit pudgy these days, though, being tall, he carried it well. He just never did any kind of exercise other than walking to his car and the occasional game of tennis, she thought.

'Hi,' he said, glancing up and smiling at her. 'Is Daisy with your mother?'

'Yes. I thought it was better than getting a babysitter.' Daisy adored her grandmother, who lived alone in her home on a clifftop overlooking the beach. Grace knew her mother and Daisy would go down to the surf first thing in the morning for a swim. 'You promised to take me out for a fancy breakfast tomorrow, remember?' Grace leaned against the door frame and crossed her arms.

'Of course. I'm looking forward to it.' He pushed his laptop aside but continued sifting through the papers on his desk, putting them in the briefcase she'd given him.

'We should leave soon. Unless you want a sundowner before we go? They're only a few blocks away.'

'Thanks, but I'll wait till we get there. Did you get the champagne for them?'

'It's in the fridge. I couldn't find the one you wanted, but the one I bought is very good apparently.'

'Are you sure?'

'The guy in the bottle shop went on and on about it. It's from 2012. Pierre someone and Sons. Do you really think the Robinsons will know a superior from a mediocre?'

'Yes, actually, I do. Give me ten minutes or so to finish off here and get ready, and then we can go.'

He seemed a little distracted so she straightened up, quietly closed the door and went out onto the patio to watch the sunset. Typical Lawrence, wanting to spend money on an expensive bottle of champagne the Robinsons might not even care about. Grace was sure they would be just as happy to share cheap bubbles with friends. Socialising was all about friendship as far as

Grace was concerned, while for Lawrence, it was about making an impression. Or as her best friend Melanie had once said, 'Lawrence always has to big-note himself. He just can't help it.'

Melanie made no bones about the fact she didn't like Lawrence. And the feeling was mutual. Grace knew that most of her friends avoided Lawrence, but Mel was the only one who'd told her bluntly that she should never have married him. And, more and more lately, Grace was wondering the same thing.

They'd been married seven years, after a whirlwind courtship. She'd met him at a cocktail party for movers and shakers in the business world after she'd done an advertising campaign for a big, newly merged financial institution. He was English, with an Australian-born mother who'd lived in England most of her life. Lawrence had come to Australia to go to university and stayed. When Grace met him, he'd recently come out of a long relationship, and he'd told her he wanted to settle down and start a family.

Grace had been on the cusp of travelling, looking for a job overseas, but Lawrence had swept her off her feet, taking her on luxurious holidays and surprising her with expensive gifts. He'd proposed after six months, with a very large Bvlgari diamond ring. He had been working on a major contract at the time and, if it came through, he'd suggested that they could live in Italy for a year or so. 'Then you can choose to work or not. Or just take assignments if you want to, not because you have to,' he'd said.

She was thirty at the time and suddenly she'd been able to see her life pattern: being a mum and working when she wanted. Come her forties she'd have kids in school and could concentrate on a career in visual advertising, finish her film and video production course, maybe start her own company. Well, it had all seemed very appealing. There was a lot to be said for a doting, older, well-to-do husband, she'd thought.

Her mother, Tina, had agreed, if not too enthusiastically. She confessed she would have been happier if Grace had chosen someone like the boys she'd gone out with when she was growing up on the Northern Beaches.

'They might look like surf bums,' Tina had said to her once, 'but some of those lads have done very well for themselves. Marty Davidson, who won all those Bells Beach championships, has his own law firm now. He still surfs here every weekend.'

'Mum, you're such an old surfer chick.' Grace had laughed. 'You've never got over your wild hippy times in Bali.' Tina had spent some time in Bali in the seventies, well before it was the tourist mecca it had since become. She spoke about it often as one of the best times of her life.

Tina had given her a quick smile. 'Yep, Kuta back then was something else!'

So Grace had married Lawrence and looked forward to the sparkling future she pictured for them. However, the big contract Lawrence had anticipated didn't pan out, and Italy was off the cards. Perhaps it had always been a pipe dream, Grace thought. Anyway, by then, Lawrence had been very keen for them to have a baby.

Out on the patio, Grace checked her watch. Just as she was thinking about pouring herself a glass of wine, Lawrence called out to her. 'You ready?'

'I'll grab my bag.' She shut the French doors and turned the key. 'Is everything locked up?'

'Yes. I've checked. You look nice.'

She smiled. Lawrence had a habit of suddenly looking at her as if he hadn't noticed her for a while, despite them sharing a house. A home. A life. 'Thanks, darling.' She'd been told often enough that she was pretty, with her naturally sun-streaked blonde hair, tanned skin and svelte figure. And when she was with Daisy, a tiny replica with bouncy blonde curls and a sunny nature, people often remarked that they should be the ones in the TV and magazine ads that Grace created.

Impulsively she gave Lawrence a hug, although he didn't hug her back. She'd got used to him not being as affectionate as she was, but sometimes, especially lately, she felt he was pushing her away. She pressed herself against his solid body. How long had it been since they'd made love?

If she were honest, her relationship with her husband was wearing her down. Lawrence could be difficult – no, actually nasty. Spiteful. But then, was that the trade-off for having a darling daughter, a comfortable lifestyle, a nice home in a good area? Could she be happy with a husband who lavished gifts on her instead of affection and fun? The thought suddenly made her feel cheap and avaricious.

In the past, she'd always fallen for the sweet guys who had nothing. She liked to think that she was generous and thoughtful towards other people. But as she stepped back from the embrace and saw the emotionless look on her husband's face she wondered, had she traded genuine unconditional love for security? Was it too late to do something about it?

Lawrence turned away. 'I'll get the champagne.'

As he slipped the bottle into the leather wine cooler, she noticed he'd changed his shirt, and was wearing the peachy-pink Lanvin she'd bought him. He patted his coat pocket. 'Right, I've got the keys.'

'It's only a couple of blocks. Let's walk, it's such a nice evening. Do us good,' she suggested.

'Me, you mean.' She had been gently nagging him to exercise. 'I'd prefer to drive. My sprained ankle from tennis still hasn't healed.'

'Oh, too bad. You are such a killer on the court,' she teased. 'You really do play to win,' she added, echoing something he'd once said to her.

'I do, darling, and why not?' he said lightly. 'Okay, let's go.'

Grace pulled the front door closed, leaving the light on outside. The air was fragrant with roses as she got into the passenger seat of Lawrence's Mercedes. Her feet bumped against his briefcase, which sat in the footwell.

'Why are we taking your car?' They usually used Grace's when they went out locally.

'I left it out the front so I thought it was easiest. Is that okay?' he asked, raising an eyebrow.

'Yes, sure, that's fine. You're the designated driver.' Grace smiled at him.

Turning out of their street, Lawrence drove past a bush block where a stand of gum trees almost obscured the view of the big homes that had been built in the 1970s and eighties.

'What's that on the road? Lawrence, stop! It's a koala!'

As he pulled over, the young koala waddled towards the trees.

'Oh, he's adorable. Let me take a photo for Daisy.'

'They're around all the time,' Lawrence said, a hint of annoyance in his voice.

But Grace jumped from the car and lifted her phone to snap a photo, saying quietly, 'Where're your mumma and papa, little fellow?'

'Hurry up, Grace. We're running late.'

'It's okay. How cute is this little guy? I hope people drive carefully round here at night.'

'No one goes out at night here. This is the 'burbs. Country style,' Lawrence said as Grace scrambled back in and the car glided forward.

'You've always been a city boy,' said Grace. 'Do you miss it?'

'And you're a water baby. Do you miss the beach?' he countered.

'Well, Mum's there so I still have a connection to it. But it's such a trek into the city from the Northern Beaches.'

'You can say that again. Okay, so who else is coming tonight?'

'Just the Robinsons and some of their neighbours. You said you wanted to get to know George Ashton.'

'The bank guy? Yes. Just don't leave me stranded with Holly Ambrose and that husband of hers. I don't give a shit about soccer and swimming and all the sports stuff they talk about.'

'Okay.' She didn't bother to argue with him. Lawrence was intolerant of subjects he had no interest in and people who he perceived to bring no value to his world. But she liked Holly, and her husband Roger did so much for the sports teams at Daisy's school.

Lawrence pulled up and parked in front of a white, ranch-style house with a basketball hoop on the garage, a trampoline to one side, and two small bicycles lying on the front lawn.

'There's Holly now,' Grace said, waving to her as she got out of the car.

*

The evening felt long. Grace had hoped they might get home early but for once Lawrence seemed in no hurry to leave. He rarely drank, but was nursing a glass of red, probing George Ashton for his views about bank rates and where certain investments were headed. George must have turned out to be a useful contact for him, Grace thought.

Finally, the other guests started to stand up. Grace carried some glasses into the kitchen and found Holly there, stacking the dishwasher. Holly glanced up and smiled. 'Been lovely to see you guys. You must come over. Bring Daisy to use the pool any time. Roger can teach her to dive properly.'

'Thanks, Holly, we'd love that. Daisy can swim pretty well now, but a few tips would be great.' It was a shame, Grace thought, that Lawrence would never want to take Daisy round to the Ambroses' place, but she made a mental note to do so herself. She and Lawrence didn't have a pool and it had been such a hot summer.

Heading out of the kitchen, Grace called to Lawrence that they should be leaving. She picked up her bag and walked with Holly to the front door, where the Robinsons were saying goodbye to their other guests.

Suddenly, they heard the thunderous boom of an explosion. The night sky lit up with a bright orange glow. They all stared in horror as a crackling red fireball erupted into the air a few streets away. Then they all spoke at once.

'What the hell was that?'

'Where is it?'

'It's not that gas storage place, is it?'

'No, wrong direction . . .'

Grace's shriek was ear-splitting. 'It's near our place! Lawrence!'

Lawrence swore as he hurried to the door where they all stood, stunned, looking into the distance.

'Where is it?' cried Grace. 'Oh, God no. I think the fire's in our street!' She screamed again and broke into a run.

'It can't be! Grace, get in the car, come back here!' shouted Lawrence.

Grace was propelled by fear, horror and disbelief. Her mind seemed frozen as she sprinted towards their home.

Lawrence jumped in the car and caught up to her.

'Jump in, Grace, for God's sake,' he called.

She was driven by some wild terror. For a moment or two her husband drove beside her, begging her to stop and get in. But she was running as if her life depended on it.

Lawrence gunned the car and sped ahead.

By the time she reached her street, the full horror had begun to dawn on her. Their house was alight, a wall of leaping orange flames and smoke. She could hear glass breaking and timber crashing.

'Oh, my God, no, no, no . . .' she panted as she saw Lawrence's silhouette and the dark shapes of other figures as they came up and clustered around him.

The flames were higher and hotter now, and she picked up the strong, searing smell of smoke.

She had fallen into some unreal, terrible nightmare. Everything moved in slow motion. She felt hands on her arms, holding her back, and heard voices bouncing around her, as if she were in an echo chamber. Her own wailing voice sounded far away, drowned out by the noises that would continue to haunt her in the nights to come. The cracking and groaning as their home, their beautiful house, disintegrated.

It was impossible to take in that everything she owned and treasured from her past and present was being swallowed in this licking orange inferno of heavy smoke and searing heat.

Sirens wailed. People held her. She couldn't see Lawrence.

'Where's my husband?' she screamed.

A man in orange overalls and a helmet put his hands on her shoulders. 'Is anyone else inside?'

'Where's Lawrence? Stop him . . .'

'He's here, it's all right, Grace,' came the shaking voice of a neighbour, who was holding her back.

More sirens, more people hosing down nearby houses. The smell, oh the smell.

Then Lawrence was beside her, pulling her to him, trying to turn her face away from the sight of their world imploding.

'Don't look,' he shouted at her.

I

SITTING ON THE VERANDAH, Grace watched her mother playing with Daisy in the garden of Tina's home at Bilgola Beach. The house overlooked the beach Grace had known since she was Daisy's age and was, now that her own house lay in ruins, the place where she felt most at home in all the world.

They'd stayed at her mother's since the night of the fire and, while several days had passed, Grace still hadn't been back to see what was left, if anything, of their home. Lawrence had done everything; dealing with the police at first and now with the insurance people.

Daisy was anxious and upset, sensing all the upheaval and seeing her mother so distressed. She knew that something was wrong and seemed to be becoming more unsettled

13

every day. The day after the fire, Lawrence had bought them some new clothes and a few basics – all impractical and not the things they needed or wanted – and when he'd given Daisy a pile of new toys, she'd burst into tears. She wanted her old, well-loved toys and couldn't understand what was going on. Grace quietly comforted her, saying they'd go somewhere special with Nana to find some new toys. Tina had offered to explain to Daisy about the fire but Grace had shaken her head. She'd tell Daisy herself when she found the strength.

Grace knew she'd have to dig herself out of the dark cocoon she had folded herself into, and face reality. She hadn't returned any of the dozens of messages on her phone. Her work on the campaign for the Lifesaving Association was falling behind. They wanted a series of ads to air on TV leading up to next summer. She had been enthusiastic and deeply involved in the Safe Water campaign, and she'd found a cameraman who'd shot some stunning drone footage as well as dramatic under-water visuals of the effects of a powerful rip. She loved her work and this job had been going so well. Until now.

She heard Lawrence's car pull up and went out to meet him. He had chosen to stay in a hotel in the city since the fire, where he could be close to his work as well as on hand in case the insurance agents needed him to go with them to the house. It made sense – it was a long commute to the Northern Beaches – but his absence made everything seem even more surreal than it already was. And Lawrence had been so busy, they'd hardly even talked on the phone. He looked tired and drawn, but he smiled at her as he climbed out of the car. He reached into the back seat and pulled out a cat carrier, out of which he lifted a grey cat, which he carefully handed to Grace as she rushed forward.

She buried her face in the animal's soft fur and sobbed. 'Oh, Sparkle. You escaped! This is a good sign.' She looked hopefully at Lawrence. 'What're the insurance people saying?'

'Write-off,' he said in a hoarse voice.

'What do you mean?' cried Grace.

'Nothing could survive that heat and smoke damage. Seems there was some sort of explosion. Gas maybe. They've got inspectors there now.'

Stricken-faced, Grace stared at him. 'Was anything saved?'

He shrugged. 'They're not sure yet, but it doesn't look like it. Maybe a few small things. There wasn't much they could do. Stopped it spreading, at least.' He walked ahead and sat down on one of the verandah chairs.

'Daisy wants her Princess Piglet.' It sounded petty, but suddenly her daughter's favourite toy seemed valuable and important. Grace sank into a chair, stroking the beloved family cat.

'Buy her another one. You can't go looking for anything there, it's too dangerous. Although the safe was supposed to be fireproof. Your jewellery might be okay.'

Grace had been thinking of their photos, books, the vinyl records, Princess Piglet.

'So what now?' She looked down at the cat settling on her lap.

'We'll just have to move forward. Can you and Daisy keep staying here with your mother for a few more days while I sort things out? The drive out here takes forever.'

'Is there any way we could move into my Paddington apartment?' asked Grace. It was small, but the apartment Grace's grandmother had left her would make a convenient home in the short-term.

'It's tenanted, remember? On a lease.'

'I know. Just thought it was an option we could explore, if the lease is due to expire soon. The Robinsons said we could stay with them for a couple of weeks. That way, Daisy could still go to school with Harry and see her other friends.'

'Do you really want to live under the same roof as another family? We're not that close and we've only known them for a year or so. Daisy can move schools, she's young.'

Grace bit her tongue. She wanted to say that no matter how young Daisy was, going to her old school with her friends and the teachers she knew was important for her – it would keep some stability in her life. But, as usual, she didn't have the energy to disagree with Lawrence. Often when she made suggestions, he would feign patience and inclusion, but nonetheless would eventually press home his point. At other times when she said something he disagreed with he'd simply lecture her. When she came up with ideas, Lawrence would rarely admit that they were sensible and practical. Instead of agreeing with her he'd just get annoyed. He was so disparaging that she'd stopped trying a long time ago.

Grace hated to acknowledge it, but she could see how she'd lost confidence in herself and her decisions as Lawrence constantly undermined her. God, could she keep on living like this?

'Oh well, I guess not,' she said. The matter of Daisy and the school was settled. Plus, in this case, having Daisy at a school nearby wouldn't be all bad. 'Mum loves having us here and I can leave Daisy with her when I have to go in to the agency. I don't have my laptop and I have no idea yet how many files I lost when it went up in flames.' She paused, biting her lip.

'Can you borrow one? I don't want to make any major purchases till we have the insurance sorted,' said Lawrence.

'I might be able to use a spare one from work and hope that I've saved everything to the Cloud.' She stood up, still holding the cat. 'I'll put some butter on Sparkle's paws. I don't want her to run away.'

*

'When are we going home, Mummy?'

Grace and Daisy were in the bedroom unpacking bags from their trip to the local shops that morning. Grace had bought them both some clothes, toiletries and shoes, the practical basics, and some books for Daisy. She paused and sat with Daisy on the bed, taking her hands.

'Daisy darling, we're staying here at Nana's, just for a while. It's a holiday for us. And for Sparkle, too.'

'Where's Daddy?'

'He's busy at his office, honey.'

'Is he going to our house after work?'

Grace paused, then chose her words carefully. 'No, we won't be going back to our house. You see, it's really badly broken and no one can live in it.'

Daisy's eyes widened and her lip began to tremble. 'Why? And where is Daddy going to live? He can come here to Nana's and share my bed with Sparkle.'

'That's a good idea, honey, and it's lovely of you to think of him.'

A thought seemed to strike Daisy. 'How did our house get broken, Mummy? Where are our things?' Her voice rose in a slight panic.

'Sweetheart, there was a fire. It was an accident; these things sometimes happen. Unfortunately, it was a big fire and our things got burned up. But you know what, we have Sparkle, and Nana, and you, Daddy and I are fine. It's sad to lose precious things, but things can be replaced. What's important is that we have each other. We are all safe and well. It'll be all right, honey . . .' She gathered Daisy in her arms as the little girl burst into tears.

Tina walked in. 'Is everything okay? What's up, Daisy? It's all okay, sweetie.' She sat beside them and stroked Daisy's hair.

'I just told her about the house,' Grace murmured.

'Oh, darling Daisy. Don't you worry. We are all here to look after you.'

'So Princess Piglet got all burned up?' Daisy asked suddenly, pulling away and staring at Grace in horror.

Grace took a deep breath. 'Yes, I think so, honey. Sometimes we lose things we love. And people. But you know what, we never forget them.' She rocked her daughter as she burst into fresh tears.

Tina stood up. 'I'm going to give Sparkle an early supper.' She raised an eyebrow and Grace nodded.

'We'll be okay, Mum.'

*

Grace came into the kitchen as Sparkle was washing her face, tail curled neatly around herself.

'Is Daisy okay?'

'Kind of, but she wants to go and see the house. I don't think that's a good idea.'

'No. I'll take her for a walk down to the beach in a minute. Is Lawrence coming home for dinner tonight?' Tina asked. 'Be reassuring for Daisy if we could all eat together.'

But Grace didn't know. She hadn't heard from Lawrence all day.

They ended up eating without Lawrence, who hadn't replied to Grace's text. Grace had to admit that the atmosphere was probably warmer without him there. She knew her mother found Lawrence's company civil if cool, but Tina mainly kept her opinions about her son-in-law to herself. For her part, Grace noticed that she had started to put on a brave front now that she was staying with her mother. Grace didn't criticise Lawrence or complain. She realised that she still wanted it to seem to others, even to her mother, that they had a comfortable lifestyle and a happy relationship. They had a delightful child they adored, both had absorbing jobs and career ambitions: surely that meant there was still hope for them?

But one layer below the surface, Grace was increasingly worried that Lawrence seemed estranged from her and from the rest of his family. His parents lived in England, and he had little contact with them or his sister. Grace had a lot of friends she'd grown up with at the beach, and she and Mel had gone to kindergarten together. Grace and her father were still close after her parents' divorce; he had moved to Perth, but she still saw him whenever she could, at least a couple of times a year.

Since they had left the city to live in their big new home after Daisy was born, Grace didn't seem to catch up with her friends as often as she used to. Melanie had a busy career as a university lecturer, but Grace knew that was not the only reason Mel didn't make the drive out to Dural.

As they finished eating and Daisy ran off to play, Grace's phone pinged with a text. It was from Lawrence.

Reading it, Grace said, 'He's going to be late. He's dealing with all the insurance stuff. He says they need to interview me too.' She put her phone down and sighed.

'Heavens, why? There's nothing suspicious, is there?' said Tina.

'It's routine, apparently.'

'This process could take ages,' Tina said. 'Don't worry, darling, you know you can stay with me as long as you want while you work things out.'

'Thanks, Mum. Thanks for everything.'

'If you want to go anywhere, you can use my car. You've had a terrible shock. Go and see your friends – talking to them might make life seem more normal for you.' Tina looked at her daughter and smiled. 'Do you think you'll start working again soon?'

'Yes, if you'd be able to watch Daisy for a couple of hours now and then. I really have to pull my big water safety project back onto schedule.'

'Take it slowly for the moment. You shouldn't put too much pressure on yourself,' Tina said. 'Don't rush into any plans. And you should decide what you want to do,' she added, with subtle emphasis on the 'you'.

Grace could tell that this was a barb aimed at Lawrence. Her mother never said it directly, but Grace knew that Tina thought Lawrence was too overbearing and that Grace acquiesced to him too much.

She pushed her own thoughts to one side. 'You're right. I can't begin to think of rebuilding at the moment. I'll always be paranoid about something like this happening again,' she said. 'I keep wondering if we caused it somehow. If we did something wrong. It was practically a new house, just six years old.'

'Yes, the surprise gift.' Tina sounded less than pleased about it. After Daisy was born, on Grace's first Mother's Day, Lawrence had surprised her with the keys to the house.

Tina had asked her at the time how she felt about not having any say in where they would live or what their home would be like. She'd spoken with Grace several times about the financial issues she'd had following her divorce from Grace's father, but she'd always been grateful that it had been a reasonably amicable split and she'd been able to keep the family home. Sometimes she thought of selling it, Tina said, as beach property was so valuable, but she loved living there and she had put so much of herself into the house.

Lawrence had tried to talk Tina into downsizing when she'd complained once about the area becoming too built up.

'You're sitting on a goldmine here, Tina. You should grab the opportunity before the Sydney housing market peaks. Sell up and invest the profits. I'm happy to help, if you like.'

But Tina had refused, telling Grace and Lawrence she considered her home to be her life insurance. 'Besides, I'd miss the beach too much.'

'How is Lawrence coping?' Tina asked now. 'He must be upset too. That collection of antique silverware of his must have been valuable.'

'Depends what you call valuable, Mum . . .' Grace's eyes filled with tears.

Tina reached over and took her hand. 'I'm sorry you've lost so many memories. I know how sentimental you are, darling. Have you talked to your dad since the fire?'

'Yes. He's worried. He thinks we should be making plans, moving forward.'

'Honey, you're suffering from shock, even if you don't realise it. It's only been a few days. Take things easy,' Tina said gently.

'I just can't comprehend how life can change overnight.' Grace paused and looked out the window at the beach, trying to hold back tears.

'I suppose it's trite to say it could be worse,' ventured her mother. 'But no one died, no animals died. You, Daisy and Lawrence are okay. I can imagine the huge sense of loss you must be feeling, the loss of a home and the special and precious things you treasured –'

'You're not going to tell me to look on the bright side, are you?' Grace turned and looked at her mother.

Tina hesitated, perhaps unsure if her daughter was going to scream at her or burst into tears. But instead Grace dropped her face in her hands and, shaking her head, started to laugh, slightly hysterically.

Tina got up and pulled Grace to her feet. 'Honey, please . . .'

Grace flung her arms around her mother. 'Oh, Mum. Yes, it's a nightmare. Yes, we'll get through it. I would give anything for it not to have happened.' She paused. 'And it's just that, well, I have this awful feeling.'

'What is it?'

Grace shrugged. 'I don't know. Just that we won't get back to the way things were.'

'Maybe it won't be the same. Maybe there'll be better, but different times ahead,' said Tina, smoothing Grace's hair as she used to do when she was little.

'Lawrence is very stressed and there's nothing I can do to help. He's keeping me at arm's length.'

'You're both in this together, even if he likes to take control of everything, so he must feel badly. It's understandable.'

'Hmm. Well, I don't want him to see me upset. That doesn't help either of us.' Wiping her cheeks with the palms of her hands, Grace walked out onto the verandah. 'Daisy, shall we go for a walk down to the beach?'

*

Lawrence arrived late, after they'd finished washing up the dishes from dinner.

'Sorry. Had to wait for an overseas phone call about a deal and send some emails afterwards.'

'I saved your dinner for you,' said Tina.

'Thanks, Tina. I'm not hungry. Where's Daisy?'

'Grace is giving her a bath.'

Later, when Daisy came to say goodnight to everyone, Lawrence rose and picked her up. 'I'll put her to bed.'

'Her book is on her pillow,' Grace said, wrapping her arms around her husband and child in a gesture of comfort, which he ignored.

When her mother turned on the TV, Grace started making notes for work. She hadn't realised how much time had passed until Tina asked her, 'Is Lawrence all right? You sure he doesn't want some supper?'

'I'll check. He's probably in the bedroom on his computer.'

But Lawrence had fallen asleep beside Daisy, who was curled up, hugging the large teddy bear that had once belonged to Grace.

She left the room, quietly closing the door.

*

The next day, an agent from the insurance company rang and asked if he could come and see Grace.

They sat at the small table on Tina's verandah, the relaxed surroundings doing nothing to help Grace's nerves as she struggled to answer the man's questions.

'I feel a bit useless – I don't know *any* details. The house was a *surprise*! My husband bought it without me knowing. He insisted on looking after everything financially. I work and I run the household and look after our daughter, but Lawrence pays the main bills and . . .' She hesitated, trying to work out what else Lawrence actually did in their family. 'The one thing I really know about is my own personal bank account, and I only use that for everyday expenses. God, I suddenly feel so inept!'

'Please don't feel like that. This is not unusual.' Then, seeing her startled expression, the man added, 'You'd be surprised how many intelligent women hand over control of their finances to their husbands, and vice versa. Money management is often taught to children at school, but in marriages I find it's rare that both partners are completely across the family finances, and that can put the less well-informed partner at a disadvantage when things go wrong. It's never too late to come up to speed, though. Now, can you tell me about items of significance that might have been lost?'

Grace sighed. 'Everything! I don't know. I lost my car. Everything in the house, including my laptop and everything in my home office. We had a safe, and it was meant to be fireproof; the jewellery my husband gave me was in there with all the valuations, I guess.'

'You're not sure? Had you opened the safe recently?'

'No. I didn't have the combination,' said Grace miserably, realising how this sounded. 'I often meant to ask Lawrence for it but I never needed to. I only wore the expensive jewellery on special occasions, and Lawrence always took it out for me. I kept the jewellery I wore every day in my bedroom drawer. It's things like photos, sentimental things I'm upset about.'

He nodded. 'Yes. It must be very distressing. Unfortunately, sentimental things have little commercial value, even though they often mean the most to their owners.'

'But we'll be reimbursed for the house, my car? Maybe my jewellery survived? Do you know what happened to things that were salvaged? And what about the big things that we had insured separately? Lawrence had a collection of silverware and some paintings . . .'

'Do you recall ever listing such items? Do you have their details?'

'You mean serial numbers or something? No. Well, I don't know.' She'd always been meticulous in everything she did, but Lawrence had insisted that he would look after their financial affairs. He'd said it was his way of helping to share their family workload. 'I'm good with budgets – I work in advertising and manage major contracts. But I've been spoiled since I got married.' She gave a weak smile. 'It never occurred to me to perhaps keep duplicates of important papers.'

'Yes. It's always useful to keep copies of important documents somewhere safe.'

'Wait, there was something.' Grace frowned, thinking back. 'I didn't make any effort to understand it at the time, but there must be a copy with the solicitor or the bank.'

'What is it?'

Grace paused, then said, 'Lawrence gave me a form to sign. He said it was a family trust that he'd set up. Like a will. All our valuables and important items were registered in that trust. It was when I was pregnant. He said it was for the baby, for her future. I think it covered my jewellery, shares, things like that. He might have added the house later, too. He didn't mention it to you?'

'No . . . Did you read this document? What was this trust called? It could be helpful.'

'Sorry, I don't know, but Lawrence will. I just signed the signature page and didn't read the rest.' She paused, feeling even more anxious now. 'It had to be sent off urgently, as I recall. Lawrence only ever referred to it as our family trust. He hasn't mentioned it since, so he might have forgotten about it too.'

The agent scribbled something down then began to put his notepad and folders away.

'Could be helpful. I'll look into it.' The man smiled and stood up. 'Thank you for your time, Ms Hagen.'

*

Life still felt so fragile and temporary. Grace woke each morning startled at where she was and wondering when things would get back to normal. Then it would hit her – there was no going back. This was her new normal. And then Daisy would come into her bed for a morning cuddle, and her mother would call out that breakfast was ready.

Sometimes it felt almost as if Lawrence had gone away somewhere, but he was just in the city, apparently overwhelmed with dealing with his business affairs and their immediate situation. Grace had offered to come in and help with paperwork, sort through whatever had been salvaged. There wasn't much, so they'd taken it to his office he'd said, and he insisted that he could look after it all on his own.

She tried to be sympathetic and supportive when they spoke on the phone. He'd asked her to stay at the beach with her mother while he 'dealt' with matters, saying he was so busy anyway he was really only returning to the hotel to eat and sleep.

'That doesn't sound very comfortable, darling,' Grace said.

'The room's fine and better than trying to commute. By the time I drive up to your mother's and back in the traffic, it takes an hour or more each way. It's all too hard. I can work late here.'

'Lawrence, let me help. I can get things organised –' But he'd cut her off.

'Grace, I am in the middle of trying to get a business deal off the ground. Plus, I'm trying to deal with the paperwork for the insurers: God knows when we'll see the money from the house insurance, it's a nightmare! So if this deal doesn't get up, we're stuffed. For the moment,' he added.

'What about renting a small place temporarily, to be together and sort things out?' she suggested.

'That would be nice, but inconvenient and . . . difficult. I might have to travel. I need to know you and Daisy are safe and comfortable.'

'That's thoughtful of you, sweetheart. But for how long, do you think?'

'Bloody hell, Grace! How do I know? Just let me worry about the finances!'

It was hard to think about juggling work, their situation, and helping Daisy to cope with losing their home and all the upheaval in her life. Grace still had nightmares about the fire, and some days she just wanted to stay in bed. She felt like a wounded animal. Her friends in their old neighbourhood were doing their best to keep in touch, but she didn't feel ready to catch up with them.

With her mother's help Grace settled Daisy into the local school, sharing the school drop-offs and pick-ups between them. Lawrence continued to stay in town, coming out on Friday nights for the weekends.

Grace knew that she had to get back into the routine of working, no matter how hard that might be as her thoughts kept going back to the fire, or wondering about their future. And, gradually, she came to realise that perhaps work was exactly what she needed. She was passionate about producing film and television projects, even if they were just advertisements and small documentaries. It satisfied a deep creative urge. Also, it was important to her, now more than ever, that she was bringing in her own income.

And Grace was getting restless. She'd soon be thirty-seven. She still harboured a desire to develop bigger projects, maybe even turn her hand to writing a film script. She'd mentioned that one evening while they were watching TV, and Lawrence had been enthusiastic and immediately pulled out pad and pencil. They'd sat on the sofa tossing around ideas. Then laughingly, gently but pointedly, he had pooh-poohed her concepts and come up with his own, which he thought were far better. He was clever and had a quick mind, if an acid wit, so she screwed up her list of ideas and good-naturedly threw it at him. He then suggested she have another baby instead and flung himself on her on the sofa.

He was ten years older than her. Grace decided there was time for her to have another child, if they wanted to, but did Lawrence have the time, or the inclination, to share the childrearing? If she was honest, he did very little of it as it was. He worked long hours, often travelling, and even when he was at home, he'd spend most of his time in his study, writing proposals and making endless phone calls. His work fluctuated in intensity and it was rather obscure, so she had difficulty explaining to those who asked just what an investment consultant did.

Grace knew it involved a lot of deal making, mergers and acquisitions, finding or creating opportunities and raising the finance for companies to develop projects, which included mines in Queensland and soya beans in India. He often mentioned shares and stock and bonds, and now he was developing business opportunities for conservative companies that were unsure how to develop an online presence. She could rattle all this off to her family and friends, but she didn't have much in-depth understanding of what any of it actually involved. And she could only recall meeting a couple of his business associates, and that was just briefly.

When she thought about it now, after their terrible loss, she had no idea how much money they actually had in the bank. Any time she discussed money, Lawrence would plunge into a complicated discussion of assets, funds and investments that made her head spin. Her own earnings went into her personal account, which she used for herself and Daisy, for food shopping and the general running of the household.

He was generous, splurging on gifts and celebrations for birthdays, Mother's Day and Valentine's Day. Then he would ask Grace, 'So did you tell your friends what I gave you?' Once, on the morning after her birthday, he'd said, 'I bet your girlfriends wish their husbands were as thoughtful and generous as me.'

Grace had nodded with a smile, but inwardly she'd cringed. She knew her girlfriends didn't care. They would laugh about their 'slack' husbands, whom they adored. 'He'll make it up in other ways,' they sometimes giggled.

Mentally Grace slapped herself on the wrist. What was wrong with her? How dare you complain, an inner voice nagged at her. Don't be so ungrateful.

Grace missed Melanie, who had been overseas when the fire happened and was still away. They'd FaceTimed since and were in touch regularly, but it wasn't the same as sitting together, laughing, talking, playing with Daisy. Mel was more like a sister than a best friend, especially since Grace was an only child. Mel had sisters and a brother but the bond Grace had with her was close. She was the one person Grace could really share her deepest feelings with, openly and honestly. She could share parts of her life with her husband, her mother, and her father over in Perth. But with her honest, blunt, caring girlfriend who had her back and was as feisty as hell, Grace had no secrets. She missed Mel at this pivotal time in her life.

For the moment, Grace concentrated on Daisy, who was still waking up at night and climbing into Grace's bed. Although she said she liked her new school, Daisy wasn't happy at suddenly being thrust into a new setting, with different teachers and no children she knew.

'So what did you do today, sweet pea?' Grace asked one afternoon as she and Daisy walked home from school, Daisy skipping along beside her.

'I'm going to a party!'

'What sort of party? And when is it?'

'Saturday. I have the paper. You know, the in . . . invit . . .'

'Invitation? How wonderful. Whose birthday?'

'Suzi. And lots of people.'

'Okay, we'll read the invitation to Nana when we get home.'

Daisy brought the invitation out of her backpack as soon as she walked in the door and showed Grace and Tina.

'Avalon. That's just around the corner,' Grace explained

to Daisy. 'Wow, that sounds fun. I'll ring Suzi's mummy and see if I can bring anything.'

'Yes, ask if we can make cupcakes to bring,' suggested Tina. 'Only three days to go until Saturday, Daisy.'

'Yay, yes, cupcakes,' cried Daisy. 'And a present.'

While Daisy was at school the next day, Grace headed into the city to look at laptops. She wanted to decide which one to buy when the insurance payment finally came through. Outside the computer store, she ran into Sophia, the make-up artist Grace often used on their shoots.

Sophia gave her a hug. 'Hi, darling. I heard the news. It must be excruciating. Are you all right? How's Daisy coping?'

Grace sighed. 'Good days and bad days. She's had a big shock, of course. We've given her new toys and clothes but all she wants are the old favourites. I do too.'

Sophia took her hand. 'That's so hard. Can I help with anything?'

'That's sweet of you. I'm just taking it day by day. Finishing a job for the Lifesaving Association.'

'Where are you living? It's a pity your cute place in Paddington isn't available anymore.'

'Yes, the tenants are locked in. I was hoping we could move there but it's a no-go. It would have been like old times, when I lived there before we were married.'

'But isn't it on the market? We went and looked at it.' Sophia stood back and stared at Grace, her brow furrowed. 'It's out of our league. And it's being sold at auction so the agent must be confident of getting a lot.'

Grace frowned. 'Wait. You mean my old place in Paddo? The one you came to for parties? It's still rented. Lawrence said we couldn't afford to break the lease to get the tenants out. That's why I'm at Mum's and he's staying in a hotel near his office for most of the week.'

'Sorry, Gracie, I'm confused. We're hoping to buy, so when we saw your old flat advertised we went over.'

'Are you sure? You're certain it's the same place?'

Sophia gave an uncomfortable laugh. 'Of course. We went there a few times, remember . . .? But maybe I've got it all wrong. You would know!' She gave her head a little shake. 'Anyway, I've got to dash – I hope the Lifesaving campaign goes well.'

'Thanks, Soph, but it's not a big deal really. Maybe you and I can work together again soon. You know you're always my first choice,' said Grace hastily.

'Thanks, Grace. Let's catch up soon – I'll give you a call.' She gave Grace a quick hug and headed down the street.

Grace watched her go. Then hailed a taxi. 'Paddington, please.'

*

Grace loved the streets of elegant terrace houses with their iron-lacework balconies and tiny formal front gardens. She'd enjoyed living there when she was single and even more so when Lawrence moved in and they'd made her little place their home. The ground-floor flat opened onto a small garden at the back. Grace was always grateful to her darling nan who'd left it to her in her will.

She paid the taxi and got out. Then stopped, in shock.

Facing her was a large real estate sign. *Flat For Sale.*

It was the photo on the board that stunned her. There was no mistaking the bi-fold doors of the sitting room opening onto the patio and garden. There were the hydrangeas her grandmother had planted.

She glanced at the buzzers by the front door. As she wondered if she should press the ground-floor bell, the door opened and a man came out and smiled. 'Hi, can I help?'

'I was looking for Mr and Mrs Nieve. They live in the ground-floor flat.'

'Sorry. I don't know them. I just moved in three weeks ago to the top flat. The real estate agent might have their phone number, though. He told me he was helping them find somewhere to move to when their flat went on the market.' He looked around and said, 'It's a great area. It'll be snapped up pretty fast.'

'This . . . the ground-floor apartment? It's not for sale!' Grace cried in shock.

He gave her a strange look. 'Sorry I can't be more help.' He went past her, turning at the little front gate and adding over his shoulder, 'The real estate agents are Sanctuary Homes, on High Street.'

'Thank you. I know them,' said Grace weakly.

She was stunned. The whole thing must be a mistake. Lawrence was autocratic, controlling, and yes, manipulative, but these were tools he used against his 'opponents'. His competitors, business rivals or investors; the people he charmed and persuaded to part with whatever it was he was after – money, a deal, a property or possessions. He simply couldn't put Grace's flat on the market without discussing it with her. She owned it. It was her superannuation. Just as her mother considered her beach house her life insurance, so Grace had always known she – and more importantly, Daisy – had the safety net of the Paddington flat.

Her heart beating wildly, she hailed another taxi and gave the driver an address in the city. Lawrence's office.

It was a plain brick building in a quieter part of town near the harbour. She glanced at the small hotel opposite, then she strode through the reception area, got in the lift and pushed the button for the third floor. There were several suites with neat plaques or signs announcing business names. She went through a set of double glass doors to Suite 702, not bothering to knock.

Lawrence was at his desk on his phone and looked up in surprise before signalling that he'd just be a minute.

Grace took a deep breath and glanced around. She'd come here when he'd first rented the space rather than work in his spacious office at home. He'd said their house was too far away and he couldn't meet with his clients easily.

The office was well set up with an espresso machine and a small bar fridge, a filing cabinet and some reference books. But what surprised her was the display of some of his antique silverware pieces. So they'd been salvaged from the wreckage of their home, she noted rather bitterly. They'd even apparently been cleaned and restored after the fire.

Then it suddenly hit her as she noticed the folded blanket and a pillow on the plush couch, the toiletries bag and some magazines, that Lawrence had been sleeping here. He'd once mentioned that there was a shower in the amenities room down the hall. She felt her anger mount as she wondered why he'd told her he'd been staying at a hotel.

'This is a nice surprise. What's up?' Lawrence came around from his desk.

'I've had something of a surprise too,' she snapped.

He perched on the edge of his desk, folded his arms, and waited.

'I've just been to *my* flat in Paddington. There is a *For Sale* sign out the front. For *my* flat! That my grandmother left *me*. What the hell, Lawrence? It's mine, you can't sell it. And you didn't ask me or say anything about it.' Grace tried hard to still the quiver of rage she could hear in her voice. She knew she needed to try to stay calm. 'I've rung the agent and told him it's not for sale,' she added brusquely.

'Yes, I know,' Lawrence replied smoothly. 'He rang me. I told him you were mistaken.'

Grace felt the bile rising in her throat, that bitter sick feeling that a fight or argument with Lawrence brought on.

'You can't do that. It was left to *me*,' said Grace between clenched teeth. 'I owned it before we got married. Don't try and bullshit me, Lawrence. It won't work.'

He moved across the room towards her. 'Grace, look. I didn't want to worry you, but we're in trouble financially. There's a delay in the settlement of the fire insurance. Also, there's a downturn in the market, so some of my investments have not quite . . . well, they haven't met my expectations,' he said, giving her an apologetic smile. 'The flat is old but it's in a good location, and it's the only asset we have that can be realised straight away. I wanted to sort things out and not bother you.'

Grace was not convinced by the apparent sincerity in his voice. 'That flat is for *Daisy*. I love it and she will love it. It was her great-grandmother's. It's for Daisy when she goes to university. And it's in *my* name, so *you* can't sell it,' she said. A gripping fear began to burn in her gut.

'Would you like a coffee?' He began to make one for himself, ignoring her as he went on, a faint hint of annoyance seeping into his voice. 'You seem to have forgotten that you agreed to our valuable possessions going into the family trust several years ago. You signed the agreement. And, as stated, in times of financial hardship possessions may be sold or relinquished at the discretion of the sole administrator and director of said trust. Which is me.' He paused as the machine hissed, spewing coffee into his mug. 'You signed everything over to me. To administer as I see fit. I'm doing this for us.' He turned around and faced her.

Grace couldn't believe what she was hearing. 'But it's *mine*!' she exploded. 'You can't sell it without *asking* me!'

'Please don't raise your voice in this building, everyone can hear you,' Lawrence said, his own voice suddenly steely. 'We'll buy her another flat. Later. She's five, for God's sake.'

Grace began to tremble. Her grandmother's beloved flat being sold from under her was bad enough. But it was the fact that Lawrence, her supposedly loving husband, hadn't even asked her. Hadn't told her anything; had deliberately misled her. Had just gone ahead and done it, whether she'd signed it over to him or not. That was too much to bear.

'Lawrence, you can't do this, you can't.' Tears began to stream down Grace's face as she shook her head. 'No. I won't allow it. It's not just any piece of real estate . . .' She choked up. The enormity of such a betrayal of trust was almost too staggering to take in. With a mammoth effort, she tried to pull herself together and think. As Lawrence sipped his coffee, she added in a more controlled fury, 'I'm not sure that you're correct about the family trust. You're trying it on. To scare me.'

'Ask a lawyer, then,' Lawrence said as he turned away and went back to his desk.

'You're sleeping here, aren't you? There's no hotel room.' As Lawrence began fiddling with papers on his desk, Grace asked as calmly as she could, 'Just how much have we got, Lawrence? What has happened to all those investments and shares and things you showed me?'

'Grace, stop interfering. You've heard about boom and bust cycles? Well, I just have to ride out the next month or so and then we'll be fine. Trust me. Have I ever not come good? You've never bothered about these things before, and I doubt you'd understand them now.'

'What do you mean, "come good"?' Grace cried, and she didn't care who heard her. 'I never knew you'd gone bad! That was our home. And everything I own was in it! I see *you* managed to keep some of your things!' She pointed at the silverware, as a thought struck her. 'And your damned car!'

'Grace. Please keep your voice down.'

'Is that why you're sleeping in your office? You can't afford a hotel?' She started to pace up and down the room. 'Oh, my God, what has happened to my life?' She dropped onto the sofa and buried her face in her hands.

'Don't be so melodramatic. I know the fire has been a terrible shock. It's sad and it's awful, but we just have to get through this.' Lawrence came over and sat beside her. 'I promise you, Grace, I'll come good. I have irons . . .' He paused, seeming to rethink the metaphor. 'I have several deals on the go. I'm trying to get together some money to fly to Mumbai to meet with the Tata people. Grace, I'm sorry. But there it is. I need money to make money.'

She was numb. 'Mumbai? In India?'

This suddenly sounded horribly familiar to Grace. The frequent business trips where he came back elated or concerned. Then in a matter of weeks, after those endless phone calls, meetings, negotiations, a deal came off or an investor came in. She always listened with half an ear when Lawrence expounded on how brilliant he'd been in a board meeting, how he'd pulled it off over a dinner or how his proposal had been ground-breaking.

As far as Grace could tell, Lawrence was skilled at presenting a case and talking it through. Then once he had delivered his pitch, the potential investor rarely hesitated to agree to the deal. At least according to Lawrence. She had watched him spend hours and weeks hunting down information, facts, examples, the whole box and dice to bolster his case, his argument. Few of the investors he targeted, Lawrence claimed, could resist his offers. He was softly spoken, charming, smiled a lot, made a small joke here and there, was conciliatory, interested in their home, family, background.

Overhearing him once, Grace had laughingly told Lawrence later that he was like a magic spider, spinning a web of dreams and riches with a dash of speculative adventure thrown in, carefully sidestepping dull details or practicalities, all to charm, impress and land his target in his web.

Lawrence had not been amused and told her crossly that she knew nothing about business. When Grace pointed out that she was very successful at what she did, bringing jobs in under budget and on time, being creative and setting her clients up in the marketplace through clever PR, he'd told her that 'dabbling in advertising is just fakery, spin-doctoring. Nothing serious. You're no deal maker.'

Grace hadn't bothered to answer him. He was out of touch with ad land, which had changed considerably from the old advertising agencies Lawrence knew. Now advertising reached across a broad spectrum of media and it was definitely more PR savvy. But there was no point in trying to tell him that. He knew everything. Or so he thought.

So now as she sat there beside the man she'd fallen in love with, the man who had wooed and charmed her, the man she had married and who had fathered her child, she felt she was sitting with a stranger. This was someone she didn't know – or like much – at all.

It was a quiet, almost calm revelation. The devastating fire had somehow burned out the passion, the respect, the love she'd had for this man. Now, after the fire, when all the comfortable trappings had been stripped away from her life, she could see that she was standing in the ashes of her marriage. With the loss of everything she had, save the most precious thing in her world, her daughter, had come a renewal. A cleansing. She saw it clearly. And in the silence, as they sat side by side, like strangers travelling forward together, but separately, she knew she would have to start over.

Alone.

2

GRACE WALKED UP TO what used to be her front door.
Or was it the front gate? In the sea of black ash, charred
timbers, blackened bricks and twisted metal it was hard
to recognise anything of her once lovely home.

Melanie, wearing thick boots, was picking her way
through the ash, bending down to retrieve small frag-
ments and then discarding them. Her long red hair was
pinned up in a messy bun and her eyes flashed with
emotion as she surveyed the wreckage. She finally came
over to Grace, who was watching with her arms hugging
her body, shivering, although it wasn't cold.

'Let's go. There's no point us being here,' said Melanie
firmly, tucking her arm in Grace's and leading her back to
the car.

'The insurance people have sifted through it all and say there wasn't much that was retrievable,' Grace said. 'Obviously some things were, since Lawrence has his silverware – I should have asked him about it, but my mind was on other things.' She sighed. 'They've got stuff stashed somewhere. In case they're needed for evidence, apparently.'

'Do they know what caused the fire?' Melanie started the car.

'Could have been a faulty gas bottle. Or possibly electrical issues. Lawrence is angry. He wants someone to blame. I'm just so, so sad. And scared, really. Scared about our future: mine and Daisy's.' She'd barely spoken to Lawrence since storming out of his office on that horrible day, and was slowly trying to come to terms with the thought of life without him. 'Lawrence looked after all the home stuff, paperwork, bills, insurance and so on, so I don't really know. But never again,' said Grace bitterly. 'I've learned that the hard way.'

'You know, that's not so unusual. You're a working mother. You have to divide up who takes care of what in a partnership. You have your child, your job, and running the house. Sounds normal to me that Lawrence would look after something, and in your case it was the finances and your insurance.' Mel turned onto the freeway heading into the city. 'What do you spend your money on?' she asked. 'I mean, Mac and I used to divvy up who paid for what. When we divorced, we went fifty-fifty. The only conflict was over books and some pictures. 'Course, we didn't have kids. God, I don't know why we bothered getting married.' She shook her head.

'I spend what I make on Daisy, the house, food, personal stuff. Lawrence looked after the big things.

And our investments,' she added. 'Huh. What a joke that's turned out to be.'

Mel glanced at her. 'So what's happening about your Paddo flat?'

'Mum's solicitor is dealing with it. It's been taken off the market for the moment. We're trying to get a copy of that trust document to see what Lawrence, as the trustee, has set up.'

'Do you know what else he's put in the trust?' asked Melanie.

'God knows. That's what we want to find out. It's all too depressing. Looking back, I can see the red flags that I should have noticed. Don't people always say you should read the fine print? But I went along with things. I trusted him – of course I did, and I should have been able to! He's my husband. Plus, he's older and a big successful businessman, or so I thought.' Grace shook her head.

'Yes, the successful businessman who managed to undermine and demean you. I hated watching him treat you the way he did. Like one of his assets. A possession. I should have butted in, but you were a bit defensive about him, Gracie.'

Grace looked away. 'I know. I guess I didn't want to admit that I might have made a mistake. On the other hand, he could be very generous. The lavish gifts, the way he kept saying that he liked to spoil me . . .'

'Did he spoil Daisy too?'

Grace thought for a moment. 'From when she was born I always paid for the practical things. Clothes, cot, stroller, doctors' appointments and so on.' She paused. 'Last birthday when Daisy turned five, he gave her a diamond charm bracelet. Said he'd add a charm to it every year.'

'Sell the bloody thing.'

'No. I don't want to find out it's a fake.' Grace burst out laughing.

Melanie gave her a swift look. 'What's so funny?'

Grace sighed heavily. 'Dunno. I just feel so stupid. It's nice to have the blinkers off. You've stuck by me. But I see now why none of my other friends keep in touch very much. It's because of Lawrence, isn't it?'

'Well, he ain't much fun. The blokes can't stand him. Pompous, arrogant, boring. Think about it: once he came into your life, you were out of the loop with your old friends. No one liked spending time with Lawrence, which meant they also spent less time with you. Jeez, he must have had *something* going for him. Was he any good in bed?'

Grace chuckled. 'Huh! At the beginning, absolutely, he worked hard to make me happy. After we were committed to each other, he sometimes demanded the suspenders and the tarty underwear . . . which he bought. I like contact, hugs, kisses and being curled up together. He became rather . . . clinical.'

'Okay, okay, I get the picture. I suspect he has a small dick and always felt inadequate. Stop – no need to say anything.' She held up her hand.

'Oh, Mel.' Grace laughed. 'No wonder you're my best friend! But I have to admit, he could make me feel special when he wanted to. It's almost like we were different people back then, at the start. I'm seeing it all from a new perspective now. I think if I had been ugly and spotty he would have behaved the same way just to get what he wanted. Not the sex. But the control.'

'What's his mother like? His family? You've never really talked about them.'

'Never met them, although I wanted to. They live in England. We get a card at Christmas, that sort of thing. Every time I talked with Lawrence about visiting, he had a reason not to, like he was too busy. Sometimes he'd make vague plans to see them, but it always seemed to fall through. We invited his family to the wedding, of course. Sent photos. It was a frantic time. He said they couldn't come to our wedding because his mum was having an operation; they're quite elderly. I just assumed we'd meet them in the UK at some stage. I figured we'd go there on our honeymoon.'

'You went to Europe, didn't you?'

'Yes. Prague. Beautiful city, but Lawrence was in business meetings most of the time. He made it up by taking me to Venice for a week. But he wouldn't go in a gondola.' She sighed. 'I wanted to go somewhere secluded and romantic. A week on the Barrier Reef would have been perfect, just lying around. But Lawrence always has to impress. Even me.' She paused. 'I suppose that makes it sound like we were never happy. That I was a spoiled princess . . .'

'Not at all. You damn well deserved a bit of spoiling,' said Mel. 'You supported your mum through some tough times. Always worked hard and paid your way. For goodness' sake, Grace, stop with the guilt.'

Grace was thoughtful for a moment. 'I know. You're right. I feel like this is a rut I've got stuck in, a pattern I can't help but follow since being with Lawrence . . . It's like he always had to prove something, show how clever he is, and I let him. And he *is* clever . . . but actually I never learned much about his childhood in England. Never heard any family secrets, his nightmares or good times, or funny stories from school. Nothing like that.

He's always been very closed off about some things. He'd tell me how good he was in business. How smart he'd been. It's as though he had no past before that.'

Melanie nodded. 'Tell me about it. Whenever I talked to Lawrence, he never said anything personal. He always had a story about some deal he'd pulled off, how he was negotiating with big-time CEOs, presidents of companies, top government officials. He was never just any old businessman doing his job.'

'He used to talk about world events, politics, and his take on things,' Grace said. 'At some point I started to go, wait a minute, that doesn't sound right. I wasn't allowed to have an opinion that didn't accord with his. And I found I had to fact-check him.' She laughed. 'Not that I would dare correct him; it wasn't worth the argument. But it just kept reality in my head and proved to me that Lawrence's interpretation of the world wasn't necessarily the true one.'

'He snowed you. Everyone, actually. He still does.'

Grace shrugged. 'Let's stop talking about him. I feel like more and more of an idiot the more I think about it.' She slapped her head in mock fury. 'How could I not have seen through him?'

'Because he's devious, clever, manipulative and a con,' said Melanie bluntly. 'And, Grace, my dear friend, it's not going to be easy to separate from him,' she added quietly.

'It's done. I'm going to stay at Mum's place for now. I know there's a mess financially. But it's over.'

Melanie didn't answer for a moment. 'I hope so. For your sake. And poor Daisy.'

'What do you mean, poor Daisy?' said Grace quickly.

'He'll always have a claim on her. Legally,' said Melanie. 'He'll always be in your life because of Daisy.'

'Yes, I know. She loves him, like a little child should love her dad,' Grace said, quietly. 'So for her sake, I guess I'll have to make sure he's always part of our family, no matter how difficult that will be for me.'

'You're right. He'll be in your life at least until Daisy is sixteen, I suppose, and probably forever to some degree. Be careful, Gracie. I suspect he won't make anything easy for you.'

'What makes you such an expert?' said Grace, a bit snippily. Melanie's words unsettled her.

'Hey, I did a psych course, remember. I wrote a paper on narcissists.'

'Is that what Lawrence is? Far out. You'd better tell me all about it.' Grace spoke flippantly but she didn't like Mel's serious expression.

'I'll just say this. You're my friend. If you are truly sure you want to leave Lawrence, then get out. He knows everything about you, your family, all your personal stuff. He knows your abilities, strengths and weaknesses. He's vindictive and he knows how to manipulate people. You know that already, even if you haven't fully admitted it.'

They drove in silence for a moment. Then Grace tried to lighten the mood. 'So. No more Mr Nice Guy?'

'You or him?'

'Me.'

'No. That's your trouble. You're a woman. You want things to be nice; we all do. To co-parent and still be friends. But I'm afraid you're going to have to walk out that door without a backward glance. Talk to your lawyer. Avoid contact.'

'Mel! That's impossible! You just said that yourself. We have a child . . . and I don't have a door . . . let alone a house!' Tears welled in Grace's eyes.

Mel looked sympathetic, but she said firmly, 'See! There you go. Toughen up, Gracie. You're going to war!'

*

Tina gave Melanie a hug as she and Grace walked into the house.

'How lovely to see you. Thanks for taking Grace out there,' she said, then turned to Grace. 'Honey, a courier delivered something for you from your work.'

'Oh, that'll be the storyboards for the ad I'm shooting. Where's Daisy?'

'Painting. We found a second-hand easel at Vinnies. You know how she loves art. She's been so miserable lately, I thought this might be something she can lose herself in. Much better than staring at a damned screen. She's on the verandah.'

'I'll go and say hi,' Melanie said.

'You okay?' Tina glanced at her daughter's tense face. 'Going back to the house must have been hard for you.'

'Yes, it was. It's all gone. Everything. The house. Lawrence.' She drew a deep breath and said the words. 'My marriage.'

Tina didn't react. 'I'll put the kettle on.'

They sat around the table at the far end of the verandah, watching Daisy paint.

'So, Lawrence was living in his office?' Melanie asked softly, so Daisy wouldn't hear.

'Yes. His choice. He actually said he was taking a hotel room to be close to his office. But he was living there. Now he's trying to do some deal in India, apparently.'

'Have you spoken with him about separating?' asked Tina.

'Not really. I told him I was leaving him after I found

47

out about him trying to sell the flat. And walked out. He didn't seem surprised,' said Grace.

'Is he likely to come here with flowers and try to woo you again?' asked Tina.

'No, Mum. I doubt it. Obviously, we'll have to discuss things. Money seems to be a major problem.'

'Let's hope he pulls off some deal. Talks some poor sucker into investing,' said Melanie. 'Although if he does, he'll probably hire the most expensive lawyer in town.'

'Grace, you'll need someone to represent you, too . . . I suppose Mr Jamison can cope for the moment,' said Tina. 'What's the next move? I mean, are you sure about this, love?'

'Yes!' said Grace and Melanie in unison.

The three women lapsed into silence as the weight of the situation settled over them. Eventually, Melanie drank the last of her tea and glanced at her watch. 'Well, I'm afraid I have to go. Thanks for the tea, Tina. Chin up, Gracie.' She patted her friend's hand and then turned to the little girl at the other end of the verandah. 'Hey, Daisy, come and give me a hug. And can I see your painting before I go?' she said.

Grace stood up and she and Tina followed Mel over to Daisy. 'I'd better go look at those storyboards; we're shooting in a couple of days. Thank goodness the location's not far away.'

'Is this the water safety ad?' asked Tina.

'Yes. I'm filming at Palm Beach so it's close.'

'Wow, that looks so cool. Excellent, Daisy,' said Melanie, admiring Daisy's picture of the beach.

'Mummy, can you take it off for me? Here, Aunty Mel.' When Grace had freed it, Daisy handed the almost-dry painting to Mel.

'Thank you, darling. Can you part with it? It's a pretty special painting,' said Melanie. 'But I'd love to put it on my fridge. Then I'll tell people I can look at the beach every morning.' She laughed, kissing the little girl.

Outside at the car, the two friends hugged.

'You're sure about this?' asked Melanie. 'It won't be easy. Or pleasant.'

'I'm sure. Thanks, Mel. I guess it's been coming for a long while. Somehow the fire seems like a sort of omen. A symbol.'

'I know the fire was traumatic, and you won't get over it for a while. And I know you lost a lot of sentimental things. But, to be corny, maybe some things do happen for a reason.'

Grace nodded. 'I've got my child, my mother and my best friend. And my work. I'm okay,' she managed to say before choking up.

'You've got *all* your friends,' said Melanie softly. 'We've missed you.'

*

It was getting dark when Grace came in from a long day of filming a sales presentation video for a seafood restaurant and boat charter business. The water safety ad was in the can and Grace had decided that work was just what she needed, and not only to pay the bills.

'Hi, Daisy darling. Hello, Mum,' Grace called out as she walked into the kitchen. 'I have some dinner for us. Fresh seafood!' She dropped a paper parcel onto the bench, nudging Sparkle away as he jumped up to investigate.

'Ugh,' said Daisy, who was sitting at the small table doing her homework. Her grandmother was sitting beside her with a magazine and a glass of wine, and got up to kiss Grace on the cheek before unwrapping the parcel of food.

'Oh, this looks so fresh. How was your day?'

'Good, thanks.' Grace opened the cupboard and took out a wok. 'This seafood's all been cleaned and there's sauce to go with it. I'll put on some rice too,' Grace said. She dropped a kiss on the top of Daisy's head. 'What did you get up to today, princess?'

'Ah, drawing and gardening. And I got to feed lettuce to Charlie, the guinea pig. But guess what, Mummy, tomorrow it's my turn to be the teacher's helper and hand out the new reading books in class. And I have to take some more lettuce to school for Charlie.'

'Wow, that sounds fun, sweetheart. And Charlie is a very lucky little guinea pig.'

Daisy nodded, sharpening her pencil.

'Here, Gracie, let me get you a drink. You might need it,' Tina said.

'Why?' Grace asked, looking at her mother.

'Here's a glass of wine. And a letter.' Her mother put them in front of Grace as she sat down.

'Uh-oh. It's from the insurance company. Let's hope it's good news.' Grace tore open the envelope.

'Why are they contacting you here? Oh, I suppose the agent who came here has this address,' said Tina, sitting down next to Daisy.

Grace read the letter quickly, frowning, then slowly refolded it.

'Basically, it's saying that there is some question about the cause of the fire, so they need an arson specialist to do further investigations.'

Tina looked startled. 'Good grief. So much red tape.

I suppose they have to be thorough. That house must have been insured for quite a sum.'

Grace stared at the letter. Arson . . . who on earth would want to set fire to their home? That couldn't be right, surely? And anyway, just how much was the house insured for? Was it even in both their names? She felt foolish that she didn't know. She decided she'd call the insurance broker in the morning. She took a sip of wine and started making the dinner.

As she was rinsing the rice, her phone pinged and she picked it up to find a text message from Lawrence.

Grace, I plan to take Daisy out for the day tomorrow. Please arrange to bring her to my office at 10 am.

'It's a school day! You jerk!' she hissed at her phone.

'Grace? What's going on?' Her mother and Daisy both looked up at her.

Grace said to Daisy, 'Can you do me a drawing of Charlie the guinea pig, darling? I'd love to know what he looks like. Mum, do you have a minute?' she added.

As they stepped onto the verandah, she held up her phone. 'Lawrence expects me to deliver Daisy to him for the day tomorrow. No mention about when he'll return her, or what they're doing. Suddenly he's interested in her. He hasn't taken her out on his own since she was a toddler.' Grace felt a rising panic.

'Well, that's just silly. She has school tomorrow. She can't just miss it on a whim. Tell him to come here and spend time with her at the beach on Saturday.'

'You don't "tell" Lawrence anything. He's gone in hard, just like Mel said he would. It's going to be a war.'

Grace thought about it then sent back a carefully worded text: *It's a special day at school tomorrow and Daisy is looking forward to it as she has a key role in the day's activities. Why not come and get her on Saturday and spend time with her up here, close to home, as I'll be working most of the day.*

Lawrence's reply was swift and to the point. *Daisy's 'home' is not her grandmother's house. It is with her parents. You are being selfish and obstructive.*

Grace couldn't be bothered to argue. Lawrence always reacted to unpleasant situations or advice by ignoring them. She was sure that if she and Daisy were to go back to him, he would act the loving and devoted father and husband in front of people, but in private he'd essentially leave them to fend for themselves. As he'd done a lot over the last few years.

The way forward seemed clearer than ever to Grace as she stood staring at Lawrence's text message. He always managed to turn things around so she was the one at fault or silly or 'selfish'. She didn't reply but went back into the kitchen and finished preparing their meal.

*

The following afternoon Grace left the shoot as soon as the filming was done. She had an appointment with her mother's solicitor before collecting Daisy from school.

Mr Jamison was sympathetic, photocopying the insurance letter and saying he would make enquiries as to the state of play. 'Especially seeing as you have no access to savings,' he added.

'I've had to buy essentials for my daughter and me since the fire,' Grace said. 'I don't have a car at the moment either, so I'm borrowing my mother's and getting public transport and taxis.'

'I'll see if I can hurry things up for you. But, Grace, as far as a divorce is concerned, it's a long process and you'll need a family lawyer. It will mean paying much higher fees than mine, too. I'll do a bit of research and recommend someone suited to your situation, if you like.'

'I understand. Thank you, Mr Jamison.' She knew that lawyers would likely cost a fortune, and worried about how she would pay for it. Tina had offered to lend her some money, but Grace didn't want her mother digging into her savings or her superannuation, such as it was.

As she was heading to the school to collect Daisy, her mobile rang. She pulled over and saw that the caller was Allison from the agency.

'Hi, Grace, I know you're up at your mum's and not coming into the office much at the moment, so I thought I'd give you a call. The boat-charter people were very happy with the way the shoot went and they're keen to see the finished product.'

'Thanks so much for letting me know, Alli. The digital guys are onto it. I've started planning that other job we talked about last week. But I need something big. Has anything else come in while I've been away?'

'Well, in a way, that's why I'm ringing, actually. We've been contacted about another job. One of your fashion clients from last year – who you did the shoot for in Cairns – emailed to let me know they'd recommended us and your work in particular. Anyway, they must have given you a great wrap because the guy, a Mr Hans Speyer, from a company called MGI, called and he'd like you to put in a pitch. It's a biggie.'

Grace felt her mood lift for the first time in a long while. 'Fantastic. That's great timing!'

'It's in Bali.'

'What? Wow! What's it for?'

'It's a big new hotel. Very up-market. They want a whole campaign. Cross video promotion, the works,' Alli said.

'Really, that sounds amazing!'

'I thought you'd be interested. First they want to brief you to do the campaign scenario. I'm not sure yet if that'll be done here or if it means you flying to Bali. Then, you'll have to present them with a pitch. If you get the go-ahead, you'll need to go there for a few weeks or even months, to oversee the shoot. Hans has sent me a lot of briefing material already, but you'll need to go to the hotel and look around before putting the campaign pitch together. They'll look after you, of course. It's definitely big-budget.'

'Alli, it would be great, but I'm a bit tied up here. We're still sorting things out after the fire.' Grace was thinking quickly. Allison was in her early twenties, unmarried and unfettered. It probably wouldn't occur to her that zipping over to Bali and back might be a trifle disruptive to family life. But the money from this job would be very, very useful.

'Oh, I understand. I can send you the materials and we can talk about the timeframe. Then we can take the next step, see whether the client needs you to go up there for the briefing.'

'Okay. Thanks, Allison. I'm in the car now on my way to pick up my daughter from school. Can I call you back later?'

'Sure. Call me tomorrow. I'll email you that material now. But I can tell Hans you're interested in pitching for it, right?'

'Yes. I am.' Grace knew this job would get a hefty fee for the agency and probably a bonus for her personally.

If she could make it work, it would be win–win. 'Thanks. Talk tomorrow.' Grace moved back onto the road.

When she arrived at Daisy's school, Grace signed in at the office and, as she was early, asked for a permission slip to wait outside Daisy's classroom. She walked down the corridor, smiling at a teacher she recognised, and stopped outside Daisy's classroom, where she peered through a hallway window. The kids were standing around the little tables, packing up their things. Their colourful art was posted all over the walls, and the place felt friendly and stimulating in a calm way.

She couldn't see Daisy so she poked her head in the door and caught the teacher's eye, and the young woman came over with a smile.

'Nice to see you, Mrs Hagen.'

'Please, call me Grace. What's Daisy up to? I know I'm a bit early.'

Instantly the teacher's expression changed. 'Oh dear. Daisy was picked up by her father this morning.'

Grace froze. 'What? This morning? I had no idea,' she stuttered. 'What did he say? I should have been notified. Where was he taking her?'

'Oh, um . . . Mr Hagen said you were working. Didn't Daisy have some appointment? Medical, wasn't it?'

'No!'

The young woman bit her lip. 'I did wonder. Daisy didn't seem too happy about going.'

'Did he say where they were going?' Grace pulled out her phone, her finger hovering over Lawrence's number.

'Not specifically. I'm so sorry, I thought everything was in order,' said the teacher in a low voice. 'I'm sure Daisy is fine.'

'No, it's my fault. I should have let the school know

55

what's going on,' said Grace heavily. She turned away and pressed the call button. The phone rang and rang, then Lawrence's voicemail came on.

'Lawrence, call me. Immediately.' She hung up, turning back to the teacher. 'What time did he turn up?'

'A bit after 10 am, I think. He said they had an 11 o'clock appointment. Is there anything I can do?' She looked very worried.

'No. I'm sorry, you weren't to know. My husband and I have separated and things are a bit . . . difficult. I'll speak to the principal about this for the future.'

'I'm so sorry to hear that. These things happen. If you let Mrs Fredericks know about it, she might want you to fill out some legal documentation. We've had issues before,' the young teacher added.

'Thank you.' Grace glanced at her phone. I bet he's not going to call me back, she thought. She reassured the teacher again and hurried back to the car, where she rang Melanie.

'What a low act. Typical. Not much you can do until you have something legal in place. He's Daisy's father, and there's nothing stopping him.'

'I'm going to make a call now. Mr Jamison said he would recommend a family lawyer; well, I might need that recommendation quicker than I thought,' Grace said. 'I'm upset for Daisy. The teacher said she didn't want to go.'

'Just think carefully about how to handle Lawrence. Don't antagonise him. If he knows you're upset about this, he'll mark it up as a win.'

'What about Daisy?'

'Don't make it a big deal. Remember, this is the way it will be now for her and for you, for the time being, anyway.'

'You mean being ripped out of school with no notice – kidnapped, essentially!'

'Until you get orders in place, he can do what he did today. It's not kidnapping, Grace.'

'No, it's a nightmare. I feel like taking Daisy and running away. To Bali!'

When Melanie didn't reply, Grace quickly said, 'Don't worry, I don't mean it. Seriously. I was invited to pitch for another job today. A huge one. In Bali.'

'What? Take it! I'll come and be an assistant!'

'It's not that easy, Mel. It's a huge project and it could be really exciting, but if I got it, I'd be away for weeks, months maybe. I can't leave Daisy for that long. Especially now.'

'Take her with you.'

'I couldn't . . . could I? Lawrence would go ballistic.'

'Find that lawyer. Talk to them and get the correct advice. You said Lawrence is always taking off on business trips.'

'True. He's always so vague about where he's going, and for how long. I wouldn't like him to take Daisy away with him, though. Besides, you can't work with a child in tow.'

'Lawrence would leave her in a hotel room with a babysitter. I reckon in Bali you could have a Balinese nanny look after her in a beautiful setting.'

'Mel, I can't think about this right now. I'm feeling really panicky not knowing where Daisy is. I'd better get off the phone.'

'Sure. Look, Gracie, she'll be fine. Bored maybe, but she's with her dad. He would never hurt her. Don't worry. Let me know how you go. Talk later.'

Grace pulled into her mother's driveway, her heart

sinking at not seeing Lawrence's car. She rang his phone again. He didn't answer, so she sent him a text.

If Daisy isn't returned to Mum's house by 5 pm, I'm calling the police.

Tina was aghast when Grace told her what had happened.

'It would have been so confusing for Daisy,' Grace said, 'knowing nothing about it. And missing school. Well, it won't happen again. I'm seeing a lawyer.'

She grabbed her phone as the message alert pinged.

I will return Daisy after dinner. 6 pm.

'Bastard!' she snapped.

'He always has to score a point,' said Tina quietly. 'He is keeping her out past five o'clock to show he's not taking orders from you. Lord knows what he'll give her to eat.'

'That's nearly two hours to wait.' Grace was really fretting now.

*

As soon as they heard his car pull up, Grace dashed to the door. Tina hung back as Grace ran to the car, wrenching open the door to unbuckle Daisy.

'Oh, Daisy darling, are you okay?' She took her daughter in her arms as Lawrence came around the car.

'Don't be melodramatic, Grace.'

Tina appeared beside her daughter. 'Let me take Daisy in and start her bath.'

'Good evening, Tina,' said Lawrence pointedly, if coolly.

'Hello, Lawrence,' she said, not looking back as she took Daisy by the hand.

Lawrence leaned swiftly down, taking Daisy's other hand. 'Give Daddy a kiss goodbye, honey. We had a magic day, didn't we?'

Daisy looked uncomfortable but she nodded. Lawrence pulled her into a hug, glaring at Grace over his daughter's head.

Daisy was the first to pull away.

'Honey, say thank you to Daddy, and go inside with Nana, please,' said Grace in an even voice. 'I'll be there in a minute.'

'Thank you, Daddy.' Daisy clasped Tina's hand and almost dragged her to the house.

Grace turned on Lawrence. 'Don't you dare do this again!'

'She is my daughter. I have every right to see her when I want, considering you have taken her from the matrimonial home without permission or authority.'

Grace knew when Lawrence became pompous like this that he was in fighting mode. He had no doubt prepared everything he wanted to say to her. But for once she didn't let that rattle her.

'We'll see about that. And what matrimonial home, Lawrence? Everything we had together has gone. Our marriage. Our home.' When Lawrence didn't reply, Grace continued, 'I've hired a lawyer. I need to get this sorted out. I hope you will behave in a reasonable and fair manner. We have to consider Daisy.'

'Yes. We do. Don't think you can just walk off with my child.'

'I have no intention of doing so. Nor will I try to kidnap her.'

As Grace turned on her heel, he threw at her, 'You can't win this. I will go for full custody if I have to.'

She slammed the front door behind her and burst into tears.

'Oh, Gracie darling.' Tina wrapped her arms around

her only child. 'Don't let him get to you. Daisy is here. She's fine. That's all that matters.'

Grace stood back and quickly wiped her eyes. 'Thanks, Mum. Did Daisy say if she had dinner?'

'Yep. They went to the zoo and had fast food crap. All day. Of course Daisy didn't think it was crap, being such a novelty.'

'I knew it!' Grace slammed a fist into the palm of her hand. 'He doesn't cook. Pretends to like haute cuisine, eats at the best restaurants, but at heart he's nothing but a drive-through junk-food moron. Who can't cook an egg.'

Tina smothered a smile. 'Well, Daisy won't be like that. She says she wants us to make spag bol for tomorrow's dinner, and she gets to roll up the meatballs.'

'Good. I'll make a chef out of her yet – despite her pig of a father.' Grace stomped towards the bathroom.

*

They were sitting in a small wine bar across from the darkened beach. It was still too early for the usual crowd.

'You know, it's been a long time since I could just walk out the door and go to a bar,' said Grace, lifting her cocktail. 'Cheers, dear friend.'

They clinked glasses and Melanie took a sip. 'Wow, that's strong. I can only have one of these. Pass the food, will you?'

'Thanks for this, Mel. I know you have to drive back to town. You're welcome to stay the night. Why don't you? Daisy could make you her famous pancakes for breakfast.'

'Thanks, Gracie. Sounds fun but I have too much on. Plus, I met a guy the other night. He's invited me to Sunday lunch. Can you believe it? Who takes a date to Sunday lunch?'

'It's a date? That's great. How'd you meet him?'

'Just through work. It's no big deal,' she added hastily. 'Now, forget about my love life. Have you seen a family lawyer yet?'

'No. I will as soon as Mum's solicitor gives me his recommendation for the best person to see.'

'That's good. You'll need someone experienced – Lawrence and whichever lawyer he gets will be going for the jugular. Be prepared to be portrayed as a bad mother, a bimbo who he supported and who dabbled but didn't really work, and who is anything from flaky to a drug addict, so not fit to care for *his* child.'

Grace laughed, then stopped when she saw Melanie's expression. 'Who'd believe that?'

'No one who knows you. But in a court, Lawrence and his lawyer can spin lies and paint you as anything they want. It's up to you and your lawyer to discredit him. With facts. Evidence.'

'But none of those things are true. He's the bastard!' Grace felt stunned. 'Shit. He's so conniving . . . I thought the truth would just be there . . .'

Melanie shrugged. 'Necessity is the mother of invention. He'll say whatever he wants to get what he wants. It's up to you to anticipate it and disprove whatever he lies about.'

Grace groaned, sinking her head in her hands, then took a long swig of her cocktail. 'This is all too hard.'

'You'll be okay if you and your lawyer are prepared. Now. The next step. Money. Do you have any?'

'Not a lot, just what I bring in from work. I haven't been able to save a lot myself.'

Melanie merely lifted her drink, raised her eyebrows and said calmly, 'So . . . show me the money. How are you going to pay the legal fees? And any bills that are in your name?'

'I'll go for fifty–fifty,' said Grace. 'It's only fair. I'll get my share.'

'Will you? Have you seen the documents? How do you know what he might have put in your name? Or only in his name? Do you know exactly what you're responsible for in the long term? I think you have to be very careful here,' said Melanie.

'He's been paying the bills. Mortgage, insurance, whatever.'

'Till now. But whose name is on all the documentation? Who's responsible if he doesn't pay? You said you signed a legal document but you had no idea what it was for. What else might you have signed, or agreed to? You *trusted* him.' Melanie leaned forward. 'I'm not trying to have a go at you, I'm just saying. But see what I mean?'

Grace went cold. She reached for a piece of sushi. 'I don't believe either of us expected to be dealing with . . . with what we're facing now.'

'The house fire or a separation?'

'It all feels like the same thing.' Grace ate her sushi, then asked, 'Do you think we'd have broken up if we hadn't had the fire?'

'Hopefully you would have realised what he is like eventually, and sooner is better than later. But it's not pretty. I'm just glad you're not planning to hang in there for Daisy's sake. Stable home and united parents, that sort of thing.'

'I know that at least a quarter or more of Daisy's classmates from her old school are from divorced families,' said Grace.

'And I bet not one of their parents has stories of their

easy divorces. But I'm worried. Lawrence is such a cunning shit; will he take you, and your mum, to the cleaners?'

'Mel, stop it! You're overdramatising. You're scaring me!'

'Good. I want you to be alert. Don't trust a thing he says or pretends to do or says he's done.' She lifted her drink. 'You should go to Bali. Put in a pitch, at least.'

'What's the point if I can't take the job? He'll never let me take Daisy out of the country. Let alone for weeks or months, or however long it would be.'

'Leave her with your mother while you go there for a few days, to see what it's all about. Maybe get the lawyer to draw up some arrangement that Lawrence can visit, but not take Daisy away from the school or your mum's place for the time you're away.'

'He'll never agree to that.'

'How often has Lawrence been to your mum's house to see her since the fire?'

'Only a few times, mostly at the weekend, and when he brought Daisy back after he stole her from school.'

'He's busy pulling his life back together. If you make the trip midweek he'll probably never even know you're gone. C'mon, a few days. It'll do you good to get away, get a fresh perspective. Have a swim and a drink and talk to interesting people.'

'That's for sure.'

'I just think this could be perfect timing. It would be a sizeable chunk of money if you got the contract. Fancy hotels have big budgets, so they can pay well. And you need the money.'

'That's all true,' Grace said. 'Okay. I'll look into it.'

'Just do it.' Melanie lifted her glass and clinked Grace's cocktail. 'Cheers. Or whatever they say in Balinese!'

*

The following day, as Grace and Tina sat on the verandah with a pot of tea, Grace talked over the idea of checking out the job in Bali with her mother. Sparkle was sleeping comfortably on Tina's lap.

'I think Mel's right, it's a good idea. Just go for a few days initially, get the lie of the land. See if it's at all feasible. And if they're paying, what have you got to lose?' said Tina. 'You know Daisy will be fine here with me.'

'Thanks, Mum. I know having us here is a big ask, especially as you're looking after Daisy so much. You haven't played tennis for weeks.'

'Oh, the girls from the club came over for tea. They adored Daisy. And it's not as though I'm not getting any exercise!'

'She does keep you on the run,' agreed Grace.

'I do things while she's at school. And this won't be forever. I feel blessed to have this special time with my granddaughter.' Tina put down her teacup. 'I think you should just go to Bali. You don't have to answer to Lawrence. Can you give me a letter of power of attorney as Daisy's carer? Frankly, I wouldn't let Lawrence know what you're doing. He'll just try and stop you. Keep it simple; you'll be knee-deep in lawyers and legal stuff soon enough.'

Grace took a deep breath. 'Okay. I'll tell Allison at work I want to go and suss it all out.'

'They must think highly of you, Gracie. It sounds like a big deal.'

'Mmm, yes, it does,' she admitted. 'Maybe that's exactly what I need.'

'And what better place to do it? I think you'll find Bali will blow you away.' Tina paused and sighed. 'Obviously it's so different now from when I was there in the seventies.'

'The big OS trip, what, when you were nineteen, right?'

'Yes, they called us the overlanders. Waves of Australian kids travelled through Asia, Nepal, Europe and then on to London. We thought we were pretty adventurous. No one had much money, and we all tried smoking pot and heaven knows what, but in reality, it was a time of innocence, of freedom. It was the era of the first Aussie surfers heading out into the unknown, the *Morning of the Earth* film and all that.' Tina stopped and smiled.

'A special time, huh?' said Grace softly.

Tina looked into the distance. 'For some of us, Bali changed our lives.'

'That sounds pretty great. Would you go back, Mum?'

'I'm not sure. From what I see in the travel supplements it looks too overcooked now, if you know what I mean.'

'Overdone and overcrowded. Yes, but maybe that's what tourists want these days.'

'There're very few unspoiled paradises around anymore.'

'Hmm . . . maybe.'

'Let's head back inside,' said Tina, gently putting Sparkle on the floor. 'It's getting too cool now. Feel like some homemade soup for dinner?'

'Thanks, Mum. Sounds good.' Grace finished her tea. Thoughts were buzzing through her mind, about tourism, attracting visitors, places on a bucket list, scenarios that might suit a hotel campaign. For the first time in months, she felt excited about the future.

3

GRACE HIT MELANIE'S FACETIME number and her smiling face appeared on the screen.

'Hi, Gracie, what's happening?'

'I'm thinking I will go to Bali and check out this hotel campaign.'

'Good on you. It sounds fantastic. Of course, it could be a nightmare too. But don't go, won't know,' she added.

'That's what I thought. Mum's happy to take care of Daisy for a few days.'

'Does Lawrence know you're going away?'

'Not yet. Do you think I have to let him know? It doesn't affect Daisy's routine. Mum will drive her to school. I don't want Lawrence throwing a spanner in the works, as Mum says, before I even know anything about this job.'

'Legally? I don't know. I guess not, but perhaps check with your lawyer. Bringing Daisy up there later could be more of an issue. Just take it one step at a time. You might hate the place. Or the people. Or the job.'

'Mum was talking last night about her time there. She was very nostalgic. I'd love to take her back sometime.'

'Really? When was she in Bali?'

'In the late seventies, before she married Dad. In the hippy era.'

'Go, Tina!' Melanie said, laughing, then sounded more serious. 'The client is paying for your travel, I assume? You can't afford to be out of pocket.'

'I know! My work is paying initially. We're all keen to get this job, it could be massive. Big-bucks budget, I'm told.'

'So what's the process? Do you have to prepare the pitch before you go?' Mel said.

'I'll do some research but really the most useful thing at this early stage will be to meet the client's marketing team and hear what they have in mind.'

'Right, I suppose they want to find out what you're like and discuss some of your ideas too.'

Grace smiled. 'Yeah, no pressure! I'll have to think on my feet from the moment I land.'

'You'll wow them, Gracie,' Mel said. 'I'm sure you'll get this contract . . . if you want it.'

'I wish you were coming,' Grace said. 'Okay. I'll keep you posted.'

'See ya.'

Grace spent several quiet hours making notes, doing some research and ordering books on Bali, until her mother stuck her head in the study door.

'Mr Jamison rang. The family lawyer he recommends

is a Mr Judd.' She dropped a piece of paper with all the details on the desk and rested her hand gently on her daughter's shoulder. 'I think going to Bali is a good idea. You know Daisy will be fine here. And I can deal with Lawrence. He's always been very polite to me. No fun and a pain in the bum, but polite.'

Grace couldn't help laughing and pressed her mother's hand. 'He's scared of you! Thanks, Mum.'

*

Allan Judd was a calm man. Middle-aged, with sandy hair greying at the temples, he came across as steady, thoughtful and seemingly unflappable. He took neat notes while Grace outlined her situation, stopping her only to ask for clarification or more detail. Grace wondered if he had always been like this, or whether the job had just inured him to hysteria and trauma. Later, when she described him to Mel, she suggested he might be on tranquillisers. Or Bourbon. 'Family law must be very draining,' she said soberly.

When Grace had finished briefing him, Mr Judd laid down his notepad and pen and plunged straight in. 'Now, I understand you want a divorce,' he began.

'As soon as possible,' said Grace.

'I'm afraid that can't happen,' he said. 'The law requires, among other things, that you have been separated for twelve months and one day. From what you've told me, you and your husband are only recently separated, is that right?'

'Yes,' said Grace. 'What does that mean?'

'It means that you'll have to wait,' he said gently but firmly. 'You are living separately now?'

Grace nodded.

'Then let's focus on more pressing issues, like this potential job in Bali.' He picked up his pen again.

'So, is this a job interview in Bali? How long would you be required to stay there, should you land this job?' he asked.

'Yes, you could call it a job interview,' Grace said. 'That would only be a few days. If I got the contract, though, I'd have to go back there for a while, maybe a month or more. A few weeks at the very least. I'm not sure yet.'

'So tell me, do you want the job? It would certainly complicate your life.'

'I know.' Grace sighed. 'It would pay well, and at the moment that is very important. And frankly, I like the idea of being out of the country so I don't have to deal with my husband face to face too often. He is difficult.'

'Well, face-to-face discussions might be limited. But I'm afraid you can't walk away easily. You'll be surprised to discover just how many entanglements there are. What about your daughter? She's five, isn't she? How do you see that working out?'

'My mother would look after her while I'm in Bali for the interview,' Grace said. 'It's already arranged.'

'Perhaps, but it won't look good to a court if you leave her with your mother. Your husband will step into the primary parenting role. It doesn't put you in a good and caring light.'

'I understand that. This initial trip would be short, five days at most. If I got the job, I would consider taking Daisy with me to Bali. I'm sure I could enrol her in a local English-speaking school and work out the other child-care arrangements. My working hours would be flexible.'

'Tricky,' he said. 'Let's just go step by step. I will draw up a document for this quick trip, to give to your mother so she has power of attorney. That way she can make swift decisions if needed. Does your husband have any such arrangements in place?'

'I don't think so. He's the one who always travelled for business. I stayed home with Daisy. My mother has been a very regular babysitter for her granddaughter when we needed her.'

'Does your daughter have a passport?'

'Yes. We were going to go to France for a holiday last year, but it didn't come off at the last moment.' Grace gritted her teeth, remembering the disappointment as Lawrence changed their plans and dumped the holiday in favour of a quick trip to Africa on his own for 'important business'.

'And you have the passports in your possession?'

'Yes, fortunately. Lawrence kept all our passports in his office safe. It was convenient for him because he travelled a lot, and he wanted to keep them together. So they weren't burned in the fire,' she added grimly. 'I asked Lawrence for Daisy's so I could get copies of her vaccination records and her birth certificate to enrol her in the local school.'

'And you have your own as well?'

'Lawrence gave me his travel wallet and I took them both out,' Grace said. 'I had no idea I'd need mine so soon.'

'As you say, that was very fortunate indeed.' Mr Judd checked his notes. 'So, as your intention is to divorce and you are supporting your daughter, a lucrative job is not to be passed up lightly. Especially as you have no financial arrangement with your husband as yet and, as you mentioned on the phone, there seems to be some issue over the insurance money.'

'Yes, that's right. And he hasn't been forthcoming with any financial support,' Grace said. 'It's not like I walked out of the marital home. There isn't one.'

'I understand. But you are living separately.' He held up his hand as Grace went to interject. 'I would say, go ahead and make arrangements to go to Bali for this first short trip. Does your husband have legal representation?'

'I'm sure he does, but I don't know who his lawyer is, I'm afraid.'

'All right. I can find out. I'll be in touch again soon, Grace.' He rose and shook her hand.

*

A week later, Grace put her bags in the boot and got into the passenger seat of Tina's car.

'All set?' her mother asked as she drove down the street away from the beach.

'Yes, but I just hate all this stuff, Mum. I feel like a criminal. I never thought I'd have a lawyer on retainer. What has my life come to?'

Tina turned and smiled at her. 'You are going off to Bali, all expenses paid! I hope this job comes through for you. One door closes and it's *Hellooooo, Bali!*'

Grace couldn't help laughing. 'Well, when you put it that way, I'm actually a bit excited.'

Tina pulled up outside the departures terminal and leaned over to hug Grace. 'Don't worry about Daisy. We'll be fine. Just concentrate on what you have to do.'

'Thanks, Mum. When I dropped her at school this morning I reminded her that I was going away and she seemed fine. I think as long as she can feed Charlie, she'll be happy!' Grace laughed, but her expression quickly changed. 'I'll miss her; I'll miss you both. I'll call every day and FaceTime with you when Daisy comes home from school.'

Tina nodded. 'I won't come in; this parking is crazy.'

Grace climbed out, retrieved her bags and waved through the window. 'Bye, Mum. Love you both!' she called as Tina drove away.

*

When she landed in Bali, the blast of sunlight and sudden humidity, the smell of *kretek*, the clove cigarettes, and the tropical fecundity hit Grace almost physically. A little bus crammed with sweaty passengers took her to the huge arrivals hall, where the endless queues at Customs and Immigration, the buzz of accents and languages, the scrum of the lines of drivers wildly holding up cards with names on them was overwhelming.

As advised by her contact from the hotel, Grace headed to the pre-paid immigration desk where she was assisted quickly. From there she was ushered outside to a waiting van by a man hired to look after the VIP guests.

The young driver greeted her as she stepped into a surprisingly luxurious interior. She reached for the chilled water and scented wet tissues, thinking that she and the seven-star guests were very well looked after. She almost expected to see a bottle of bubbles and a couple of glasses. It seemed that no one else was joining them, so the driver took off.

They drove through congested streets lined with shopping complexes, fancy stores, cafés, bars and entertainment joints. It's Party Central with bells on, she thought. The traffic snaked around massive fountains with white stone statues that, while dramatic, looked like a mock Italian city square minus the spaciousness. Between the crowded buildings there were glimpses of palm trees and a beach crammed with sunbathers.

The driver slowed as they passed what looked like untamed jungle dropped into the middle of the commercialised chaos. Leaning forward, Grace saw there was order to the wilderness. Two massive palms marked an entrance where large wooden gates slid open as the driver touched the screen on his dash. It was like dropping out of the world through a secret door, like Alice going down the rabbit hole, she thought. But then reality hit her, as a boom gate dropped down in front of them and several uniformed men came forward. They checked the van for bombs, sliding a trolley with a mirror beneath the car, inspecting the motor, opening the boot and moving her luggage around, glancing into where she sat alone but ignoring her. Finally the boom lifted and they were waved on.

Grace caught her breath when she saw the brilliant white driveway, lined with tropical trees and plants, that wound towards her destination, the Kamasan Hotel. The tyres made a gentle *crunch* as they rolled forward.

'What's this driveway made of? It looks like pearls!'

'Crushed shells, old coral, special sand,' the driver answered, obviously used to people's reactions when they first saw it.

'It's like a secret island jungle,' she exclaimed, noticing the filigree metal torches stabbed alongside the driveway. But there looked to be order and calmness to the great green forest, now that she could see it close up. Sunlight slanted through the trees, the filtered light making the branches look soft and yielding, and the bamboo and palm fronds swayed gently. It was inviting and peaceful.

A flash of colour in a tree caught her eye. 'Are there monkeys in there?'

'No. Special birds. Monkeys make trouble.'

'It's stunning. Magical.'

'No more place in Bali like this.'

'Hard to believe we just left the crowds and the shops outside the gate.'

'Very special place. This must be the most special place in Bali,' the driver said enthusiastically.

Before Grace could answer she caught her first glimpse of one of the buildings: a spacious pavilion that seemed to be floating above the ground. Its soaring peaks hinted at its Balinese inspiration. It looked light and airy, as if woven of delicate strands of bamboo by some giant master weaver. The landscaping and water features were unfinished but the trees and plants, living green sculptures, were stunning despite being surrounded by the detritus of a building site.

The van pulled up at the front entrance and Grace climbed out. The effect of the jungle all around was even more intense now, as the sounds of birds filtered through and the bamboo clacked softly in the breeze. Turning towards the beach, she saw the line of ocean shimmering beyond the gardens.

Breathtaking, she thought. Grace felt embraced and protected by the lushness of the nature that surrounded her. This truly was a jungle paradise.

As she walked into the main pavilion, which was still a work in progress, Grace's first impression was of a sense of lightness. The building's construction looked delicate, but she knew it was strong and flexible. In the briefing documents Alli had sent her, she'd read that the hotel met the highest standards for cyclone and typhoon proofing. And while the design was innovative, it was obviously inspired by traditional Balinese buildings. With its large spaces and soaring ceilings, it was a marriage of elegance and natural beauty. The quality of the building materials immediately impressed her – carved wood, polished stone, glass and tiles. It was clear no expense had been spared; everything around her was tasteful and carefully designed.

A young woman approached her. 'Ms Hagen? Welcome. I am Sutini. I'm the assistant to Mr Wija Angiman, the CFO for the company. Let me show you to your suite. We have a few rooms that are finished, and we want you to experience what the hotel will be like when it is complete.' She led the way, adding, 'I hope that is all right with you.'

'It sounds lovely,' Grace said, following behind. 'Thank you.'

The suite was like nothing Grace had ever stayed in before, including on her trips with Lawrence. She couldn't believe the sumptuousness and thought put into its every detail. After unpacking and freshening up, she barely had time to appreciate the luxury before Sutini knocked on her door and suggested they should head over to the briefing.

'Do you know who will be there?' Grace asked as they walked.

'I understand that a representative of the owners, the managing director, the architect, and the head of marketing will be attending, and perhaps some others. As you can appreciate, some areas still aren't finished and so the conference room is very basic.'

'I understand,' Grace said. 'Are you Balinese, Sutini? You have an American accent.'

'Actually I am from Java. I went to college in the US,' Sutini answered. 'Please, watch your step here.' She pointed to some building materials and workers' tools. 'They are putting up some handmade glass sculptures on these walls.'

'I can see that it will be stunning when the work's done,' Grace said. 'But more than that, there's a feeling of tranquillity here,' she added. It was true; even though she knew her problems at home hadn't changed, her physical and mental distance from them in this place was making her feel calmer about tackling them. But first she had to focus on the briefing.

Grace was thoughtful as she walked with Sutini to the conference room. Luxury hotels, no matter how beautiful, often had similar, familiar elements. But this one was utterly different, dreamlike in a way, because of its setting in a landscape that seemed almost untouched. In these surroundings, she could imagine how the whole island must have been like this once.

The conference room might have been a temporary setting, but it had the aesthetics of an art gallery. In the centre of the light-filled space was a magnificent long wooden table with about ten chairs around it, and a contemporary sculpture of lava rock in one corner. An eye-catching though deceptively simple arrangement of flowers and greenery sat in the centre of the table. Hand-blown crystal water glasses were set at each place. Sutini's description of the room as being basic made Grace wonder what Sutini might consider 'elaborate'. Grace stopped and looked at the beguiling vistas from the huge windows.

Almost immediately, a tall, well-dressed man entered the room and strode towards her. 'Ms Hagen, how do you do. I'm Hans Speyer, the marketing manager for MGI,' he said, and shook her hand. 'Welcome.'

Grace had read about him and knew that he'd worked around hotels in Asia for years.

Other people followed him in, and soon the room was filled with greetings and conversations. Hans's assistant, a Javanese man, escorted her around and made all the introductions.

The marketing manager, the head of finance, and the hotel's architect had all been invited to be part of this briefing for Grace. She was particularly interested to meet the son of the owners, Johnny Pangisar, a handsome Balinese-Chinese man who looked to be in his late thirties.

The architect had a face she wouldn't forget. Samuel Mandura wore small, dark-framed, round owl glasses that gave him a rather penetrating stare. His long dark hair was carefully styled and smoothed into a ponytail, held in place by an ivory clasp. He wore an immaculate linen shirt and pants with funky raffia sandals and carried, though didn't use, a silver cigarette holder. Grace later discovered that he used it to stab at things for emphasis, knocking it on the table, pointing it at people, or holding it against his nose in contemplation before launching into a tirade or a serenade of effusive praise.

Arriving late and apologising with a shrug and a grin was another Australian. He was deeply tanned and wrinkled as a result. Noticing his tangled mop of grey hair, Grace thought he was probably in his late sixties. He introduced himself to Grace as Andy Franklin. It didn't surprise her when he explained that he'd 'come to Bali in the old days to surf and never went home'. Andy was setting up and would be managing the hotel's bars and overall food and beverage – or 'F and B', as Andy called it – as well as its entertainment program. 'Nothing loud and flash, very classy but fun,' he was quick to explain.

'Fabulous.' Grace smiled and wondered if he'd guessed that she'd first thought he was just an old surf bum rocker.

'If you want, I'll take you for a spin later around the clubs and bars so you can see what's happening on the scene,' he said to Grace.

'Thanks for the offer, I'd enjoy that,' she said.

With the introductions over, Hans called everyone to the table and they got down to discussions in earnest. There was a lot to cover, and even though Grace had read the copious briefing papers, her head soon started to spin.

Eventually, they agreed that as the venue was not finished to a degree suitable for filming, her pitch should focus on the stage one online teaser campaign.

'It can use the artful branding that combines the venue's lofty artistic and culinary direction,' said Hans. 'The next stage of the campaign will feature our brilliant celebrity chef with his vision for the venue and his aim for culinary excellence.'

'Chef is brilliant, and mad as a meat axe,' Andy said to Grace.

Ignoring this remark, Hans continued, 'And, as Grace has suggested, stage three could reveal more of the venue, the accommodation and the staff. Stage four will feature the beach club, bar and entertainment, and its international roster of superstar DJs.' He gave a nod towards Andy, who gave a cheerful thumbs-up to Grace.

'Any additional thoughts?' Hans asked, looking around the table.

Grace said, 'Perhaps as it's an international campaign we could include some footage of some other parts of the island. Then, later, we could film the official Balinese blessing ceremony at the hotel opening, and maybe an interview with the Minister for Tourism, to use in future campaigns.'

Johnny Pangisar added, 'My sister is planning to have her wedding here. My mother would love it to be filmed and included in the package.'

There were immediate murmurings of acquiescence. It was quickly apparent to Grace that had the mother asked for a parade of elephants or a circus performance, it would have been instantly agreed to. From her background reading and research, Grace had ascertained that the Pangisar family were international billionaires. They'd made their money through dealings in petrochemicals and tobacco. This hotel was a new venture for them, which they'd handed to their son to oversee.

Grace had been told Johnny was in the international jetset, while his father was more a traditional Balinese businessman whose Balinese-Chinese wife came from a wealthy family. There were two daughters, one a businesswoman in her own right married to an American, while the younger daughter, an artist, was about to marry an antiques dealer from Sumatra. Neither had any interest in the hotel.

Grace glanced around the table. 'This is a major campaign. Every concept here is tasteful, innovative and inspiring. I would want our visuals to reflect that. There is a big story here. I'd like to flesh it out a little more as we go along, of course, but to start with we have plenty to attract potential customers and visitors in our stage one online campaign. I'll come back to you with my ideas and a formal proposal,' she said to Hans directly.

Hans cleared his throat and smiled as the room went quiet. 'Thank you, Grace,' he said, 'I think everyone will agree that this has been an extremely productive meeting. Your ideas seem to align with our vision for the campaign. Spend the next couple of days soaking in the essence of our hotel, and talk to us individually, if you like.' He looked across at Johnny, who gave him a quick nod. 'Then get your pitch to us as soon as you can.'

'I will, Hans. Thank you.' Grace realised that everything about this job felt right. 'I'm very grateful for the time you've all given me today. I'll develop the ideas we've discussed and work on the pitch now,' she added.

It had been a long meeting, and when Johnny also thanked them all for their time, then stood up, everyone was ready to leave.

Andy pulled out Grace's chair for her as she rose, and Hans joined them.

'I hear you are very good and people like to work with you.' Hans smiled. 'We are looking for the best team to launch our project.'

'Absolutely,' Andy said. 'Who would you have in mind to direct this extravaganza?' he asked her.

'One or two people. My first choice might be tied up with a film, but I'm not worried. I know I'll get a good crew together.'

'You ever do any movies?' Andy asked her.

'Only a few projects where a film production wanted to use a client or have something styled, or to arrange a contra deal for a client,' she said. 'A lot of people in advertising want to move into drama, though,' she added.

'We have arranged to take you to dinner this evening if that suits you, Grace?' said Hans.

'Yes, then you'll see what we're up against.' Andy laughed. 'The island is full of five-star restaurants and bars. You wouldn't believe the top-class chefs who come here,' he added. 'The hotels and other venues are constantly poaching each other's staff. But there's always some new star on the horizon. It's very competitive.'

'Really? I'm sure people will be rushing to work here when it's opened,' she said to Andy, then turned to Hans. 'Dinner sounds lovely. Thank you. Where and when?'

Johnny joined them. He gave Grace an appraising smile, and instantly she saw a rich, confident man used to getting what he wanted. 'You are clever as well as beautiful. I will see you all at dinner. Thank you for sharing your ideas with us, Grace. They sound excellent.'

'We have a driver at your disposal,' said Hans. 'He is available twenty-four/seven during your stay, and he'll meet you in the foyer at six.'

Back in her suite, Grace called her mother and spoke with Daisy, relieved her daughter was happy and 'busy baking cupcakes, Mummy'. They chatted and blew kisses before Daisy passed the phone back to Tina.

'How did your meeting go?'

'Gruelling. But my ideas were well received, I think. It's such a massive project. Mum, you should see what they're doing! It really is stunning. Magical. Very, very clever. It's exciting.'

'That's great! Good to hear you excited about something. So you want to do this?'

'I do. It's pretty groundbreaking. The architect and his team are really creating something out of the box, and money seems to be no object. But I just don't think I could do the whole job. It'll take months. I can't be away that long.'

'Why not? Why should Lawrence travel for his work any time he likes, and no one bats an eyelid, but you can't? You'll have to negotiate some deal with him.'

'You think he's going to make that easy?'

'Gracie, by the sound of this job it could set you up. Not just financially, but if it's as good as you say, it could really make your reputation. I haven't heard you this upbeat in ages.'

'What's exciting is the visual aspect. The whole place is like a movie set, a dream job in a location you can't imagine. I feel as if I'm in the last paradise on the planet.'

'I like the sound of that.'

'Listen, I have to get ready to go out to dinner. They're showing me some of the opposition – well, the culinary side of it. There's an old Aussie surfer dude here, Mum. You'd get a kick out of meeting him. Came here in the late seventies and never went home. He's setting up the entertainment, the bar and stuff. This island seems very buzzy. I don't think it's the laid-back place it was when you were here.'

'Go have fun. Send me some photos! Worry about Lawrence when you get back.'

When Grace finished the call, she sat for a moment, deep in thought. She felt completely torn. After what she'd seen and heard today, she wanted this job very badly. It had been a while since she'd worked on a project of this scale, but she'd run large campaigns before, and she could already see how she'd manage this one. If things at home were different, it would be a no-brainer. But as it was . . . Grace shook her head to clear it. She would just have to cross that bridge when she came to it.

The dinner at Johnny Pangisar's favourite five-star restaurant, Mejekawi, on the beach in Seminyak, was tasty, elegant and up-market, but Grace had the feeling she could have been anywhere in the tropics. When the others left, Andy took her on a tour of some of the most popular entertainment venues in the area. As they made their way along the busy streets, she started to see a more local side of Balinese nightlife.

'Aren't we going to anywhere in Kuta or Sanur?' Grace asked.

'Boofheads and bogans in one, and the other is the "elephants' graveyard", y'know, only for the ancients,' Andy replied. 'The night scene is pretty wild in some places,' he added. 'Bali's always been a place to let your hair down.' He grinned.

'So tell me more about what Bali was like when you first came. There wasn't much tourism here in the seventies, was there?' asked Grace.

'Nah. I was a teenager then, and a mad surfer. It was that film Albe Falzon did, *Morning of the Earth*. I just had to come here and see it for myself.'

'My mother talks about that film too!' exclaimed Grace. 'She came here in the seventies herself.'

'Yeah, the film and the music turned a lot of us on to surfing places like Bali. I came up here with mates and just surfed. We found some magic places no one had been to, so we kept them quiet.'

'How come you never went home?'

'Oh, I did, but just to see the folks and pick up my gear. I married a local girl. We started a little *warung* that grew into a café and then a bar. I started a band here, too. My wife and I stayed in hospitality for years, until she died. I closed the bar down after that – too many memories. Now I'm busy setting up the deal here for Johnny's family.'

'And your band? What happened to that?'

'Ah, I gave it away. Our main guitarist did pretty well, though. Sang with a group in the States.'

'And do you ever get back to Australia these days?'

'I go back every year. I still have family there, though they're getting on now, and my son has just moved to Sydney. But this is my home.'

'I haven't stayed out this late in years,' Grace said, laughing. 'Thanks, Andy, it's been fun, but now I need some sleep. Tomorrow I'll have to start talking to film people to see who would be available if this project comes off for me.'

'Hey, I know the local crews. The best video production teams here are the ones who do the up-market wedding videos, which ain't cheap. Bloody mini movies!'

'How amazing, is that a niche market here?'

'No. Big-time. The kids making them are creative, smart and well travelled.' He leaned forward and looked at her. 'But seriously, the person you should try to get to direct is Steve Boyd. He's been over here quite a few times from Australia. He'd have a ball working with these crews.'

'Oh yes, I've heard of him. He's brilliant. He won an award recently for a short film he made in the Kimberley, didn't he?'

'Yeah. I met him when he was up here doing a documentary on the artists in Ubud in the old days. He still does commercials, those big-budget jobs for Indian cinema and stuff. He doesn't mind a surf. I took him out to a few of the less well-known spots while he was here.'

'Sounds great. I'll call you tomorrow to get his details. Can you give me your mobile number, please? And I'll talk to the local video and digital guys. But right now, I'm ready to crash.'

'How about a surf one morning? I swim out the front of the hotel at sunrise most days. You should try it. C'mon, let's find your driver.'

*

Grace spent two days talking to creative video and digital companies, looking at their facilities and examples of their work, and discussing their availability. She had already roughed out her pitch for the stage one launch and was now working on the details.

She was busy all day and met with Hans in the evenings, and reported back to the agency every day, too. She made sure she spoke with Daisy and her mother at least once a day, no matter how busy she was. She hadn't seen Andy again, but rang him a few times for advice and the contact details of various creatives. She was beginning to think of him as a friend, an uncle, and, as a fellow Aussie, someone she could talk to directly and easily. He also knew just about everyone on the island and their history. He warned her to be wary of Johnny Pangisar, whose reputation as a playboy was pretty fierce.

'I never mix business and pleasure,' she said. 'Of course, you're a bit of an exception.' She laughed. 'Don't tell anyone.'

'I'm hugely flattered,' said Andy. 'Y'see, I look in the mirror and still see the handsome suntanned stud I used to be. Sun-bleached locks, fit and skinny.' He patted his paunch and grey head. 'And each morning when I get that first wave, I feel sixteen again.'

On her last day, Grace agreed to meet Andy on the beach out the front of the Kamasan at 5.45 am. She'd swim while he rode his board. He'd been insisting all week that she had to experience the sunrise.

And she was glad she did. She had grown up at the beach in Sydney, and she'd experienced holidays on tropical islands on the Great Barrier Reef and Fiji. But this place hit Grace emotionally and she couldn't understand why.

Further along the beach, where old coconut palms arched over the sand as if weight and age were tiring them, a rock wall of artfully tumbled rocks formed what looked like a natural barrier, subtly dividing the beach from the other resorts further along towards the township. Tucked away on this southern end, the Kamasan was blooming in splendid isolation. In the distance she could see figures moving, probably early morning surfers, walkers and hawkers. But if she turned her back on that end and looked to the golden horizon, the empty beach and trees, the shining unbroken line of endless waves, she felt she was on her own desert island.

Sitting on the sand, drying off after her swim, Grace tried to put in words how she felt, but Andy cut her off.

'Just soak it up. I get it. Some places grab your heart the moment you see them. Why do you think I never went back home to live? My friends in Australia think I'm an old hippy seeing out my days here. Which I am. Since my wife died, as I told you the other day, I don't really have anything keeping me here. But I couldn't imagine living anywhere else.'

They sat in silence for a moment.

'I just can't help feeling there's a reason I'm here. I don't mean for a job; I mean for my soul. It's very special.' Grace sighed. She wasn't ready to share her problems yet. Giving voice to them would spoil the moment, she thought.

'Yep. I can imagine how old K'tut Tantri felt. Why she flung herself into everything she did here.'

'Who's that?'

Andy turned to Grace. 'The heroine of Indonesia, although she's not known as that anymore. Sadly she's mostly been forgotten. Hey, come with me, there's something you should see.' He pulled her to her feet.

They walked along the beach, then Andy turned into a grove of coconut palms, pandanus and tangled bushes.

As the dried palm fronds crackled beneath their feet, he pointed into the undergrowth and Grace saw a tall, carved pole. Near it were several large stones that were pitted and covered in lichen.

'What was this?' she asked.

'The remains of the Suara Segara. It means "Sound of the Sea". K'tut Tantri's hotel.'

'A hotel? Here? How fabulous this must have been. When was this?'

'In the 1930s. She claimed it was the first hotel on Kuta Beach. There was no one like K'tut. Her original name was Muriel something . . . Walker, I think it was. She was a film reporter in Hollywood for a while. Had a big run-in with Noël Coward, apparently.'

'Really, Noël Coward? He was such a big name. She must have been pretty brave to take him on.'

'She was a legend. I don't know all the details. After the war, she kind of disappeared. But she stayed here after everyone fled when the Japanese came in. She wasn't Balinese; Scottish, I think, but she fought for the Balinese. As you can understand, she adopted Bali and they her.'

Grace stared at the forgotten ruins, trying to visualise how the hotel might have looked. She turned and faced the sea. A light breeze rustled the fronds above her head and lifted her hair.

'How beautiful, how evocative this setting is. It must have been a wonderful place to stay.'

'I agree. She had the right idea. God knows what she'd make of Kuta Beach now.'

'So you don't know what happened to her? Is there anyone I could ask? Who owns this land?'

Andy shook his head. 'I assume it belongs to our Kamasan Group. The Pangisars' land comes all the way through here. Maybe that's why this block has never been touched. I think K'tut was always something of a mystery woman. I could ask some of the old Balinese people, if you're interested.'

'I am. Very interested, thank you,' Grace said. 'I'd like to find out what gave her the strength to stand up for what she believed in. She must have been incredibly brave.'

Andy nodded but didn't say anything more. They turned and headed back along the beach towards the Kamasan.

'I can't thank you enough for bringing me here, Andy.'

'I don't tell many people about it. It's all forgotten now. Bali is booming again. Hadn't you heard?' He laughed.

'It certainly is,' agreed Grace. 'The Kamasan Hotel is contemporary and groundbreaking in so many ways, yet its roots are buried in a lost dream.'

*

That afternoon Grace met Andy once more for a goodbye drink before leaving for the airport.

He put a fluted glass in front of her.

'Wow, beautiful glass. I love it. What is it?'

'The glass or the cocktail?'

'Both.' Grace laughed then took a sip. 'Mmm. Tangy, sparkling, refreshing. I suppose it's dangerous too. Not sure what I like better, the beautiful glass or the drink!'

'It's called Sunrise. We also have Sunset, which is richer and heavier. This is lime, mangosteen, locally made gin, mint . . . maybe another secret ingredient or two. I'd have to kill you if I told you. Actually, it's not very alcoholic. And the glass is made from recycled glass.'

'Stunning. Is this your signature drink for the bar?'

'Maybe. We keep experimenting. Cheers, and *selamat jalan*.'

'*Selamat tinggal*. Thank you for all your help, Andy.'

'Come back soon,' he said, raising his glass. They clinked glasses and sipped their drinks. 'So, did you find a director?'

'I took your advice and contacted Steve Boyd,' Grace replied. 'He's based in Sydney at the moment. I'm meeting him when I get back.'

'Great. Everyone is very impressed with you, you know.'

'That's reassuring. Thanks for letting me know. Your bar and the entertainment are going to be sensational. I still can't believe what a huge project this is. I would be thrilled to be part of it.'

Finishing her drink, she stood and picked up her bag, ready to say her goodbyes. She was impatient now to get back and see Daisy and Tina.

'Tuck this in your bag.' Andy handed her a gift box. 'Two of the cocktail glasses. Think of us when you have a sundowner. And I have something else for you too.' Andy handed her a book.

'Andy, this is too much . . .' Grace began, but Andy waved his hands in protest.

'Not at all. I had this lying around at home and after today I knew you'd be interested. It's the book K'tut Tantri wrote about her time in Bali, *Revolt in Paradise*. It's out of print now, but there are still copies if you know where to look. I've read it several times and I'd love it to go to someone who'll appreciate K'tut's story. Enjoy, Grace, and see you soon, I hope.'

He kissed her on the cheek and escorted her to the entrance where Surya, the driver, was waiting.

Grace gazed at the lush green haven around her as Surya drove towards the exit. The gates swung open and they drove from the quiet gardens into the chaos of Kuta traffic as the two worlds collided.

Grace pulled out her phone and checked her messages and email. Still nothing from Lawrence. She hadn't told him she was going away and he usually called her every few days, so she had expected to hear from him. His silence seemed a portent of bad news, and she dreaded what would be waiting for her when she arrived home.

4

GRACE SAT AT THE kitchen table working on her borrowed laptop as Tina stacked the dishwasher after they'd shared an early dinner.

Daisy sashayed in, wearing the batik sarong and lace kebaya top Grace had bought for her.

'Ooh, how sweet you look,' said Tina. 'Can you do a Balinese dance for us?'

Grace smiled as Daisy twirled, and then closed the laptop, stood up, and gave her a hug. 'That was beautiful. I missed you, darling girl.'

'I missed you too, Mummy, but Nana and I had a good time. We went to the beach every day after school.'

The performance over, Daisy sat on the floor and started to play with Sparkle.

'That traditional outfit brings it all back. I loved the dancers at the temples and ceremonies,' Tina said, turning on the dishwasher and sitting down at the table.

'I only saw some traditional dancers in a hotel garden. I wanted to go to the temples and art places up in the hills, but I didn't have time. I never left "sunset strip",' Grace said, sitting back down opposite her mother. 'Everywhere I went was crowded with tourists and locals, except for the grounds of the Kamasan. I really can't get over how untouched it seems, in among all that development. The area around the hotel complex has been landscaped, but they had so much wild growth to work with. That's part of what makes it such a unique place.'

'The land must be worth a fortune. I remember what that area was like, basically unspoiled, with only small shacks, dirt roads and local souvenir stalls. I can't believe the photos now of all those resorts along the beach,' said Tina.

Grace sighed. 'I know, but it seems to be what people want; big swimming pools with waterfalls, yoga retreats and cocktails in coconuts at sunset. You could be at any island resort.' She shook her head.

'Is there anything left of old Bali?' Tina asked.

'Mmm, I'm not sure. The serious adventure tourists go to the outer islands to surf and scuba-dive,' Grace said.

'Can we go one day, Mummy?' asked Daisy.

Grace laughed. 'That's a good question, sweetheart. We'll see.'

'Well, those generic resorts are not my idea of an island holiday. I'm glad I went to Bali when I did. Anyway, why would I want to go anywhere? Look what we have on our doorstep!' Tina waved at the darkened window and in the silence that followed they could hear the surf rumbling on the rocks below. 'Now come on, Daisy dear, time for bed.'

'I'll take her,' said Grace, getting up. 'C'mon, honey bear, brushing teeth and story time. And you can tell me everything you and Nana did while I was away.'

Daisy gave Sparkle a goodnight pat and skipped out of the room beside Grace, holding her hand.

*

'Would you like a nightcap? You look rather worn out,' said Tina as Grace walked in and sat down on the lounge.

'No thanks, Mum. It's just that Mr Jamison emailed today. He's liaising with the insurance brokers for me, and it seems they still need more information about the house contents. I feel like I'm drowning – with everything I have to do for the claim as well as for work.'

'Grace, darling, you can only do the best you can and take it day by day.'

'I don't even want to think about the stuff in the house.' Grace sighed, remembering how Lawrence had insisted they use the furniture he owned already when they moved in together, and if they bought anything new, he chose it. 'You know, I never liked Lawrence's taste. It was so fake-opulent and over the top,' she added.

Grace preferred a simple look, with touches of shabby chic, which Lawrence loathed. He'd told her that his furniture was too valuable not to use, and it gave a better impression when people came over. Grace had always laughed at him and joked that most people had stopped visiting since they'd moved into their big new house anyway. It didn't seem like such a joke anymore.

'Didn't you itemise everything when you took out your home and contents insurance?' asked Tina.

'Lawrence would have done it, I suppose. But I don't care about any of the furniture and most of the other things. It's the sentimental things I'm really sad about. You know, photos, letters, Daisy's baby things . . . I don't know, Mum. I mean, how do I put a dollar value on those things? They're priceless to me.' She sighed again.

'It's okay, Gracie. I know this is hard for you,' Tina said. Then she frowned. 'I'd have thought Lawrence would have finished doing all that paperwork for the insurance by now. It's been weeks.'

'Me too. Actually, one of the insurance agents called me today and asked a few questions about the value of some of the things in Lawrence's home office that I'd listed for them. Maybe to compare my estimates with Lawrence's or something?' Grace grabbed a cushion and hugged it to her chest. 'Maybe they think what Lawrence is claiming is more than the correct value. Plus, I'm wondering what was salvaged from the fire. Like, what happened to the safe? It had my jewellery in it – or at least I thought it did. Lawrence bought the jewellery as gifts for me, and it would be worth a bit. Maybe I could sell it.'

'Ask to see the claims he's put in,' said Tina. 'You need to make sure anything valuable you have is in your name now.'

'You're absolutely right. I won't ever let Lawrence hoodwink me again,' said Grace. 'Now I just want to take back control of my life!'

'Good,' said Tina briskly. 'I never liked to say anything, but I hated the way he took the lead all the time. You were so confident and together before you met Lawrence and then suddenly, he took over.'

Grace nodded slowly. 'You're right. I didn't realise that all control of my money and, well, my everything was slipping away from me. He made such a big deal about being "old fashioned" and looking after me. He always said he loved to spend money on me and spoil me.'

'He spent money on himself too, I noticed,' said Tina. 'He had the expensive car and you had the family wagon. He had his suits tailor made, you bought clothes from the local shops. Oh, I could go on. I couldn't help noticing, but I kept my mouth shut.'

Grace shrugged. 'If you'd said anything I would probably have jumped down your throat. I think subconsciously I knew it was all a mistake, but I couldn't face admitting it. And with Daisy, the light of my life, well, you just keep on, eh?' She tried to smile.

'Until there's a big wake-up call like the one you've had. And it's precisely for Daisy that you're taking back control now, isn't it? It'll be hard in the short term, of course, but I think all three of you will be better off in the end. Just my two cents!' said Tina. 'Time to move forward now, my girl.'

Grace got up. 'Thanks, Mum, I will. I'm going to bed; it's been a huge week.'

*

On Thursday night, Grace's phone beeped.

I will collect Daisy from her new school tomorrow afternoon. Very inconvenient for me to have her out there at the beach. I will return her to your mother's on Sunday at 5 pm.

When Melanie arrived the next day, Grace was pacing around the house.

'Let's go have a coffee before you pick up Daisy,' Mel said.

'Lawrence is collecting her. And he's keeping her for the weekend. He's never had her on his own that long! Daisy has never spent a night away from me, except with Mum. Now he's keeping her for two!' Grace was furious

95

and close to tears. 'I know he's her father and he has a right to see her – and Daisy misses him – but this doesn't feel right!'

'Listen, one step at a time,' Melanie said. 'Start cutting all ties to Lawrence, other than regarding Daisy, and get him to give you some financial support for her.'

'Much easier said than done. I so need this job in Bali, Mel. It would be fantastic – financially rewarding, and it could set me up career-wise. It's such a great opportunity,' Grace said. 'But if Lawrence knows how much I want it, he'd probably throw every obstacle in my path just to spite me.'

'Honey, you need the money, and this is your work! Has he given you anything to help you – and Daisy – since the fire?'

'Nope. He assumes Mum will pay the bills, I guess. He hasn't contributed to the fees for Daisy's new school either. I just can't believe I have no access to our money. Mum doesn't mind helping for the moment, but she shouldn't have to.'

'Can't you take money from your joint account?' Mel asked.

'Well, no. Look, I know this is embarrassing but I never asked Lawrence for the password or even the account number.' Grace stared down at the floor. 'I'll talk to him about it and if that doesn't work, maybe the bank can help me, but I doubt it.'

'What does he say when you ask him about contributing to school fees and so on for Daisy?'

'If I mention anything he says to stop being petty and mean. He goes on about the pressure of trying to pull off a big deal, replace a *home*, and that I'm fussing over *small* domestic issues!'

'He's such an arsehole. Sorry, Gracie. But there's no other word for it.'

'Yes. I have to agree. I get so mad at myself for not seeing or admitting it before. But you know what? In part it's my own fault – I ignored all the signs. I could have made the effort to be across our financial issues, and I didn't. Don't –' She held up a hand to stop Mel protesting. 'No matter how unfair that sounds, it's true, Mel. But I'm awake to it all now. C'mon, let's go for that coffee.'

In the sunny little beach village they settled at an outside table and ordered coffees. Mel picked up the thread of the conversation again.

'It's not just you, Gracie. You and I both need to think about our finances – not only now but for when we retire. Women don't often think of their old age. Doesn't matter whether you meet another guy or not. You have to look after you,' she said firmly.

'Mel, the way I feel now I can't even look past the end of the week,' Grace said wryly. 'But it's true, I will need to think about my future if I'm on my own.'

'And think about Daisy. Lawrence is unpredictable. He might say he'll do the right thing by her and that she will come first. But from what I've heard of his rather mercurial business career, I'd say money is the driving force in Lawrence's life. He needs money to do all the stuff he thinks is important . . . that is, big-noting himself and surrounding himself with the "best" stuff.' Mel made quote marks in the air with her fingers. 'He doesn't have an altruistic bone in his body. Everything is all about him.'

Grace nodded. 'I know you're right. He won't do the right thing unless it suits him, or if it makes him look good, or so he can be the big important guy. I just don't know how I didn't see it. I'm so mad at myself.'

'You didn't see it because he didn't want you to see it. He paints this glowing, exciting, positive picture of himself, and he projected that at you for a long time. That's how he gets money out of people to invest in his businesses, too. It's an art form.'

Grace sighed. 'I felt so sad this morning, sending Daisy to school with a little backpack with her clothes, her favourite teddy bear, her toothbrush . . . it's not how I imagined things turning out.'

Mel reached over and patted Grace's arm. 'It's hard. But you know that Lawrence will take care of Daisy over the weekend, in his own way.'

Grace nodded. 'He'd better,' she said tensely.

When the waitress brought their coffees they sat quietly for a moment, sipping their drinks, and Grace started to relax, and decided to change the subject.

'Hey, did I tell you I'm meeting with the guy I really want to direct the filming for the Bali job?' she said. 'He's a cinematographer, and he's technically smart and very creative. He's won some major awards.'

'Wow, he sounds great – but also expensive and in demand. Is he available? And no offence, but if he's on the up and up, why would he want to do a hotel ad campaign?' Mel raised an eyebrow questioningly.

'Well, I hope he'll be available, and that I'll be able to persuade him!' Grace said with a grin. 'I can only try. He was in Bali a while back doing a documentary and loves the place, apparently. The Aussie guy who runs the bars and entertainment at the Kamasan, Andy Franklin, knows him and told me he thought Steve would jump at the chance to go back there. So I've outlined the brief, the creative approach, emailed him some mood boards to show him how I see the emotion, the energy, the lighting, the vibrancy, and the colours. This isn't your average hotel campaign; this will be something special. A challenge. I'm hoping that'll be enough to tempt him – and that he'll have space in his schedule to fit it in.'

'Do you know what he'd be like to work with?' Mel asked.

'No, but I know his cinematic style and that's important. He's an influencer, sets the trends, plus he's worked with big-name stars and with big budgets. It's lucky he just happens to be in town between jobs.'

Melanie thanked the waitress when she came to clear their empty coffee cups, then asked Grace, 'What exactly is your job title these days?'

'I'm Chief Creative Officer at large of The Carson Agency, responsible for the overall look and feel of the marketing, media and all branding connected to the client,' said Grace.

'Impressive, but that's a lot of work for one person, isn't it?'

'Not really. I only sign on from job to job,' Grace said, leaning forward and playing with the sugar sachet from her saucer. 'I didn't want to be locked in to the agency, having to take on too many projects at once. This way I choose and control what I want to do and have some security as well as some freedom.'

'That's unusual. But if they're giving you that sort of flexibility it shows you are damned good at what you do.'

'Like you, Mel! Whoever thought maths would be stimulating and interesting and entertaining! I don't know how you inspire those teachers.'

'Hey, mathematics makes the world go round!' Mel laughed, then said seriously, 'People just don't realise that it's part of everything we do every day. Maths rocks!'

'So do you!' Grace smiled and glanced at her watch. 'I'd better get back home.'

'Okay. I'll drop you back and head off.'

When Mel pulled up outside Tina's house, Grace reached over and gave her friend a hug. 'Thanks for taking the time, Mel. I really appreciate it.'

'Always a pleasure,' said Mel with a chuckle. 'I won't come in. Say hi to your mum. And let's do something tomorrow night, since you won't have Daisy.'

Inside, Grace called out to her mother. 'Hello! I'm back. How was tennis?'

'Mummy, Mummy!'

Grace stopped in surprise as her daughter ran down the hall towards her. 'Daisy! What are you doing here? You're supposed to be with Daddy. Where is he?' Grace picked up Daisy and hugged her.

'Hi. Her daddy isn't here.' Tina appeared in the kitchen doorway, eyebrows raised.

'What happened? Did you collect Daisy?'

'Yes. The school principal rang me. Said she couldn't reach you. And Lawrence was "tied up".'

'I'm so sorry. I was with Mel, I had my phone off.' She brushed Daisy's hair off her forehead and put her down. 'I wasn't expecting any calls . . . especially from the school. Where's Lawrence?'

'I have no idea,' Tina said quietly. 'Apparently he rang just before bell time and told the school that something had come up and he was unable to collect Daisy.'

'What! Thanks for collecting her.' Grace turned to Daisy. 'Have you unpacked your lunchbox, honey?'

'Um, no . . .' Daisy ran off to her room to get it and Grace took out her phone and began scrolling through her messages.

'So you didn't hear from Lawrence?' Tina asked when Daisy was gone. 'He really is a sod.'

'No, nothing,' Grace said, holding up the phone to show Tina. 'Just the message from the school. I'd better let Mel know. I was going to go into town with her tomorrow night . . .'

'Go anyway, sweetheart. Daisy can stay with me. I certainly don't have plans!'

'Mum, what would I do without you?' Grace gave her mother a hug.

'Grace, what are you doing about Lawrence?' asked Tina later, after Daisy had delivered her lunchbox and a handful of drawings she'd done at school and gone off to play.

'I'm still not sure,' Grace said, sticking one of the drawings on the fridge door. 'I'm glad he's not taking Daisy for such a long time, though. Maybe it hit him that a whole weekend is an age to have to entertain a little girl.'

'Yes, and where would they have stayed?'

'I assumed they were going to stay in the hotel across the road from his office. But Daisy might have been scared to be in an unfamiliar place like that.'

'He has to work up to these things and give us fair warning. He's not a planner, is he? Never mind any plans *we* might have had.' Tina shook her head. 'Selfish. Thoughtless.' She glanced at Grace, then burst out laughing. 'Every time I hit a good shot at tennis today, I wished it was Lawrence's head!'

'Mum! That's terrible.' Grace laughed. 'I will have to say something to him. He can't just inconvenience everyone by collecting Daisy when he feels like it. She has a schedule too!'

'Well, at least he has shown little interest in having

her so far, and been unreliable when he does make plans. That won't look good if custody becomes an issue down the track. I guess it might be best to let sleeping dogs lie, for now. Especially if your job in Bali comes to fruition,' said Tina.

'That's true.' Grace pulled out a chair and sat down opposite her mother at the kitchen table. 'I'll keep it simple.'

Grace picked up her phone and sent Lawrence a cool but polite text asking why he was unable to collect Daisy, and to please give her notice if it happened again.

His reply was curt. *A business issue came up. I am busy organising my life, Grace. But I am going to seek full custody of my daughter.*

*

On Monday morning, Grace sat in Mr Judd's office. Lawrence's text message had sent her into a tailspin, and she'd worried about it all weekend. She found Mr Judd's completely unruffled demeanour soothing.

'The first thing to do is not to panic. He hasn't filed anything yet, hasn't sent you any official documentation seeking a parenting order, and until he does so it's just an empty threat,' Mr Judd said calmly.

'But what if he *does* file something formal?'

'You'd be in a good position. You have always been the primary caregiver, and you're offering Daisy a relatively stable home with you and her grandmother, compared to the somewhat erratic living arrangements you've described Lawrence having at the moment. But the courts will always look at what is in the best interests of the child. There's a process. Step one: you are both required to enter into mediation under court supervision, before proceeding to the next step,' he said.

'I suppose that's to save everybody's time and money, is it? To be really sure about this big step,' said Grace.

'That's the general idea. Also, we can identify where the trouble spots and issues are. It saves the court's time and money in the long run. Yours, too.'

'My mother is paying my legal costs, so I hope so. I appreciate your help,' she added quickly.

Mr Judd stepped her through the stages that would follow, not just for parenting orders but for divorce, too, adding, 'That's if we don't run into any difficulties. I've yet to see a divorce case go through without hiccups.'

'Oh dear. Knowing Lawrence he'll make it as difficult and drawn-out as possible. He likes to win. Or to be seen to win.' Grace looked down at her clenched hands in her lap and tried to calm down.

The solicitor nodded. 'I know the type. Difficult people. I hope he doesn't follow that pattern, but we'll do our best to address it if he does.'

'What do you mean?' asked Grace.

'Some people stall and drag it all out to make you and yours suffer rather than taking the logical and smooth path. Ego plays a large part.'

Grace groaned. 'Yes. Well, that can be tricky with Lawrence. He is careful to make sure he always appears to be very successful. But I've learned he does sail a bit close to the wind, and that beneath all the bluster, he can be rather insecure – which surprised me when I finally saw that in him.'

'Well, nothing formal is in train yet, so let's concentrate on the present, shall we?' said Mr Judd. He looked over his glasses. 'Tell me now that you are convinced in your heart to move on from this marriage. How many times have you thought of leaving and he's persuaded you to stay with him? Is this the last straw? I'll be blunt: there's no point wasting your time and money, if there's any chance you will go back to him.'

Grace didn't hesitate. 'No. This is it. I feel like I'm breathing clear air for the first time in a long time. It's scary doing all this with no idea how I'll manage. But anything is better than feeling I'm slowly suffocating every day.' This all came out in a bit of a rush, surprising her.

'Good,' said Mr Judd, nodding solemnly. 'And to confirm: Lawrence hasn't actually sent you paperwork seeking parental orders for full custody. If he does, come straight to me, and we'll deal with it. Like I've said before: one step at a time. This is a long, slow process – nothing will happen immediately.'

'That's a sensible approach. On one hand, I'd like to rush in and get the process over with, even though I know the divorce will take a while. And on the other hand, the last thing I could do at the moment is go to court, if it came to that.' Grace looked at Mr Judd and said softly, 'I just don't have the strength for that yet.'

She left the lawyer's office feeling reassured but also nervous at the idea of an uncertain future. Underlying it all was the knowledge that Lawrence wouldn't make anything easy.

*

On the drive to her meeting with Steve Boyd later that week, Grace tried to put her concerns about Lawrence aside, and instead played over in her head the pitch she planned to use to persuade Steve to direct and film her Kamasan launch.

The looming issue of the job in Bali both excited and worried her. If she couldn't stay there for the job's duration, would it be feasible to commute up there every few weeks? At the moment she was going on her gut instinct to just plough on, hoping the logistics could be worked out later. From what Andy had said, she seemed to have made a good impression on the management team with her initial ideas and discussions during the few days she'd spent in Bali, and that was the main thing.

Steve Boyd's office turned out to be in a rambling old home in Lavender Bay, overlooking the harbour in the shadow of the Sydney Harbour Bridge. A young man opened the door, introduced himself as Henry and ushered her inside.

Loud music, probably a soundtrack, was coming from the front room, which Grace noticed had been turned into an edit suite. Two people were hunched over their computers.

'The front part is the working area; the back of the house is more sociable,' Henry explained as they walked down the long hallway. They passed rooms that were being used as an office, a small studio and maybe a recording studio, Grace thought. Then Henry opened a door to a large sitting room off a kitchen.

Covering one wall and spilling along shelves and in a glass showcase in an alcove was a display that stopped Grace in her tracks – the awards Steve had won.

'Wow, this is amazing!'

Gold, silver and bronze statuettes and a few plaques adorned the shelves, awards from film and advertising festivals and competitions all over the world. Proof that this guy was at the top of his game, Grace thought.

The young gun escorting her smiled. 'Yup. The wanker's wall. I'm allowed to say that. It is pretty serious though, isn't it? Steve's work is genuinely amazing.'

'You're not wrong,' Grace said with a smile. 'What do you do?' she added.

'I'm the resident barista.' Henry laughed. 'Actually, I'm also the nerd data wrangler and drone operator. I've run sound a few times when we haven't got an audio operator – we don't use them as much these days, what with the technology.'

'Of course, I see. Good for you.'

Outside the kitchen was a covered patio where a few people were seated around a large table, deep in conversation. One of them rose to greet her, and she recognised Steve Boyd from the picture she'd seen when she'd researched him online.

'Hi, you must be Grace. Sorry about the noise back there,' he said, nodding towards the hallway. 'We're just trying to finish up a sound job. I'm Steve.' He shook her hand warmly.

He had a direct gaze and radiated enthusiasm. He wore jeans and a pale blue linen shirt, loosely unbuttoned over a T-shirt with a logo she didn't recognise. He was one of those people who appeared comfortable in his own skin, Grace thought, and she envied him that. A calm person, she decided, and gave him a mental tick. This was a useful trait for the director, who was captain of the ship on a set, juggling diplomacy with the sometimes warring factions, temperamental egos, and logistical hiccups, all in an environment where time was money.

The group at the large table began to gather up their cups, computers and phones, and return inside, saying hello to Grace on their way.

Steve led her to a small table under the shade of a large tree. 'We can sit here.' He pulled out her chair and then sat opposite her.

Henry walked over to them and Steve glanced up and smiled. 'Would you like a coffee, Grace? Henry makes a mean brew. The usual for me, thanks, Henry.'

'Yes, please. Milk, no sugar. Thanks, Henry.' Grace looked across the garden and back to the house. 'Do you do all your post-production here?' she asked. 'You seem to have everything under one roof. Is this also your home?'

'It is. Not forever, but at the moment it suits me. I can get a lot done here, and then we're across all the elements of every production. The crew don't live here, though,' he added, laughing.

'I know your work, but I didn't realise you'd received quite so many awards for it,' Grace said. 'The collection inside is very impressive.'

He shrugged. 'Helps swing some clients to our side. And the ones who don't know what all the awards are, act like they do!'

'While I was in Bali I met Andy Franklin, as I mentioned in my email. He gave you a big wrap. Said he loved the doco you did on the artists of Ubud.'

Steve nodded. 'Andy's a great character. I suspect he has quite a story. I've only met him in his hippy-Aussie-seventies-surfer-dude role, though. He took me surfing to some unreal breaks while I was there. But I hear he's a mean foodie. Interesting guy.'

Henry brought them their coffees, then Steve got down to work.

'So, I read the material you sent me, and your notes. What else can you tell me about this hotel? It's a new one, isn't it?'

'I don't mean to sound like a cliché, but this is not just any hotel,' Grace began. 'What they're planning for the Kamasan breaks new ground. I'm still trying to get my head across all the levels of management. MGI – Masari Group International, have you heard of it? – is a specialist hotel management group that looks after hotels across Asia, a bit like the Marriott Group. The hotel owners, the Pangisar family, are Balinese-Chinese. They're based in Jakarta and are involved in a lot of different investments: telecommunications, real estate, tobacco, and they also have philanthropic foundations. The family don't want to be bothered with the day-to-day running and staff dramas of the hotel, which is where MGI comes in.'

'Yes, I've heard of the Pangisars,' Steve said. 'They seem to keep out of the limelight but they're very clever businesspeople, and powerful.'

'That's right. Their hotel and real estate investments and holdings are financially managed under the Kamasan brand. Their son, Johnny, is the front man for the family. I haven't exactly worked out what his role is yet, but he seems to be a shrewd operator.'

Steve leaned his arms on the table. 'Okay, to start with I'd need to do a comprehensive location survey. Not just for inspiration but to develop the concept and narrative as I see it, along with the brief you gave me. And that will determine my budget and crew and so on.'

'Of course,' Grace said, putting down her coffee mug. She felt a frisson of hope shoot through her – did this mean he was interested? 'Who do you think you'd need in your team? This has the potential to be a major job so you could need a large crew.'

'I'd initially allocate a drone operator and some tech people, and take it from there. We'd need to liaise on all this when there's a clearer script direction.' He spread his arms, giving a disarming grin. 'I'm very collaborative. It's just that my name sits out there in front of it all, so I like my projects to live up to expectations. I'll give you my latest show reel for your next round with them. I assume the hotel management group are footing our bill, not your agency?'

Grace nodded. Allison had told her the initial launch budget would be generous and covered by MGI, but she merely answered, 'I do need your reel, I'm sure it's impressive, plus your fee estimate for the concept development, survey costs, travel, accommodation, per diem.' She knew that the survey was necessary to develop their creative approach and to help them gauge accurate production costs. 'Once that's calculated I'll do a presentation to the management of the hotel group. Then we'll need to wait for their decision to know whether it will all be approved.'

She smiled, knowing she had moved the chess game forward.

Steve tapped his fingers on the tabletop, thinking. 'I like it,' he said finally, and Grace, while careful to keep her expression composed, felt a flush of exhilaration. 'From what I read in your emails, this sounds like a challenge. I like the idea of turning a hard-nosed commercial business into something that's also beautiful, evocative and cutting edge, yet still meets the sales brief.' He leaned back. 'And it's in Bali! I have a soft spot for the place, I admit. Could you fill me in on some more background on the family?'

'I don't know much more about them, I'm afraid. When I arrived at the hotel, I thought it was unusual that the land was still with one family and they are only just developing it now. There's a story there, I suspect, other than that they're very rich and the land has always been in their family. But I assume I'm only getting the simple version . . . that the project is family controlled, no outside investment. As you probably know, only Balinese can own the land in Bali. The family are Chinese originally, but now they're Balinese-Chinese and they changed their family name to make it more Indonesian. There must have been a convenient marriage sometime that meant they could say they are partly Balinese, I guess.'

'Yes. It was a more casual arrangement in the early days, I think. The foreigners – the *bule* – had to team up with a local, sometimes by marriage or just on trust. They brought in the sales and marketing expertise, and the locals had the land and the labour,' said Steve.

'Yes, I see. The Kamasan concept took me by surprise a bit,' said Grace. 'I expected to see that same slick cookie-cutter tropical resort you find all though the Pacific and Asia. You know, with a superficial smattering of Balinese culture and design but otherwise no different from any other hotel or resort.'

'I know what you mean,' Steve said. 'A tourist's view of Bali with all the stereotypes attached to it.'

Grace leaned forward. 'But there in the middle of the tourism madness is the last piece of untouched beachfront land. Serendipitously, it's owned by a family with not only the money but the inclination, style and taste to develop it in a way that's utterly different from everywhere else. I was blown away.' She stopped, noticing Steve's expression. 'I can see you think I'm showing all the signs of someone fresh from their first trip to Bali. But I can honestly say this development is like nothing I've seen. It's outstanding and original,' she said, smiling.

He laughed, crossed his arms and tried to look serious. 'I apologise. Bali is a mad, magical, mysterious and soul-stealing place. I love it. So what are they selling that's different?' he asked. 'The ultimate experience, the latest in products, services, technologies? Robots serving cocktails?' He chuckled. 'Sorry, I don't want to seem face-tious, but have you seen the rollout of resorts, villas, new style *losmen*s, everywhere? Seminyak, Kuta, Sanur . . . even Ubud in the hills. And then there are the other little islands, like the Gilis. It's a crowded marketplace with plenty of competition.'

Grace held up her hands. 'I know, I know.' She leaned forward again. 'What they're doing is very different, and yet for those who want that high-end Bali experience it meets the brief.'

'Yep. That set who go to the classiest bars and clubs and can drop fifteen grand US plus in an evening. I've seen them do it,' he added.

Grace pressed her point. 'Take the setting, for example. It's magical. It's a chance to reinvent old Bali, the lost and forgotten Bali; to be creative and bring together innovative, modern influences with traditional design and Balinese culture.'

'That won't come cheaply.'

'No way,' she agreed. 'But the family owns the land already and it's in a prime location.'

'Cheaper than knocking down one of the older resorts, I guess.'

'Its beauty is that it's virtually untouched land, and they've been smart about embracing that and making it a feature, not bulldozing everything to make way for just another resort,' said Grace. 'It's a remarkable situation.'

'Okay,' Steve said slowly. 'How do they think they should sell this paradise? Where are they coming from? I have my own thoughts, as do you, I'm sure.'

Grace pulled out her iPad to show him some new images of the hotel. 'This might give you some idea of what they're building.'

Steve nodded as he skimmed through some photos and drawings of the complex.

'You're right, it's different from the glitzy, rich, tropical extravagance I've seen in some of the resorts up there.'

'Yes. And even though they're not finished, you can see how stunning the gardens will be. It's natural and wild, but cleverly cultivated into these amazing, almost theatrical landscapes,' said Grace.

'Ah, no doubt inspired by the work of Made Wijaya,' said Steve. 'He was a Sydney boy named Michael White, who jumped off a ship and swam ashore to Bali in the early 1970s. He found his calling in Bali, and changed his name. He established most of the fabulous gardens in big homes and in the first resorts and hotels. He died quite young; a big loss. I can imagine what he would have done with your paradise.'

'It's fascinating to learn how Bali has evolved to be so contemporary, yet it never let go of its culture,' said Grace. 'But tourism is God there now, it seems.'

'Yes, that's true. The foreigners who went there in the early 1970s were welcomed because the government saw them as a means to an end. The country was broke and it had come out of a purge of mass killings and famine.'

'I know, I recently watched the old movie, *The Year of Living Dangerously*.'

'From what I've read, the government infiltrated every-thing, and they saw the expat foreigners as bringing in lots of cash. So they embraced them, thinking that was the way to the future. But it backfired. Those first tourists didn't have money for travel as they know it now,' said Steve.

Grace nodded. 'My mother went up there in the late seventies. She didn't have two pennies to rub together then, she said, but she loved it.'

'It was the hippy era! They weren't looking for four-star hotels; it was free love on the beach, dope and drugs, surfing and mysticism. Bali was the travellers' pot of gold at the end of the rainbow. Not quite what the government had in mind.'

'Well, they have their tourist money in spades now.' Grace laughed. 'You seem to know a lot about the place; why's that?'

'I met some wonderful characters when I was filming the art scene doco in Ubud. You couldn't make them up! And I only scratched the surface. As well as the artists, the dance and music culture is breathtaking.' Steve leaned back in his chair. 'Tell me, the name Kamasan. Does it have any connection with Kamasan village?'

'I have no idea. What's in Kamasan village?'

'It's where traditional Balinese art evolved, going back centuries. It's a very interesting archaeological site, and art continues to be a focus there. It's considered the "heart" of Bali.'

'Fascinating, I didn't know that. Hmmm, could be a theme for the campaign perhaps,' said Grace thoughtfully.

Steve stood up and stretched his legs. 'I agree it's effective to have a story hook for the project, rather than just a tourism hard sell. Certainly gives us more creative opportunities,' he said. 'Which market do they want to appeal to? Trippy-hippy backpackers have no money. So that leaves the rich international older set or the international players, the children of the jetset, the playboys and their trophy wives ... Or people with taste who appreciate style and have the money to afford it, or all of the above?' He grinned. 'I'll need a bit of time to think about this.' He picked up the iPad and scrolled through the images again.

Grace felt her heartbeat pick up. She asked tentatively, 'So, what do you think, Steve? Are you interested?'

He looked at her, and she hesitated.

'Sorry, I don't mean to rush you.' She smiled and forced herself to relax.

'It's all right. I'm just trying to think about how we could sell this in a different way. I don't usually do stock-standard commercial projects anymore –'

'That's why I'm here,' interjected Grace.

He laughed. 'Let's get another coffee and talk a bit more.' He went into the kitchen, returning a few minutes later with two fresh coffees, and sat down.

'So tell me about you. How come you landed this gig? Are you the exec creative at your agency?'

She bristled for a moment but then saw that no slight was intended. 'I had meetings with the marketing people and others from the hotel up in Bali and presented them with a pitch. First off, though, I gather MGI liked the package the agency sent them – my bio and demo reel. I have to admit I'm a very keen film person. And I've had a few successful campaigns,' Grace added modestly.

Steve leaned back and sipped his coffee. 'I'm with you. Movie buff. Storytelling rules. You can tell a story in a thirty-second ad and move people emotionally.' He tilted his head and asked, 'Do you want to make movies, too?'

'Me? No . . . well – I don't know. I haven't really thought about it. I just try to bring the heart into each job as a way to connect with the audience. I guess I actually try to hide the sales pitch angle and get to them by enter-taining them, capturing their attention so they can be fully engaged with what I'm "selling" them.'

'It's not something you can really learn,' said Steve slowly. 'Sure, you can follow the trends, the shooting style and imagery, but to make someone put their hand in their pocket . . . that's the test.' He put his cup down. 'I like the way you think, Grace. If you get the job, count me in.'

Grace couldn't help the smile that flashed across her face. 'That's wonderful. Thank you, Steve. I'm so pleased. It's going to be an exciting project.'

'Yes, and now comes the best part. Tell me your ideas,' he said.

Grace straightened in her chair. 'Well, as I mentioned, the setting is what bowled me over. I would want to make the jungle around the hotel – the natural landscape – a big part of the backdrop to the campaign. You'll see what I mean when you're there.'

'I look forward to it.'

'How's your schedule looking?' She knew this was probably the only remaining hurdle: if he couldn't fit the job in, they could be back to square one.

He gave a small smile and shrugged. 'As it turns out, I have a gap. The finance just fell through for a movie. Happens all the time. So this could work for me if it all comes together. What's been the feedback so far from the group running the show?'

Grace felt a wave of relief wash over her. 'MGI are receptive, as is Johnny Pangisar. And, of course, you'll get to work with Andy.'

'I'm definitely up for that. Not to mention the surfing! Andy is one of the originals. Straight out of *Morning of the Earth*.'

'You know that film? My mother talked about it. She said it was one of the first Bali surf films.'

Steve nodded. 'There's some amazing footage out there of early Bali, going back to the thirties. Did you know that Charlie Chaplin went there with some of his friends? I found it hard to reconcile that spunky guy I saw in the film footage with the character of The Little Tramp! Bing Crosby and Bob Hope did a "road" movie supposedly set in Bali in the old days. Bali's culture is the same as always – it's the visitors and the modern world that's changed,' said Steve.

Thoughts of old Bali suddenly reminded Grace of the book Andy had given her. It was still in her bag, though she'd been so busy and distracted since she got back that she hadn't had a chance to start reading it. She reached into her bag and pulled it out, showing Steve. 'Actually, Andy gave me this to read. *Revolt in Paradise*. Have you heard of K'tut Tantri? Andy took me on a beach walk one morning and showed me the remains of an old hotel there – on the Kamasan land, incidentally – which apparently K'tut established,' said Grace. 'It must have been amazing. It was in a coconut grove right beside a deserted Kuta beach.'

Steve grinned. 'Not only have I heard of her, I've read that book! I stumbled across a copy when I was in Ubud. I'm a bit of a history buff, actually. You'll enjoy it – it's an incredible story. She was an inspirational woman. Scots-American, wasn't she, and a writer in California before she came to Bali?'

'Yes, it sounds like she hit the big time. Andy said something about a run-in with Noël Coward!' Grace replied.

'And her hotel is on the Kamasan land, you say? Now that's something.' He looked thoughtful.

'I wonder what happened to the hotel?' Grace mused. 'We could try to find out. Could be another angle we could use in the campaign. But for now, the important thing is, you're interested,' she added, smiling.

'Yes indeed, in theory. Let me do the numbers and I'll get back to you.' Steve stood up and held out his hand. Grace stood too, and they shook on it.

*

Feeling elated after her successful meeting, Grace decided to swing by the agency while she was in the neighbourhood and catch up on any news while relaying her coup of getting Steve Boyd on board.

However, her heart sank when she walked into the big open-plan area where staff hung out to relax, chat, talk through ideas, or work away from their hubs, and heard the fast, high-pitched, nasal whine of Spencer's voice.

Spencer Campbell was the new young chairman of the agency and most of the staff considered him a hotshot with too much attitude. He'd been ruffling feathers in his sweep through the company to rev things up. While he considered himself a hands-on chairman and not a 'conference room chief', his arrogance and gung-ho, new-broom persona had caused a lot of angst.

Grace, and many of her colleagues, found Spencer irksome, to put it mildly. He'd had one clever idea once, which had become a popular campaign, and he'd milked it for all it was worth ever since. Some of the senior staff saw him as a Wunderkind, whereas he was more of a one-hit wonder in the eyes of the creative staff. Grace was glad she kept out of office politics as she worked virtually independently of the agency. However, she knew Spencer was annoyed by her 'wilful freedom' and had been attempting to rein her in by requesting that she base herself in the head office. She was relieved the assignment to Bali would take her even further from the sphere of Spencer.

'It was just *awwwwwful*, one of the worst campaigns I've *eeeeever* seen. Talk about a frog going off in a sock . . . *he* thought it was bloody marvellous. It was the pits! I would've fired the director on the spot . . . Oh, look who's here, *Gracing* us with her presence!'

'Hello, Spencer,' said Grace serenely. Then she turned to greet Allison and a small group lounging on a sofa, spreadsheets and drawings on the table in front of them. 'How's it going, guys?'

'Pretty good. How're you going with the Bali job?' said one of the young producers.

'Yes, what's Steve Boyd like? I love his work,' said Allison.

'Oh man, I'd kill to work with him. What's happening, Grace?'

Spencer turned on his heel towards her, his tight skinny jeans and leather jacket out of step with his pale skin, thinning yellow hair and pinched features. Grace noted he had new tortoiseshell-framed glasses and a glittery stud earring. Real or fake? she wondered idly, before deciding it was fake. Spencer was too mean to spend actual big bucks on something that might not be noticed. He wanted people to know when he was splashing money around, mostly on his expense account.

'Report to me about the film crew and director before you leave,' he said coolly, tapping one high-heeled tooled cowboy boot loudly on the floor.

'Oh, I can tell you right now, Spencer,' Grace said with a smile. Nothing was going to spoil her mood today. 'Steve Boyd and his crew are on board. Thrilled at the whole concept. Pretty good, huh?'

The group around her exclaimed in delight, congratulating Grace on such a fabulous win.

Spencer said nothing. He nodded curtly to Grace, then spun back around and stalked away, his shoulders as clenched as Grace's jaw.

*

Driving back to the beach in her mother's car, Grace thought how lucky it was that Steve had agreed on the spot. She knew there were still some hoops to jump through regarding money and logistics, but she'd seen the spark of enthusiasm in his eyes. He knew Bali and obviously wanted to film there again. And how great it had been to let the obnoxious Spencer have it between the eyes!

Her mind was racing with ideas. It was wonderful to be on a job that was so stimulating, fascinating and challenging, she thought. Don't get ahead of yourself, it's not a done deal yet, she cautioned herself. There's hard work ahead. But the signs are good! She glanced at the clock on the dashboard and worked out that she'd have time to get some notes down before going to collect Daisy.

But then she felt her excitement fading and the familiar tightness in her chest returned as she thought about Lawrence. She was worried he'd try to jeopardise this job, if he found out about it. If she landed some big contract, he wouldn't be pleased for her, he'd be jealous and obstructive. Every day that passed that she didn't hear from Lawrence about custody of Daisy made her a little bit calmer, but she knew he could change his mind at any time. She took a deep breath and repeated Mr Judd's words in her head: one step at a time.

*

Grace was making herself a pot of tea when her phone rang and she saw it was the local solicitor.

'Hi, Mr Jamison. How are you?'

'I'm very well, Grace. And you?'

'Well, okay. Bit more of a standstill, as far as my husband is concerned. I thought things might pick up once we'd agreed to separate. The living arrangements are an issue, for him, anyway. We really need that insurance money. One of the insurance brokers emailed and asked me to submit another list, this time about the items in Lawrence's home office. I've sent it to them.'

'Right, well, the managing broker contacted me. There seems to be an issue.'

'Oh no! What?' She sat down at the kitchen table, feeling the constriction in her chest tighten further.

'It seems there was nothing of much value left after the fire, which I think you knew already, but that even includes what was in the safe.'

'Wait, wait . . . You mean the safe in the house? But it was fireproof. It should have had all our valuables in it. What happened?' Grace could hear her voice rising.

'I believe the safe did survive the fire. They retrieved some papers that were in it, apparently, but nothing else, I'm afraid.'

'How's that possible?' she cried. 'You're telling me some papers survived but my diamond jewellery did not?'

'I'm sorry, Grace. I'm sure the jewellery meant a lot to you, but it's something you'll have to talk to your husband about. It wasn't in there.'

'No! Mr Jamison, the jewellery didn't mean a lot from a sentimental point of view, but it meant money! I wanted to sell it. I need cash!'

'Oh, I see. Well, if you're positive it was in there,

you'd better speak to the insurance broker and the investigator the company uses, a Mr Tony Freeman, I believe.'

'Well, I can't be positive. I never had access to that safe. It was my husband's . . .' She paused, feeling embarrassed. Again she berated herself. How had she been so, so . . . helpless? So trusting? *So stupid.*

'I think you'd better ask your husband,' Mr Jamison said again, quietly. 'And, if necessary, inform your family solicitor.'

'Thanks for letting me know, Mr Jamison. I'll do just that.'

Grace hung up, and felt like throwing her phone across the room. 'Damn you, Lawrence,' she shouted.

'What now?' Tina came in from the garden.

'Lawrence appears to have done something with my jewellery from the safe in our house. The investigators said there was nothing in there when they found it.'

'What! Why? How? He has money, doesn't he?'

'As I've learned, Lawrence always likes to give that impression. It's feast or famine with him. Honestly, Mum, I really have no idea what he does for money. All these business deals he talks about. Development in oil wells, gas, soy-bean production, futures, bitcoin, commodities . . .'

Tina frowned. 'And he always makes it sound like such a big deal. Doesn't he ever do anything local, modest, ordinary?'

'Sadly, it seems like he doesn't, or I wouldn't be looking around for something to pawn or sell,' answered Grace. 'Mum, I need to do this job in Bali. I really *want* to do it.'

'And you should. How did it go with the film director? Is he interested?' Tina asked.

Grace grinned. 'Steve agreed. I'm really delighted – he's terrific. It's exciting.' She paused. 'But I just can't see how I can go away without taking Daisy. I'll have to see Mr Judd again.'

'Listen, sweetie, you know she can stay with me, but I understand there could be legal issues with Lawrence. And as her father he has rights. He could leverage that to his advantage. But the fact that he's left you without any money, unless you take a job in Bali, means you don't have much choice. Knowing him, he'll twist it to make you look like you're an uncaring mum, dashing off for a tropical holiday. You'll have to be ready for whatever he throws at you.'

'I know. And who gets a high-paying job in Bali anyway, he'll say. It will be interesting to see how he spins the disappearance of my jewellery. It just doesn't add up.'

Tina gave her daughter a quick hug. 'You look so down in the dumps. Let's go out and have a coffee before we collect Daisy,' she said. 'My treat.'

*

That afternoon, Daisy seemed out of sorts, refusing to eat her dinner and crying broken-heartedly when Grace insisted they turn off the television after her favourite show, old re-runs of *Sesame Street*.

'Daddy wouldn't make me turn it off, you're mean!' she shouted at Grace, folding her arms and stamping her feet, her angry little face wet with tears.

Without making a big deal of it, both Grace and her mother knew Daisy was still feeling destabilised and confused at the upheaval in her life. They hadn't told Daisy about the separation yet, as the little girl was already coping with a lot of change. They'd just told her that Daddy was working in the city and they were staying with Nana near the beach until they found a new house.

It wasn't as though Lawrence used to see Daisy a lot even when they all lived under the same roof, so that, at least, hadn't changed much for Daisy. But it was clear she was picking up on the tension and uncertainty in the adults around her.

At bedtime, an exhausted Daisy clung to Grace and asked, 'When are we going to our new home, Mummy? Sparkle wants to go home.'

The cat looked perfectly content on the bed beside Daisy, but Grace knew her darling girl missed her home, her toys and clothes – and the sense of normality that her old life had had. This extended 'holiday' at her Nana's was worrying her, even if she couldn't articulate it.

'Honey, you're happy here, aren't you? And you like your new school, don't you?'

Daisy nodded.

'And being with Nana, and near the beach?'

'Yes, Mummy.'

'But you miss Daddy?'

'Yeah. Can Daddy come and live here too?'

Grace chose her words carefully. 'He has to work at his office, honey, and that's right in the city, so it's easier for him to stay there. Maybe one day soon you and Daddy can go and do some fun things together.'

'Okay.' She seemed reassured, reaching to pat the cat. 'Tomorrow I get to turn the pages when Miss Thomas reads our story.'

'That's wonderful. When you come home I'd love you to tell Nana and me all about it.'

'Uh-huh.' Daisy's eyes closed and she snuggled down to sleep.

*

123

After the long day she'd had and the emotional afternoon with Daisy, Grace decided to have an early night. As she climbed into bed, she remembered the book Andy had given her. A bit of escapism was exactly what she needed, she thought, and after the good rap Steve had given it, *Revolt in Paradise* sounded like just the thing. Snuggling down under the covers, she opened K'tut's memoir. The pages were thick and starting to yellow. She breathed in that old-paper smell, one she'd always loved. Flicking through to the first page, she began to read . . .

This is the story of a white woman who lived for fifteen years in Indonesia – living, not visiting – knowing the country and its people, from the highest to the lowest, and sharing their joys and their sorrows. This woman is myself. Which makes it more difficult for the telling because it is always difficult to be completely honest about oneself.

I spent the first fourteen years of my life on the Isle of Man, and then I went to school in Scotland. My stepfather was killed in the First World War. After his death my mother decided to go to the United States. We settled in Hollywood . . .

I myself was really an artist. It was largely through chance that I became successful in another field. I found myself writing interviews and articles about the film stars and the high moguls of Hollywood which were published abroad in British trade and film magazines. Yet I became increasingly restless. I was discontented. I was unhappy. I often wished that I was an archaeologist and would thus have a real excuse for going to far places. I thought the people I knew shallow and superficial. Their aims, their ambitions, were wholly apart from my own.

I must now come to the year 1932, which is another beginning for my story – perhaps the one that matters most. It was a rainy afternoon. I was walking down Hollywood Boulevard. I stopped before a small theater showing a foreign film and on the spur of the moment decided to go in. The film was entitled *Goona Goona, The Last Paradise.*

I became entranced. The picture was aglow with an agrarian pattern of peace, contentment, beauty and love. Yes, I had found my life. I recognized the place where I wished to be. My decision was sudden but it was irrevocable. It was as if fate had brushed my shoulder. I felt a compulsion, from which I had no desire to escape . . .

Escapism indeed, thought Grace, and felt a wave of empathy for this woman. Going to Bali from the Western world in 1932 must have been like going to the moon, and yet K'tut was bravely taking control of her life and directing her own fate and future. If she can do it, so can I, thought Grace, and she put the book on her bedside table and turned out the light.

*

Over the next few days, feeling freshly inspired, Grace concentrated on the contemporary angle of selling the Kamasan. She wanted their campaign to be stylish and creative while also being accessible to a wide range of people.

She contemplated finding a beautiful, exotic couple who might epitomise the type of guests who'd be attracted to, and could afford to stay at, the Kamasan. But it seemed too much of a cliché so she abandoned the idea.

Then came a text message from Lawrence.

I'd like to take you and Daisy to lunch tomorrow. I'll collect you at 12 midday. Your mother is welcome, but I would prefer to just discuss matters between us in private.

What the hell? Grace thought. One minute Lawrence was cold, brusque and combative – or just absent – and the next . . . this strange polite courtesy. What did he want? She steeled herself. Whatever it was, it was no doubt all part of his strategy. She would go in with her eyes open.

Lawrence arrived a little early, with a bunch of flowers for Tina, and swept Daisy into his arms.

'Hello, beautiful gorgeous adorable girl! Are you happy to see your daddy?'

'What have you got for me, Daddy?' Daisy began searching all his pockets.

'What makes you think I have anything for a little girl?' he teased.

''Cause it's *meeee*, Daisy,' she squealed. Then she discovered a package in his coat pocket and darted away with it.

'Where do you plan to go for lunch?' asked Grace. 'If you'd prefer to just take Daisy, that's fine.'

'Of course not. I enjoy being seen with my beautiful wife.' He smiled at Tina. 'You're welcome to come, Tina. There's a stunning new café at Palm Beach right on the water at Pittwater.'

Grace couldn't believe what she was hearing. Hadn't Lawrence specifically said he didn't want Tina to come?

And 'beautiful wife' . . .? What was going on? Grace saw Tina grit her teeth and smile tightly.

'Thank you, Lawrence, and for the flowers, but no, I can't join you. I'm meeting my tennis friends.'

'Daisy! Come and say goodbye to Nana. We're leaving. See you after lunch, Mum.' Grace kissed her mother on the cheek as Tina squeezed her arm.

Lawrence lifted Daisy up onto his shoulders, grasping her by the ankles, and called out, 'Have a lovely afternoon, Tina.'

Grace and her mother exchanged a surprised look as Grace followed Lawrence out of the house. He and Daisy were singing loudly. Grace used to think this was sweet. Now she felt irritated, but she bit her tongue. She would not say a thing against Lawrence to Daisy. It wasn't fair to drag little children into the issues between their parents. Daisy will figure him out as time goes on, she thought.

The restaurant near the water was surrounded by manicured lawns. It was clearly up-market and expensive. But the service was slow, and Daisy was soon bored with the small colouring sheet and two pencils she'd been given. Grace was not inclined to linger and wanted to order immediately, while Lawrence went through every dish on the menu with Daisy, describing it in detail.

'Lawrence, she doesn't want abalone. Just order something simple.'

'Grace, she has to learn there's more to food than hamburgers and chips.'

Grace bit her tongue, almost literally. He knew very well that she and her mother were healthy eaters. Lawrence was the one who opted for fast food. She recalled what he'd fed Daisy on their day at the zoo and fumed inwardly.

Lawrence and Daisy compromised on fish and chips.

'My daughter will have the beer-battered barramundi fillets with the duck-fat wedges. Do you do hasselback potatoes? No? Okay, just the wedges, please.' Lawrence smiled winningly at the waitress.

'Why are we here, Lawrence?' asked Grace tightly after she'd ordered and the waitress had left. She wondered if she should raise the issue of going to Bali or not, but she hadn't yet spoken to Mr Judd so she decided to keep quiet for the moment.

'I miss my beautiful daughter,' said Lawrence lightly.

'Tell Daddy about school,' said Grace, to distract Daisy.

Daisy was immediately enthusiastic and began to talk about her new friends, Charlie the pet guinea pig in the classroom, and her teacher, but Lawrence cut her short.

'How is your schoolwork, though? Reading and writing?'

'Good,' said Daisy in a bored tone.

'When I come back, I think we should find you a new school. In the city. Much more convenient. And I'm going to find us a new house,' he told her.

Daisy looked distressed. 'But I like my school now, Daddy!'

Grace tried to suppress the flash of irritation and alarm she felt as she patted Daisy's hand and suggested that she go and play on the grass while they were waiting for their meals to arrive. Daisy seemed happy to scramble off her chair and go to practise handstands on the lawn.

'What are you saying?' said Grace in a low voice, when Daisy was out of earshot. 'There's no new house. We're separated, remember. And what do you mean by "when I come back"? Where are you going?'

'Overseas. On business,' said Lawrence curtly. 'An opportunity's come up unexpectedly and I have to jump on it. I brought us here because I want to have a few matters cleared up before I go.'

'So if you're going away, then you're not seeking full custody?' said Grace quickly.

'I will not discuss private matters with you in public,' hissed Lawrence.

'Lawrence, you said yourself in your text that you wanted to discuss some matters today! So where are you going? When will you be back?'

He shrugged. 'India. Probably to and fro for a bit. I won't know until I have the initial meeting in Mumbai.'

'I see. Well, we're perfectly comfortable at my mother's house for now, in case you were wondering. And if you won't be around for a while . . .'

Grace let the subject drop as the waitress appeared with their entrées and drinks. When she'd gone, Grace said, 'Lawrence, look. I'll need money to help support us. There are school fees, and I need to replace clothes and things. I can't let my mother pay for everything and my income only goes so far. It's not reasonable that I'm paying for our daughter's needs entirely on my own.' Grace expected Lawrence to jump down her throat, but instead he pressed his hands together and leaned back in his chair.

'It'll get sorted. Just red tape with the insurance. Please, Grace. Let's enjoy our lunch.'

Fuming inside, she wanted to ask why the safe was empty but didn't want to upset Daisy with a scene. It would have to wait, or perhaps it was time for her lawyer to talk to his, Grace thought.

*

Lawrence dropped them outside Tina's house. As he helped Daisy out of the car, Grace said to Daisy, 'Tell Daddy thank you for the fancy lunch, please, sweetie.'

'Thanks, Daddy.' Daisy turned and skipped to the front door without looking back.

'Thank you for lunch. I hope your Mumbai deal goes well,' said Grace stiffly, figuring she may as well take the moral high ground and be polite.

Lawrence gazed at her for a minute, saying nothing. Then he got in his car and drove away, leaving Grace more confused than ever about what he was up to.

5

A STORM WAS COMING. Lightning flashed on the horizon behind the clouds out at sea.

Grace walked alone along the sand. It was cold, the sun had set, and a breeze had sprung up. Arms wrapped around herself against the chill, she turned and headed for home. On the rise above the beach she could see the lights glowing warmly in the windows of her mother's house. How grateful she was for her mother's generosity and love. She knew Tina enjoyed having her and Daisy there, but still Grace felt it was an imposition.

She'd also just got off the phone with her father. Until now Grace hadn't burdened him with the news of her separation and problems with Lawrence. He'd disliked Lawrence from the moment he'd met him. Her father had said his piece privately to her after one visit with them a year after the wedding, and that was it.

But today she'd been missing him, and she'd been struck with a pang of guilt when she remembered it had been over a year since he'd seen Daisy. She didn't want him to feel left out, to feel that he wasn't important in her life. She'd hoped he wouldn't say, 'I told you so.'

In the end, her father had been wonderful: he'd taken the news calmly, saying he wasn't surprised, and telling her she was a strong, independent woman and that he was thrilled she was standing up for herself. 'Go get 'em, Gracie,' he'd said. He'd asked if she was okay financially, and she'd assured him that she'd be fine once the insurance money came through, and that Tina was helping her in the meantime.

Now, as she walked along the beach, she thought how lucky she was to have two parents who loved and supported her so much. Then a thought struck her: if both her parents had always disliked Lawrence so intensely, why hadn't they said something earlier? She rather wished they had. But then, to be honest, would she have taken kindly to her parents intimating she'd married the wrong man? Probably not, she thought.

Although this walk had helped to clear her head, Grace felt more conflicted than ever. She was worried about her and Daisy's future, about Lawrence's threat to challenge her over custody of their daughter, their financial mess, the loss of everything she owned, and the fact that her marriage had failed. She wished simply that she had recognised all the danger signs long before things had gone beyond the point of no return with Lawrence. What upset her now was that it had taken her so long to see the truth of it all.

When had she stopped trusting her instincts? wondered Grace. She'd had misgivings on her wedding day, that was true, but why hadn't she been able to see that those were not just nerves but a deep intuition shouting at her, 'Don't do this'? Over the years of her marriage her trust in her own judgement had become eroded; she saw that now. She had to learn to trust herself again, and she'd make sure to teach Daisy to pause and listen to herself, and think hard before leaping.

Grace turned and headed back up the hill track away from the beach.

*

Later that evening, when Daisy had gone to bed, Grace came out of the study and announced to Tina, 'This presentation has to be perfect, but I've had enough for one day. Daisy is sound asleep. Feel like watching a movie, Mum?'

Tina glanced up from where she was reading on the couch and stretched. 'I'd love to another night, but I might just go to bed. I'm in a big tennis match tomorrow. Oh, by the way, have you started that book your friend in Bali gave you? The one about K'tut Tantri?'

'Yes. I've been dipping in whenever I can, although with everything that's going on I'm not very far in. But it's a fascinating story, and it's all true. K'tut is still known as Muriel in what I've read, and she hasn't arrived in Bali yet. She's just about to arrive in Indonesia, I think. She was a showbusiness writer, but became disillusioned with the Hollywood scene, and in 1932 decided to take a leap of faith and travel to Bali for a completely different life . . . imagine that. Pretty brave for a young woman alone back then.'

'Almost unheard of, I'd say,' said Tina.

'I'm finding it very inspiring,' Grace said. 'And, Mum, it put some things in perspective for me. There were so many more obstacles for women back then. At least I have a great work opportunity right at my feet.'

'Oh wow, I really will have to read it after you, if it makes you feel that way,' said Tina. 'Speaking of work, when do you do the presentation and talk to the hotel people again?'

Grace shrugged. 'I didn't get a chance to tell you, but they emailed me today saying they want to have the meeting in Singapore, for me to do my pitch to the family's hotel management group, MGI, as well as the money guys – the bigwigs of the Kamasan family and the CEO of MGI. Talk about layers of power.'

'Do you present your ideas, figures and strategies to them?' asked Tina.

'Yep. I'm explaining my overall grand plan then breaking down the strategy into its various components, beginning with cross-media initiatives. After that comes the big creative detail on how it will integrate into the media. This is the cue for me to then show the cross-media concept mock-ups and finally the fantastic animatics Steve put together from his past work using my creative concepts for the hotel. I think it's pretty genius. I'm using Coldplay's "Up and Up" as the background music. Then straight after the video, I present the costs documents, which include Steve and his production costs, my costs and the agency overhead.' Grace took a breath. 'This is probably my biggest job, ever.'

Tina shook her head. 'It sounds amazing. I'm so proud of you, Gracie. So, when are you going?'

'In a week or so. I'll be there for a night. I've decided not to let Lawrence know. If he asks I'll say I'm tied up in meetings. Which will be true. He's keeping his distance at the moment anyway.'

'He hasn't made good on his threat to go for full custody?'

'Not yet – and I'm taking no news as good news. It was probably just an empty threat anyway, and then when this opportunity in India came up, it didn't suit him to have full custody anymore. Really, I don't exactly see how he *could* sue for full custody from India. But still, it's awful to live with this hanging over me; I'm waiting for the axe that could drop at any second.' Grace felt her stomach churn at the thought, but shook herself out of it. 'So you're okay to look after Daisy, Mum?'

'Of course. I'm not going anywhere exciting,' she said with a smile.

'Thank you. And yes, I think I've got enough excitement on my hands for both of us at the minute,' replied Grace.

*

Johnny Pangisar had chosen the venue for the Singapore meeting, as well as Grace's accommodation, and as Grace expected, everything was first class.

She'd arrived in Singapore early after an uneventful night flight from Sydney and cleared Customs in record time. After settling into her room at the Fullerton Hotel, which had once been the central post office on the water-front, Grace spent time exploring its surrounds on the reclaimed land where Singapore was continuing to expand. She was impressed at this avant-garde city–state; its greening, a clever combining of nature with the urban streetscape, from trees on rooftops to hanging gardens on skyscrapers; stunning landscaping; the massed orchids at every turn. Sydney seemed rather moribund and cement-bound in comparison, and made her think again how valuable was the little world of ancient nature, just lightly retouched and directed, that embraced the Kamasan Hotel. Old nature, even in the lush tropics, was not easily replicated. This was part of the 'something extra' they could bring to the Kamasan in the competitive world of international hotel tourism, she reminded herself.

Her dinner invitation had been left in her room along with a gift: an exquisite finely woven seagrass handbag on a long slim plaited strap with a beautiful tortoise-shell clasp engraved in gold with her initials. This was no flimsy beach bag, she thought. She looked at the invitation: *Please join us after today's meeting for dinner at Odette, National Gallery, 8 pm. And après at the 'Marquee', Marina Bay Sands.*

This was going to be a long day, a late night, and an early flight home the following day. Grace decided to go over her presentation and then take a nap in her luxurious suite before getting ready for the afternoon meeting. Looking around, she wished she could share all this with Melanie, so she sent her a wish-you-were-here text and photos. A few moments later Mel texted back: *Enjoy! You deserve it!* and attached an emoji of a big smile followed by *Good luck, you'll knock 'em dead!* and a thumbs-up.

Feeling buoyed, Grace switched on her laptop and got to work.

*

Grace arrived early at the Fullerton Hotel's conference suite to check that all the necessary technology was in working order. Then she went to freshen up in the ladies' room and calm her nerves.

When she walked back into the conference room the MGI executives were there. They introduced themselves and made small talk as Grace glanced at the door. This was it, she thought. Breathing deeply, she checked and rechecked her notes and equipment. Finally the Pangisar entourage were announced and made something of an entrance, their lateness annoying Grace, rattling her somewhat, though she was careful not to show it.

After some introductions and pleasantries, the CEO of Masari Group International, whose name was Farrouk Eljoffrey, finally opened the meeting, outlined its purpose and introduced Grace. He then introduced the consultant who'd be doing all the hotel's publicity, an attractive young woman named Rosie Chow, who ran the biggest public relations company in South East Asia, and also re-introduced Hans Speyer, the MGI head of marketing, whom she'd already met. The group settled around the long conference table. The immediate Pangisar family was present: Johnny, his father, plus a sharp-eyed, scarlet-lipped, mature-aged Chinese-Indonesian woman wearing serious diamonds, who was introduced as Madame Pearl Kutarian. Grace later found out that she was the sister-in-law of Mr Pangisar Senior and an investor in MGI.

Grace was nervous. She'd put so much effort into this pitch. She really wanted this job and she knew she could do it well, though she also knew that was no guarantee of success. But nothing ventured, nothing gained, she told herself, and, taking a deep breath, she launched in.

She began by going through the strategies she was planning to employ, and how they would influence the creative plans she had in mind. The centrepiece of her concept was to release video segments and filmed vignettes through social media every week or so to attract potential clients to make bookings well in advance of the hotel's launch. Using the techniques of storytelling, the short films would illustrate the hotel itself, its setting and staff, things to do, highlights of the local area and other amazing places around Bali. She felt her knees quiver as the faces around the table remained immobile, giving away nothing. A ripple of doubt ran through her but she pressed on, and when no one challenged her ideas, and her strategies seemed to be accepted, her confidence began to rise.

But as she came to the video presentation her heart was in her mouth. She knew that if they didn't like this, she was in trouble. She dimmed the lights, creating a sense of drama and flair for this crucial portion of the presentation, and the room went quiet as she started the video. Action burst onto the huge screen.

Steve had warned her that typically Chinese business-people were difficult to present to, and so she was prepared for a low-key reaction. When the video ended, the room was silent.

Then, from the head of the table, Mr Pangisar Senior spoke. 'Play it again, please, Ms Hagen.' His tone was noncommittal. As she hit the icon again, the lead weight in the pit of her stomach grew heavier.

But this time around there was a rumble of mutterings, and Grace sensed her audience was appreciative. There was even the odd 'Ooh' and 'Aah'. Then she heard Johnny's excited whispering and saw him leaning towards his father. As she brought the lights back up at the end of the ninety-second video, she saw, with relief, smiling, excited expressions. There was even a smattering of applause – a rare event at presentations such as these, she guessed. She allowed herself to hope.

Grace started in on the last part of her presentation: the financials. She had always feared that perhaps the budget she was requesting would be too high. As she was about to run through the figures on the screen, Mr Pangisar Senior interrupted her and asked a question about the editing technique of the video. As she started to answer, Grace was suddenly shocked when Johnny reached over and slid her financial notes away from her, pushing them instead in front of Farrouk Eljoffrey, saying, 'Just give this to MGI's CFO and make it work, will you? The family have no problems.'

Her heart lifting, Grace continued addressing Mr Pangisar Senior, briefly explaining the video technique as a combination of real footage, CGI and special effects. He nodded and then smiled.

'Please forgive my reserved reaction initially. To show no emotion is the old Chinese way, as my father taught me. Times change and Jonathon, of course, does not agree. Regardless, I feel this will be a very good campaign for us. Thank you, Grace, and welcome on board. Let's get this done.'

As the group broke into applause and smiles and nods, Grace let out her breath in relief and said, 'Thank you, Mr Pangisar. I am delighted to be a part of the project.' She began to gather her papers together with slightly shaking hands.

This was a huge step. She wished she felt as confident as she sounded. While she'd got the gig, she now had to pull it off. Thoughts of the job and all it entailed brought with them the problem of Lawrence and the separation, and moving to Bali with Daisy for possibly an extended period of time. But she put them aside for the moment: the night ahead would be a celebration of all her hard work, as far as Grace was concerned.

Before she changed and headed out to dinner, she had just enough time to dash off an email to Spencer at the agency telling him the good news. He'd been emailing constantly over the past week, insisting she keep him updated. Put that in your pipe and smoke it! she thought.

The dinner was held at the elegant Odette restaurant in the National Gallery building, in a private space with personal supervision from chef Julien Royer. Grace was glad she'd bought a new outfit for the occasion: fitted silk pants, stilettos that would likely rarely see the light of day again, a lace top and loose matching silk jacket, all in the palest of apple green.

Johnny Pangisar acted as host, making sure the Dom Perignon flowed and the mood was upbeat. Grace, seated between Farrouk Eljoffrey and Madame Pearl, as the others called her, was very conscious that she was playing in the big league. Johnny paid Madame Pearl particular attention, his manner hovering between solicitous and flirtatious, although only once did he elicit a partial smile from the older woman. Watching this handsome hotshot, Grace couldn't help but admire the easy style of a man she knew to be a shrewd operator, one who knew just who held the aces and who could be useful to his family business.

When everyone had arrived, Johnny welcomed them, and then handed over to Farrouk Eljoffrey, who rose and thanked everyone, giving a nod to Madame Pearl. He went on to say that this was an exciting and auspicious time for everyone present. He gestured to Grace, welcoming her to 'the world of the Kamasan' and adding that they were excited now that their dream had found its path to reality, thanks to The Carson Agency, especially Ms Grace Hagen and her team's creative inspiration. He lifted his glass and the waiters stepped forward to pour more Dom Perignon as he proposed a toast to 'Paradise. The last paradise and the most magnificent paradise in Bali – *to the Kamasan!*'

Grace raised her glass and accepted the accolade with a smile. When the toast was over and everyone had gone back to chatting, Grace noticed that opposite her, Rosie and the marketing manager Hans Speyer were deep in a conversation about music trends and hot DJs. Johnny overheard a remark and leaned forward.

'Have you heard Mr AJ? The DJ *du jour*? You must come with us to Marquee after dinner, we've booked a table. You'll come too, Grace?' Johnny turned his smile on her.

'Okay. Lovely.' She knew of the latest clubs in Sydney but nothing compared with what she'd heard about Singapore's fabulous new club.

Limousines delivered them to the Marina Bay Sands, and walking into Marquee, Grace was taken aback at how slick, glitzy and classy it was. And costly! She overheard one of the executives mention that the table had cost $40,000 to book. Shaking her head in disbelief, Grace caught a glimpse of the star DJ on a dais prepping for his set.

She studied the spacious open-plan, three-storey wonderland, with dizzying tube slides between floors that would have sent Daisy into a spin, and gasped at the full-sized, fluoro-lit ferris wheel! Its cabins also turned out to be photo booths to record the experience.

The cleverly designed dance area meant there was plenty of space for people to show off their moves. There were pockets of comfortable leather banquettes, island tables and a massive decorative peacock that overlooked a long bar. Comfortable lounge seats had space for at least forty people, and a bar was strategically placed at all corners of the club so there were no long waits for the super-stylish drinks. At least two dozen waiters worked the club, too. Grace took mental notes to pass on to Andy: here was a venue doing everything in an exciting way.

'Woah!' Grace watched as the immersive sound and 8K-resolution screens flashed to life.

Johnny was jigging up and down. 'This technology won't be available in your home for at least five years,' he enthused loudly.

'Not in my house! It's ear-splitting!' she shouted back, laughing.

Rosie came up to join them. 'Wow, they've done a good job. *Crazy Rich Asians* meets *The Great Gatsby*!'

As the others were ushered to their reserved banquette, Johnny held out his hand. 'Come on, Grace, let's do it!' he said, and pulled her onto the dance floor.

The rest of the evening hurtled past like an out-of-control meteor, as she later described it to Melanie. Mr AJ was like a magician, controlling them all as he punched buttons and switches, and lighting effects, more like fireworks, exploded and zoomed around the room, punctuating the throbbing music. At one time, Johnny clasped Grace to his damp silk shirt, his sinewy body pressed against her, before spinning them apart. For a moment Grace thought about letting her inhibitions go and flirting right back at him . . . No. What was she thinking? This was the biggest project of her life. She had to keep a cool head. Nevertheless, as she moved to the throb of the music, she felt the years slipping away, as though she were peeling Lawrence away from her life and she was a free spirit again.

'Just how out of control were you?' asked Melanie on FaceTime the next morning as Grace drank her breakfast coffee before getting ready to fly home.

'I wasn't, really, it was just so nice to let my hair down properly. Wait till you see what the club was like – I'll send you and Mum some pics,' Grace replied.

'Great. I'm glad this is all working out so well for you. It's come at just the right time, hasn't it? Bali could be really good fun.'

'It's also going to be hard work. I have to get all the paperwork in order. Thankfully MGI are sorting out my KITAS, the work permit that's good for six months. They'll help me find accommodation too. I don't want to live in a hotel no matter how plush. And I need to find a school for Daisy.'

'And they'll pay for it all, I hope,' said Melanie. 'What does your lawyer have to say?'

'Last time we met he said to take it a step at a time. Well, it's time for the next step! So I'll see him when I get back. I'd forgotten what it's like to be free, have a bit of fun, to have a challenge – in a good way – with my job.'

'Well, don't let Lawrence know any of this! He'll deliberately throw a spanner in the works, knowing him. Frankly I think he'll be jealous that you're so stunning at what you do.'

'I know. But at the same time, I don't think I can just take Daisy out of the country without telling him: he is her father, and I'd be furious if he did that to me. I just have to hope he doesn't make a fuss. He can't exactly look after her while he's in India, anyway. No doubt he's busy greasing palms and wheeling and dealing.' Grace heard Melanie's snort of derision down the line. 'Hey, let's catch up when I get home, I've got to head to the airport now,' said Grace. 'See ya, Mel.'

*

The minute Grace walked in the door, Daisy ran and clung to her.

'Mumma, Mumma. Come and see, quick.' She tugged at Grace's hand as Grace smiled at Tina, giving her a quick hug. Then Daisy dragged Grace to her bedroom. 'I did it all myself!'

Grace clapped her hands to her face when she saw her bedroom as Daisy danced around her. 'Oh, wow! This is gorgeous, darling!'

'See, see. Surprise, Mumma!'

Grace ooh'd and aah'd at the drawings and decorations Daisy had painstakingly made and hung up all around the room. A drawing of roses, carefully coloured in, was on her pillow.

'We couldn't find real roses, Mummy, but you can keep these ones forever and ever!'

Grace kissed her daughter and hugged her fiercely: she would never let Lawrence take her away. 'I certainly will. Much better than real roses. So, tell me, what else have you been doing?'

'Reading! Nana is teaching me new words. I can read my book to *you*, tonight!'

'Great idea.'

Sitting at the kitchen table with a pot of tea, Grace brought out the gifts she'd brought home for her mother and daughter. This time it was their turn to ooh and aah. Daisy opened a hot pink box and took out a small red handbag, perfect for her little hands. Tina's present was a golden silk shawl that she immediately draped over her shoulder.

'The shopping in Singapore is incredible; there are towers, palaces of shops. I only shopped around the hotel, had no time for anything else. But a serious shopaholic would be in heaven.'

'Is everyone still very status conscious, label and brand oriented?' asked Tina.

'Absolutely. No fakes for Singaporean shoppers. I even saw people rub a business card when they exchanged them. If it was embossed and good quality, I'm sure it went in a special pocket,' Grace laughed. 'So, Mum, any news?'

'Not really. Not a peep from Lawrence, you'll be glad to know.' Tina smiled at her reassuringly. 'So, what next? Will you now assemble your team?'

'Yes, we start preparations in earnest now. That reminds me, I must ring Steve and fill him in. I sent him a text when I knew the job was a done deal; I think he's pretty keen to get started.'

'It's a big project, pays well. No wonder.'

'Hmm, I think it's more than that. I feel the same way. Yes, it's a huge project, but it's selling it in a way that's really special that matters. We have to highlight the hotel's originality and difference in a show-stopping way . . . I'll have my work cut out, but I have lots of ideas of how to bring it all together. And you know the book Andy gave me? I think it might turn out to be really useful: I can't wait for K'tut to arrive in Indonesia and hear about what it was like back then.'

'You and me both.' Tina laughed.

*

Grace was now in a whirlwind of preparations to head off to Bali, bouncing between meetings or calls with the agency and with Mr Judd and Mr Jamison. She had a brief discussion with Steve, who had cleared the decks and was getting his crew together for the Kamasan project.

Her biggest worry was money. When she'd rung Mr Jamison, he'd said nothing had happened with the insurance claim as far he knew, which he thought was unusual. He promised to make some follow-up calls and get back to Grace as soon as possible.

He rang back the following day to report his findings. After the call, Grace walked into the kitchen as Tina was unloading the dishwasher. Tina glanced up at her daughter and her face fell when she saw Grace's expression.

'What's up?' she asked in alarm.

'Mr Jamison just rang about the insurance money from the house. It's been paid.'

'What? Well, phew, that's a relief then. Isn't it?' Tina stared at Grace.

'It was paid two weeks ago. Lawrence hasn't said a word – and he must have told them not to tell Mr Jamison either – and there's nothing in my account, even though Mr Jamison had given the broker my account details.'

'Surely they can't have just paid it all to Lawrence, when they had your details too. They shouldn't just do whatever Lawrence tells them!' exclaimed Tina.

'Yes, that's what I said. Mr Jamison said it might have something to do with that wretched, mysterious trust document. He still hasn't been able to get a copy of it, but he said it's possible that a document like that might give Lawrence that kind of power.'

'Well, you get on the phone and demand to know where your share is. You need that money, Gracie. And what about your jewellery? Did Lawrence claim for it?' Tina closed the dishwasher and leaned against the kitchen bench. 'Is Lawrence in the country?'

'He's still in India, from what I can gather. I'll send him a text, and ask him about putting some money in my account. Maybe they mailed a cheque and it's slow.

Possibly this is all a misunderstanding.' Even as she said it, she knew there was no way this was a simple mistake.

'Have you told him about the Bali job yet? And taking Daisy with you?' asked Tina gently.

'I spoke to Mr Judd yesterday and his advice is that I'll have to tell him, as I thought. I don't want it to look like I'm kidnapping Daisy! I'll gather as much information as I can about the job, accommodation, schools, nannies, et cetera, to prove that Daisy is going to be well looked after. Lawrence doesn't even have a home – isn't even in the country! – so I don't see how he could think Daisy would be better off with him. He'll have some time to think about it while I go to Bali ahead of Daisy to get settled. It's only fair.'

'What about formal court orders? What did Mr Judd say?'

'I'm hoping to avoid having to go through the courts. Mr Judd said that if there are no court orders in place, I'm not breaking any orders or laws by taking her. But I don't want to be seen as trying to prevent Lawrence seeing her: if it did get to court, the court wouldn't like that, it doesn't look good. But I don't see how he can argue that if he's in India anyway, and if I tell him about it well in advance and show that she's looked after.' Grace sighed.

'What if Lawrence objects?' asked Tina.

'There is a chance that he could make an urgent application to stop it: force me to deliver her passport to the court, that sort of thing. I just have to hope that he's too busy in India and doesn't try. I won't stoop to his level and try to hide things from him.'

'The court process sounds like a nightmare,' said Tina.

'Absolutely,' Grace agreed. 'Mr Judd explained it to me last time. What a palaver it all is. It could drag on for months! It could take six to eight weeks each time to get into private mediation. Public mediation would take much longer. And then getting into court, even for a hearing, is likely to take months after that. I need that insurance money! Not just for the lawyers, but for day-to-day living.'

'What about the job?' Tina asked. 'I suppose you don't get paid till the job is done?'

'More or less. They give me a debit card to cover living expenses and travel, and then the agency is paid after each tranche of the campaign is finished. It's a kind of package deal.'

'Would Lawrence agree to mediation? He's doesn't seem one to compromise and, well, mediate. He's a "his way or the highway" sort of a guy.'

'I know. Mr Judd agreed and was pretty blunt. Said I'd feel as though it is resolved or almost sorted, and then he'll raise something else. I can look forward to this pattern in a never-ending, heartbreaking loop.' Grace's shoulders slumped.

'Well, that's a lot to look forward to,' said Tina dryly.

'One step at a time,' Grace said. 'It's becoming my mantra! And for now my focus is on getting me, and eventually Daisy, to Bali. Would it be okay with you if Daisy stays here for a few weeks while I go there and sort all of that out?'

'Of course, sweetie. But you need to get the finances worked out. And, I did have an idea . . .' Tina gave Grace a big smile. 'When the time comes, why don't I bring Daisy up to you in Bali? I'm intrigued now to see it again. I can stay a while and help look after her. I have time – one of the benefits of being retired!'

Grace felt a rush of happiness, relief and gratitude. 'That's a *great* idea! Thanks, Mum. My mind is so full of my job, I just don't want to know about all the Lawrence hassles. This makes the case for Daisy coming with me even stronger. She'll have the two of us to look after her there.'

'Wonderful.' Tina beamed. 'And speaking of Lawrence, I had another idea too, Grace. Why don't you contact that woman who works for Lawrence and say you need to get into the safe? Do it in person. Say you want Daisy's passport.'

'But I already have it, Mum.'

'She won't know that for sure, though. It seems to me you need to find out a few things. He's been too secretive and controlling. You'll be in Bali for a while and might not get another chance while he's out of the country.'

'Mum, I wouldn't have thought you had such a conniving streak in you. Great idea. Let me check out the time zones. I don't want her calling Lawrence to ask permission.'

*

Grace was at her most charming with Jenny, the part-time personal assistant Lawrence had been using for the past eighteen months. She was fairly sure Lawrence would not have shared any of their personal issues with his PA. He'd always been very firm about keeping their private lives private, which in this case Grace planned to use to her advantage.

Grace had spent a lovely evening with Melanie and had sent a late-evening text to Jenny saying she was spending the night in town and had an 8.30 am appointment, but needed Daisy's passport to enrol her officially at school and also some documents from the safe for the meeting. Could Jenny let her in early and open the safe for her, please? It would only take a few moments.

Jenny answered her text at 6.15 the next morning, agreeing, if hesitantly.

Grace arranged to meet her at the office at 7.45 am. Melanie went along with her.

They waited on the footpath below Lawrence's office, until Jenny hurried towards them, fishing the keys from her bag.

'Sorry to keep you. I only live a few blocks away.'

Grace introduced Melanie to Jenny as they caught the lift up and she opened the office door.

'I've been so overwhelmed with things, paperwork and such since the fire . . .' stammered Grace, hoping she seemed flustered.

'Oh, yes. What a horrible thing. Just awful.'

'I'm so relieved Lawrence had the sense to keep some papers and things here in his office,' added Grace sweetly.

Melanie rolled her eyes behind Jenny's back as Jenny put her bag on her desk and went into Lawrence's private area.

Grace stood by Lawrence's clean desk as Jenny punched in the safe numbers. Melanie sat on the sofa watching Jenny open the safe door with a clunk, and straighten up. She stood to one side as Grace took her place. She was surprised to see another passport in the safe, so she quickly took it.

In the outer office Jenny's phone started to ring and the PA hesitated and then dashed out to answer it. Mel was beside Grace in an instant, reaching over her shoulder and grabbing two large, unsealed envelopes marked *Personal and confidential*, one of them very bulky. She stuffed them into a tote bag.

Grace scanned what was left in the safe and recognised

the insurance papers so she snatched them up and put them in her own handbag.

They could hear Jenny saying, 'Hello . . . hello . . .?'

She came back into the office as Grace straightened up.

'Thanks so much, Jenny. I have the passport.' She held up the crinkled leather passport holder. 'Sorry for the rush and being so early. It was one of those now-or-never appointments. You know what bureaucrats are like.'

'Nice to meet you, Jenny. C'mon, Grace, can't be late.' Melanie was almost pushing Grace across the floor.

Jenny nodded. 'You're welcome. I'll let Mr Hagen know you came by. He's probably not up yet. It's very early in Mumbai.'

Out in the street, Melanie's phone rang. She glanced at it and smiled. 'Jenny. Checking who rang her.' She disconnected the call and put her phone in her bag.

'Oh, Mel,' gasped Grace. 'You're incorrigible. Did you ring Jenny to distract her? How did you know her number?'

'I saw it in your contacts when you texted her yesterday and thought it might be useful. Turns out it was!'

'Wow, good thinking. I need a coffee, I feel quite shaky. Let's go in here.' Grace walked into a café.

It was a little rundown, bordering on old-fashioned, with dim lighting and a printed menu featuring Devonshire Tea as their speciality.

Grace was clutching the tote bag. 'Should we look at the stuff in here?'

'Stop feeling like a criminal, you haven't done anything wrong,' said Melanie quietly. 'Of course. What did you grab?'

'Well, I got the insurance papers.' She pulled out and opened one of the envelopes Mel had picked up. Scanning the document inside, she said, 'I think this is the trust document. The one that Lawrence said gave him the right to sell my Paddington flat. Mr Jamison is still trying to get his hands on a copy, I think.'

'Oh fantastic!' said Mel. 'Whatever happened with the flat?'

'Mr Jamison came down on Lawrence like a ton of bricks. I think he spooked him and Lawrence backed down. Said it was a "misunderstanding" on my part,' Grace said, rolling her eyes. 'Mr Jamison threatened taking out an injunction, but we didn't have to take it that far.'

'That's a surprise. How do you know he won't try it again?'

'I suppose I don't,' said Grace.

'Well, we'd better give a copy of that trust document to Mr Jamison and find out just what it gives Lawrence the power to do.'

Grace nodded and turned back to the insurance document. 'Here they list the contents of the house that were saved from the fire . . . it's all odds and ends. But no jewellery. It's not that I loved the jewellery; it's the money it must have cost. I could do with that now.' She went back to scanning the insurance document. 'What did you get?' she asked, without looking up.

'Ta-da!' Melanie tipped the contents of the bulky envelope, which proved to be a number of small boxes, onto the café table. Grace recognised them immediately and gasped. Mel took one and, opening it up, she showed Grace what it contained: a pair of diamond and ruby earrings.

'My jewellery! Oh no. Those were a wedding anniversary gift. I've hardly worn them. Was always scared I'd lose one.'

Melanie opened a few more boxes. 'Look at this stuff. Bit OTT; doesn't seem your taste.'

'It's not,' Grace said. 'The word "gaudy" springs to mind. I like sweet, sentimental, simple things. I so treasured a necklace Daisy made for me at school. I'd much rather have saved that from the fire. Over the years I tried suggesting nicely to Lawrence that he didn't need to buy me expensive jewellery. I hardly wear it and he won't let me choose anything. I think at one point it wasn't insured, which is why I didn't want to wear it. So I was happy to leave it in the safe. Don't know why he thought it'd be safer in the office.' She was pondering this when her thoughts were interrupted by the waitress bringing their order: the tea came in a metal pot with a dangling teabag string and the coffee was basic. Having deposited their drinks, the waitress was about to walk away but then paused in some shock, looking down at the jewellery.

'It's okay, we're not thieves,' smiled Melanie. 'She just left her husband.'

'Good for you. All I left with was a black eye.' The waitress gave them a crooked smile and turned away.

'So what am I going to do with this? I can't sell it; he'll notice it's missing. I need to copy the documents and put it all back in the safe.'

'While I keep Jenny busy!' Mel laughed. 'You know, you could sell just one or two pieces of this jewellery, just to give you some cash while you sort out the insurance money. It is yours, after all. We'll put the empty boxes back in the safe and hope it's a while before he notices.'

Grace nodded slowly. 'Yes, that could work.'

'Well, that settles it then,' Mel said, handing the ruby and diamond earrings to Grace. 'We'll get the documents copied this afternoon – and properly witnessed. I know a

JP, he can notarise them. Do you know when Lawrence is due back?' Mel started closing the boxes and putting them, including the now empty earring box, back into the envelope.

Grace said suddenly, 'Actually, there are a few pieces missing. Were there any other boxes in the safe?'

'I don't think so.' Mel put the envelope back in her bag. 'I'd say Lawrence is probably selling your stuff for urgent funds. I guess he thought you'd swallow the line that it was all destroyed in the fire.'

'Well, if that's the case, the joke's on him,' said Grace darkly.

As they prepared to leave, Grace, who was rifling through the remaining papers, gasped.

'What on earth . . .' She was looking at the passport she'd taken, which she then thrust at Melanie. 'It's one of Lawrence's old passports. But look inside.'

Mel stared at it. 'Seems this is an early one. Why would he keep it?' She looked at Grace. 'What's up?'

'It's from the UK. Look at the name . . . Mel, it's him, see the photo . . . but the name?' said Grace. She stared in shock at Mel. 'Who the hell is Justin Odford?'

'What!' Mel glanced at the passport again then looked at Grace. 'This is his real name, or it's a fake passport. Except it's expired . . .'

'What on earth is going on? Who did I marry?' said Grace hoarsely. She dropped her head in her hands.

'You okay?' Mel reached over and put a hand reassuringly on Grace's arm.

Grace looked up. 'What else don't I know about this man? It's scaring me now.'

'Calm down. He thinks he's clever and everyone else is stupid. Like I said, we'll get these documents photocopied and witnessed, and we'll put everything back in the safe.' Mel leaned forward. 'We could start doing searches on this name. But you know what? You don't care, Grace! You don't want to know! Just disentangle yourself from this man as soon as you can. You must send copies of all this to your lawyer and keep a set yourself. Say nothing to Lawrence. He'll figure it out soon enough. Then he can't bluff you and you've got ammunition.'

'He'll know I saw it all. Jenny will tell him.'

'She doesn't know that you took anything other than the passport, and we're going to return it all. And right now, who cares? Say nothing. Carry on. We can use this to your advantage, Grace. Drink your coffee; I hope it's better than my dishwater tea. We have a few errands to run, and a return trip to Jenny. And after that, you're going to Bali!'

*

The next week or so passed in a frenzy of preparation. Grace sold the earrings for a decent price – not as much as they were worth, but enough to give her some money to tide her over. She could start contributing to her lawyers' fees – and there was a lot of work for them to do. She gave Mr Jamison the certified copies of the insurance document and the trust deed so he could advise her on what they meant. She also gave him a copy of that creepy old passport, for safekeeping.

The fact that Lawrence seemed to have had a different name, a different past that Grace knew nothing about, coupled with the fact that she'd heard nothing from him about the insurance money, tipped the scales for Grace. She told Mr Judd that she wanted to seek parental orders, and that he should do whatever was required to get mediation rolling. She had to protect her little girl. Then, instead of heeding Mel's advice, she googled 'Justin Odford'. So many references came up that she quickly abandoned that approach. She thought for a moment, then logged on to Facebook. She hardly ever used it, and knew that Lawrence didn't use it at all, so it was unlikely he would have an old profile she could search for. But maybe his sister would be on there. Her name was Beatrice, or so Lawrence said. Hoping that he hadn't lied about her first name, Grace typed 'Beatrice Odford' into the search bar. Of all the entries that came up, there was only a woman in the north of England – Lawrence had always said his family was from Sussex – who looked like she might be around the right age. Grace sent her a brief, polite message, explaining that she was trying to find relatives of Justin Kenneth Odford. She included the date of birth on his passport. That would have to do for now: she turned her mind to the seemingly endless list of things she had to do ahead of her departure.

Next, she had to gather as much information as she could about her Bali living arrangements, to show Lawrence that it was the best thing for Daisy over the next few months. Fortunately, both Johnny and MGI made it easy for her, lining up top-notch accommodation and helping her choose a school.

The Kamasan had organised a villa bungalow close to what would be Daisy's International School in Canggu. Grace's accommodation and living expenses were covered by the company, as they were for Steve and his key people: Henry, his tech and drone assistant she'd met in Sydney, and Mateo, the cameraman. Steve had already lined up several whizkids from a local production company to work with him, including negotiating the use of their studio and facilities. He and the crew had opted for a large shared villa in a complex near where Grace would be staying. There was, she was informed, a cook and staff at her villa. And a driver, of course. She, Daisy and Tina would want for nothing.

Once she'd gathered this arsenal of information, she sat down and wrote to Lawrence, copying in both his PA, Jenny, and Mr Judd, trying to keep it as short as possible.

Lawrence
As you have not responded to my messages, I am forwarding this to your assistant, Jenny, as well. If you have engaged a lawyer, please let mine, Mr Judd (copied in) know.

Please respond to my text messages about the insurance money. I understand it has been paid entirely to you. Apart from the fact that half of it belongs to me, it proves that you at least have the funds necessary to support our daughter.

As you have not cooperated in any way to financially support your family since we lost everything in the fire – house, car, belongings, etc. – and as you have control of the finances, I have found it necessary to take what employment has been offered to me, in order to support myself and our daughter.

I have accepted a position that requires me to spend some time in Bali, Indonesia. My mother is caring for our daughter, using her own finances, until I can make arrangements for Daisy to join me in Bali, where I will be working for the next couple of months.

You have no home, no belongings and are travelling overseas. I feel Daisy will have a more stable and secure life with me in Indonesia in a comfortable home and she can attend school in the expatriate community. She is old enough to value the experience and learn from it. I have attached details regarding Daisy's accommodation and schooling while we are in Bali. My mother will also be with us. I'm sure we can agree that Daisy will be well looked after. I don't want to prevent Daisy from seeing you – you are her father. If you let me know when you will be back from India, we can work something out, I'm sure.

I want our marital and financial situation settled as soon as practicable. You'll be hearing from my lawyer.

Grace

After carefully re-reading the email, Grace hit 'send' and sent up a silent prayer that Lawrence wouldn't cause problems. She knew she'd done the right thing in informing him. Then she turned her mind to the next important issue: explaining what was happening to Daisy.

She held her daughter on her lap and told her that Mummy had to go away for a little while for work, but that very soon Daisy and Nana would come and join her for a while in a magic place. 'It'll be like a special holiday.'

'But I want to go with you *now*, Mumma.'

'I know, sweetheart. But I need to go and get things ready for you and Nana. Then when you get there, you'll get such a lovely surprise. You know how you have to wait for big surprises . . . like your birthday, holidays, Christmas? Well, it won't be fun if you come and nothing is ready. It's going to be so amazing, you won't believe it.'

Daisy's lip trembled but her interest was clearly piqued. 'Like what sort of surprise?'

'If I tell you it won't be a surprise.' Grace tickled Daisy and she squirmed, giggling.

'Gimme a clue.'

'Well, this place is like summer all the time. Lovely and warm. There's sunshine, swimming pools, beaches, funny monkeys, yummy food, special music and dances: you'll get to wear your sarong and kebaya that I bought you . . . I think you'll have a lovely time.'

Daisy clapped her hands. 'Really?'

'Promise. And because we're going for a little while, you'll need to go to school there, too. But guess what, I've found you a super-cool school. That way you can keep learning new words and get better and better at reading.'

Daisy grinned. 'Maybe they'll have a guinea pig too? Like Charlie?'

'Maybe they will,' said Grace with a chuckle.

Daisy's brow furrowed. 'But I like my school here. Will we come back here?'

'Yes, darling. This trip will be for a month or two, but then we'll be coming home, and you'll go back to school and see all your friends again.' Grace hoped that Lawrence wouldn't stick his oar in on the schooling issue in the meantime.

The questions went on and on as Daisy's mood switched from happy to worried, and back again. Finally, when Grace had reassured her that after their holiday in Bali they would come home, Daisy hugged her.

'Yay!' she yelled and hopped off Grace's lap. Flapping her arms with excitement, she ran to find her grandmother, shouting, 'Guess where I'm going, Nana!'

*

Grace handed her boarding pass to the flight attendant and walked into the air bridge tunnel towards the plane that would take her to Bali. She'd thought she'd never

159

get there: every day during the past week she'd checked her phone and email, dreading seeing something from Lawrence that would make all her plans go up in smoke. But no email came, no text message, no call – nothing at all. Grace's intense relief was mixed with bitterness. Did Lawrence care so little about his own daughter that he could not even be bothered to call her, or ask about her? After finding her seat, she checked her phone one final time before switching it off for the flight – there was nothing there other than fusspot Spencer bothering her with more irrelevant questions.

By some miracle there was no one sitting beside her. Grace finished the mimosa a flight attendant had brought her and pulled out K'tut Tantri's book, glad she didn't need earphones to block out a chatty neighbour. She couldn't wait to leave her problems with Lawrence behind and sink back into Muriel's world. Muriel had just set sail from New York and was about to set foot in Indonesia for the first time . . .

We dropped anchor at a cluster of wharves and warehouses called Tandjung Priok, the disembarkation point for Batavia, some six miles inland. That golden island where I hoped to live, that enchanted paradise of Bali where life would prove uncomplicated and exquisite, was still some distance off, waiting tranquilly between two oceans, the Indian Ocean and the Java Sea.

The dock laborers of Java were lithe, agile brown men, their bare shoulders and strong legs gleaming like metal in the equatorial sun. Lordly Dutchmen and other Caucasians, cool in starched white duck or seer-sucker, stood aloof from the antlike activities of the Javanese, and satisfied themselves that all was in order before they signaled for the shiny American-built motorcars, the taxis of Java, to take them home or to their clubs.

To reach Batavia, where I must arrange for my final objective, I drove along concrete-paved, canal-bordered roadways. The hotels in Batavia surprised me. There was the swank Hotel Des Indes, the comfortable Des Galleries, and the Netherlander of older fashion. All excellent. Important guests were received in the great houses whose green lawns surrounded the Koenigsplein, or King's Square, and whose windows looked grandly out on the Governor General's Palace. Java, like all the other islands of Indonesia, was then part of the Dutch East Indies, and Batavia reflected all that was best in colonial elegance.

I had planned to buy a motorcar and drive through Java to the little harbour of Banjuwangi, at the other end of the island, and then cross Bali Strait by native ferry. Dutchmen speaking good English were most eager to help me exchange dollars for guilders and negotiate the purchase of a motorcar until they learned that I intended making my journey alone. In Java, where every car owner has a chauffeur, it was not considered proper for a white man to be at the wheel himself, and for a woman it was unthinkable! I was implored to abandon my original idea and instead to ship my car and travel in comfort by the Dutch KPM steamship line. I listened politely to this advice, and verified information I had already obtained. There were fishermen at Banjuwangi who could be hired to sail a motorcar across the strait in one of their native praus.

I bought a small drophead car and decided to set out alone that same night. I wished to see the people of Java and the countryside at close quarters, and to me there was nothing frightening in driving alone across Java. I had often driven alone from coast to coast in America. But I am forced to record that this Java drive proved quite a different matter.

The roads were strange and I knew neither the language nor the value of the money. At night I found myself in a veritable jigsaw puzzle of twists and turns with unlighted oxcarts blocking the way. And as for lights, my car lamps proved to be of limited use. Gleaming faces seemed to absorb them and overhanging tree branches blotted the moonlight that crept fitfully through clouds. Java was a motorists' nightmare, and I began to realize why my Dutch acquaintances had been so dissuasive. The air at least was pleasant with a smell of wet earth and the fragrance of strange flowers.

There were many false turnings and fruitless gesticulations of inquiry to local people who couldn't understand me any more than I could understand them. I could see that I had started my drive grossly unprepared, but it didn't matter. I was on my way to Bali and never doubted I should arrive there.

Then at close to midnight, though it seemed later, I was jerked to a stop by a child too close to my path. I saw him quite plainly, a smiling, ragged little vagabond thumbing a lift. He had long blue-black hair and a pixy face. He couldn't have been more than nine. And he spoke amusing pidgin English.

This must be a trick, I couldn't help thinking. He might be a decoy for robbers. Or, if I took him into my car I might be accused of kidnaping. For what would such a little fellow be doing alone so late and so far from any village?

'Lady,' he said, 'you like me? I be your eyes. I be your tongue. I get you right change for your money, and I show you right road. I protect you from evil spirits at night. And I speak English good.'

When I could interrupt his flow of speech I asked him many questions. Unexplained, he was much too unbelievable. How, for instance, had he learned such fluency in pidgin English, which could not have been his native tongue?

'I pick it up from tourists around the hotels since as long as I can remember.'

'And your parents?'

'My father, he taken by Dutch soldiers to the land beyond the moon to die. My mother she die of broken heart, and her jiwa [soul] carried off by *leyaks*.'

'Leyaks?'

'Evil spirits. I told you – they roam at night.'

Pito proved an expert navigator and an excellent teacher. He knew money values and taught me the Javanese equivalents of yes, no, want, how much, too much, and other simple and useful phrases. I was in luck to have found him.

These days were pleasant adventure, and this child – with no home, no family, and no future apparently – was an amusing companion, quite aside from his practical use. At night we stopped in villages at a series of resthouses maintained by the Dutch administration for the benefit of Dutch officials and

163

commercial travelers. Despite the fact that these places were usually run by Eurasians, Pito was always refused admission. His colour was wrong. But unperturbed he slept in the car along with the dusty luggage.

Soon I couldn't bear the thought of parting with Pito. He must come with me to Bali. His body, starvation thin, needed care and food. These he could have. I would see that he went to school – received an education. It would be a pleasant life.

'No,' he said, 'a Java boy needs no schooling.'

It was this that had brought his father to ruin. The gods are angered by too much white man's learning.

But I couldn't desert Pito. I decided to cross Bali Strait at night with the boy asleep in the car, and afterward try to persuade him once more to remain with me in Bali.

The first part of my plan was successful. Pito slept soundly while the fishermen, signaled to be quiet, rolled the car into place on the light vessel, a craft so narrow it was impossible either to enter or leave the car while we were on the water. Sails were hoisted silently and the prau, heavy laden, bobbed slowly into the darkness.

All went well until we reached the uninhabited and deserted beach of the island of my dreams. As the car was being unloaded, Pito woke up. I had to tell him that we were in Bali and that Java was five miles across the strait.

For a moment he stood rigid. Then his eyes distended and he screamed.

'Take me back – take me back!' he shouted. 'Bali full of *leyaks* – I die here –' Then he collapsed into complete hysteria. He wept while the fishermen whispered among themselves.

So Bali was not yet attained. It was Pito who suggested that the car be left on the beach while we sailed back across the strait to Banjuwangi. I had desired freedom for myself. I could not take freedom from another.

It was an anticlimax, our arrival in Banjuwangi: the purchase of a train ticket to the village nearest where I had first seen Pito; the giving of a little money, food for the journey, some new clothing; and the writing down of my name should Pito ever wish to come to Bali, with the address of the American consul who might know where I could be found. At the end Pito was calm, silent and somewhat moody. His glances were sidelong and his underlip quivered a little. He removed the new and tightly rolled sarong from around his waist and drew forth an oddly shaped and hammered silver box. From this he took out a small carved wooden figure.

'This is a good luck charm,' he said. 'Saved me many times from evil spirits. Very powerful. So you take this, kind American lady, and keep it with you always. The train comes now. I go. I thank you very much.'

'*Selamet tinggal*!' he shouted as the train moved away. That means, Live in peace.

'*Selamet djalan*, Pito.' Go in Peace.

It is difficult for me to describe how I felt as I stood there, once again alone. My adventure had now begun in earnest.

Grace stepped from the plane and took a deep breath, wishing she had her own Pito beside her, guiding her. Still, it was a good feeling to be familiar with the bustle of passengers on arrival at Denpasar and know her path would be smoothed as much as possible, thanks to the influence and connections of MGI.

Mr Angiman's assistant, Sutini, met her at the airport this time, 'In case there are any problems with your KITAS,' she said with a smile. But all went smoothly, and they were soon driving towards Grace's accommodation.

'I think you'll find Villa Ramadewa very comfortable,' Sutini said. 'The Carrefour supermarket has everything. And the local fresh market close by is excellent. Or you can use the Recreational Club.' She smiled. 'The expatriates seem to have everything they need.'

'They certainly do,' said Grace.

The villa was an enclosed world of its own, with a luxurious pool surrounded by open-sided pavilions for dining and relaxing. The indoor sitting, lounging and entertaining areas opened onto the pool and garden or could be closed off in the rainy season if needed; the bedrooms upstairs each had a verandah overlooking the grounds but were discreetly private. It was beautifully furnished in the up-market 'modern Balinese' style that Grace knew could be found in most tropical five-star-plus locations throughout Asia.

Sinking into a rattan chair and stretching out her legs, sipping an exotic drink with fruit and flowers in it that the chef had whipped up, and looking at a frangipani flower that had fallen onto the emerald grass, disturbing the perfection, Grace sighed. As over-the-top as this all was, she appreciated it.

But guilt struck within minutes. All this indulgence,

all this space. She missed Daisy. What was all this for, if not for her? 'Sheesh, I'm not on holidays,' Grace said with a sigh, and picked up her phone and called Steve.

'I'm here, you settled in okay?' she asked.

'You might say that.' He chuckled. 'Not bad digs. So when are we meeting?'

'How about this afternoon? I'd like to bounce some ideas off you. Shall we meet at the Kamasan by the front entrance?'

*

Steve strolled towards her looking relaxed in board shorts, a T-shirt and yellow tennis shoes, his sunglasses pushed up on his head. He carried a camera and gave her a grin. 'Do I look like a tourist?'

'Are you going undercover or something?' she said with a laugh.

'Taking stills is easier than making notes, and a better reference. Besides, I enjoy using a proper camera. Good to see you. Thanks for including me in this adventure.'

'What can I say? You're the best for the job. Have you met Johnny or any of the others yet? We've been invited for drinks at one of the beach bars for the sunset ritual.'

'Johnny introduced himself when we arrived. Haven't had the pleasure of dealing with the management fellas; I'd prefer to leave that to you. But I caught up with Andy. Who else is going to be talent?'

'The star chef, apparently. And other staff as we identify their jobs and their appeal plus camera likeability.'

'I heard the old retired head gardener is a character, very traditional Balinese gentleman. But I guess it's food, drinks, playtime, relaxation and indulgences that people come here for.'

'There are the earnest travellers who want to experience the *real* Bali, too,' said Grace.

'That's getting harder. Though sometimes you stumble over a local ceremony on a street corner, stuff like that, but most tourists still like to come back to comfort and cocktails after a day of experiencing rural life and culture,' Steve said. 'Let's go for a walk. Soak up the atmosphere. Like you said, this hotel is a one-off. The trick is going to be how we pitch its uniqueness.'

'My thoughts exactly,' said Grace.

They talked easily as they walked through the gentle garden jungle then, as they approached the beach and the grove of coconuts, Steve touched her arm.

'Listen . . .'

She paused then smiled at him. 'The sound of the sea . . .'

He nodded. 'Magic, isn't it? Imagine sleeping on the beach here.'

'Mosquitoes.' Grace laughed. 'But yes, essentially, the magic of this place is the reason I wanted us to meet here. There's something I want to show you.' She stopped and looked around. 'Now where was it? Andy showed me . . . we have to go onto the beach and walk further down, I think.'

Steve paused as they reached the beach, which was deserted save for a small fishing boat pulled up on the sand.

'Not much surf. Gentle enough for tourists, which is good. The serious surfers will have to find the best breaks.'

'You a serious surfer?' she asked.

'When the mood and opportunity strike. And the water is clear. Good that this strip of beach is clean and empty. Guess they've put that breakwall there deliberately for privacy, even if it does look natural.' He grinned. 'Okay, where now?'

'Down this way.'

They walked in silence as Grace studied the tree line along the beach. Steve stopped and bent down, picking up a small shell. He handed it to Grace. 'Don't see too many of these anymore. There used to be beautiful big shells by the truckload on these islands. All picked over now, to sell.'

Grace studied the shell and put it in her pocket. 'How delicate. Well, at least it's not a bit of plastic.'

Steve nodded. 'Sadly, it's out there. They say the government is working on it, but a lot of locals just want the convenience of plastic. I hope the international hotels are more conscious of it because of their guests.'

'I'm pretty sure Andy is on top of it in the bars – paper straws instead of plastic, things like that – but I'll check it out,' said Grace. 'Ah, here we go. I recognise it now.' She turned and headed up the sand into the pandanus, date palms and coconut grove.

'Where're we going?'

'It's the old section of the Kamasan land that they're not developing for the hotel just yet. But look, over there . . .'

Steve slowed to a stop and whistled. 'What is this place . . . or was . . .?' He began taking the lens cap off his camera. 'How amazing . . .'

She smiled at him. 'This is it! K'tut's hotel!'

Steve gazed around him in silence for a moment. 'No way . . . this is incredible. I had no idea it would be like this.' Moving forward, he stepped carefully among the few remains of the old stone walls and what might have been a carved gate, almost lost in the tangle of growth, taking photos from all angles.

Grace sat down, hugging her knees as she stared at the strip of beach and sea between the old trees.

Steve finally returned to her and sat down beside her,

swiping through the photos he'd taken. 'How bizarre. Almost sad, isn't it?'

She smiled. 'I wanted to show you this because I think it's the key to the promotion of the Kamasan. Like a phoenix rising from the ashes . . . paradise is restored . . .' Grace looked at him, her face alight. 'Here are the ruins of the original hotel on Kuta Beach – The Sound of the Sea. There's our story! I just have to find out more about the extraordinary woman who did this.'

Steve looked at Grace, nodding slowly. 'It would be fantastic if we could use this somehow. How are you going with K'tut's book?'

'I'm not far in – she's in Indonesia and about to arrive in Bali, I think. I can't wait to read about Sound of the Sea. She was such an adventurous woman – so brave, really, so intrepid. Her journey across Indonesia sounded hair-raising, but also fun. I wish I could have met her.'

Steve nodded. 'Me too. Not many people take real risks anymore . . .' He looked around again. 'Why was the land abandoned? I wonder why they aren't developing here.'

'All I know is that it's family land.'

'Maybe they think it's haunted. The Balinese – and the Chinese – are very superstitious.'

Clambering to their feet, they walked back along the beach, and when they reached the spot where Steve had picked up the shell, Grace paused, pulling it from her pocket and putting it to her ear.

As if from some far-away place she heard the gentle breath; the sound of the sea, like a soft sigh. All of her troubles – Lawrence, finances, doing the best for her dear, dear daughter – seemed to blow away.

Gently she put the shell back on the sand to be touched by the incoming tide.

6

AFTER A CASUAL DRINK and dinner with Steve and Andy, who'd stopped by after work, Grace headed to bed. It had been a long week of meetings, research, brainstorming and filming, with dawn starts most days, and she was exhausted. But she also felt wired and very much alive. She admitted to herself that she hadn't felt so engaged with a project in years, and apart from the separation from Daisy, which she was finding very tough, she was enjoying the experience hugely.

Now curled in her bed, a mosquito net dropped around her and the door open to let in the breeze, Grace felt safe and cocooned. She opened her book, ready to unwind and keen to see what Muriel was up to now that she'd arrived in Bali.

My plan was simply to fill the car with benzine, drive into the interior of the island, and keep on driving until the car ran dry.

When the car finally spluttered and died, I found myself in a beautiful, medieval village high up in the hills and outside a handsomely carved wall of red brick with an open archway guarded on both sides by four stone figures representing Balinese gods. Behind the stone wall seemed to be a mysterious-looking temple hidden in tropical foliage. Hearing weird music coming from within the imposing-looking walls and knowing that the Balinese people have no objection to strangers entering the temples if they do so with proper respect, I timidly entered the courtyard.

A sumptuous Oriental feast was in progress. Temple bells were ringing, and gamelans (Balinese instruments) were softly playing hypnotic melodies from a bygone age. High priests, like Buddhas, were seated cross-legged on bamboo platforms six or eight feet from the ground and surrounded by columns and pyramids of fruit, flowers and carved palm leaves, fantastically shaped offerings to the gods. Behind each priest sat a priestess handing him the different flowers needed for the distilling of holy water.

On other bamboo platforms sat the Rajah with the nobles. Their golden bodies also were bare, but from the waist down they wore a kain (a long strip of cloth) of brilliant hue. Tucked into the back of their sarongs were handsome krisses with gold handles carved in the shape of a Balinese god, and studded with precious gems.

Just as I was moving towards the gate a handsome young man of about thirty came up to me saying, 'Excuse me, perhaps I could be of some assistance to you. Are you looking for someone?'

I stared at him in amazement, noticing his princely clothing, and then foolishly stammered, 'Oh, you speak English.'

His dark eyes danced with amusement as he replied, 'Well, is there anything remarkable about the ability to converse in the English language? A few of us have attended universities abroad, you know. May I inquire how you came to be in our village, and how you found your way into the palace?'

'Palace!' I exclaimed. 'This is a temple, is it not? I came in to hear the lovely music and to admire the beautiful offerings.'

The young man threw back his head and laughed heartily.

'It gives me great pleasure to hear you refer to the puri as an abode of the gods. You have in fact entered the palace of my father,' he said. 'May I introduce myself? My name is Anak Agung Nura. I am the only son of the Anak Agung Gede. I bid you welcome to my father's palace. I am most curious to hear how you found your way here, for you are an American tourist, are you not?'

'No, Anak Agung Nura, I am not a tourist. I came to your lovely island with the intention of staying for the rest of my life, hoping to be able to paint and follow the peaceful, contented way of your own people.'

I explained how I could not endure living in the Dutch tourist hotel another day, how I had started for

173

the interior of the island, vowing that with the help of the gods I would stay wherever the car ran out of petrol. 'The car spluttered and stopped dead outside your palace gates.'

Anak Agung Nura smiled and said, 'It seems to me that your fate has been decided by the gods you so wisely invoked – it is evident that you are destined to stay at my father's palace . . . Come, I shall introduce you to my father. He is an even greater fatalist than I.'

He took my arm, led me to the verandah, where his father was seated with his nobles. The Rajah's sweet old face wrinkled up in smiles as he heard his son tell him the story of my defiance of the Dutch officials; and the nobles laughed heartily. After Anak Agung Nura had finished the story of my adventure, the old Rajah studied me thoughtfully. After a few moments, he said, 'What is written in stars must be. I think that you did not come to my puri by chance. I bid you welcome, daughter.'

Grace put the book down for a minute as she thought about her own trip to Bali. She wasn't sure the gods had brought her there, and smiled at the idea, but she did know that this was exactly where she was meant to be at this time. She picked it up again.

I could not provoke the gods. The Rajah's offer must be accepted. I must stay at the palace as a daughter.

The Rajah's broad smile needed no translating. His speech was always translated by his son.

'Now I have three daughters and one son.' The old man spoke so gaily that I was inclined to think the entire matter had turned to jest. But then his tone

174

turned serious. 'We shall call you K'tut, which is Balinese for fourth-born child. Soon I shall summon the high priest and, after the custom of our ancestors, we shall give you another name, which will be the name of your destiny.'

A month later I found myself playing the star role in a ceremony, part medieval and part pagan, in which the name K'tut Tantri was bestowed upon me. I have kept the name ever since.

During the next month I learned a great deal – language, customs, and – more than anything – a wholehearted acceptance of a way of life which was alien to me. It was, I do believe, my destiny. How, otherwise, could I so soon have regarded the palace as my rightful home? Agung Nura, with his European training, was responsible for gently introducing me into it. He never let me see too much at once. In the evenings Nura himself taught me to read and write in 'high Balinese'. I became steeped in the history of the country and in the works of the writers and philosophers.

Grace read on, knowing she should get some sleep, but she had to find out how K'tut fitted into her adopted home.

By now I knew that Bali, the country of my adoption, was my place in the world. And I decided that I must learn more about it than I could see from the perspective of the puri. I must go forth by myself and live within the kampongs.

By this time I was known to the people all over the island. News travels fast in Bali, and the peasants knew that I was friendly. And Agung Nura had introduced me to many of them at temple feasts and dances. It was therefore easy for me to stay at the kampongs. I just went in and said that I should like to stay with them for a few days. The peasants were delighted with the idea.

I was gone from the puri for more than two months and I did everything I had been warned against doing. I went to all corners of the island, living in unspeakable conditions in the very lowliest of kampongs, and everything that Nura had said about them was true, and more besides. Night after night I slept on a mat on the floor in dank huts without windows. I ate food prepared by women with filthy hands and dirt-caked nails. I drank unboiled water from their earthenware jugs, and their fermented palm wine out of dirty glasses or broken cups with dead mosquitos floating on top. I bathed in the creek with the other women and for toilet facilities wandered into the bushes. I watched old women with betel-stained mouths chew food to a pulp and then stuff it into the mouths of children who lacked the teeth for chewing. I remained in excellent health, free from dysentery or malaria, though both diseases were rife. I never showed that I was shocked at anything or that I considered myself above anybody. And I received nothing but affection.

Despite the filth, the discomfort, and the meagre meals from which I always arose hungry, I found the kampongs the paradise for which I had left Hollywood. To me they contained a curious quality of peacefulness which I had not found in the palaces of the rajahs. It was an artistic, an uninhibited way of life. Most of these poor peasants were artists of talent and power of expression.

I finally came to the village of Kuta on the west coast facing the Indian Ocean. The beach was magnificent and without a house or a hut. There were a few temples and numerous fishing smacks or praus moored close. What a site for a house! I revisited the beach frequently and it was here that the idea entered my head of building an exclusive hotel. It was merely an idea. What would I be doing with a hotel? A hotel took capital and I had by this time given most of my money away . . .

One day, sitting on the beach, I asked my artist friends, 'What are we going to do now? My money is almost gone.'

'I will tell you what we will do,' Wyjan replied calmly. 'We will start to build a hotel – the kind of hotel of which you have dreamed. It will be right here on this beach, and built like a rajah's palace. It will be famous and everyone will help you. And when it is finished the foreign guests will surely come to you and you will make a fortune. We will call it Suara Segara – The Sound of the Sea. We will pound our own rice on the grounds. We will have Balinese maidens who will weave. We will have our own gamelan – Maday here will know about that – and Njoman will dance and bring in other dancers. Everyone who works at the hotel will be in some way an artist. We will have painters and sculptors. It will be an enchanted garden by the time we get it finished. We will build a coral temple and the village priests will prepare a feast and bless the ground. Beneath the

177

temple we will bury offerings of gold and silver. If we follow all these customs all will be well and we shall prosper.'

Wyjan was interrupted by the others with many exclamations of 'beh adoh', which means approval and applause. Then Njoman and Maday added to the fairy tale: 'We will have our own pigs, ducks and chickens – we will not cut down any of the coconut or palm trees, but build in between and around them. It brings bad luck to cut down trees without making offerings to the tree-gods. Besides, we can always sell the coconuts. Oh – we can be self-supporting!'

I almost cried as I looked at the three earnest faces. 'Lads,' I told them, 'it's a beautiful dream . . .'

'A beautiful dream', these words circled in Grace's head. She could see the vision K'tut and the people around her had for the hotel.

At last the hotel was completed – completed, that is to say, as much as it would ever be, because we kept having to add new pavilions in order to accommodate the swarms of guests. From the outset the place was a tremendous success, and no wonder. It might have come straight from the Arabian Nights, with its lush gardens, wall of white coral, and its ancient stone statues. It was a replica of a rajah's palace. There were very few concessions to Western comfort – bathrooms, deep mattresses, and later a large powerhouse to generate electricity. Foreign magazines reported it as the unique hotel of the entire Far East.

Inevitably legends grew about a place as unique and successful as Sound of the Sea. The spirit of camaraderie was so marked that the guests frequently spent time in the kitchen learning from the cooks how to prepare the dishes. It was said that mine was a place where you waited on the servants instead of the servants waiting on you. There was a joke – and it was not entirely a joke – that if I liked you and you had ten guilders in your pocket you could stay at Sound of the Sea forever . . .

The following evening, after a day's shooting with Steve and Henry, Grace flopped into a deck-chair by the pool and checked her phone for texts or emails before calling Tina and Daisy.

At first, she'd looked at her mobile constantly, just waiting for a bomb to drop from Mr Jamison, or Mr Judd, or from Lawrence: that he really was seeking full custody, that he was going to get the court to prevent Daisy coming to Bali. But as the days had passed and she'd heard nothing from him, she'd started to relax – or at least to put it out of her mind. Mr Jamison had said that he would email her once he had finished reviewing the insurance documents and the trust deed, so there was nothing she could do in that regard but wait.

Grace spoke to her mother and Daisy every day, some-times several times a day, and so far they'd had no news of Lawrence either. However that evening, after the usual hellos, Tina said, 'I think Lawrence might be back from India.'

'What makes you think so?' asked Grace, slightly alarmed. 'From what he said I thought he was going to be there for quite a while, or at least moving constantly back and forth.'

'I don't know, but he called my home phone this morning and asked to speak to Daisy. I overheard him saying to Daisy that he was planning something special and looking forward to spending time with her. Has he contacted you?'

'No. I'm leaving it to the lawyers and trying to have as little contact as possible. My strategy is to be brief and polite, and keep any communication to exchanges about visits with Daisy, those sorts of practicalities.'

'He also sent her a present,' said Tina, and Grace could hear the edge to her mother's voice. 'It arrived via courier just after we got home from school.' At that point, Daisy clamoured in the background, demanding to speak to Grace.

'Daddy got me the *beeeeeest* present, Mummy!' Daisy's voice got louder as she took the phone.

'What is it, sweetheart?'

'Daddy called it a "smart watch". It does lots of things and it tells me the time, so I don't have to learn how!'

Grace bit her tongue to stop the expletive that sprang to her lips.

'Honey, maybe you can learn to tell the time properly before figuring out all those bells and whistles. But how lovely, I can't wait to see it. How was school, sweetie?'

'Yep, good. We had running this afternoon and I came second.'

'That's great, Daisy. You can practise by running along the sand. Now I better talk to Nana again. Would you put her back on the phone, please? Love you lots, darling.' She heard Daisy singing as she skipped away, having handed the phone back to Tina. 'Mum, can you believe that present? Stupid and extravagant.'

'I know! Typical Lawrence,' said Tina.

'I don't hear from him for weeks about the care of his daughter, and then he sends her an expensive, inappropriate gift, without even consulting me? What does a five-year-old want with a smart watch?'

'Tell me about it. She almost broke it two minutes after opening it. But don't worry,' said Tina. 'She'll forget about it soon enough, since most of the functions are of no use to her. Tell me more about what you've been doing.'

Grace made an effort to calm herself before she began. 'Well, we've started shooting, which means there's a lot of editing. The crew here is excellent and Steve is so good to work with; he just has such an eye, and he's very creative. I'm really enjoying it, Mum, but I can whip back home if you ever need me to.'

'If anything else happens with Lawrence I'll let you know, but we're fine for now, love. Send me some more photos when you get a chance so I can show Daisy. She's been wondering about where you are. You know, what it's like and who's there.'

'Will do. I hope I can get you both over here soon. I can't wait for you to see everything. The holiday scene seems a bit crazy, though. Some people think that when they're away they can go mad and do stuff they'd never do at home. The celebrity chefs, the millionaire DJs, the jetset in the A-list bars, the bogans in bean bags with beers . . . I had heard it was like this, but I think I needed to see it to believe it.'

'Well, I'll brace myself,' said Tina dryly. 'I'm starting to get excited about coming over there, though. Your place sounds amazing. Like I said, send more photos. I loved the ones you sent from the disco in Singapore.'

'AJ the DJ. Yes, it was pretty wild. Haven't let my hair down like that for a while. That's Johnny, the owner's son I'm twirling with. Just about everyone hit the dance floor.'

'It was nice to see you having fun, Grace.'

'It was nice to have fun – and the place was incredible.'

Grace farewelled her mother with a promise that she'd call again the following day. After their chat, Grace ached, missing her daughter's little arms hugging her. But now that the project was well and truly under way, she hoped she could get an advance from MGI, and set the wheels in motion to fly Tina and Daisy to Bali.

*

'Bali is perfect for the camera, isn't it?' Grace said to Steve when they were packing up after the early morning shoot. 'The colours, the flowers and the temple offerings. Every scene you shot looked like a vivid still-life painting.'

Steve smiled at her. 'Sure is, and the light's great too.' He closed the last of the camera bags. 'Do you want to come back to my place and we'll check we have everything planned for the filming this evening?'

At first light they'd been at the open-air food and flower markets as the vendors had set out baskets piled high with produce and plants before the first customers arrived. The Kamasan's sous chef and an assistant had carefully chosen only the freshest produce to take back to the hotel's kitchens. Grace knew that the chef and his team sourced special ingredients from the best producers from the area, or had them flown in as needed: fresh truffles, Australian seafood, New Zealand lamb. But most of the food was local or grown in the produce gardens at the Kamasan, which would also be a part of this particular video segment.

Mateo and Kadek, from the local production crew, were already at Steve's place when he and Grace arrived. They were having coffee and bonding with Henry as tightknit and committed film crews did. Steve had once told Grace that he found each shoot a bit like a marriage or an intense affair for the duration of the job. The crew lived in each other's pockets, dealing with the same dramas, highs and lows, each long day.

Steve cleared a place for Grace at the table crowded with papers, photos, diagrams and iPads. She greeted everyone and sat down. They were working on the series of vignettes that would be released weekly, leading up to the opening of the Kamasan, which focused on the key people who would be working there. And there were plenty of interesting stories to choose from.

While the gardens were run by a team of fit and well-trained young men and women, Steve was keen to showcase the retired head gardener, who was now the curator of the 'offering temples' scattered around the grounds. There was also Maya, a smart Javanese woman, who was in charge of guest relations. She'd had international experience in hotels around the world and was multilingual. The manager of housekeeping, Komang, had trained as a classical Balinese dancer as a child and still performed in ceremonies – she'd be part of the Kamasan's special blessing and opening ceremony outside the front of the property's main temple, which would be filmed with several cameras to capture it all. Grace knew when the first guests were booked in, but she hadn't been given a definite date for the official opening. She hoped the leisurely pace would pick up when they'd decided on a suitably auspicious day.

Andy would also be featured in the video portraits of the behind-the-scenes running of the Kamasan. They'd promote him both as the charming and affable Aussie-surfer-who-stayed, a man who knew how to party, and the sharp, creative mind directing the hotel's bars and entertainment. One of Andy's segments was going to show his preparations for a planned weekly competition for his staff, where each Friday they'd submit their cocktail invention or concoction. The winning cocktail would then become the Kamasan 'special' for the week.

And then there was the executive chef, Stephano Bianchi. The food was a big selling point for the hotel. As the chef had garnered several Michelin stars and was an international celebrity, he was hardly ever in residence. So it was left to his long-serving second-in-command, Belgian head chef, Emile de Franco, to run the show. He had worked his way up the ranks in Bianchi's various kitchens around the world.

However, Emile had proved rather elusive, and Grace hadn't been able to pin him down to discuss doing a video segment. The assistant food and beverage manager, Wayan Toni, a quietly spoken man who controlled the culinary engine room of the Kamasan, had the most to do with Emile, and the previous day he'd pulled Grace aside and delicately explained the situation. Now, as she sat around the table with Steve and the crew, Grace told them what she'd learned.

'Monsieur Emile is a bitter man, apparently. They were the exact words Wayan used. He's jealous of his boss and feels that he is the better chef.'

'That's not unusual,' said Steve, tapping his pen on his notepad.

'Pressure was put on him to transfer here from Stephano's number one restaurant, a Michelin-starred affair in New York. It seems he was told it would be good for his career, but he hated the idea from the start and he's only here under sufferance. So the upshot is, he's not a happy camper here in Bali. Now the delicate bit: Wayan tiptoed around this, but he said that Emile abuses the kitchen staff terribly and is an arrogant misogynist to boot. The staff don't complain as they don't want to lose their jobs.'

'I've heard it's not uncommon for foreign *bule*s to boss the local staff around. He'll either be found with a *kris* in his back, or get a bashing from one of the local gangs,' said Steve.

'Well, perhaps someone should tell him that. Wayan said his temper often goes right off and when that happens, everyone finds him impossible to work with. And if that weren't enough, he's nurturing some unfortunate habits.'

'He's a drinker?' said Henry. 'Lot of chefs are, I'm told.'

Grace raised an eyebrow. 'He has a serious cocaine habit, but manages to keep it below the surface day to day. How he turns out such superb food I can't imagine.'

Steve shrugged. 'There's a heavy drug scene here even though you get the firing squad if you're caught. It seems the high-enders' habits are generally ignored so there're a lot of expensive drugs about.'

'Do you think Johnny knows about Emile?' Mateo asked.

'He'd have to.' Steve turned and looked at him. 'Someone has to be doing any PR damage control that's required – Rosie Chow, I'd imagine.'

'Let's hope we can catch Chef in one of his rare moments when he's smiling and sober,' Grace joked.

'We want the food too . . . that's why we're featuring him,' said Steve. 'I'll go and talk to Wayan and some of the kitchen staff. See if there's any other talent, and maybe get some more lowdown on Chef Emile.'

Grace sat forward and said, 'That would be great. Okay, what do we need to arrange for this evening?'

They planned the shoot and worked out who was needed when they'd film the garden and bar scenes at sunset. Before that, Steve and his team were going to get some footage of Andy surfing, if the waves were up.

Grace stifled a yawn. 'That all sounds good. Now, if you guys don't need me anymore, I might take a few hours off – it was an early start this morning. Sometime I want to take a day off and go exploring. I haven't been anywhere except within these couple of blocks for days.'

'Good idea,' Steve said. 'It's easy to forget that we can have fun in this amazing place as well as getting the work done.'

Grace nodded. 'Not that I want to go into the throbbing heart of visitor-ville, though. It is incredible that within a few kilometres you can go from the sublime to the seedy with brash bogans in the middle.' She paused. 'Makes me think . . . Are we just showing one side of Balinese life – an island within an island – by limiting ourselves to the Kamasan?'

'We're selling the hotel, an image, a world of its own . . . old Bali in jungle aspic, morphing into the height of travel indulgence,' said Steve. 'It's not a documentary.'

'True,' said Grace. 'But I wonder if the campaign would be stronger if we put some of that sort of thing in as well.'

'You mean, showing sights that aren't connected to the hotel?' Mateo asked. 'I like that. Break away from the clichés.'

'It might be a good idea,' Steve said. 'Let's think about other places that we could film.'

'Thanks everyone.' Grace got to her feet. 'See you at the hotel later. Hope the surfing shoot with Andy goes well.'

*

By mid-afternoon Grace had had a delicious lunch and a siesta and was feeling refreshed. Switching on her phone, she rolled her eyes when she saw that there was an email from Spencer in her mailbox. As usual there was no preamble or niceties. She could hear his snippy tone of voice as she read:

I want to get on top of your progress and check what you're doing up there. I want to see concepts so far. The general outline we have here is pretty flimsy. I need the full brief. Spencer.

His curt email annoyed her, and she decided he could wait to get a response. When Kamsi, the cook, brought her some fresh fruit and a creamy iced coffee, she calmed down. She was here, Spencer was there. Thank heavens.

Grace was deep in thought when she heard the house-maid Sri quietly call, 'Ibu Grace? You have a visitor . . .'

Turning, Grace saw Andy at the door and stood up. 'Hi, Andy. How did the shoot go?'

'Better ask the boys. Steve seemed happy. I caught a few waves and had a great time. Nothing to this movie business.'

Grace laughed and invited him over to sit at the table by the pool. 'Would you like a coffee, a drink?'

'Thanks, no. I'll take a load off for a minute, though.' He pulled up a chair and sat opposite Grace. 'I was just on my way to the hotel to get ready for tonight's bar run-through and I thought I'd call in and see how you're doing.'

'That's nice of you. It's going really well, I think. It's all so stimulating and so much more than just another job.'

'That's a good sign. It's a bit chaotic, I know. You don't throw up a multi-million-dollar, state-of-the-art, innovative complex like the Kamasan without a few dramas,' said Andy with a wry smile.

'True. Although we've been lucky so far. It helps that Steve and the guys he works with are all so professional,' Grace said, then stopped and thought for a minute. 'What can you tell me about Johnny? There's the family and the Kamasan group, there's the MGI executives, and then there's Johnny who has a foot in both camps. And always a lot of hangers-on who dance around him, seeming to run errands and do things while Johnny holds the strings.'

'He might look and act like a lightweight sometimes, but don't underestimate him. Because of their heritage, the family is extremely cautious in all their dealings, and Johnny is no exception,' Andy said, leaning forward. 'Johnny is very close to his father and completely loyal to his family.'

'The heir apparent, I gather.'

'Who can do no wrong,' added Andy. 'Like father, like son. Johnny went to uni in Sydney, did a law degree that he "topped up" at Yogyakarta State University.'

'Wow, I didn't know that. He comes across as . . . well, a playboy. But he is smart, I can see that. A great front man to sell the Kamasan.'

'Yes, he knows the old rich list, plus the new jetset. Apparently he's also best mates with the president of some big bikie gang in Australia.'

'So no-one tangles with Johnny?'

'No way. He's also a respected martial arts expert, especially in Silat.'

Grace smiled. 'Well, a man of many talents.' She paused. 'Tell me, do the big drawcard stars the Kamasan has employed have contracts?'

'Like Stephano, the executive chef?'

'I was thinking more of our head chef, Emile. We're featuring him, but what happens if he throws a tantrum and leaves? Are they on tight contracts?'

'Yes. Pretty watertight. It's big money. Their reputation and business depends just as much on the Kamasan being a success as the Pangisars' does. It's in everyone's best interests for the guests to want to come as much for the food experience, or my bar experience, as for the culture, the world-class service, the scenery and setting.' He grinned. 'If we get it right, the Kamasan brand will become self-perpetuating. Put it this way: it'll be like a great big dazzling piñata, and when you whack it, goodies will rain down on everyone.'

Grace laughed. 'What an image!'

Andy reached over and touched her hand. 'Grace, I don't want to pry into your financial affairs, but I hope you've done a deal, to share in whatever success comes if all this works as we hope it will.'

Grace glanced at him. 'Hmm, funny you should say that. I've been talking to my mother about this. She reminded me I should take control of my life again. I used to manage very well. Then I got married and handed over my money as well as my head and my heart. Thanks, Andy. I'll pay more attention.'

He smiled. 'Glad to be of service. Now, I better go and do some work and leave you to yours. See you tonight.'

*

They were filming in a quiet corner of the gardens as the sun set. Nyoman, the retired head gardener, was setting an offering in front of the remains of a mossy, carved stone statue at the temple ruins, the afternoon sun's rays lighting the grooves in the old man's gentle face.

'Cut. Lovely,' said Steve softly.

'You'll take a movie of my garden now?'

'That would be great, if it's okay with you,' replied Steve.

They followed Nyoman through the coconut trees to a fence, where he unlatched a bamboo gate.

'Oh, wow,' said Grace, stopping in surprise.

She had known the hotel had a kitchen garden, but had not expected what she now saw in front of her: the area was filled with an abundance of vegetable beds and lush climbers on trellises, different types of lime trees, as well as mango and pawpaw trees.

'We pick all the Kamasan coconut trees,' explained Nyoman. 'For meat and oil. Much of our cooking oil is from our trees. And used in the spa.'

'Yes, I remember, the spa products are all coconut based. They're divine,' said Grace.

'You did all this?' Steve asked the elderly man as the crew trailed in behind them, exclaiming in admiration.

'I make the garden using permaculture,' said Nyoman. 'I get seaweed from the beach and make fertiliser.'

'Look at those capsicums and eggplants – oh, and little beetroots. They look perfect but they're all miniature,' exclaimed Grace, looking at a tray of fresh beetroots.

'I grow baby vegetables for Chef. He likes them.'

'Where did you learn all this?' said Grace, after she asked Mateo to set up the camera.

'My family were from Bedugul. We all lived on farm. I bring some seeds from there.'

'What's in the shed over there?' asked Mateo, pointing. 'Anything to film?'

Nyoman chuckled and replied, 'Many chickens. And quail. For their eggs. They spend the morning running around and go inside when the sun starts to set.'

'I've heard about the indulgence breakfast the Kamasan is going to be serving,' said Steve. 'Twenty quail-egg omelette garnished with these baby vegetables. Unreal.'

Grace wandered around while Steve and Mateo filmed the old gardener tending the overflowing beds of vegetables for the kitchens of the Kamasan. She found the whole place endlessly surprising. After a little while she said, 'We should finish now or you'll be worn out, Nyoman. Thank you so much for all your time and for showing us your magical garden.'

The old man smiled, clearly enjoying taking the visitors around, and he handed them each a flower he'd picked from one of the colourful beds.

They all thanked him profusely and Steve glanced at his watch. 'Okay, let's head over to the bar and catch Andy at work.'

As they walked, Grace said, 'Steve, I've read more of the book on K'tut Tantri that Andy gave me. I've been chatting with him about it. It's mind-blowing. Better than a novel, it's mesmerising.'

'I know, right? It really opens your eyes to a different world, doesn't it?'

Grace was thoughtful. 'It really does. I'm not sure what it is about it that's got me so intrigued – K'tut herself, or the times, or how different old Bali was from the one we know today. It's amazing to be here, reading it. I'd love to talk to you about it when we're not working.'

'Sure. Every day here is getting filled up, isn't it?' He shrugged. 'No matter how well you prepare for a day's shoots, there's always something that doesn't go to plan, or something unexpected comes up that we really want to film.'

'I guess that's showbiz, eh? C'mon, let's find Andy and his amazing cocktails.'

*

The design of the main bar, the ambience, the exquisite setting, the music, flower arrangements and flickering candlelight blending with the contemporary lighting, all against the backdrop of the bleeding sunset sky, was inviting, sophisticated and friendly. It promised fun and pleasure.

Leaving Steve and his crew to the filming after helping them to get set up, Grace said, 'I might go check out the kitchen while I'm here.'

There were well-equipped food-serving areas dotted about the complex, but Grace headed to the heart of the food empire, the main kitchen. As she approached, she heard the clatter of dishes and pans, and smelled a delicious aroma. But suddenly she heard shouting coming from inside.

Hurrying through the doors into the main part of the kitchen, she saw several frightened staff standing back against a wall as Chef Emile shouted at and shook a young chef.

'Stop that. Immediately,' shouted Grace, hurrying forward. The red-faced chef let the younger man go and spun around to face her.

'*Sortez d'ici! Allez-vous-en!*' he screeched.

Grace stood her ground. 'Chef, leave that man alone!'

The frightened young chef hurried towards the group huddled in the corner.

'What is going on? What happened?' demanded Grace. 'Where is Wayan Toni?'

The head chef straightened his kerchief and wiped his hands on his apron. 'It is not your business. This is my staff.'

'I know they are your staff, but I can't stand by while you treat them like that . . .' began Grace in a furious voice, annoyed at the chef's actions, when the doors behind her banged open and Wayan Toni hurried in.

'Madam, please leave. Thank you, but we know what to do.' He nodded his head at the frightened young chef, who fled outside as the other staff went back to what they'd been doing. Chef Emile hurried away through another door as Wayan gave calm directions in Balinese to the remaining staff.

Grace hastened after the young chef. She caught up with him in the corridor outside, grasping his arm.

'Are you all right? '

'It is all right. I am okay.'

'Has this happened before?' she asked gently.

He looked down and didn't answer.

'It's all right, you won't get into trouble,' said Grace.

The young man nodded. He seemed to be barely twenty. 'I want to keep my job,' he murmured.

'I'm sure you won't lose your job. Why was Chef so angry?'

He hesitated. 'We see him. He do bad things.' He stopped, looking fearful.

'Okay, there's no need to say anything more if you don't want to.' Grace gave him a small smile and patted his shoulder.

'Thank you. I will go outside, to the fresh air, then I'll get back to work,' he said, looking around nervously.

Grace watched him walk away, feeling anger welling inside her. She thought briefly of Lawrence, and of Spencer; she was becoming increasingly fed up with people who thought they could bully and mistreat anyone who stood in their way.

Back in the main bar she found the others busy shooting. She decided not to say anything for the moment.

The bar food appeared, and it looked exquisite.

'It's more than picture perfect,' she exclaimed. 'The presentation is stunning.'

'That's why it's called edible art,' said Steve.

They'd filmed the 'guests' – staff and friends invited to fill the room for the filming – as well as the rows of bottles of rare and expensive wines, the exotic and original cocktails, the stunningly presented food, Andy in a wild silk shirt, his ponytail tied back and wearing a gold chain, managing to look like a raffish ageing movie star.

'Are you ready for your close-up, Andy?' called Steve.

'I want to see this.' Grace laughed as she sat down at a table with a few of the staff, who were tucking into some delectable tapas.

On cue, Andy grinned and took his position behind the bar. With a great flourish he lifted two impressive, ornately garnished, deep red drinks onto the bar in front of him.

'I have, after many years experimenting with exotic Asian flavours, perfected what will become my Kamasan signature cocktail,' he began. 'You might think this looks like a Bloody Mary. But no!'

'This is a triumph created from our home-made tomato-based vegetable juice, with a generous dash of beetroot juice, *sambal terasi* for depth and flavour, fish sauce for saltiness, fresh lime juice, a dash of fresh ginger juice, heaps of good vodka, a shot of extra dry vermouth – or a good very dry sherry – a teaspoon of Moringa, and instead of the predictable celery stick as a swizzle, we bash the end of a stalk of lemongrass and let the emerging oil add another layer of Asia-ness.

'And we're not done yet! On top we sprinkle some crunchy freeze-dried rendang and finish it off with what

I reckon is the world's greatest flavour maker . . . the zest of a kaffir lime. That's the great smell wafting towards you . . .'

He lifted a glass and held it high. 'And here we have the Kamasan Kamikatsi! Here's to the Kamasan and all who sail in her!'

To laughter, cheers and applause, he tilted a glass and drank.

'Cut! That's stupendous. You're a natural,' said Steve with a broad grin. 'Man, I've got to try one of those. C'mon, Grace, you have a try too!'

'That's utterly delicious,' declared Grace, taking a sip. 'Well, I guess we can call it a wrap.'

When he was free, Grace took Andy aside and explained what had transpired in the kitchen. Andy rolled his eyes.

'Bugger. Emile's probably trying to keep off the coke and whatever else while he's here, and he's taking out his frustrations on the staff. I don't quite know what to do next. He's had one "consultation" and a warning. But we need him. He can't get out of his contract and he'd lose his job, not just here, but with Stephano's whole group, if we fired him. He's just such a damned amazing chef. Is the guy he attacked okay? Who was it, do you know?'

'I'm not sure. I didn't catch his name.'

Andy frowned. 'All right. Keep this quiet, if you don't mind. Not sure how we're going to manage it. I feel like I'm trying to keep a saucepan lid on top of a volcano.'

*

Waking with the dawn sunlight, Grace stretched luxuri-ously then, as she did every morning, checked her email for news from Lawrence, Mr Judd or Mr Jamison. This time, there was an email from Mr Jamison. Grace sat up in bed and quickly opened it.

First he discussed the insurance. He could confirm that, while there'd been a small hold-up initially, eventually the claim had been approved on the order of the man Mr Jamison had mentioned before – Mr Tony Freeman – and paid in full to Lawrence. Which led him to the trust document. It looked valid, Mr Jamison reported: it gave Lawrence the right to deal with things such as Grace's Paddington apartment, and probably the insurance money, without consulting with her. As both Lawrence and Grace were signatories to the trust, if Grace wanted to vary it then both she and Lawrence would need to sign again. Fat chance of Lawrence agreeing to that, thought Grace.

The only other way to be free of it, Mr Jamison said, would be taking him to court and proving he tricked her into signing it, which, for now, Mr Jamison recommended against. Grace felt her belly tighten: would she ever be free? And just what on earth did all of this mean?

At that moment, her phone pinged with a message from Allison at the agency, asking her to call Spencer as a matter of utmost urgency. That was unusual: Spencer emailed her a lot, but he rarely sounded stressed or hurried, and hardly ever bothered to go through Allison. Grace picked up the phone and dialled Spencer's office phone at the agency. The call was diverted to Allison.

'Oh hi, Alli, it's Grace. I'm just calling Spencer like you asked. I suppose he wanted me to call him on his mobile.'

'Oh,' said Alli, and Grace thought she sounded hesitant. 'Yes, he, um, he wants to talk to you.'

Grace paused, not liking the tone of her voice. 'Why's that, Alli? What's happening?' she asked.

'Look, Grace, Spencer isn't happy . . .'

Grace groaned. When was he ever happy? He obviously hadn't liked her lack of response yesterday when he'd asked for all her creative and logistical concepts for the Kamasan account, and she guessed he'd probably thrown a tantrum.

She sighed. 'What's bothering him now?'

There was a moment of silence before Alli said, 'He says he wants to pull you off the job. I'm so sorry, Grace. I'm just repeating orders.'

Grace felt her stomach drop. 'He *what*? That's ridiculous! The whole campaign is mine. I created it, I won it for the agency, I'm managing it. And it's going well . . . what's his problem?' she demanded.

'It's stupid . . . but he saw some photos online. He wants to look at your concepts again. He says they're vague, not enough use of Carson Agency creatives, you know the sort of thing. It's all rubbish, I know –'

'What is he talking about? What photos?'

'Somewhere on Facebook. There's a couple of photos of you lounging by a pool, dancing in a club. He says you're wasting time and money for the agency and the client.'

'That's such crap!' Grace exploded. 'They're photos I sent my *mother* to show my daughter I'm okay . . . oh, for God's sake. The one time I take a half-hour break, I wanted to show my daughter the pool. The other photo is of me socialising with the client, who insisted I dance with him. This is all madness.'

'Yep. He's really gone nuts. The photos are just an excuse, we know that. He says you're too independent, not part of *the team*. He wants to have someone else take over the job. In other words – he wants it himself. He fancies himself prancing round Bali, I think.'

Grace could feel the tension in her body growing as she gripped the phone tightly. 'Over my dead body. No one else can just walk into this campaign. It's in my *head*, it's how I work and collaborate and create with my team; it's not a list of instructions that just anyone can follow!' Her voice was rising. 'He must know how much this whole Kamasan deal is worth to the agency.'

'That's for sure,' said Allison quietly. 'This is our biggest account at present.'

Grace paused for a second, and the penny dropped. 'That's why he wants this gig: so he can take credit for its success, to show the bosses in New York that he was a good pick as Australian chairman. That he's a hands-on creative chairman. Bastard.'

Allison said nothing, which only confirmed Grace's suspicions.

'Well, I feel like quitting. And if I quit, good luck to whoever has to go back to square one and start over. I have a strong professional relationship here with the client, and a commitment. I'm passionate about this project. It's more than just a job to me, Alli.' Grace surprised herself, suddenly realising how much the Kamasan campaign had etched itself into her being. She had started to sense that it was going to be a greater success, both for herself and for the companies involved, than anyone had expected. Plus, she was challenging herself at a time in her life when one part of her felt a failure, and now she was finding strength, independence and faith in her abilities. It felt good.

'I'm not letting go of this.' She spoke calmly. 'I will go and discuss it with the executive of the company here and see how he feels. I will also talk to the CEO of MGI.'

'What will I say to Spencer?' asked Alli.

'Nothing. If he asks, just tell him I returned his call, then had to go to a shoot. Give me a couple of hours.'

'Okay. Good luck, Grace. I'm so sorry to be the bearer of bad news.'

'Yeah, I know.' Grace sighed. 'It's not your fault, Alli. Thanks for being upfront.'

Grace ended the call and started to shake. What else could possibly go wrong in her life? How could she lose this job, right at a time when she needed money more desperately than ever before? Damn Lawrence. Damn Spencer. She felt tears spring to her eyes. What were the odds of her mother putting those pictures up online for her friends, and someone spotting them? She wouldn't mention it to Tina; she'd only feel bad about it. Quickly, Grace opened her laptop again and checked her bank account: with the money she had left from selling the jewellery, she had a small safety net.

She stood up and was going to have a shower when her phone rang. It was Allison again.

'That was quick. Good news or bad?'

'Sorry, Grace. Bad, I'm afraid. It seems Spencer has already notified the CEO of Masari Group International that you have been taken off the account.'

'What? How dare he! Spencer, that nasty little jerk, doesn't even have the decency to speak to me *first*.'

'I know. He expects you to work back here under his lead and with his ideas or else he's assigning you to production on the Clementine account. I'm really sorry, Grace,' said Alli miserably.

Grace chewed her lip, thinking hard. She knew everyone hated working for the Clementine people. It was the account equivalent of the poisoned chalice.

'You still there, Grace? Is there anything I can do?'

Grace felt the well of anger that had been growing in her since she'd seen Chef Emile attacking the young chef the previous day harden into steely determination. She would fight this all the way. It wasn't fair, and it wasn't right. She would no longer let things like this happen without pushing back – not for any reason. She said, 'Not for the moment. But there's no way I'm working under Spencer on anything. Especially this Kamasan project. Thanks for the alert, Alli.'

After a shower and taking her time to get dressed and gather her thoughts, Grace sat with a cup of coffee, her breakfast untouched.

Her phone beeped again. She saw it was a text from Spencer.

I am advised that you are less than happy at the prospect of working under my leadership on the MGI/ Kamasan project. That is a shame, but get used to the idea as it begins now. MGI have been advised accordingly. Be back in my office in 24 hours with my Kamasan brief . . . Spencer.

The speed of this response shocked Grace, but this was the final nail in the coffin. She found the situation, and the way Spencer had handled it, unacceptable. There has to be a showdown, she decided. She would fly home and deal with this immediately.

Grace called Sri, who hurried in, looking concerned.

'I have to pack and fly back to Sydney. Can you help me, please, Sri. I have to book a flight.'

'Your family, your little girl . . . they are okay?'

'Yes, thank you,' Gracie said, smiling to try to reassure her. 'It's just business, Sri, but thank you, they're fine.'

Hands shaking, Grace sent a text to Johnny and then to Andy, saying she had been recalled urgently. She decided against alerting Steve and the crew that she might be off the job until matters were settled.

Half an hour later, Grace jumped in the villa van as her driver, Putu, put her bags in the boot. She was on the phone booking her airline ticket. There had been no reply from either Andy or Johnny.

At the airport she thanked a worried-looking Putu, checked in and went through immigration to the VIP departure area, showing her Kamasan credentials. With her boarding pass in her hand, Grace sat and tried to clear her head.

She debated about sending her mother a message. She didn't want to alarm her, or have her jump in the car and drive the hour or more to the airport to collect her. Grace was so distracted that she didn't notice two figures approaching her table until they were right beside her. Moving to lift her carry-on luggage out of their way, she looked up.

Andy was grinning at her. 'Where do you think you're going, missy?'

Johnny was standing next to him. She was stunned to see them. Of course only Johnny would wield enough influence to get into the departure lounge as a non-passenger, she thought. She couldn't help smiling at his white suit, dark glasses and purple silk shirt.

Grace decided there was not a lot left to lose and that honesty was the best policy. 'Trouble at the agency, unfortunately. The chairman, Spencer Campbell, wants to take me off the job. I have my suspicions as to why, but I don't think it would be very professional of me to repeat them. Let's just say that he's offered me an ultimatum – work under his lead on the Kamasan project from Sydney or take on our agency's least-popular project. Don't worry, I'm flying there now to fight for this, even though Spencer has apparently already advised Farrouk Eljoffrey that I am off the job.'

'So I heard,' said Johnny dryly. 'Farrouk called me. I had to ask, who the hell is this Spencer?'

Grace gave a crooked smile.

'Anyway, after Farrouk told me, I said, fire this Spencer bastard and withdraw the account from The Carson Agency. How dare they try to take Grace away from us.' Johnny was obviously used to dealing with bigger fish than the likes of Spencer, Grace thought. 'I advise you to quit and then we'll hire you directly,' he added.

Grace's heart skipped a beat, but reality quickly set in. 'I'd like nothing more, but my contract would prevent it. Also, the agency will never allow their biggest account to walk away. Never.'

'We'll see about that,' said Johnny coolly. 'Can you get this Spencer on the phone, please, Grace?'

Grace found Spencer's number and called it, handing her phone to Johnny. Spencer must have been vetting his calls because the call went through to Alli again. Grace and Andy listened to Johnny say, 'This is Jonathon Pangisar of the Kamasan Group speaking. I wish to speak to Spencer Campbell immediately.' After a short pause, another voice came on the line.

'Spencer. Jonathon Pangisar here. How good of you to take my call. We've all had rather a nasty surprise here this morning.'

They listened as Spencer spoke on the other end, but Johnny cut him off.

'I'll be blunt. My family, and the Kamasan management, and MGI, are most unhappy about this turn of events. We are dispensing with The Carson Agency's services as of this moment. I am offering to pay your agency a fair severance fee to cover your losses so you won't be out of pocket. Also, I intend to hire Grace Hagen. Please be advised that she will be handing in her notice immediately, and we expect that you will free her from her contract with no conditions.'

The sounds of an outraged Spencer came down the line, but once more Johnny cut him off. 'I suggest you take me up on the generous offer we will make your agency. Unless, of course, you want to take on not just the Pangisar family lawyers, but also MGI's lawyers? I hate to think how that would play out . . .' There was a long silence on the other end before Spencer said something in reply. And then Johnny hung up and smirked. 'Spencer saw reason, funnily enough.'

He reached over and picked up Grace's boarding pass and crumpled it in his fist.

'You are now on your own, Ms Hagen, commissioned by MGI directly and responsible to me. We'll sort out the paperwork later. Now, let's get out of here and celebrate. I haven't been to bed yet. Big day for you, Grace . . . Oh, and text me your bank details so we can send you some operational funds. We don't need you stressing out further.' He started to walk towards the door of the lounge then stopped and turned to Grace, who was following behind, her bag in hand. 'I heard you've been hoping to get your daughter and mother over here – let's get that done, too. I'll have someone contact you about it.'

Tears of gratitude sprang to Grace's eyes but she quickly blinked them away.

'Thank you. This means a lot to me,' she said simply.

Johnny dropped his arm around her shoulders as Andy reached for her carry-on bag.

'Let's get something to eat,' Johnny said. 'I need rice, fish and lots of coffee after last night.'

7

THERE WAS SOMETHING UNIQUE about airports, Grace thought as she waited for her mother and Daisy to arrive. They were a kind of time capsule, filled with a sense of excitement mixed with anxiety; so many people in one space, all going in different directions, lives intersecting perhaps only for a few seconds.

Daisy was clutching her nana's hand, looking totally overwhelmed when Grace caught a glimpse of her. At that moment, Grace felt the tension in her shoulders ease and her heartbeat slow to normal. Lawrence or his lawyer could have stepped in right up until the last minute before the plane took off, and even though it seemed they hadn't, it wasn't until Grace actually laid eyes on Daisy that she could let go of the gripping stress she'd been feeling.

Tina and Daisy both looked a bit tired and cranky as they emerged through the Arrivals gate and started searching for Grace among the sea of Balinese drivers holding name signs and calling out for their unknown passengers. Grace rushed towards them, breaking into a jog when she noticed that Daisy seemed really frightened now.

'Daisy, over here, hello, sweetheart,' Grace called, a huge smile on her face.

The little girl turned her head and her pinched expression changed to one of joy. She dropped her grandmother's hand and ran to Grace, squealing, 'Mumma, Mumma!'

Grace swept her daughter up, holding her tight as Daisy threw her little arms around her mother's neck. They were both crying and raining kisses on each other.

'Oh, it's so wonderful to have you here,' exclaimed Grace as Daisy slid to the ground, then, holding Daisy's hand, Grace embraced Tina. 'Thanks so much for taking such good care of Daisy, Mum.' She blinked back fresh tears.

'It's my pleasure, darling girl. We're glad to finally be here!' said Tina happily. 'But I don't recognise a thing in this new airport. I feel like an ant in a castle! And getting through Customs and finding our luggage took forever. Where to now?'

Grace introduced the smiling Sutini from the Kamasan, who stepped in and took charge of their luggage trolley. 'It's lovely to meet you both. Please, follow me,' she said.

'Well, that was kind of easy,' said Tina. 'Apart from the slow baggage, I'm impressed.'

'Sutini has a local SIM card for you. If you give her your phone, she'll put it in,' Grace explained as they walked towards the exit.

'Thank you, Sutini,' said Tina, handing over her mobile. At that moment they stepped outside into the humid, soupy air that is the first sense of Bali, and Tina stopped still, closed her eyes and took a deep breath. 'Ah, I'm back.' She smiled. '*Kretek* cigarettes. The cloves. Now this, I recognise.'

Sitting between Tina and Grace, Daisy snuggled up to her mother as Putu drove them out of the chaos of the airport. Daisy and Grace talked and giggled nonstop. Grace held her daughter's hand, delighting in her excitement and her stories. Tina stared out the window and said to Grace that she was trying to spot anything that was familiar to the nineteen-year-old girl she'd been. So far, she said, it was all very new and different.

Sri was smiling a welcome as they arrived at the Villa Ramadewa and Putu carried their bags inside.

Tina exclaimed with amazement as they toured the pavilion rooms, and when Daisy ran through to the garden, she squealed as she saw the pool and the huge pink elephant inflatable bobbing in the middle.

After a quick swim, they showered and wrapped themselves in specially woven sarongs, which were samples of gifts for the future guests at the Kamasan. At a table by the pool, Kamsi had laid out a welcome lunch, a delicious chicken satay, *nasi goreng* and a fruit platter.

'Oh, I remember this fruit!' said Tina delightedly. 'Mangosteens and rambutans – I lived on them when I was first here. There were trees in the *losmen* where I stayed; we just picked the fruit up as it dropped.'

Grace smiled at her mother, noticing how slim and fit she looked, and with wet hair and no make-up, she was even more energetic and youthful.

'You look great, Mum. And you're pretty damn hot in

a swimsuit, too.' She smiled at Daisy. 'And you're looking full of beans now, too! Shall we dress up and go out for a nice dinner tonight? I'm dying for you to see some of these ritzy high-end places, Mum.'

'Sounds like a plan,' replied Tina.

'Yes, I want to dress up and go out,' said Daisy firmly.

'Right. We're going. But it might be a good idea to take a nap this afternoon to adjust to local time. I have to do some work, but I'll be back in a few hours. Sri can help you unpack and iron your clothes, if you ask her politely, and Kamsi can get you a snack or a drink if you feel like one.'

Daisy's eyes looked ready to pop out of her head at the idea of all this indulgence, and she ran off to explore her room, whooping and clapping her hands, as Tina stretched out on a deckchair.

'What luxury, how relaxing. Though you deserve it – I know you work hard, too. Is everything sorted out now with your job?'

'Yes. Well, so far so good. I don't want to take anything for granted, of course,' Grace said, sitting down in the deckchair next to her mother. She had filled Tina in on everything that had happened with Spencer and Johnny as she knew her mother was worried about it.

'Okay, that's a relief – I think. Have you thought about what you'll do once this assignment is over?'

'If this campaign is as successful as I hope, it's likely I'll be offered more jobs on the same basis – executing a major branded content campaign. It's pretty amazing to work directly with the client, with no agency in the middle – so in a way what happened with Spencer might turn out to be a good thing. If I can make this campaign work without a middleman, it bodes well for the future.'

Her mother smiled at her and Grace felt that her life really was changing. Her family was with her and the future, in terms of her work, anyway, looked bright.

'It's better for me financially, too,' she continued. 'Johnny Pangisar insisted that all the submitted costs stay the same. That means I'll pick up the agency mark-up on the job as well, which is pretty hefty.'

'I'm pleased to hear that,' said Tina. 'I just want the Lawrence issue to get sorted. Has he been in touch, or sent you any money? What happened to the house insurance?'

Grace sighed. 'Not a peep. I haven't heard anything from him about money or about Daisy coming here for a visit. Mr Judd has put in the application for Family Dispute Resolution, but with the long waiting periods it could be ages before we get the compulsory mediation session. And who knows what Lawrence might do in the meantime? Plus I have that trust document to deal with. I don't know when I'm going to find the time to get it all sorted. Has he contacted you since the smart watch episode?'

Tina shook her head. 'Maybe he's still in India. I hope he pulls something together with his work. That might get him out of your hair. I've noticed he always seems easier for you to deal with when he's working and has money.'

'Mmm. Yes, you're right.' They sat in silence for a few moments, both lost in thought, then Grace checked her watch and said, 'Well, I have a meeting with Steve, the director. Will you and Daisy be all right if I leave you for a while?'

'Of course, darling,' Tina said, looking around at the pool and garden. 'We are in paradise here.'

'Thanks, Mum. It's so good you're here.' Grace smiled

and stood up. 'I'll be back to change for dinner. We'll go to La Lucciola, on the beach. I'll ask Putu to drive us.'

*

When Grace arrived at Steve's villa, he was sitting at a long table facing the compact garden and pool.

'Where're the others?' Grace asked as she sat down.

'Henry is getting some equipment sorted at the studio with the production guys, and Mateo is out doing some stills. So, did Daisy and your mum arrive okay?'

'Oh yes. It's wonderful to have them here. Daisy is thrilled to have her own pool. We're going out to dinner at La Lucciola.'

'Cool. Want an iced coffee, juice?'

'I'm right, thanks, Steve. I had a fresh fruit juice on my way here.' Grace pulled her laptop from her bag.

'All right, what's up next?' Steve saved the document he was working on and opened the spreadsheet containing the data for the segments they had decided on for the campaign.

'Infrastructure and environment.'

Steve screwed up his nose. 'Ugh. Not so photogenic!'

'That makes it a challenge for you, and with your talent I know you'll make it exciting, dramatic, cool and current,' said Grace cheerfully.

Steve chuckled. 'Righto, boss. Should we recap first on where we are?' His fingers were poised over his keyboard.

'Good idea.' Grace scrolled down through her notes. 'We've covered a lot of the ambience, the look of the hotel architecture and grounds in a scenic way, profiled venues, food, key staff. We still have to do the Pangisar family; they're proving a bit reluctant.' She looked at Steve and they both laughed, saying in unison, 'Except Johnny.'

209

'So, what do you want to showcase in these new pieces about the infrastructure?' said Steve.

'I think we need to give people a glimpse of what's behind the façade; you know, some insight into the inner workings of the hotel buildings and its environment. We could show that the hanging gardens, the rooftop gardens and the "green" growing walls are not just design décor, they serve an ecological function. Then there's the recycling, all the enviro-friendly, state-of-the-art technology. There's Nyoman's permaculture garden. The hotel's a top-tier development in terms of sustainability – people will be amazed when they find out more about it, I reckon. Listen, I made some notes.' Grace clicked open a document and read aloud: *'The Kamasan property recycles all water, so it can be re-used for sewerage and gardening. All rooftops on the property are clad with solar panels or covered with plants. There is an extendable wind generator that is hydraulically raised skyward each night in the windy season and hidden during the day. The management is consulting with the government about bringing in charging stations for electric vehicles. In the near future, nothing on the property will be powered by engines requiring fossil fuel. It will all be electrical or biofuel. Apart from the distinctive front driveway, the property's road system and paths are made from recycled plastic.'* She looked at Steve. 'You get the picture?'

'You betcha. Bloody amazing. Good on them.' He studied his spreadsheet. 'There're many layers to this story,' he said thoughtfully.

'I know. My mind keeps going back to the old hotel.'

'Have you finished reading the book yet?'

'I keep dipping in and out. She makes the old days sound so romantic.'

'Yes, maybe they were; certainly there must have been some wild times in Bali. When I made the film about the art colony at Ubud in the twenties and thirties, I researched the German artist Walter Spies and his amazing life up there. His paintings sell for a bundle these days – one went for eight million dollars recently at Sotheby's. You should go up to Ubud when you have time. It's a totally different atmosphere in the hills,' Steve said. 'Anyway, Spies's home is now an up-market rental to the stars and royals. Bowie loved it; Jagger got married there. It's been beautifully restored.'

'Really? Will it be in competition with the Kamasan?'

'Well, not really, although they both appeal to top-end clients. One is in the mountains and one's at the beach, plus the Kamasan is a hotel, not a house,' said Steve. 'But both have their own unique appeal, and the Kamasan's privacy and solitude at the beach is pretty hard to come by compared to most places.'

'That's what K'tut thought. I wonder what she'd make of Kuta Beach now.' Grace smiled.

'I think she might be happy about the Kamasan. It's still got the privacy, the secret garden vibe . . .'

'You're right.' Grace glanced at her notes. 'Jumping ahead, we'll have to film the blessing and opening cere-monies, when the hotel officially launches. Plus the big glittering opening party, of course. Has Johnny said anything to you about it?'

Steve shrugged. 'No date has been set for it yet, as far as I know. But they have the money to buy any big name they want to launch it, I'd say. Johnny knows everyone. And if he doesn't, his father does.'

'That'll be a pretty exclusive invitation. Okay, I'll put a query next to that one.' Grace made a note.

They talked on, developing ideas for the upcoming segments, making notes and finalising plans. Eventually, Grace pushed back her laptop and stretched. 'We've covered a lot of ground this afternoon. I should head back now and get ready to go out to dinner. It'll be a bit different from what Mum remembers – she told me on the phone last week that when she was here before they'd have suckling pig feasts on the beach. A group would get together for the festivities and a local family would have cooked the pig all day . . . I just can't imagine that happening anymore.'

'We should mention that to Andy. He'll want to do suckling pig feasts at the Kamasan, for sure. You can imagine it – traditional preparation but with a modern and stylish twist.'

Just then Kadek, one of the local production guys, came running towards them, panting and looking distressed.

'Hey, man, what's up? Take it easy,' said Steve, getting to his feet. 'Sit down.'

Kadek shook his head, waving his arms and trying to catch his breath.

'You all right? I'll get some water.' Grace jumped up to run to the kitchen.

Kadek waved his hand, gasping. 'No . . . no. It's the chef. Chef Emile. He's dead.'

Grace stopped still. 'No way!' she said. 'What happened?'

'Bloody hell.' Steve put his hands on Kadek's shoulders. 'Where is he? Are the police there? We need to check this out. Does Johnny know?'

'He's been murdered, by the gangs probably. The big boss Johnny is coming. They're trying to keep it quiet. I was over near the kitchen when someone started wailing.'

'So where's the chef now?' asked Steve briskly.

'Emile, he's on the beach,' said Kadek, his voice shaking. 'In the water.'

'Maybe it was an accident and he drowned? He could have been zonked out with drugs,' Grace said.

Kadek just shook his head.

'You go to the kitchen and see what's happening. I'll go with Kadek. I'd better find Henry and Mateo.' Steve paused, touching Grace's arm. 'Are you okay? If you want, you can go to your villa and we'll get in touch when we know more.'

'No. I want to check that everyone in the kitchen is all right. I'm sure there're people helping, but –'

'Okay. I'll catch you up,' said Steve, and he and Kadek hurried out.

The staff were gathered outside the back entrance to the main kitchen. As Grace approached, Andy was speaking to the young sous chef de Franco had been shouting at the previous week.

She kept her distance, not wanting to interrupt. Then Johnny strode along the verandah accompanied by two senior-looking police officers.

Grace spotted Bakti, a young kitchen hand she knew from one of the shoots, looking distressed and standing to one side. She had witnessed the chef's bullying – had probably endured it herself, Grace suspected – but Grace knew she'd still be in shock.

She went to her and said gently, 'Are you okay, Bakti?'

The young woman looked solemn. 'He was a bad man. Trouble man.'

'Because he lost his temper?'

Bakti shook her head. 'He did bad things,' she said in a low voice. 'I saw him sometimes, with bad people.

Chef Emile, he is . . . was . . .' She struggled to find the right word, screwing up her face in distaste and giving a shudder.

'Creepy?' It was a word that had come to mind when Grace met him. 'Because he used drugs?'

Bakti shrugged. 'Lot of rich *bule* buy drugs. He was friends with bad people. They come from many countries – Russian, French, Arab people, Java people. Bad men.' She glanced around and stopped speaking when she saw Andy hurrying over to them.

When he reached them and glanced at Bakti, he said quickly, 'It's okay. You go home, Bakti. If the police want to interview you, we will come and get you. This could get a bit messy.'

As the young kitchen hand hurried away, Andy turned to Grace and sighed.

'You heard what happened? Nasty, but not totally unexpected, I have to say – de Franco was asking for trouble mixing with that mob.'

'Was it something to do with drugs?'

'Could well be. From what I've heard, de Franco would do anything to get the drugs he wanted, even if it meant mixing with the grim underbelly of Bali. Maybe it was a debt? Whatever it was, someone meted out rough justice. Poor bloke.'

'Do you think he got so far into drugs because he wasn't happy here?' said Grace.

'Who knows? Actually, I would have said things had been improving with him lately, but he ended up in a bad circle. I know more than I want to about some of the clubs he often went to. They can seem harmless enough if you wander into them. Hosted by ladyboys, and the drinks are cheap. But go further in and you discover they're a front for a really sinister crime world,' Andy said. 'I warned him once, but it was like water off a duck's back.'

'It's so sad. In spite of his temper, he was doing a brilliant job. He could have really made his name here.' Grace sighed.

Johnny and Rosie Chow strode from the kitchen, followed by the police officers. Johnny paused and spoke to the police, who nodded and then quickly left. Rosie pulled out her iPhone and started furiously texting as Johnny approached Andy and Grace.

'We have to keep this quiet. Get a lid on it. Rosie's onto it now,' Johnny said to Andy. Looking at Grace he said, 'When we get the new chef, film him straight away, get him out there, make a fuss on social media. That way, people will be distracted from de Franco.'

'Do you have someone in mind? Luckily we hadn't shot much with the chef himself, more the food, the setting and the sous chef. It won't be a huge problem to feature whoever replaces poor Emile,' said Grace quickly.

Johnny spluttered. 'There's no "poor Emile". Looks like he got some well-deserved rough justice.'

'Has his family been notified?' asked Andy.

Johnny nodded. 'Farrouk spoke to them. They agree this is a private matter. Rosie will help make arrangements with the family so there is no publicity.' He started to turn away. 'See you later,' he said to Andy. 'You too, Grace. Around 10 pm at Forty Thieves? We will all deserve a nightcap by then.' Johnny nodded at Steve who had just walked over, and then hurried off.

'Do you want me to swing by and we'll go together?' Steve asked Grace, when she and Andy had filled him in on everything that had happened and the plans for the night.

'Yes, please,' said Grace. The chef's apparent murder had unnerved her and the last thing she wanted was to go to a fancy bar. As it was, she didn't know how she'd get through dinner.

*

Watching Daisy and her mother admire La Lucciola's setting and enjoy its attentive service helped Grace to calm her nerves. She'd decided not to mention anything to Tina yet about the chef; she wanted them to enjoy their evening together first.

They had a drink before dinner as Daisy practised handstands on the lawn and played in the sand in front of the restaurant. Then Grace waved to her to come in and clean her feet and put her sandals on as they were going upstairs to their table.

On the balcony overlooking the beach, they watched the sky change from pink, to orange, to gold.

'You never forget the Bali sunsets,' said Tina softly.

'Feeling nostalgic, Mum?'

'Oh, yes. We'd eat dinner on the beach, right down there. Sit in the sand, and a local family would bring food and snacks and drinks, for pennies really. We'd light a fire, other friends might roll up, hire a *bemo* or a bike, or walk along the beach or down the sandy village lanes behind the palms. Some might share a joint, drink Bintang beers, or just talk. Occasionally someone might have a guitar. I used to carry a little torch because once the sun had gone down, there were hardly any lights and it could be pitch black. Then I'd go back to the little bamboo hut I rented for a couple of dollars, where there was a kerosene lamp, the smoky glass cleaned by the *pembantu* each day, and fall into bed. I remember my sheets were always dried in the sun and neatly folded with a flower left on my pillow.'

'That's a lovely custom that I notice is still followed,' Grace said.

'In the morning the *pembantu* would leave offerings in the house, at the shrine in the garden, and would sweep all the frangipani flowers off the sandy grass.'

'And you'd head out for another day at the beach.' Grace laughed.

'Yes, a morning swim, then we'd move around, following the boys surfing. Or hire scooters and go into the hills to Ubud or up the coast. Kuta was the hot spot to hang on the beach and there were a few casual little bars. Occasionally we'd share a scooter over to the Rum Jungle Club in Legian, bumping over the potholes . . .'

'And Sanur?'

'It was quieter, a bit snobbier. I s'pose there's still a bit of a class divide around here. Your hotel sounds like it's going to be very exclusive.'

Grace nodded. 'I can't wait to show you around the Kamasan, especially Nyoman's secret food garden and the place where the old hotel was.'

Daisy was getting a bit impatient, even with the colouring book and pencils they'd brought to entertain her, so it was a relief when the food started to arrive. Grace enjoyed Daisy's delight as each dish was brought to the table, festooned with flowers.

By the time they arrived back at the villa, Daisy was nearly asleep on her feet, so Grace bundled her off to bed. She and Tina were sitting in the cool night air in the garden when Steve came by to collect her for their meeting with Johnny. Grace introduced him to Tina.

'How was dinner? You chose a good spot,' Steve said.

'Lovely. Terrific food. Daisy had a ball,' said Tina. 'We all did.'

Grace smiled. 'It brought back a lot of memories for Mum.'

'The changes since the late seventies are mind-boggling,' said Tina. 'I can't quite get over it.'

'I'm sure some people would prefer that it were still as it was then,' said Steve. 'But if you know the island well, there are still places that are more or less unchanged, where you can step back in time.'

'I'd love to travel around again like I did then,' said Tina. 'But not on a scooter, given the traffic I saw today.' She rose. 'Nice to meet you, Steve, and good luck with your production up here. It sounds challenging. Even a bit dangerous; Grace was just telling me about the poor chef.'

'I know. It was a shock for all of us in our crew,' Steve replied. 'That reminds me, Grace, we've been told not to mention it to your *pembantu* – Sri, isn't it? – as it will spook her. The local people are very superstitious.'

They all went back inside and Grace kissed her mother goodnight. 'See you in the morning, Mum. Daisy is out like a light. I hope I won't be too long. There's a guard who minds the villa, so don't worry, it's very safe.'

'I'm going to sleep like a log. Though I'd love to see the sunrise. Perhaps take an early morning swim.'

'I'd pass on that if I were you, Tina,' said Steve. 'A walk's okay, but there're sometimes issues with the water quality around here depending on the tides and weather.'

'We'll find a spot for a swim in the next couple of days,' said Grace.

'You could take your mum to some of the outer islands. There're some great beaches there,' Steve suggested.

'Otherwise swim in front of the Kamasan. It's clear there, no drains.'

'When we have time,' Grace reminded him. ''Night, Mum.'

*

Forty Thieves was packed, but as usual Johnny had an island table to himself. Andy and Rosie were there as well as two people Grace didn't know.

Seeing Rosie, Steve did a double-take. 'Woah, Rosie has let her hair down. Literally!'

The beautiful Chinese woman, who usually wore her dark hair in a French knot, had let it spill down her back and over one shoulder, almost to her waist. She was wearing a clinging bright-red silk jumpsuit with strappy gold stilettos. Dramatic gold earrings swung almost to her shoulders, and from a long gold chain hung a large piece of carved jade.

She was sitting right up close to Andy, whose arm was resting behind her along the banquette. Johnny was in a casual white linen suit with loafers and no socks, his turquoise silk shirt was half unbuttoned, displaying a heavy gold chain. Andy was in what Grace considered to be his uniform of Hawaiian shirt and cargo pants.

Johnny waved at them as they approached. The other men were deep in conversation. Grace noticed that Johnny was smoking Dji Sam Soe Black, the expensive brand of *kretek* cigarettes. This was a sign he was uptight, she'd been told. Smoking was banned indoors, but rules never seemed to apply to Johnny Pangisar.

'Thought this was a serious meeting, not cocktails,' muttered Steve. 'I'd rather be in bed.'

'Me too. No choice, though,' murmured Grace.

Steve and Grace greeted Rosie and Andy before Johnny introduced the other two men by first names only.

'They're Balinese lawyers, fixers, "cleaners",' Andy whispered to Grace as she and Steve sat down. 'They know what the law is and how to break it "legally". The justice system in Bali is complicated. These types of guys simplify it.'

Grace ordered an espresso martini. Steve had a Corona beer with a wedge of lime in the neck. Then Johnny leaned forward and the group around him huddled closer as he spoke in a low voice.

'Our two friends here are part of my legal team, to help with details regarding Chef Emile. This event is tragic, if not entirely unexpected.'

One of the legal men cocked his head. 'Indeed, we thought something like this might happen. The chef's habits were well known among the staff, and to us. He was a difficult boss and we were aware of the degree to which he was involved in other activities outside meeting his Kamasan requirements. He was exceptionally good at his job, very creative, a great talent.' The man stopped and took a sip of his drink. 'Stephano, the executive chef, had asked us to overlook some bad issues with him so long as it didn't affect his work,' he added.

'His work was brilliant, but he *was* tough on his staff,' said Andy. 'A few people are talking about that now, as the threat of retaliation has . . . disappeared.'

Rosie leaned forward to reach for her glass. 'That has to be stopped straight away. We can't risk people spilling the beans on him because they think he can do no harm now that he's gone. That's how information gets out there, and it could damage the hotel's name,' she said.

Johnny glanced around at everyone seated at the table,

then said quietly, 'de Franco met an unfortunate end. He was mixing with dangerous people – people who do not wish to be known. So any friend of Emile de Franco, or anyone who hints that they know who the perpetrators are, puts themselves in a dangerous position. The mob I'm talking about are seriously brutal if displeased or if you owe them something as, sadly, de Franco discovered.'

One of the legal guys nodded. 'If you cross them, or don't pay your debts, they'll kick you till your guts come out your mouth. Who knows what state he was in when he went into the water.'

'He would've been alive for a while,' the other lawyer said grimly.

Grace shuddered. 'Did he drown?' she asked quietly, not certain she wanted to know the answer.

The first man turned to her. 'You might say that. He was, well, bashed. But it seems they managed to keep him alive for a while longer. They tied his hands and feet and buried him in the sand to his neck, facing the sea.'

'Until it came in over him,' added the second man. 'The idea is that you see your death coming. Slowly.'

Grace spluttered into her drink. 'Oh, no! That's appalling. Nobody deserves that.'

'Apparently someone thought de Franco did,' Johnny said.

'What is his family doing?' asked Grace.

'A relative is coming to collect his ashes. Officially, he has gone back home. We just won't say that it's in an urn,' said Rosie dryly. She turned to Johnny. 'What's the hotel's position on why he left?'

'Health problems,' said Johnny quickly.

Everyone looked at Johnny as Rosie asked the obvious. 'So . . . who's going to replace him?'

'It's not that simple,' said Andy interjected. 'Stephano is pretty unhappy. I am too. For all his excesses on the dark side, de Franco could bloody cook.'

'We've already done some research,' said Johnny. 'Stephano is in London and he has contacted Wayan Gede Antara.'

'Yes!' Andy punched the air. 'Fabulous idea. He's a star now. Talk about local boy makes good. Would he come back to Bali, though? He's been working in starred restaurants in France and the UK for the last couple of years.' He turned to Rosie, who had her iPhone in her hands and was typing quickly. 'Gede's a great story. He's Balinese, trained at the Cordon Bleu Culinary Institute in Paris, and he's been on the celebrity "must-have" chefs' lists for some time.'

'So is he on board?' asked Rosie, leaning forward.

Johnny took a drag of his cigarette. 'We made him an offer he'd be crazy to knock back. Depends if he's ready to come home or not, I suppose.'

'He's certainly at the top of his game,' said Andy enthusiastically.

'Has he done any media? TV, masterclasses? How old is he?' asked Steve.

'Full details when he signs on with us, but as Andy said, his is a great story,' said Johnny. 'Perfect for the Kamasan.'

'Sounds like he could be,' said Steve. 'With a Bali background to add to the picture, too.'

'Sounds good to me,' said Grace.

Rosie nodded. 'He's a big enough name, that's for sure. Local star comes home . . .'

'I think he's acting coy. I made a flat offer. Take it or leave it,' said Johnny. 'He knows who we are. I also understand his grandfather is not well; that's a big incentive for a Balinese person to come home. He has family obligations.' Johnny looked at Rosie. 'I want media ready to go as soon as he signs the contracts.' He turned to Grace. 'You might want to visit his family compound – there's a story to film in the good, successful son returning for ceremonies, family stuff.'

Grace looked at Steve. 'Could be poignant, a family reunion. Joining the Kamasan family while he comes home to his own family, that sort of thing . . .'

Steve nodded. 'Sure. Maybe we should wait until he's accepted before committing to the idea?'

To Johnny it was all settled. Grace was tempted to ask what his plan B was if the chef didn't accept, but she kept quiet. It was clear not many people ever said 'no' to the Pangisars.

Johnny turned to his two lawyers. 'How thoroughly are you looking into who's responsible for de Franco's death?'

'As far as we need to.'

'There won't be any public noise about it,' said the other man. 'The word will go out. Your man was a warning to others to pay up and keep quiet. He was obviously getting too deep into their world and rocking the boat. They don't like outsiders.'

This enigmatic comment seemed to satisfy Johnny, who lifted a hand and a waiter stepped forward.

Grace shook her head and stood up. 'Nothing else for me, thank you, Johnny. It's time I hit the hay.'

Steve rose too. 'We have an early start. Thanks, Johnny.'

Andy dropped his arm around Rosie's shoulder and Grace noticed how comfortable they looked together. 'We'll have one for the road, Johnny. Thanks,' Andy said.

As Grace and Steve headed towards the door, Steve glanced back. 'Poor Emile. Those lawyers of Johnny's will hush this all up.'

'Bit scary actually, and sad. What a horrible way to die.'

'Yes. There's another layer of life here that visitors don't see. Family. Reputation. Funds. Money talks.'

'I guess so.' She sighed and changed the subject. 'Did you see Andy cosying up to Rosie? She's younger than me, and much younger than him – maybe thirty?'

'C'mon, Grace! Andy is a red-blooded Aussie bloke. He's fit. Still a good surfer. Successful and fun,' Steve said, chuckling. 'I'm not surprised Rosie would be keen on him, just as he is clearly keen on her.'

Grace shook her head. 'Yes, you're right. Today has been too much to take in, that's all. There seem to be surprises at every turn. I'm exhausted.'

Steve looked at her then dropped his arm around her shoulders. At first Grace stiffened, wondering what was happening, but then she realised she liked the feeling, and made a conscious effort to relax.

'Let it all go for now, Grace,' he said. 'Think about Daisy and your mum. What have you got planned for them the next few days?'

'Well, Daisy doesn't start school until next week. And after Johnny's directive it seems we'd better visit the chef's family compound, if he accepts the offer. I may as well invite Mum and bring Daisy along too,' Grace said, turning to look at him, 'if that's okay with you.'

'Of course.' Steve smiled, then added, 'Here's your driver. Goodnight, Grace. I'll text you about it first thing tomorrow.'

*

It was close to midnight, but Grace's mind was in over-drive and there was no way she could get to sleep. After tossing off the sheets and sighing, she pulled out K'tut's book. She'd reached a chapter where the war in the Pacific had started and Grace was reminded that whatever was going on in her own life was calm in comparison with what K'tut went through.

Surabaya we found in a state of chaos. Roads leading out of the city and the trains we could see from the highway were jammed with Dutch soldiers. They were, we quickly learned, trying to reach military headquarters at Bandung, on the other end of Java. Panic-stricken Javanese were fleeing by the thousands to the safety of kampongs in the interior.

Agung Nura was concerned, not about himself – the Japanese could have no particular enmity for a Balinese – but for me, as a white woman and an American. My nationality, even more than my color, might mark me for brutal treatment. The prince decided he must go to Solo in West Java to find out if there would be a hiding place for me in the Sultan's palace.

I remained, comfortable for the moment but insecure, in Surabaya's leading hotel, the Oranje.

It would have been a welcome relief to escape . . . but it was unthinkable that I should leave this troubled island. What of the prince, and all of my other adopted Indonesian friends? What of Agung Nura's dream of freeing his people from all foreign oppression? What of my promises, during those days at his coffee plantation, to do everything in my power to help bring about a free Indonesia? With the Dutch forfeiting the reins, perhaps for all time, the Japanese might be most willing to hand over the power to the Indonesians.

There was another prospect also. High Dutch officials were confident that the Japanese had overreached themselves and that the war could not last more than three months. If they were right, this was still the time for Indonesia to assert its bid for independence. I could still be of service to my adopted land.

I would remain in Surabaya, awaiting developments. Agung Nura warned me not to push my luck and to stay out of sight of the Japanese as much as possible.

The Japanese commander of Surabaya ordered all Europeans to come to headquarters and register. Agung Nura went with me to the commandant and asked that I be given an order exempting me from internment, and that I be granted also a traveling pass between Java and Bali. He explained that I was his adopted sister, having lived at his father's palace for many years, and that I was an artist, completely divorced from war activity.

Apparently my native clothes, my sandals, my dyed black hair and my ability to speak both Balinese and Malay impressed the commandant. 'A white Balinese,' he murmured. Obviously sceptical of the prince's account of our relationship, he gave me a knowing look and good-naturedly wrote out an exemption order and a traveling pass for 'one Balinese by adoption, K'tut Tantri'.

While the Dutch were feeling the weight of the invader's heel, the Indonesians too began to learn more about their new rulers. The men from Japan began confiscating food and goods to meet their pressing war needs. As produce and supplies became costly and scarce, less and less made their way into the hands of the Indonesians. Wherever it suited their purpose the Japanese roughly thrust Indonesians out of their jobs. Many Indonesians were thrown into prison on slight pretexts, without fair trial.

Agung Nura and his friends moved back and forth between Bali and the key cities of Java. They told me that Sukarno, in spite of his fiery radio speeches in support of the Japanese, was in sympathy with an underground movement that had sprung up under a Christian Indonesian, Amir Sjarifuddin. The whole purpose, I was told, was to prepare Indonesia for self-government – since the Japanese were obviously not disposed to grant this – the moment it might prove possible.

So it was that Agung Nura became involved in an underground resistance movement against the Japanese.

Anak Agung Nura would go back to Bali to organize his many friends into a resistance group and to further the movement in the nearby islands.

My role was to become known as the girlfriend of Frisco Flip, and be introduced to Japanese officials and to mix generally in Japanese circles, and to paint pictures of pretty Balinese maidens and sell them very cheaply to the Japanese.

By day, then, I painted canvases, the quickly done,

calendar-type pictures which I loathed, but which were greatly admired by the Japanese. I couldn't turn them out fast enough to keep up with the demand. And at night I became a playgirl, an habitue of the night clubs, a friend of the Japanese and especially of Frisco Flip. For a city at war, Surabaya was surprisingly lively – in fact, almost gay – at night. The fighting had moved thousands of miles to the east.

An interesting addition to the after-dark attractions of Surabaya was a group of geisha girls and a theatrical troupe, recently arrived from Tokyo. They were to tour Asia, entertaining the troops. The geisha girls were bright and charming, not at all the rough type I had expected. And full of informative chatter about conditions in Nippon and elsewhere. The members of the theatrical troupe were most gracious. It was hard to associate them in any way with a war.

Weeks had passed since I had heard from Agung Nura and I was beginning to worry. Then a courier arrived, with an envelope from Bali. The young man's face was very familiar; I could see that he was not a Balinese. 'Don't I know you from somewhere?' I asked.

The courier gazed at me intently for a moment and then his face lit up with a pixie's grin. 'Good American lady,' he chanted. 'You like good guide. I show you the way.'

Pito! It couldn't be, but it was! The nine-year-old ragged urchin I had picked up on my first midnight ride in Java years ago, now grown into a handsome young man.

'Your father, Pito, what of him?' I asked. 'Remember you told me the Dutch had kidnaped him and sent him to the land beyond the moon to die?'

'Oh, yes, indeed. My father was liberated from Tanah Merah when the Japanese came. He has always been a freedom worker for his country. That is how I have become a courier.'

Pito said that when Anak Agung Nura asked him to take a letter to K'tut Tantri, he did not realize that this was the American lady he had met as a child.

Pito promised to visit me each time he passed through Surabaya.

The letter from Agung Nura asked that Frisco Flip send money and small firearms to Bali as soon as possible. All bank accounts in Bali had been frozen while the Japanese sorted out Dutch accounts from Native accounts. The need for firearms needed no explanation.

At the factory, Frisco Flip had managed somehow to fashion a crate with a false bottom. He brought it to my house, packed small weapons and ammunition into the bottom part, and filled the top part with books. Our problem was to get the shipment to Bali.

Some days later I learned that the Japanese theatrical troupe and the band of geisha girls had been ordered to go to Bali to entertain navy personnel. They would travel by special train to Banjuwangi, and then by a Japanese patrol boat across the Bali–Java Strait.

Calling at the hotel to say good-bye to my little friends from Tokyo, I noticed that their stage props had been nicely crated, ready for transportation. Suddenly it dawned on me; here was the way to get our shipment of firearms to Bali. I got in touch with Frisco Flip immediately, and we worked out the details. I would ask the head of the theatrical troupe if I could go along with them to Bali. If they agreed, Frisco Flip would put our crate among the stage props. Since he was a Japanese, it should not be difficult to deceive the Indonesian guard.

All went well. The head of the troupe was delighted that I would accompany them. 'We need someone to speak Balinese, to interpret for us,' he said. 'It would be pleasant, too, to have you as a guide.'

Frisco Flip delivered the crate to the prop manager, and I saw it stowed with the rest of the baggage. Then Flip and I had dinner in seclusion together, laughing at our private joke that the Japanese would be transporting the firearms that might be used against them.

The long train ride to Banjuwangi was another of the ironies of my life in the early part of the war. Here was I, a white woman in Indonesian dress, sharing in the song and revelry of show girls from Tokyo whiling time away. The geisha girls were hilarious, and sang the whole distance. I sang too, partly to banish worries over what might lie ahead for me. I am thankful now that I did not know what the future held in store.

The Japanese cutter took us across the strait and in to Gilimanuk just after dark. All the way I was worried about how I would retrieve my crate from the show props. I might better have eased my mind. It turned out to be almost too easy. My friends found my crate and loaded it on a dokkar. 'How heavy it is,' one commented. My heart skipped a beat. I replied with what I hoped was nonchalance, 'My books, I am taking them to the home of a Swiss artist, a friend living a few kilometres outside of the town.'

Anak Agung Nura had given instructions that the firearms be delivered to a certain hideaway. It was

almost midnight when I reached the place. Anak Agung
Nura was astonished at first, and then – after hearing
my story – horrified that I had undertaken such a risky
venture. 'How could Frisco Flip have been so foolish?'
he raged. 'Letting you travel with geisha girls, and on a
warship! You might have been taken to Japan.'

'Please, Nura,' I replied, 'it was not at all that
bad. I was safe and comfortable and we had no
trouble. We could think of no other way of getting
the things here.'

The arms were removed, and the books replaced,
with speed.

Good sense dictated that I remain in the house,
in hiding, for the next few days. But good sense
has never been one of my conspicuous features.
My thoughts now turned to my beloved hotel, and
to Wyjan, Njoman and Maday. I must find them.
Nura had told me that the hotel had been completely
destroyed but I wanted to see for myself. Early the next
morning I found a local with a dokkar and set out for
Suara Segara, my 'Sound of the Sea' hostelry.

My heart leaped as we came in sight of the sea,
and the lovely white sweep of Kuta Beach, and my
grove of date and coconut palms along the shore. But
where was the hotel? And where were the beautiful
guest bungalows that had blended so perfectly with the
landscape that they were almost part of it?

As the rugged little horse pulled nearer, I could
see that not one brick stood upon another. The great
carved-stone statues were gone. The grove looked as
though it had not been disturbed. The driver, seeing
my distress, turned his eyes away. He murmured,
'I thought you knew.'

Stumbling to the ground, I ran to the spot where my own cottage had stood. Not a piece of bamboo remained. I ran about frantically, looking for a brick, a stone, some evidence that there had been a building anywhere. The only sign of human habitation was a row of ketalas, or native yams, planted across the ground.

My legs gave way under me. Sinking into the grass, I burst into tears. Could wars planned and declared in far lands do this to peaceful Bali? Why should such beauty, so lovingly wrought, be so wantonly destroyed?

After a frantic day and night of phone calls, emailing and making plans, Grace, Daisy and Tina, Steve, Henry and Andy all crowded into the hotel's minibus after breakfast, and Putu took off.

'Where're we going, Mumma?' asked Daisy.

'Into the mountains, where it's cool and beautiful. We're going to visit a special house. Well, a big family compound.'

'What's a compound?'

'It's where all the family live, the grandad and nana, brothers and sisters, cousins, uncles and aunties. You'll see.'

'Are they expecting us?' asked Tina.

'Yes. Gede's family knows we're coming. Now that he's agreed to move back here and work for the hotel, they're very happy,' Grace said. The call had come through the previous day, just as they'd firmed up the arrangements to visit. Johnny had worked his magic again, it seemed.

'He'll have a bit of pressure on him back here, though, as he's pushing thirty and that means it's time to start taking on family obligations,' said Andy. 'In a gentle way I need to explain to his family that he will have a lot of duties at the Kamasan, and what a great honour it is to work there.'

'We want to link his family story with our presentation of the hotel,' Grace explained to Tina.

They wound into the verdant terraced hills, passing picturesque villages, but soon the garish 'tourist-ville' sprawled out before them. Tina caught her breath and sighed loudly when she saw all manner of accommodation, shops, stalls, clusters of 'art centres', restaurants, spas and yoga retreats. Signs covering many of the shops were advertising adventure trips on rivers, in canyons and down waterfalls, on kayaks and bikes, as well as 'organic' farms, coffee plantations, the elephant caves and monkey forest tours.

Tina looked aghast. 'Oh no! I don't believe this! Ubud was where you came for peace and simplicity; for Balinese culture. All the little villages have joined together so it's one huge town,' she said. 'No! Look at all the tourist buses.' She dropped her face in her hands.

'Nana, what's wrong?' Daisy looked concerned.

'It's all right, sweetie,' Tina soothed. 'When I came here a long time ago, this was a quiet, sleepy place. I'm surprised at what it looks like now, that's all.'

Andy chuckled. 'Yeah, it was a very different scene up here in the mountains compared to the beach culture. But it was all pretty benign back in the day, eh?'

'Depends,' said Tina, and they laughed.

They drove past the monkey forest and up into the hills. Henry and Daisy were keen to see some monkeys and, when they did, their excitement made Putu burst out laughing.

'These are just regular monkeys,' he said. 'Not far now,' he added. 'It's through this next little village.'

In a dusty, shaded, tree-lined lane the minibus took up most of the road as they drove slowly, looking for the gateway and shrine outside the walled compound they'd had described to them.

'That must be it – there's an ornamental gateway in that big wall, with the little shrine by it,' said Grace, pointing. 'Unfriendly spirits not welcome.'

Putu parked under a tree and Andy led the way through the gate, where there was another angled wall, 'To confuse evil spirits,' he said. In front of them was the family temple, a covered platform raised on pedestals, with a shrine in the centre. It was surrounded by several smaller houses and open-sided pavilions.

Two curious, smiling children ran towards them, and a young woman sat on the stone steps of one of the pavilions, brushing a little girl's hair. They smiled at Daisy.

'The kitchen will be on the south side; I want to see that. The design of this place might look random but everything here is placed according to custom and tradition,' said Andy softly.

'It's a whole little town,' said Grace. She was already enchanted by this private and peaceful little family world, seemingly unchanged for generations.

Two young men came out of a small house to greet them. Andy spoke to them in Balinese and introduced everyone.

'These are Gede's younger brothers. Their mother and father are over near the kitchen.'

A dog frolicked beside them as they followed the

young men towards a pavilion where smoke was rising and the tantalising smell of food drifted in the warm breeze.

A group of women were working around an open-sided cooking area. Grace could see that the room next to it was filled with cooking utensils, food storage pots and a preparation table. Behind the kitchen she glimpsed fruit trees and gardens.

They were introduced to Gede's mother and father, sister and his brothers' wives, who lived in their own dwellings in the compound. Finally, a stooped, white-haired man, who was possibly younger than Andy, came forward with a gap-toothed smile to greet them.

'This is Gede's grandfather,' said Andy respectfully.

They were all invited to sit down on stools outside while the old man settled in a chair and lit a cigarette. Two of the women went into the kitchen to prepare some snacks for them.

The little girl who'd been having her hair brushed came and stood next to Daisy and spoke to her. Daisy smiled shyly and looked to Andy to translate.

'She wants to show you the animals,' he told Daisy. 'They have new baby piglets. Over there behind where the granary is.'

Daisy smiled and looked at Grace.

'Sure, honey, go and explore. But be careful of the mama pig!'

Gede's mother, Chandri, spoke some English and was very happy that her first-born son was returning home.

'Did you teach Gede to cook?' asked Grace.

She smiled as she nodded. 'He help me. He likes food.'

She reverted to Balinese to explain further to Andy, who told them, 'Because Chandri had three boys first and no daughter to help with the cooking for a long while, Gede used to prepare vegetables and always watched her cook.'

'He likes to eat,' Chandri said.

'Can I take a look around please, maybe take some photos?' asked Steve.

'May I go with you?' said Tina, as Chandri and her husband nodded their assent.

As they wandered off with two young boys in tow, to admire the ornately carved doors on some of the pavilions, Grace asked Chandri, 'So your mother taught you to cook? Now you teach your sons and daughters?'

Chandri held up a finger. 'Just number one son cook. All girls learn to cook. Sometimes I cook for *bule* lady.'

'She's being modest, Grace,' said Andy. 'Chandri is famous. She and her mother started one of the first little *warung*s near the beach. Just a stall, really, she'd cook snacks and take them to the tourists in Kuta. She'd walk along the sand carrying them in a basket on her head. Then a couple of Aussie surfers got her to cook a version of Aussie meat pies and sausage rolls . . . Balinese-style, as it turned out. Maybe the recipes got a bit lost in translation but they were delicious and a huge hit,' Andy added, laughing. He translated his words for Chandri, then said, 'Warung Baba got bigger and became a place to sit down outside and eat. Gede grew up watching his mother cook for tourists.'

'Oh, that's a fantastic story. Does anyone have photos of her stall and Gede when he was younger?'

Andy asked her and the older woman called her daughter and spoke to her. The young woman smiled and disappeared.

'Andy, how serendipitous is this? Is there a dish that could be unique to Gede's family that we could promote?'

'Meat pies? Sausage rolls?' He laughed. 'No one makes them like Aussies do.'

'Maybe you could do a little stall of snacks at the Kamasan's beachfront for the guests,' said Grace.

'Steady on, we want them to eat in our great restaurants and bars. But we do run food down to the beach. Hmmm, maybe reviving Warung Baba isn't a bad idea for Gede to think about once he's settled in.'

Tina rejoined them, sitting down. 'Warung Baba, did you say? I remember that. It was on the little path from Bemo Corner that went to the beach. It sold delicious snacks.'

'Get outta here. Well, I s'pose that's no surprise,' said Andy, grinning. 'You were around in the good ol' days too. Gede's mum started it.'

'Oh, my heavens!' Tina clasped her hands and turned back to Chandri. 'I'm honoured to know you. You are famous. Like your number one son.'

Chandri laughed when Andy translated this, and then her daughter returned, handing her a glossy magazine carefully wrapped in plastic. Chandri took it out and gently opened it and showed Grace and Tina. There was a photo story on the little Bali beach shack doing a roaring trade in '*Balinese-style Aussie meat pies*'.

'*Tracks* magazine, 1980,' said Grace and handed it to Tina.

'Yep, that's it. Well I never, how magical to meet you, Chandri, after all this time,' Tina exclaimed.

Suddenly Daisy called out, 'Mumma, look!' And they all laughed as Daisy walked very carefully towards them with a plump, pink, wriggling piglet in her arms.

'Quick, photo op,' Grace laughed as Tina pulled out her phone.

By the time they'd had milky sweets and *kopi susu*, Balinese-style coffee, pressed on them, Steve and Henry had taken lots of photos with Chandri and her husband and all the family, and it was time to leave.

Daisy asked for some extra sweets, and as Grace was about to say no, already a little worried about tummy upsets, Daisy whispered, 'They're for Putu, Mumma.'

Putu had been sitting in the shade, smoking and chatting to Gede's two brothers, and he scrambled to his feet, putting out his cigarette.

'I will bring the car.'

Daisy handed him the sticky sweets and he smiled, giving her a pat on the head.

There was a lot of chatter about favourite haunts and food as they drove back.

'What a gift Chandri turned out to be. Mother and son. Great stuff,' said Grace.

'From humble beginnings, eh? All very visual too, in that beautiful compound,' said Steve.

Daisy scrolled through the photos on Tina's phone and announced, 'Nana, can we get a pig when we go home? For Sparkle to play with.'

'That little piggy will grow into a big fat sow. We'd have to move out of our house.'

As they headed away from Ubud, a tourist bus sped past, honking its horn, forcing Putu to take evasive action. Grace checked that Daisy had her seatbelt on, as no one seemed to bother in Bali.

'Do you mind dropping me off in the main Kuta drag, Putu? I have to meet a supplier there,' said Andy.

As they drove down Jalan Pantai three large motorbikes driven by bare-chested young men wearing board shorts, thongs and back-to-front baseball hats, with girls in bikini tops behind them waving their arms, careened past, taking selfies as they rode, screeching with hilarity. Putu swerved to avoid them when the bikes weaved alongside. He only narrowly missed hitting one of the women on the bikes and several cars.

'Drunken hoons,' exclaimed Andy. 'They wouldn't do that back in Australia.'

'Drunk as skunks. No helmets, no shoes, no brains,' said Grace.

'It's the thing the Balinese dislike most about tourists, especially off-their-head Aussies, and who can blame them?' Andy said. 'There's a couple of people killed or injured every fortnight up here. At least. And if there's a sniff of alcohol involved, their travel insurer walks away. It can cost them a bucket of money – if they survive. Listen, Putu, pull in near the shopping complex. I'll take a short cut through the mall. Thanks.'

Andy hopped out of the minibus and Putu headed back to the quiet streets and made a stop at Steve's place, then pulled up at Grace's villa.

As they climbed out, Sri came hurrying out, looking concerned.

'What's up, Sri?' asked Grace. 'Everything all right?'

'You've got a visitor, Ibu Grace. He won't go away. I tell him to come back later but he wait.'

'What do you mean, Sri?'

She turned and waved an arm.

'Oh. My. God,' hissed Tina.

Sitting in the large carved teak chair, which was purely ornamental as no one ever sat out the front, was Lawrence, inscrutable behind dark glasses. He was wearing a polo shirt and cotton blazer as if he were on a cruise.

They stared at him in stunned silence, even Daisy,

239

who was clearly trying to compute her father suddenly being there in this place far from home and where he was not expected to be.

'Afternoon, ladies,' said Lawrence with a thin smile.

8

GRACE WAS SHAKING, HER breath coming in short sharp gasps as she tried to talk to Melanie.

'Gracie, calm down, take a deep, slow breath. So you had no idea he was coming? I thought he was in India?'

'So did we!'

'Where is he now?'

'Sitting calmly by the pool watching Daisy swim, being waited on hand and foot by Sri and Kamsi, because, of course, he's being charming to them. As usual. Mum is in her room.'

'Where are you?'

'In my bedroom.'

'Well, don't let him have the run of the house. Where's he staying?'

'I have no idea. I suspect he thinks he'll stay here! Thank goodness we don't have a spare bedroom.'

'Listen, get him out of there. Tell him to go to a hotel and you'll see him tomorrow. You don't need to be friendly to him. Just lay it on the line,' Mel said firmly. 'Say to him: What do you want? Get out of my life. I've registered my separation and, as soon as I can, I'm filing for divorce.'

'I wish it were that simple. He knows how to get under my skin. I was so happy here, doing so well in my work. Daisy and Mum are having a great time, and then he shows up and I go to pieces. I'm scared.' Grace could hear the tremor in her voice.

'Stop that right now!' Mel said. 'That's exactly how he wants you to feel. Did it occur to you that *he* might be rattled and afraid? You have your family with you, and they're having a blast. You have a stupendous job. What's going on in his life? He has no home, no family, and who knows if he even has any money? What happened to the big deal in India, huh? Have you asked him? How come he can just drift into Bali and annoy you *at your job*? Push him as far away as possible. Call in some of your buddies up there. Frighten the shit out of him.'

'Mel! I can't do that. God, he might end up with cement boots at the bottom of the ocean.'

'So?'

Grace couldn't help but laugh, and she felt some of the tension in her body easing. 'Stop being so outrageous – though it does make me feel better. I'll tell him he can't just walk in on me like this. That he needs to stop acting like we're still married –'

'But you are,' Melanie interjected. 'Is your separation legal?'

Grace sighed. 'As I said, nothing is simple. You have

242

to be separated for a year before you can file for divorce. And Mr Judd told me not to rush into that. I don't want to do anything that will make Lawrence more difficult to deal with than he already is. And I don't have time to do anything while I'm over here anyway.' Grace could feel her anxiety levels rising again. 'He could try to use Daisy as a bargaining chip, I suppose. That happens, Mr Judd says, and then the woman tends to cave in.'

'No, you don't want that. What does he want from you anyway? He'll say he wants to see Daisy, of course. I only hope he doesn't use her to get at you.'

'I'd say that's exactly what he has in mind. And I'm worried about money, too. If he says he's here on holiday, then he's got to be hiding money and saying he doesn't have any. Or he's spending the insurance payout without having given me my share.' Grace took a breath and tried to think clearly. 'At least I know that he can't say I kidnapped Daisy by taking her out of the country. Mr Judd told me that Indonesia is one of the few countries that is not a signatory to the Hague Convention on Child Abduction, which I think would make it more difficult for Lawrence to make an application to have her returned to Australia – if that's what he has in mind. Anyway, Mr Judd has copies of the correspondence between Lawrence and me about my job, and leaving Daisy with Mum, and the plan to bring them here temporarily. And if Lawrence didn't answer, that's his problem.'

'Well, he's gone to Bali for some reason, and you need to know what it is.' Melanie paused, then added, 'Y'know, Gracie, I think there's another layer to this. It's been months since the fire, but Lawrence hasn't made any move – that you know of – to buy a flat or even rent something. Shows he has no intention of having Daisy move in with him, don't you think?'

243

'Could be,' said Grace thoughtfully. 'In a way, I hope so, because it would make a custody claim by him harder to justify. I suspect that for all his posturing, he has no savings and no long-term plans. Maybe that's why he's stalling on handing over my share of the insurance money.'

'You should prepare yourself, Grace. Once he realises you've got his number and know what he's really like, he'll drop all pretence of being nice. He'll draw the equity out of any property, syphon the money overseas, invest in cryptocurrency or just lavish it on girlfriends to ensure there are no funds left to be divided. I've heard so many stories like this.'

'I doubt there's a girlfriend,' Grace said. 'Listen, I'd better not leave him too long with Daisy. I want him out.'

'Call your friend Johnny. He has interesting mates who could help you with that, by the sound of it,' said Melanie.

'Don't joke,' said Grace. 'But thanks for the call, I feel a bit better. I'll call you again soon.'

After farewelling Mel, Grace put her phone in her pocket and hurried through the villa to the garden. Lawrence was frowning, looking at his mobile and ignoring Daisy, who was frolicking in the pool. He probably hadn't watched her at all, thought Grace. Just as well she could swim, but Grace never left Daisy unattended in a pool; even if she was only playing near the pool Grace always kept her eyes on her. Grace sat in the deckchair next to Lawrence and spoke softly, though she found it difficult to keep the anger out of her voice.

'So, Lawrence. Just why are you here?'

He looked up from his phone. 'Such hostility!' he said. 'Is that any way to speak to the father of your child? It's bad enough that you've dragged my daughter out of the country without my agreement.'

'She's my daughter too. You were fully informed of my every move. There's not much more I can do if you don't communicate with me. As you have not contributed anything to her support in any way, I had to take this job to pay the bills and feed us.'

'I'd say you are all eating very well,' he said snidely, waving his arm vaguely towards the house.

Grace chose her words carefully. 'This might look very glamorous, but I am not paying for it, and my pay only comes in instalments, when I finish the various stages of the campaign. This is a huge job, and a job in which, although you have demeaned me and made me feel inadequate for years, I am respected and encouraged. I've been given a lot of responsibility, and I'm getting a lot of kudos for what I'm doing.'

'Terrific. Bully for you. Then you won't be needing anything from me.' Lawrence smiled coldly.

'It is your responsibility as a parent to contribute your share of Daisy's upkeep.' Grace could feel the familiar fury and frustration rising in her. No, don't let him bait and rile you, an inner voice reminded her. She took a deep breath. 'Lawrence, why can't we be civilised about this? Our marriage is over, but we need to do the right thing by Daisy.'

Lawrence's face darkened, his emotionless expression changing to one of barely controlled rage.

'Don't you ever give me any credit for having feelings?' he hissed. 'You always think the worst first. Don't you think I miss my daughter? My family? That I'm also upset because we've lost our home?'

Grace almost laughed. '*Our* home? You mean the house *you* bought, *you* furnished, and you ran *your* way?'

'And that I paid for!'

'It's always about money, isn't it, Lawrence?' Grace sighed. 'I feel as though we never had a real home. We were never a proper family. When did we ever do things together just for fun, as a family? You didn't come to school events, sports days, group activities, even things like the movies . . .'

'I was working, dammit! To make money to spend on you. You didn't contribute much.'

The outrageousness of his comment stuck in Grace's throat and she almost laughed again. Instead she folded her arms and took a deep breath. 'Well, if I'm such a loser who doesn't contribute anything, you're better off without me, aren't you?'

Daisy climbed out of the pool, seemingly oblivious to her parents' argument.

'Mumma, where are we going tonight?'

'I have to go to work for a little while, sweetie. I'm sure Nana will have some plans. We can ask her when she comes back.'

Daisy pulled her towel off the back of Lawrence's chair. 'Are you coming too, Daddy?'

'I'd love to, sweetie. Better still, why don't you and I go out exploring and find somewhere to eat?' he said to her. 'Seems your mummy is too busy tonight.' Lawrence took the end of Daisy's towel and began to dry her.

'Honey, go and get dressed,' said Grace as smoothly as she could manage. 'Daddy has to go to his hotel right now and he'll come back later. Or should you start making plans to fly home now, Lawrence?'

'Not at all.' Lawrence laughed. 'I can stay here for a few days, at least. Daisy, do as Mummy says and get dressed. Then when I come back we'll go out and you can show me around.'

Lawrence stood up, dropping Daisy's towel onto her shoulders and smiling at her. 'Have you missed your daddy, sweetie? Daddy has missed you.'

'Uh-huh,' said Daisy dutifully, then ran inside.

Grace's anger was rising but there was nothing she could do. At least they were on an island, she thought, with Daisy's passport locked away in a drawer with her valuables. 'All right,' she said. 'Look after her this evening and make sure she's back early. She's had a big day. Text me when you come back and I'll meet you at the front door,' she added. 'There's no need for you to come in.'

'Charming of you, Grace. Can you ask your driver to take us?'

'I'll ask Putu if he minds,' she said, standing up to go and find him. Putu would keep an eye on them; he wouldn't let anything happen to Daisy, she decided. 'But first, tell me why you are here, Lawrence. Just what do you want?' Grace said in a low voice.

'I missed my beautiful girls!' he said loudly.

Grace snorted in disbelief, and then left to find Putu.

*

'Hi, Daddy.' Daisy opened the door and led Lawrence out to the garden. 'Come and see my drawings of the chooks I saw at the markets this morning.'

Grace closed her laptop when she heard Daisy and looked up as they came over to the garden table. 'Lawrence, back so soon. Did you enjoy dinner last night? Daisy said you bought her Coke and chips.'

Before he could answer, the gong sounded again at the front door and Tina called out that she would answer it.

Grace stood up as Andy and Tina came out.

'Hi, Grace.' Andy gave a big smile. 'Hey, Daisy Doll!'

Daisy ran to him. 'Hi, Andy! What's happening?' This was how he'd started greeting Daisy and she had latched onto it.

Andy chuckled. He patted her head and strode over to Lawrence, extending his hand. 'Hi, I'm Andy Franklin.'

Lawrence shook hands. 'Lawrence Hagen. Grace's husband. Daisy's father.'

'This is nice, eh, Daisy.' Andy held back any comment about the surprise arrival, but he glanced very briefly at Grace.

Daisy tugged at Andy. 'So what's happening?' she repeated.

'Daisy, I'm sure we can find something nice to do together,' said Lawrence.

Andy looked at Daisy. 'Your mum is working with Steve to shoot the action out at Uluwatu this arvo,' he said. 'So I thought I'd go along, be an extra and have a surf. Would you like to come too, Tina?' He smiled at her.

'Yes, thank you. I don't think I'll be riding that wave, but a beach walk and to see it again would be lovely.'

'Doesn't sound like our sort of thing. I'll take Daisy for an early dinner again,' said Lawrence.

'After what you bought her to eat last night? I don't think –' began Grace.

'What's Oo-loo . . .?' interrupted Daisy, looking disappointed.

Andy turned back to Daisy. 'Uluwatu. It's pretty cool out there. It's one of the best places in Bali to watch the sunset, and there's a performance of a monkey dance on this evening.'

'Monkey dance!' squealed Daisy.

'Not real monkeys, honey,' said Andy. 'But there're lots of real monkeys out at the temple. Maybe we can have a walk along the beach then make our way up to the clifftop, that's where the temple is.'

Daisy turned beseeching eyes on Lawrence. 'I want to go, Daddy, to see the monkey dance.'

'Maybe your dad's not very interested.' Grace was damned if she was letting Lawrence join them when she was working.

But he gave one of his winning smiles. 'I'd love to see the monkey dance. Or we can see the real monkeys. Then afterwards we can have a nice family dinner. Shall I book a table somewhere nearby?'

Tina and Grace exchanged a look, but Andy stepped in quickly.

'How about I get a table for all of us? The restaurants around Uluwatu can get booked out, especially on a performance night. But most places generally hold a table back, just in case, and I know lots of the restaurant managers. I'll let you know. What about Steve and co, Grace?'

'I'll check and send you a text about what the crew wants to do.' Grace was thinking quickly. If they were all out there, Lawrence could have time with Daisy but she'd also be close by. She knew Lawrence had a right to see his daughter, but she didn't want him to have too much time alone with her. She shuddered and reminded herself to stay strong. She hated Lawrence intruding on her life. Apparently even Bali wasn't far enough away.

Andy glanced at his watch. 'Right, we're set then. See you all later.' He gave a wave, and Tina walked with him to the door to see him out.

'Pleasant fellow,' said Lawrence. 'Australian, I gather. Old friend of Tina's? Or yours?' He gave Grace a smile but his look was hard and challenging.

'Neither. He's a colleague from the Kamasan,' said Grace shortly.

'I see. All one big happy family, eh? Nice work if you can get it.' He glanced around.

'Daisy, go and play in your room for a little while,' snapped Grace.

Daisy started at her tone. 'Aren't we going out, Mumma?'

'Not yet. It will probably be late by the time we get home so you need to relax now, sweetie,' she said, her voice softening. 'Say goodbye to Daddy, you'll see him in a while out at Uluwatu.'

Tina reappeared. 'I'll get her settled.' She took Daisy's hand. 'What're you going to wear tonight?'

'Sawong kebaya,' Daisy answered firmly.

'See you later, sweet potata,' called Lawrence.

Daisy turned and ran back and gave him a hug around his waist, and then skipped over to Tina.

When they'd gone, Grace turned to Lawrence. 'Look, can you make your way out to Uluwatu? Our van will be full with us and the film crew and their gear. And, as your visit is interrupting my work, I need you to tell me why you're here and how long you're planning to stay so I can plan accordingly.'

His face shifted from the pleasant, friendly expression he'd shown Andy to cold hardness as he looked at her. The mask has fallen, thought Grace. He doesn't even bother to pretend. It was hard to believe they'd ever been in love. Or had she? Had she ever really loved Lawrence? she wondered.

'I'll get a taxi. Let me know where to go. I came here to spend time with my daughter, seeing as you've taken her out of the country without my consent. I shall stay as long as I please.'

'Lawrence, that's simply not true. As I've told you more than once, my lawyer has copies of the correspondence and details I sent to you, which you never answered. I copied Jenny in as well to make sure you received them. If you don't like me doing it this way, give me some other contact for you. I don't want to send off personal emails to just anyone without you knowing. But you left us with no alternative contact details, no itinerary, no response to any of my messages, and NO money!'

'You have a good job. I'm the one dealing with all *our* debts. And trying to get a deal set up in India so I can get on my feet again. I paid for that house, so I've lost money. You just walked in the door of a beautiful home.'

'In which I had no say at all! There was absolutely no need to give me a whole furnished house in an area where I didn't know anyone, and we both had a long commute from there to work. It was absurdly, ridiculously extravagant.'

He leaned towards her, shaking a finger. 'See, that's the trouble with you, Grace. You're ungrateful. How many women would have killed to have that house? And I've given you plenty of other lovely things too. Nice handbags. And perfume. Not to mention jewellery.'

Grace was about to snap, her temper was at boiling point, but she forced herself to respond rationally. 'Yes, you gave me a lot of nice presents. And some not-so-nice presents. You never noticed or cared that I didn't really need or want any of them. If you want to stock up while you're here, they're plenty of good fakes around! And speaking of the house, what happened to the insurance money?'

'I paid for that house and everything of any value in it. Why should I give you any compensation?'

'Feeding and clothing your daughter doesn't count?'

'You have a job.'

Grace took a deep breath. Here we go again, she thought. If it's not this, then it's something else. It was the story of her marriage. She just wanted out of it.

'Yes, I have a job. A challenging job, with a lot of responsibility. But I'm paid in instalments, so money is tight.'

'So who pays for this place? Your boyfriend?'

'Don't be pathetic,' she snapped, then bit her tongue. It wasn't worth the energy to argue. 'Will I call you a taxi?'

'Sure. But I'd like to say goodbye to Daisy first.'

She showed him to Daisy's room and walked away to call a taxi, adding an extra request to the driver as she did so.

Grace could hear the murmur of Daisy talking to her father. How she wished things were easier. All little girls want a devoted, comforting daddy to spoil them and love them.

As she walked Lawrence to the door, Grace said they'd see him at Uluwatu in the late afternoon. 'As soon as I hear from Andy I'll let you know where he's booked us in for dinner.'

'I can call him, what's his number?'

'No. I'll text you,' Grace said. She didn't want him nosing his way into her business and her friends. She'd learned that lesson.

A short time after Lawrence left, Sri called to Grace that the taxi driver was back at the front door. As Grace picked up her wallet, Tina looked up from reading on the lounge.

'Don't tell me Lawrence didn't pay him!'

Grace chuckled. 'I offered the driver a good tip to come back and tell me where he dropped Lawrence.'

'Grace!' Tina laughed. 'Why?'

'Doesn't hurt to know these things. Is he paying to stay in a large hotel or cheap digs? Is he meeting anyone here? Why the hell is he *really* here? Lawrence doesn't do anything for altruistic reasons.'

When she came back from seeing off the driver, Tina asked, 'So? Where is he?'

Grace shook her head. 'He's staying at The Stones – five star, from what I've heard, and not far from the Kamasan. Seems a coincidence. I just can't help but think he's come here to make trouble for me.'

'Oh, Grace, don't say that. You sound bitter,' said Tina. 'He hasn't seen Daisy for weeks.'

'That's not new. He went away on business trips all the time. He left on a work trip two days after she was born, if you recall. And he has stayed away on long trips, too, like those five weeks he was in America last year.'

'Yes,' admitted Tina. 'And I have to say the times I spent with you, I never saw him do much with Daisy. He was always working in the city or in that wretched home office of his.'

'With the door shut. Well, let's move on. I'm meeting the crew briefly before we head to Uluwatu. If you don't mind getting Daisy ready and asking Putu to bring you guys to Steve's place and pick us up in an hour or so, we'll head out there together.'

*

The boys glanced up when Grace walked into the meeting in their villa. Steve kept his eyes on her a beat longer than the others, then smiled, seeming embarrassed, and quickly went back to work on his laptop.

'You're all dressed up, Grace, you look great. Who're you seeing after work?' asked Mateo.

Grace was flattered by the compliment. 'Hate to say it but no one special. My hopefully soon-to-be ex-husband is here. He walked in unannounced, which was a bit of a shock. But I certainly didn't dress up for him. No, Andy is booking us in for dinner somewhere at Uluwatu after we're finished shooting, so I thought I'd make an effort.' She laughed. 'Would you like to join us? With Lawrence there, I'm not guaranteeing fabulous company. Though to be fair, when I first met him, he could be very charming. I'm sure he'll put his charming face on for you.'

'Would it be helpful if we came along to defuse the situation?' asked Steve.

'Yes, it sounds like heaps of fun,' said Henry jokingly.

'Sorry. Actually, I'd really like you to come along and I'm sure Andy will find somewhere fabulous.'

'Okay, count us in,' Steve said, and Henry and Mateo nodded.

'Thanks, guys, I appreciate it. Right, let's get to work and figure out what we'll film there.'

'Remind me again why we're doing a shoot at Uluwatu?' said Henry, pulling up a document on his laptop. 'I mean, it's about an hour's drive from the Kamasan.'

'Well,' said Steve, 'it's a bit like the filming you and I did up in Ubud, Henry. We weave these short sequences in with the stuff about the hotel itself. Give potential guests a full picture of Bali beyond Kuta and Legian.'

'That's right,' said Grace. 'To feed a constant social media campaign, we want to shoot anything here that's unusual and will draw people in; those potential guests who want to see Bali itself, as well as come to the Kamasan. We'll appeal to a wider audience this way.'

Steve looked at his notes. 'There're several options.

The scenic visitor version; the best place to see the sunset, the amazing surf break, the temple, the monkey dance show.' He paused and looked at the others. 'Actually, it's not the historical classical dance tourists think it is. Walter Spies and a famous Balinese dancer adapted it for tourist consumption. It's vaguely inspired by a male ritual trance ceremony. But now tourists think they're seeing an original ancient Hindu ceremony.' He laughed and shook his head.

'Does that matter for our purposes?' Henry asked.

'No, it's still a stunning dance and the performers are professionals,' Steve said and looked back at his notes. 'We'll also take some drone shots, Henry, of the cliff and the beaches, the cave entrance to the sea . . .'

Henry started typing some notes.

'So what's the story of this Uluwatu?' asked Mateo.

'*Morning of the Earth*,' the others chorused.

'Okay, I'll bite,' said Mateo with a grin. 'What's with this *Morning of the Earth*?'

Steve leaned forward. 'It was 1971, in a house out at Whale Beach in Sydney –'

'Near where my mum lives,' interjected Grace.

'There were three guys who worked on producing *Tracks* surfing magazine: David Elfick, a music entrepreneur; John Witzig, an amazing earthwise architect; and photographer Albe Falzon. They were all surfers, so the mag was pretty out there, promoting pot, pop surf music, hippies and anything anti-establishment, but above all, surfing. They were in seventh heaven working on it. So they decided to make a surf film,' said Steve. 'But they had no idea that their little surf movie would become, and remain, the icon it is. Its music has a cult following too.'

'You don't think they knew what they had when they made it?' said Grace.

'I'm sure there was no grand plan. They filmed in Australia but Elfick felt the film needed a bit of adventure. So he did an advertising deal with an airline, got tickets to Bali, even though no one thought of it as a surfing destination then. No one in Bali surfed, so they needed some talent. And Elfick found this fourteen-year-old kid from Narrabeen, Stephen Cooney – a killer surfer,' Steve said. 'Elfick needed a mentor for him in the film. It so happened that the 1965 USA surf champ, Rusty Miller, was living in Byron Bay . . . And the rest is history.'

'So did they go to Uluwatu?' asked Mateo.

'No foreigners even knew it was there till Albe and another guy hired a *bemo* to take them up the Bukit Peninsula. The driver dropped them off at the temple on top of the cliff at Uluwatu. As they scrambled around the clifftop they saw that unbroken wave rolling from horizon to shore. Steve Cooney was the very first to surf it, that we know of.'

'They'd found their nirvana!' exclaimed Henry. 'Albe must have been stunned.'

'That's an amazing story,' said Grace.

'Sure is,' Steve said. 'If you get a chance to see the film, you should. It's best to watch it on the big screen, with the music blaring out.'

*

'Man, this is amazing,' said Henry as they drove along the winding road past the clifftop temple, where tourists were taking photos and monkeys darted about, looking for treats and making a nuisance of themselves.

'Look at that surf break!' Mateo said, craning his

neck to check it out. 'I can see why people say this is so incredible. The sunset will flood the whole place and the ocean. Stunning. Shame there're so many people.'

'Let's drive down and shoot from the beach first. Andy should be there,' Grace said. 'Get the surfers on the sand then going into the water, and swimmers going between the rocks and the cave. Save the high-angle shots till the sun is going down. Then we can come back up here for the monkey dance spectacular. Get the temple in the sunset too.'

'Where're the monkeys? I want to see the dance,' said Daisy, almost jumping out of her seat behind Putu.

Tina took her hand. 'Honey, we'll go to the temple and see the monkeys while Mummy and the others are working.'

Grace's phone pinged. 'It's Andy. He's booked us in at Sundara for dinner. It's on the beach on the way home, he says. Mum, I'll text Lawrence to meet you at the temple and I'll tell him about dinner.'

'Do you think the restaurant will be very expensive?' Tina said, sounding worried.

Steve smiled at her. 'My guess is that it will be excellent, and Andy will sort out the bill. The hotel will probably pay for it,' he said. 'C'mon, let's hit the road to get there before sunset.'

'Let Daisy and me out first,' Tina said. 'We're going to explore the temple and look for monkeys.'

As they were getting out of the minibus, Grace told her mother where they were going and arranged to meet them again later. Then Putu drove Grace and the crew down the steep incline to the beach.

They spent some time filming Andy and several other surfers gliding on an endless curling wave out from the beach at Padang Padang. Steve looked like he wanted

257

to get into the surf too. He called out to Grace, 'This is amazing. We could do a whole film at this beach – the water's an incredible colour.'

As they were looking out at the ocean, Grace was surprised to see her mother walking towards them along the sand. She gave a cheerful wave.

'Where's Daisy?' called Grace.

'With Lawrence. They're fine and I didn't really want to stay with Lawrence. A couple of girls were driving down here so they gave me a lift.'

Grace's heart sank but she didn't want to say anything. She just hoped everything would work out okay.

Tina sat with Grace as Henry sent the drone camera scooting above a wave, filming Andy gliding inside its breaking curl. He studied the screen, mumbling to himself, 'Bloody brilliant . . .'

'Was Lawrence okay?' asked Grace.

'Seemed to be, and don't worry, for all his faults, I'm sure he will take care of Daisy for half an hour. They were getting tickets for the monkey dance, although somehow I don't think that's going to be his cup of tea,' said Tina.

'Probably not, but Daisy wants to see the show,' Grace said as she went over to talk to Mateo, who was looking at the angle of the sun.

Andy walked up the beach, shaking his wet head, a spray of glittering water circling him.

'Some things never change, eh?' He smiled at Tina as he put his board down.

She tossed him his towel. 'Yes. Thank goodness. Looking out to sea, it's like it was yesterday.'

'Mateo, get that last shot and we'll move up to the top,' Grace said, worrying about the fading light. 'You right, Andy?'

'Yep. Can't get enough out there.' He grinned and started towelling himself dry.

With the beach filming finally over, Grace said, 'Okay, Steve, let's go back up to the temple.'

After the ten-minute drive, they all walked along the path where tourists were heading to visit the temple, beginning to gather to watch the sunset and taking their seats for the monkey dance performance in the amphitheatre.

Henry and Mateo stopped to take some stills, and Tina said she was going to find somewhere to sit on her own, away from the other sightseers, to admire the sunset, leaving Steve and Grace to walk together, both silently enjoying the view. Steve was carrying the video camera he used for extra pick-up shots and reference footage.

'I might get some quick shots here of the tourists,' he said, and stopped.

'Fine.' Grace pulled out the little notebook she carried with her everywhere and checked her scribbled notes from earlier.

Suddenly Steve gasped. 'Bloody hell . . .'

'What's up?' Grace looked at him.

Then, following his gaze, she was about to scream but Steve grabbed her arm.

'Shh, don't startle her!'

'Oh my God, the bloody fool!' hissed Grace.

Lawrence and Daisy had left the path and walked around to the edge of the cliff that dropped away with no fence or barrier to the rocks, which looked to be about a hundred metres below. They were standing with their backs to the edge as Lawrence held up his phone, taking a selfie of them both.

Two steps backwards and they'll be over the edge, thought Grace.

'Just walk over and call calmly. Let her come to you,' whispered Steve.

Several tourists had stopped to watch in horror.

With a fixed, if grim, smile on her face, Grace stepped off the path and began walking slowly towards them.

Daisy spotted her, dropped Lawrence's hand and ran towards her. 'Hi, Mumma . . .'

Grace clutched her, holding her tight. As Steve led them back to the path, Lawrence took one more photo of himself and strolled over to them.

'Daisy, stay with Steve for a minute, please.' Grace hurried towards Lawrence. 'Are you *mad*? What were you thinking? You were far too close to the edge. That was so irresponsible!'

'Nonsense. There were metres behind us before the cliff edge. Don't be such a hysteric, Grace. You can't keep her wrapped in cotton wool, you know.' He walked back to the path, where Steve was holding Daisy's hand.

'Are we going to the show, Dad?' asked Daisy.

'Sure. But let's go and look around the temple some more first. See you at the amphitheatre in a little while, eh?' Smiling pointedly, Lawrence took Daisy's hand and led her towards the temple ruins.

'I don't think I can stand this.' Grace dropped her face in her hands.

Steve touched her arm. 'It's okay. Don't think about it. Daisy is fine.'

'He did it deliberately, you know,' she said. 'He didn't want that photo; he wanted to scare me. He saw us coming.' Her breath was escaping in strangled gasps. 'That was spiteful of him,' she said, 'but what if he was feeling desperate or angry? Would he ever take it out on Daisy?'

Steve gently took her arm. 'Hang on, Grace. It's all right. Take a deep breath.'

Grace looked at him, trying to calm down. 'I keep seeing him . . . if he'd taken any more steps towards the edge . . . would he . . . would he . . .?'

'No. It looks closer than it really is. Your deep fears have rushed in; just close your eyes. It's all right, truly.' He put his arm around her as she took several deep breaths.

'Sorry. It just seems that if my life is going well, he always has to rattle my cage, deliberately it seems.'

'Why is he here? Just to see Daisy or to stir you up? Is he checking on you?' asked Steve softly.

'All of the above, I guess. Not that my life is any of his business anymore. We're separated.'

'It's not my business either, I know. But can you pretend you didn't see that scene at the edge of the cliff? If he likes to upset you, then the best thing is to pretend to ignore it now. For a man with a big ego, being ignored, politely, would be very annoying.'

'Thanks, Steve,' said Grace quietly. She took another slow breath and felt herself relaxing a little.

'Let's sit and wait for the others. I have enough shots here.' Steve led her to a section of the crumbling low wall beside the path. They sat and stared out to sea.

'I've been meaning to tell you,' he said conversationally, 'since you've got so interested in K'tut's book, I did a bit of digging. Did you know there's a recent book – well, from a few years back – that a professor from Melbourne Uni wrote about her?'

'No. Really? What's it about? Her contribution to Indonesian politics?' Grace was instantly interested and appreciated the change of subject.

'Not sure. I've ordered a copy. Though from the synopsis it sounds like he deconstructs her book. Analysing whether her account is all true or not.'

'What? But there're all sorts of stories in newspapers that I read online about her. It has to be true. I've been reading about how she smuggled arms to Bali for the Prince. In the chapter I'm up to, I think she's about to get arrested.'

'Oh, yes, there's no question that she was some sort of heroine. It sounds like the issue is more how she told her story, but then an autobiography is that person's reconstruction of their life, isn't it? His book seems to go into a lot of detail. Apparently he knew her.'

'Really?' Grace was intrigued. 'This is a recent book, right, so the professor's still alive?'

'Yes. For sure. He's still teaching.'

'I can't wait to read his version. But that doesn't take away from K'tut's own story.'

'I agree. You're really into K'tut's life, aren't you?'

'It's a story that seems larger than life. So, even if this professor guy is nit-picking, her life is completely fascinating. And now, being here, I get it. I see it. Steve.' She grabbed his arm. 'It's a film. It would make a great big bloody brilliant feature film!'

'Ah, so you've got the film bug. I know that feeling.' Steve laughed and Grace joined in, feeling the earlier wave of anger and fear rolling away.

'It makes sense,' she said. 'I need to see that book. What's it called? Would Andy's bibliophile friend in Ubud have it?'

'I'll check for you or I'll lend you my copy when I'm done. The professor's name is Tim Lindsey, and the book is called *The Romance of K'tut Tantri and Indonesia*.'

Grace looked up when she heard Daisy's giggles.

Running to them, Daisy called out, 'The monkey took Daddy's sunglasses!'

'Oh, dear. Expensive ones too, I suppose,' said Grace, looking at Lawrence striding towards them.

'Hang on to everything, Daisy, the monkeys are very naughty. Keep away from the ones up here,' said Steve.

'I will. But when's the dance?' she asked, looking crestfallen. 'I've been waiting and waiting.'

'C'mon, Daisy, let's go and find our seats.' Ignoring the adults, Lawrence handed Grace her ticket, then took Daisy's hand and began to pull her away to follow the stream of visitors.

'You'll need to shoot some of this,' Grace said to Steve, 'the fire in the middle and the men in the circle starting the clapping and drumming. Once the sun goes completely we'll be done,' she added. 'Where's my mum, I wonder?' She tapped a message into her phone.

Tina replied straight away. *I ran into Andy. He's going to drop me at the restaurant. See you there. Watch Daisy with those monkeys!*

Leaving Steve to get some more footage, Grace followed Lawrence and sat on the other side of Daisy, who was watching the large circle of young men in poleng sarongs, the symbolic black-and-white checked cloth representing shadow and light, with red sashes and bandanas. Their bronzed torsos gleamed in the lights as they formed a circle.

'Aren't you directing proceedings?' asked Lawrence. 'I thought you were in charge.'

'Steve and the crew know what to do,' Grace answered.

They sat in silence.

'Well, this is a nice family outing, isn't it?' said Lawrence after a while.

Grace didn't answer.

'Where are the dancing monkey people?' asked Daisy.

'It's called the *Kecak* dance, honey. It's called the monkey dance because the sounds they make can sound like a whole bunch of chattering monkeys,' Grace said.

Daisy didn't last the distance to the finale, though she loved the lights and the rhythmic movement of the dancers in the circle. The elaborate, even grotesque figures of the Ramayana characters scared her as they appeared on stage.

'I want to go now,' she whispered.

'Let's go eat then, hey?' said Grace, feeling relieved. It had been a long day.

They found Steve.

'We're going to head to dinner. Are you guys ready?'

Steve was checking his camera. 'Thanks, but I'm not completely happy with some of these shots of the performance. I'd like to try to get a few more. Then I think we'll go back to the villa and sort through some of the footage before tomorrow. Perhaps Putu can come back and pick us up after he's dropped you off at the restaurant,' he said. He glanced at Lawrence, then returned his gaze to Grace. 'Do you mind? Will you be okay?' he added quietly.

'Yep, no worries,' Grace replied, though she found herself feeling a bit disappointed.

When they arrived at the restaurant, they saw Tina and Andy sitting at the bar. Andy had changed out of his board shorts; Grace knew he always carried a clean outfit in his car.

'We've been reminiscing,' said Tina. 'Would you believe we have a lot of overlapping stories of places and people we knew back in the day?'

'Not so unusual, I s'pose. There weren't many tourists here then, and a lot of the same visitors came back each year,' Andy said. 'Fancy a drink?' he asked them.

'I think we'll go to our table and get something for

Daisy, she's starving,' said Grace, taking Daisy's hand. 'See you both when you're ready.' She felt tense, dreading the thought of an awkward dinner with Lawrence. Just as she was wondering how she'd deal with it, she heard her name being called and spun around to see Johnny and Rosie Chow with a young Balinese man and a couple of other men in expensive but casual outfits.

'Oh, it's Johnny Pangisar, my boss!' She waved them over, introducing Lawrence as 'my daughter's father, Lawrence Hagen'.

'And this is my daughter, Daisy, and my mother, Tina, coming over now,' Grace said. 'She and Andy have been reminiscing.'

Johnny and Lawrence shook hands and then Johnny said to Grace, 'How fortuitous is this? Chef Gede is here. We're doing the rounds to update him on some of the opposition.'

'Really? You arrived quickly,' said Grace, greeting the chef, Rosie, and their entourage.

Rosie explained, 'Chef Gede sadly had to rush home as his grandfather is unwell.'

'Oh, I'm so sorry to hear that,' said Grace. 'We visited your family this week, Gede, and met your grandfather then.'

'Thank you,' said the young chef. 'It's my mother's father, who lives in his own compound with his younger brother's family. He has been ill for a while, but it's quite serious now.'

'When Gede accepted the offer to come and work with us, he decided to catch a flight here straight away,' Johnny explained.

'That's right,' Gede said. 'I didn't want to miss saying goodbye to my grandfather, even though I'll have to make a quick trip back in a week or so, to tie up a few things at my old job.'

There were more introductions as Andy and Tina came to join them.

'Sorry,' Andy whispered to Grace, 'I didn't know they'd turn up. I was going to introduce you tomorrow.'

Johnny asked if they would like to join his party, and before Grace could answer, he had waiters running to add chairs and extend their table. Lawrence held out Rosie's chair and without invitation sat himself between Rosie and Johnny. Andy sat next to Tina and Daisy. Grace was next to Chef Gede. Johnny signalled to the waiter to bring tapas and drinks.

Grace found the chef a delightful man, well travelled and modest about his great success. He admitted he was glad to be back home.

The two men sitting on the other side of Grace were introduced as the chef's manager and a writer Rosie had hired to do a profile on Gede for a leading international travel magazine.

After the plates for their main course had been cleared away, Grace could tell Daisy was tired and bored, but she was being well behaved. Grace leaned across to her mother. 'I think I'll take Daisy home. You stay for dessert and a nightcap. We'll get a taxi back, and I'll text Putu and ask him to be here in an hour to bring you home.'

'It's all right, I'll come, too,' said Tina, glancing at Lawrence who was deep in conversation with Rosie.

'Don't worry, Mum, you stay. I don't want to break up the party.'

Grace quietly excused herself, telling Daisy, 'Go and say goodnight to Daddy. He's going to his hotel.' Then she walked over to Andy. 'See you later. I'll be in touch in the morning. Thanks for booking this. I'll settle our bill,' she began.

But Andy waved a hand. 'No worries. I am sure this will be on Johnny, or the hotel can pay. It's research, after all,' he said, smiling.

*

Back in their quiet villa, Grace put Daisy to bed and settled outside with a glass of wine and her laptop to address a stack of emails.

One from Allison sent from her personal email address caught her eye.

> *Hi Grace,*
> *Hope all is going well for you. You're well out of the chaos at work. Spencer got chewed out by head office for losing the Kamasan campaign and he's spitting chips and stamping around the office. Good luck with it all. If you ever need an office manager, don't forget me! Like everyone else here we're all looking for new jobs! Good luck, Grace.*
> *All best,*
> *Alli*

Poor Allison. Grace made a mental note to offer her a job in the future if given the chance. Well, thank goodness she was out of the Spencer tantrum city.

A short while later, she received a text from Steve.

Are you home? Want a drink? I could come over to run through some of the footage we got today if you want? Otherwise, what's the schedule for tomorrow?

Grace glanced at her watch. It was nine o'clock. She texted back, *Great idea. See you soon.*

She was finishing her emails when the security man let Steve in through the side gate.

'Hi. Is everyone in bed?'

'Daisy has crashed. Mum is still out gallivanting. I hope she didn't get stuck entertaining Lawrence. Did I tell you I found out he's staying near the Kamasan, at The Stones? Makes me nervous when he starts getting nosey.'

'Have you worked out why he's here?'

'Not really. Just prying, I'd say. Pull up a chair. How does today's stuff look?'

'I brought it to show you. There're some great shots of Andy on that really big wave.' Steve handed her a bottle of cold wine. 'Here you are. How was the dinner? I'm sorry we couldn't make it.'

'That's fine. Don't worry about it. I brought Daisy home straight after the main course. Would you believe Johnny and his entourage turned up? He had the new chef in tow. Chef Gede had to come back even sooner than expected as his grandfather's ill. He seems really nice. He's going to work well on camera, I think.'

'Perfect. Okay, here's the footage Henry shot with the drone.' Steve opened his laptop.

They ran through the shots from the day, Grace making notes about the bits she liked or felt could work.

Tina came in just as Grace and Steve were finishing up their notes, schedule and plan for the next few days.

'Hey, Tina, did you have a good night?' asked Steve, standing up to greet her.

'Lovely place, the food was delicious. I enjoyed chatting with Andy. He knows so much about Bali. We remember a lot of the same things.'

'Did Lawrence stay on? And Johnny and the others?' asked Grace.

Tina rolled her eyes. 'Lawrence was in Johnny's ear the whole time. I think Rosie got a bit fed up with him.'

'Do you want a nightcap, Tina?' Steve said.

'No more for me, thanks. I'm heading to bed. What's happening tomorrow?' she asked Grace. 'Shall I just take Daisy somewhere easy with Lawrence?'

'You don't have to do that, thanks, Mum. If he comes over demanding to do something with Daisy, I'll just have to trust that she'll be okay with him for one day,' Grace said. 'We're supposed to go to the school and pick up some info, though. Maybe you could do that, if you don't mind? If Lawrence doesn't appear, Daisy can go with you. It would give you the chance to see her school and maybe meet the teachers. It's a great place. She starts next week,' Grace added, for Steve's benefit.

'I'd love that. G'night, Steve.' Tina gave Grace a kiss. ''Night, sweetie. This has been such fun.' She winked at Steve. 'Even with you-know-who skulking around.'

''Night, Mum.' Grace laughed.

'Your mum is good value,' said Steve when Tina had walked up the hallway. 'She's so energetic. Do you think she's lonely on her own?'

'I sometimes wonder. She keeps busy and she's involved in lots of things,' Grace said. 'She's great company. I'd be lost without her. I really don't know how she and my dad got together – they're so different. He's a bit serious, an academic.'

'Your mum's lightness and her sense of humour are probably what attracted him,' said Steve. He held up the wine. 'One more glass?'

'Why not. Let's go and sit in the garden. I'm finally relaxing. Having Lawrence around makes me so stressed. Sorry. I shouldn't bother you with my personal issues.'

As they walked outside into the warm night Grace was tempted to ask Steve about his personal life. He didn't seem to be seriously attached to anyone. But then, how would she know?

He poured the last of the wine into their glasses. 'Listen, to get back to what we started to talk about earlier this evening . . . *Revolt in Paradise*. I've tracked down Tim Lindsey.'

'The professor? No kidding. What have you discovered?'

'He's young, judging by his photo on the uni's website. He's a media commentator, a specialist on Indonesia. He knew K'tut when he was a graduate student.'

'That's amazing. I so want to read his book.'

'Read K'tut's book first. That's what he advised.'

'You spoke to him?'

'Email.' Steve grinned at her. 'I told him what we're doing, and where. And as it happens . . .' He lifted his glass. 'He's coming here in two days' time and he said he'd be happy to meet up. He has stories about K'tut that he'll tell us.'

Grace could hardly speak. Was it the wine, the warm night air tinged with the perfume of frangipanis, or something else . . .? But suddenly she felt a shift, a shadow at her shoulder, a sense of . . . something. She shivered and wrapped her hands around her glass.

'Are you thinking what I'm thinking?' she asked.

'Take it slowly,' Steve said. 'Let it unfold. Who knows what he'll have to say? Maybe leave an offering at the shrine outside your gate.'

He said it lightly but Grace decided she'd talk to Sri in the morning and ask her to make an offering for good luck, and to get benign spirits in her corner. She'd been told the gods and spirits were powerful, and she wanted to do the right thing.

'I might ask Sri how to get the spirits to deal with pain-in-the-butt husbands.'

'Good idea.' Steve laughed and stood up. 'It's late. We can talk more before we meet him.' He tucked the laptop under his arm and picked up the empty bottle and glasses. 'I'll put these inside and let myself out.'

'Thanks, Steve.' She looked at him and said softly, 'Thanks for everything today. You were calm when I was about to completely lose it. It was what I needed to deal with everything.'

'No worries. See you tomorrow,' he said quickly, then turned and went inside.

Grace suddenly felt weary. On the way to her bedroom she gently opened the door to Daisy's room and peeped in.

Her daughter's gentle breathing and curled shape, clutching her bear, reassured her. Grace went to her bedroom where she could hear the murmur of Steve talking to the security guard outside.

Feeling comforted, she fell into bed.

*

Tina was reading the *Bali Advertiser* with her morning coffee and Daisy was sitting at the laptop, watching a journalist named Jackie Pomeroy who did the morning volcano activity report on Mount Agung, which they could see in the distance. Daisy had become fascinated with the occasional puff of smoke rising from the famous volcano, and she loved the movies and photos that appeared on the daily morning report.

'All good,' she declared.

'Can I have the laptop now?' Grace said. 'Have you had breakfast?'

'Not yet, Kamsi is making me noodle eggs.' Daisy pushed the laptop over to her mother.

'*Nasi goreng*, it's called. Okay. Thanks, honey.'

Grace skimmed through the list of new emails, pausing when she saw that there was an email from the solicitor, Mr Jamison. Its subject line had the word *Skulduggery?*

Dear Grace,

I hope your mother is having a lovely visit and young Daisy is settling in to her new surroundings.

Some information has come to hand I felt you should know about, though quite possibly it might not concern you.

I was contacted by the insurance company re the fire at your house. As you know, the insurance was paid out in full to Mr Hagen as the claim was made in his name. They are notifying claimants that the investigator they were dealing with has been charged with fraud and theft. I hasten to add this will not affect the payout for your house. But it has come to light that in several instances of cases dealt with by that particular investigator, the claims were inflated, and/or the circumstances suspicious. It seems he was in collaboration with some owners to defraud the insurance company for a commission.

The matter is being looked into and some owners are being investigated, along with said investigator. I'm not making any assertions, but you may wish to add your name to the list of parties wanting to know more details. Just FYI.

Regards
Howard Jamison

'Good grief! Mum, listen to this.' Grace read the email to Tina.

'Heavens. What are you going to do about it? Is it a class action suit?' Tina said. 'Will you tell Lawrence?'

'I don't know. I'll take advice on that. If I add my name, it's as much as accusing Lawrence.'

'Maybe the investigator will sing and spill the names of people who paid him off?'

'I'll sit tight for the moment. But it's a case I'll watch with interest.'

'Well, you never got a red cent, so you're not going to get caught up in it unless you choose to, at least,' said Tina.

Grace worked in silence for a while till Sri brought in bowls of *nasi goreng* for them all.

'Tell me more about last night, after I left,' said Grace, closing the laptop and pushing it aside.

'It was fun. Andy is good company – he's an interesting character. He misses his son, and his late wife, of course. Loves it here, has put down roots, but wonders what he might have done with his life if he'd gone back and settled down in Australia, like most of the other fellows did. He said his mates back then all seemed to be drifters, hash-smoking surfers, with no real ambition. Yet they've turned into bankers, salesmen, executives. It makes him laugh, but I think he's kinda lonely. He's in his sixties but acts like a forty-year-old.'

'I don't think Andy is lonely for female company,' said Grace dryly.

'Just not those in his own age bracket, eh?' Tina smiled. 'Maybe that's why we had such fun and a lot of laughs. We can speak in shorthand. No games. No big act, just be ourselves. I can't say the same for Lawrence.

Everything seems like an act with him. He monopolised conversation with Johnny all night.'

'Oh dear,' said Grace. 'But Johnny's smart, no one puts anything over him.' She thought for a minute. 'Hey, I wonder if that's the real reason Lawrence has come here. He's heard, or figured out, who I'm working for, and he knows Johnny's a big fish.'

'Yes, you may be right. Listen, Gracie, stop worrying about wretched Lawrence. Go do your job. That's more important. He's like the bad smell from the drains here . . . hangs around all the time. Ignore him.'

'I wish I could. I just hope this isn't going to be the pattern of my life. I don't feel I can ever threaten him or successfully get my lawyer to force him to butt out. Daisy is in the middle, so she'll always tie me to him.'

'He can have his time with her, and the rest of the time he should stay away. That needs to be a binding legal arrangement,' said Tina firmly.

'Y'know what, Mum? What I'm learning is that Lawrence will never make a clean break and move on. His mission in life is to make mine as miserable as possible. And I think it's inevitable that Daisy will get caught in the crossfire.'

'You don't think he'll find a girlfriend? Maybe one with kids? That might change things,' said Tina.

'Maybe.' Grace tried to smile. She knew her mother was trying to soothe her. 'Okay. I'm going to get dressed and meet Steve to plan today's shoot. I might try to get some info out of Johnny, too. He sent a text to say he wants us to go to Ubud for some big art auction.'

'Are the boys going to film it?'

'I have to find out what it's about. I have a meeting with Johnny later this morning. Are you okay with going to Daisy's school?'

'Yes, no problem. And if Lawrence shows up, I'll just take him with us.'

'Oh, Mum, you're an angel. Let's hope he steers clear, but if he does come, try not to let him interfere, or make any changes to what I've arranged.'

'He's entitled to see her school, I guess. He said something yesterday about wanting to take her somewhere this afternoon, too. Don't worry. I'll keep an eye on them.'

Grace headed to her bedroom to dress, but the conversation stayed with her. The freedom she'd felt in her first few weeks in Bali was gone. She felt like she was suffocating, the walls closing in on her.

'Damn you, Lawrence,' she muttered.

Very early, a pounding on the door jolted me out of my sleep. Dazed and frightened, I called out, 'Who is there?'

'Open the door,' shouted a man's impatient voice. 'The Kempetai.'

The Kempetai! My spine froze. Jumping up, I dropped my night sarong and started to pull my dress over my head. Then I ran to the door, on which the pounding had risen to a crescendo.

Two Japanese officers stepped quickly out of the shadows. They marched in, holding themselves stiffly erect, and without a word of explanation began to search the living room. I scurried into the bedroom to finish dressing.

'Come on outside and get in the car.'

'Where are we going?' I asked, my voice quivering with fear.

'For a ride. You'll find out soon enough.'

We drove away. After an eternity of two, three, perhaps four hours, the car slowed. We stopped beside a grim, gray structure – a prison, I knew, by the look and feel of it. A guard led me into a cell – a cage, really, closed on three sides, with the fourth side an iron grille looking onto a narrow hall where Japanese sentries paraded back and forth. On the floor of my cell was a filthy mat of palm and another mat rolled around a handful of straw. The only other feature to be seen was a hole in the earthen floor – the toilet, I discovered later.

For five or six days or maybe a week – it was hard to keep count – nothing much happened. Twice a day a banana leaf of rice was handed to me through the bars; little better than a starvation diet.

At daylight each morning the guard came down the corridor, down the line of tiny cells just like mine, each with its occupant. We had orders always in the daytime to kneel, with hands clasped in front of us. The guard carried a long pole, with which he prodded us like beasts if we were not already on our knees. All day long we were required to remain on our knees, never allowed to sit no matter how sharply our muscles pained.

There had been no charge against me. But a day came when I was called out of my cell and taken to an interrogation room around which were seated several Japanese officers. For some minutes, questions were put to me, based obviously on my papers which they had seized.

My replies gave them no satisfaction. 'Of what am I accused?' I cried. 'Why are you holding me here?'

'You are an American spy! You must give us your FBI number.'

I almost laughed. 'That is ridiculous, and quite untrue.'

The seated Japanese officer showed impatience at my responses. My chief questioner scowled fiercely.

'Take off your clothes,' he ordered. I stiffened, paralyzed with shame, and a young lieutenant tore off my one garment.

'Stand on one leg!' the interrogator barked. 'Now raise the other with the knee bent.'

Sobbing with humiliation, I complied. Later, much later, I grew so hardened that I began to undress automatically as soon as the door of the examination room was closed behind me, but on this first morning the emotional torture was worse than that of any burn or blow.

I was returned to my cell for another day of filth and lice and waiting. Each morning I was brought back to the room, and again stripped, grilled, and subjected to beatings and indignities.

My failure to confess to knowing anything stung my inquisitors. They decided to try a new refinement of torture. 'If you will not tell the truth, you shall walk the streets of Kediri naked,' they said. 'Everyone shall see your shame.'

They ripped off the last pitiful bit of covering I had. And with bayonets they forced me to walk down the very centre of the street.

But the Japanese had not reckoned with the Indonesian mentality. The Javanese are frank about the facts of life, but modest. One glimpse of what the Japanese were doing to me and they were horrified.

They fled in every direction. Doors and windows were slammed shut. My tormentors hurried me back to the prison for another severe beating, and then tossed me into my cell. But they knew that they had, somehow, lost face.

After three weeks of almost daily interrogation, the commandant, for some inscrutable reason, set me free.

I found my next confinement quarters to be a cell underneath the Surabaya Kempetai Headquarters. I was quickly informed that what I had suffered at the hands of the Japanese in Kediri had been as nothing compared with what I would go through in the Surabaya Kempetai.

At first they were reasonably gentle, trying to make me talk. I insisted that of all the Japanese I had associated with not one discussed anything with me except art and literature. The grilling became sharper. Before long I had been battered into semiconsciousness.

They stood me on the table, tied my hands behind my back, fastened my elbows together, and then – twisting my arms backward in their sockets – looped my hands over the hook that dangled from the ceiling. Inch by inch they moved the table away, demanding with each pull that I tell them what information I had received, and from whom. With a last pull the table slid from under my feet. I was hanging. I screamed in unbearable agony. When my mind cleared I was on the floor. Then the guards carried me back to my cell.

The tortures went on.

The Japanese officers came to my cell late at night, and talked to me in very quiet and serious voices. 'We have decided that there is no use going on with this,' they said. 'We know that you are guilty of espionage. Therefore, tomorrow at daybreak you will be shot.'

I knew that if I confessed to my dealings with my friends I would not save my own neck, and would certainly bring them to torture and death. So if one had to die, better to die alone, saying nothing.

The Japanese officers came very early the following morning. They bound my hands behind my back, and tied me against a banyan tree with branches that hung down to the ground like the tentacles of an octopus. 'You still have time to confess. I will count to three. If you say nothing, on the third count you will be dead.'

I heard the count in Malay. 'Satu.' I braced myself. 'Duah.' Now, now it will come. 'Tiga.' The shattering roar of the rifle staggered me. I felt something hot and sharp hit my chest. I fell to the ground.

Several days later I awoke in an Indonesian hospital. The Indonesian doctor and nurse said the Japanese had fired their rifles into the air, and at the same moment had hit me with a stone from a catapult. The intent had been to make me think I had been shot. It succeeded only too well.

And then came August, 1945, and the final defeat of the Japanese all down the chain of islands they had won so easily. All we knew at the hospital was that the war was over. Shouting Indonesians stormed the hospital and also the camp at Ambarawa, disarming the Japanese. All of us cheered and wept, and threw our arms around each other. It was a wonderful time.

The Indonesian soldiers who took the hospital by force quickly learned my story, and that I was still in a critical condition. I was taken to the mountains to the chalet of a highly respected Indonesian doctor. I weighed less than half my normal weight. I regained health rapidly.

And what of Anak Agung Nura? I would have no news of him until communications with Bali were restored. I was sure that this would not take long and that I myself might soon travel back to the puri that had for so many years been my home.

9

GRACE WALKED ALONG THE beach in the fresh, early morning air. It was a lovely way to start the day. The tide was out and the wet sand shone like gleaming glass. This part of the beach was deserted, though once guests were in residence at the Kamasan, Grace knew this pristine strip would be 'claimed' for them, with beach lounges, deckchairs, sun umbrellas and staff in attendance.

As Grace turned into the hotel grounds she caught a glimpse of Nyoman collecting fallen palm fronds from the immaculate lawns. The gardens were flourishing; she noticed some plants had grown even in the short time she had been here. Artfully trained bougainvillea spilled in controlled clumps, while frangipani, white jasmine, hibiscus and trailing orchids looked as if they'd always been there. The huge hibiscus, heliconia and, in the shady spots, exotic anthuriums all made for a dramatic backdrop.

She picked a sweet blossom and, waving to Nyoman, turned off the path and went through the bamboo and pandanus grove to the hidden back garden and the remains of K'tut's hotel. A startled bird screeched at being disturbed and darted away into the greenery.

Passing the crumbling, lichen-covered remains of a carved stone gateway, Grace spotted a simple shrine with the sculpture of the Hindu deity, Vishnu, on top. A flower offering had already been placed on the pedestal. Grace tucked her blossom in her hair, its perfume trailing behind her.

She recalled reading about K'tut's despair – coming back here to see her beloved hotel in this peaceful setting ruined by the Japanese invaders. It was almost unfathomable to Grace that K'tut had suffered torture and solitary confinement for many months on another island, only to return to further hardship and disappointment – and yet she had survived it all, and gone on to make a positive difference to the world around her in spite of it. Grace thought about K'tut's strength, perseverance and fortitude. It didn't seem right to her that K'tut Tantri had been forgotten. She sighed and turned away, taking the short cut through Nyoman's kitchen gardens to the back of the hotel.

She followed the smell of pungent Balinese coffee and the murmur of voices and found Johnny, his father and, to her surprise, Madame Pearl, seated at a table on the terrace.

Johnny waved her over. 'Grace, hello. Have you had breakfast?'

Grace grinned and walked towards them. 'Not yet. Good morning, Pak Pangisar . . .'

'Harold, Harold,' the older man said, smiling.

Johnny pulled out a chair for her and Grace sat down. 'Thanks, Johnny. How are you, Madame Pearl?'

'I am doing quite well,' the elegant older woman replied. 'Very much looking forward to this evening.'

Grace wondered if Madame Pearl was spending the day at the hotel, as she was already dressed formally enough to be ready to go to the evening's art auction in a silk dress with multiple strands of fat pearls and large diamond and jade earrings. She was wearing a narrow Cartier Tank watch. Daywear, thought Grace, rather bemused.

'Oh yes, please tell me about this evening.'

'Breakfast first. Have anything you like,' said Johnny.

A waiter who'd been standing nearby came over and smiled at Grace, ready to take her order.

'I'll have creamy eggs with smoked salmon,' she said, 'and sourdough toast, please.'

After they had given their orders for tea and coffee, the waiter bowed and left, having not taken a single note. Johnny gave a nod of approval. 'He's going to be good. They have to keep every detail of every order in their head.'

'So what's happening tonight, exactly?' asked Grace again.

Johnny leaned forward. 'Auctions like this one are for serious collectors. A lot of money will be spent and a percentage will go to charity,' he said. 'There's significant Balinese art going under the hammer tonight. Some of the works are culturally very important; I'd hate to see them leave the island.'

'We are only interested in the pieces from Kamasan village,' Harold reminded his son.

'Naturally,' added Madame Pearl. 'Make sure they are

283

well insured, Johnny, before you put anything you buy up on public display in the hotel.'

Johnny nodded, seemingly unconcerned that he was planning to purchase hundreds of thousands of dollars' worth of valuable art to hang around the family's hotel.

'Do you know about Kamasan village?' Johnny asked Grace.

Grace nodded. 'I've heard it's an important centre for Balinese art, but I don't know much more than that.'

'Very old classical art was produced there, based on the *wayang* puppet stories – stories that come from the heart of Bali. They bridge two worlds, the spirits' and ours,' Johnny explained.

'It's always been a collaborative effort. To this day, the whole village paints and creates the artworks,' said Madame Pearl. 'You should go there sometime, Grace, to Klungkung, to see the village.'

Johnny grinned at Grace. 'More to film!'

'I'm going to end up with a full-length feature film about the Kamasan.' Grace laughed. 'Though we *do* need a lot of online material. MGI have started releasing the TVC teasers on Instagram, YouTube and Facebook – the online ads and infomercials, that is – leading up to the hotel's opening,' she said, turning to Harold. 'The ads and teaser will be released in Australia and on iflix across South East Asia. They expect a viewership of forty million plus. The travel tourism magazine editors and travel bloggers will start coming in soon too.'

'Excellent. What great show are you planning for the opening?' Harold asked his son.

'You'll know soon enough.' Johnny smiled. 'We're tying up a few loose ends, locking in the last big name.' He winked at Grace.

'We need to fill this place,' said Harold.

'Well, just don't overspend on art tonight, Johnny. I know you consider yourself quite the collector,' said Madame Pearl.

'Oh good, here's breakfast,' said Johnny cheerfully, perhaps happy to change the subject.

*

Grace was working at her computer when she heard Daisy and her mother return after Daisy's second day at school.

Daisy ran to her, waving a few sheets of paper. 'I have to get some books and things, Mumma.'

Tina followed her. 'Gosh, that school is great, lovely staff. Lots of amenities and a pool with its own water-slide! Daisy will be swimming lengths and diving before you know it.'

'Did Daddy like your classroom?'

'Um, I don't know, Mum,' Daisy said and dashed away. 'I have to give a drawing to Sri,' she called over her shoulder.

'He didn't see it,' said Tina, rolling her eyes. 'Said he'd seen the school the other day, before she started, and he didn't have time for her to show him the classroom. Had a meeting, apparently.'

'Story of his life. My life. He went to a "meeting" one time and I found him a few blocks away near the park, sitting in his car on the phone,' said Grace.

'He excused himself just when the subject of spending money came up,' said Tina. 'I mentioned to him that there are fees to pay and a uniform and books to buy. The usual expenses that come with starting a new school.'

'That'd be right,' sighed Grace. 'I just wonder what the hell he's up to.'

'He mentioned possibly going to Singapore.'

'Did he? He used to go there fairly regularly on business. But mainly to have his suits made. Bet he can't afford them anymore.'

'He asked if he could take Daisy to an early dinner tonight. Just the two of them.'

'Where?' asked Grace. 'She loves La Lucciola and it's close by. I'll text him. That works out well as I'm going to that art auction in Ubud I was telling you about. Steve and the boys are coming too as there's sure to be some action worth filming. Would you like to come along?'

'No thanks, honey, I might stay in tonight,' said Tina.

'No worries. If you decide to go out, Sri will be here to look after Daisy and help her get ready for bed when she comes home from dinner. I don't want Lawrence to come in here on his own,' she added. 'Maybe I'm being paranoid, but I worry about him snooping around.'

'It's hard to move on when he's under your feet like this,' her mother said. 'You have to get the mediation process worked out soon, darling.'

'I want to, but I don't know how to stop Lawrence stalling and refusing to cooperate,' said Grace with a sigh. 'I've spoken to Mr Judd about it. We're still waiting on a date for our mediation – the family courts are so clogged up, a wait this long isn't unusual, apparently. I've asked Mr Judd to try to get Lawrence to agree to parenting orders now – apparently we can do that at any time on our own and lodge them with the court to make them legally enforceable. But so far, of course, Lawrence's lawyer has told Mr Judd that "his client" is not prepared to do anything yet.'

'He does like to be in control, that's for sure.'

'Well, I hope he leaves soon. It's so distracting having him hanging around. He might say he came here to see

Daisy, but I'm pretty sure he also wanted to nose around and upset me. And it's working,' Grace muttered crossly.

'You know, I heard him say to Rosie Chow at dinner the other night that he might go to London,' said Tina. 'Time to see his family, he said; his father's getting on. Went on about them still going to the polo and shooting weekends in the country.'

'Oh, give me strength,' said Grace. 'For a start, where's he getting the money for the airfare? And who the hell are his family, anyway? Are they Odfords or Hagens?'

'Have you got to the bottom of that strange business with the passport yet?' Tina said.

'No, I really don't know what the story is,' said Grace, hiding her face in her hands for a moment. 'Copies of the expired passport are in Mr Jamison's safe and I sent that message on Facebook. You never know what might come out of the woodwork.' She stood up and paced around, trying to ease her anxiety.

At that moment Daisy walked down the stairs wearing her swimmers and with a towel draped over her shoulder, and Grace smiled, welcoming the distraction.

'Can you come for a swim with me, Mum?'

'What a good idea, sweetie. I have time for a quick dip before I have to go back to work. Wait here for me while I get changed. I'll be back in a minute,' she said, and, gazing at her daughter for a moment longer, it occurred to her that Daisy was growing up. The 'Mumma's and 'Mummy's were getting fewer and farther between. Daisy plonked down on a chair looking onto the garden and swung her towel around, obviously keen to get into the water.

Grace turned and said quietly to Tina, 'I'll pay for whatever's needed on the school list. If I let Lawrence pay for those things, he'll start telling Daisy what she can or can't do, because *he's paying for it.*'

'Being here really is a wonderful experience for her,' said Tina. 'Lots to occupy her developing brain; new people, different language, and an exciting school. Not to mention all the delicious new food she's trying.'

Grace smiled, guessing that her mother was trying to lighten her mood. 'Did you see what she wrote in her homework book yesterday?' she said. '"I love dragon fruit but I hate durian."'

She relished these light conversations; they helped her overcome the dark moments. Sometimes she felt as if she couldn't fit anything more into her head. Just as things had been going well, along came Lawrence to throw a rock into the smooth pond of her life.

She squeezed her mother's shoulder affectionately and went to get changed.

Later, when Grace had finished editing the latest script and Daisy was busy with Sri, 'helping' her cook noodles – Sri had the patience of a saint, Grace often thought – Grace settled down in the garden with K'tut's book.

Really, thought Grace, how could she complain about her life, compared with what K'tut went through? And so many of the people K'tut knew had died or simply disappeared. Grace found it hard to imagine this sunny, happy island under the terrible cloud of war, and it had all happened so close to Australia.

By this stage in the book, as K'tut recounted, the Japanese were mortified at the lowering of their flag. That was nothing in comparison to the Dutch colonials' anger. They had expected to return to their elegant homes in Indonesia with their servants and countless labourers who worked, indeed probably slaved, on their plantations and in their factories.

K'tut seemed proud to record that Sukarno, the leader of the freedom movement, had stepped forward. In the square in front of the palace of the Dutch governor-general, which was filled with thousands of local people, Sukarno had declared his country's independence on behalf of the Indonesian people. The thousands gathered in the square had begun weeping and shouting, '*Merdeka . . . Merdeka . . . Freedom . . .*'

Then, read Grace, British troops moved in. Mountbatten, their commander, was misled and manipulated by the Dutch, who were hoping to reclaim their hold on Indonesia with the backing of the British soldiers. So, if the British were fighting for the Dutch, the Indonesians, against their will, would have to fight for their freedom. And, as K'tut wrote, the Dutch smiled and waited, biding their time.

Grace poured herself a glass of pineapple juice and returned to her book.

During the first month after my deliverance from the Japanese prison hospital I lived in the shadow of death. Under the gentle care of the Indonesian doctor I gained strength, day by day. Every morning and evening he unfolded for me the story of the Indonesian declaration of independence. He read the daily news to me. Later he brought me a radio.

One day I asked the doctor the reason for his kindness and consideration. Why had he nursed me, a stranger, back to a semblance of life?

'You are not a stranger to me, K'tut Tantri,' he replied. 'It is important to me that you get well.'

The news of Indonesian freedom had filled my heart with gladness. How happy Nura must feel. But as I thought of him, something told me that he was in danger. I could not shake off this presentiment, although I told myself it was foolish. But was it foolish? The radio said that the Dutch had reinstated themselves in Bali. Guerilla warfare in Bali against the Dutch was rampant. Nura was bound to be in the middle of it.

One morning the doctor came to my room with a bigger smile than usual, and said, 'K'tut, make yourself pretty. You have company.'

I replied, 'What company could I have? No one knows that I am here.'

I was astonished when the doctor ushered in four Indonesian men in their early twenties. I gazed at them blankly for a moment, and then recognized one.

'Pito, darling little Pito,' I sobbed.

He came over to my bed, bent down and rubbed my nose with his, drew in his breath. Such is the custom of the Indonesians when embracing.

Pito was dressed, as were the others, in khaki shorts and a khaki tunic on which was sewn the rank of a first lieutenant. He introduced me to the other young men. I smiled at their titles, but then remembered that these young men were in the midst of a revolution.

'How did you know I was here?' I asked.

'I am in the intelligence department. In any case, the doctor sent word that you were here.'

'The doctor!' I exclaimed. 'How would he know where the guerilla headquarters were?'

'He is one of our most important guerillas.'

I sat up in amazement. The doctor! A member of Bung Tomo's ragged bamboo army of freedom fighters. What next!

After the pleasantries were over the doctor joined us, and his pretty wife brought native coffee – *kopi tubruk* – and rice cakes. We sat around talking about the revolution. One story led to another until Pito suddenly broke into the general discussion.

'K'tut,' he said, very serious. 'We came here to find out how you were getting along, and to see if you were getting the proper care. But we also came to ask you to consider two propositions. We hope you will find one of them agreeable.'

He drew a paper from his pocket and began to read in his soft, musical voice.

'K'tut Tantri: We, the guerilla fighters of Java Timor, know only too well the suffering and torture that you have been subjected to by the Japanese, just as we know how the Dutch persecuted you for so many years in Bali.

'Because of the love and understanding you have had over the years for our people we pledge ourselves to help you in every way possible to reach your own countrymen at Batavia. This will mean smuggling you through Dutch and British territory, but we will see that you are delivered safely to the American consul. Then you can be evacuated to your own country where you will have the proper medicine and food, and peace away from the strife in Java.'

Pito halted and looked at me for my reaction. My face must have shown how deeply touched I was.

I knew that any effort to get me through the British lines would require these young men to risk their lives.

'Go on, Pito dear,' I whispered. 'What is the second proposal?'

Pito tightened his lips and cleared his throat.

'It is our hope that K'tut Tantri, health permitting, will not desert us in this great hour of Indonesia's destiny. It is our hope that K'tut will find it in her heart to stay in Indonesia and help to bring our beloved country to the same state of freedom that her own people enjoy.

'But before any decision is made we should like to point out that the road to freedom will be fraught with danger. We have nothing to offer K'tut Tantri in return for such a sacrifice, except the love and esteem of seventy million Indonesians.'

If I remained in Java I definitely could not have the care, the medicines, the good food I required to build up my health again. My thoughts turned to the American Revolution, and to the men of other lands – Poles, Frenchmen, Germans and Englishmen – who had played important parts in shaping the destiny of that great democracy. I thought of Thomas Paine, who wrote in his book *The Rights of Man*: 'There can be no freedom for one unless there is freedom for all.'

My decision was made.

To the lovable golden people standing before me I said, 'Come what may, I shall throw in my lot with the Indonesian people.' To Pito, quoting his child's words to me so many years ago, I mischievously added, 'Take me with you, gentle Pito, for now I shall be your eyes and your tongue. I shall help you get the right change, and I'll show you the road. Or I will die in the attempt.'

Pito fell to his knees, hid his face in the bedclothes and wept.

Just before he was leaving, Pito asked me what had become of the charm he had given to me when we first met, knowing that I had worn it constantly around my waist on a silver chain.

I told him that the Japanese had ripped it off when they questioned me at Kediri and that I had never seen it again.

'I have another charm for you,' Pito stammered shyly. 'This one is much stronger, and must be worn next to the skin. It will protect you from all harm in these dangerous days that are ahead of you.' He pulled from his tunic pocket a long strip of white cloth stitched with designs of gods and demons and with magic words of protection in ancient Sanskrit. Handing it to me, he said, 'May Allah protect you always, K'tut.'

We said good-bye, rubbed noses, and drew in our breath. '*Selamet tinggal* – live in peace,' said Pito. '*Selamet djalan*,' I replied. 'Go in peace.'

'Mumma, Mum.'

Daisy squeezed in beside Grace on the sun lounge. 'Nana asked what am I going to wear tonight?'

'Let me see. What would *you* like to wear?' For a moment Grace was tempted to suggest that Lawrence could take Daisy shopping, but then thought better of it. If he was broke, Daisy would be disappointed. 'What about a sundress? It's fun to dress up to go out to dinner.'

'Okay. Maybe the yellow one . . . no, the green one. With the hearts on it . . .' She ran off.

Looking at the time on her phone, Grace said to herself, 'I'd better think about what to wear too.' She picked up the book that had fallen to the ground and tucked it under her arm just as her phone rang.

'Hi, it's me,' said Steve. 'We're heading up to Ubud now. Mateo wants to see what the light is like and how the gallery is laid out. Sounds like it could be a bit ordinary from a visual point of view.'

'Hopefully the auction will make it more interesting. I'll ask Putu to take me and I'll see you there.'

'Sounds good. Do you want to have dinner afterwards? There're some great places in Ubud. Maybe Apéritif or Room 4 Dessert?' He paused, then said, 'Or do you want to come straight back and start editing?'

'Dinner sounds good. Let's see how we go, but it should be fine. We're pretty much on schedule,' Grace said. 'I'm trying to find the right music to go with the rough edit, before we send it to the music production company. Something upbeat,' she added. 'Any suggestions?'

'Well, I could ask Johnny to buy the rights from Coldplay or someone,' Steve said.

'Don't joke and don't suggest it. That'll blow my budget – I've already used their music once in this campaign and you wouldn't believe what I had to pay for it.'

'I can guess! Let me think about it and I'll come back to you,' he said, laughing. 'Meet you there around five thirty?'

'Fine. See you then.'

Grace went inside and opened her laptop. Before checking her emails, she looked at her Facebook page, which she'd been far too busy to check lately. She was surprised to find there was a message for her from a Beatrice Odford.

Shakily she opened the message to read:

Hello. My name is Beatrice Odford. You say you are searching for relatives of Justin Kenneth Odford. From the full name and date of birth you provided, it sounds like you're talking about my brother. We have had little contact with him, as we are estranged. After he left for Australia years ago, he cut off any connection with his family. He didn't get on with our father. But I think my mother regrets not hearing from him. Mum feels he thought we were never good enough for him. My father is retired but worked in the fishing industry at the port. I run a hair salon in Grimsby. I'm sure my mother would like to know how he is. Does he have children? That sort of thing. Our parents are in their eighties and my father's not well. It would be good for them to know he is doing all right.

If it is the same Justin Odford, please message me with a photo. We won't bother him. I am sure he is successful, and, we hope, happy in his life. I apologise for taking so long to respond. I don't use Facebook very often. And, of course, your message surprised me somewhat. I will check my Facebook more often now, though, for your response.

Kind wishes, Bea Odford

'Mum!' Grace called shakily. 'Come and see this.'

'What's up?' Tina raced over to Grace and peered over her shoulder to read the message. 'Good grief! How sad.

Didn't you write to his mother when Daisy was born? I thought you said you sent photos, and of your wedding?'

'I did. But I didn't post them myself. I always gave the mail to Lawrence to send when he went in to the office. I was home such a lot with Daisy, it was easier that way. He probably gave me a fake address and never sent the packages. When we didn't get a reply, I talked to Lawrence about it and he just said they weren't close, and not the sort of people who sent presents or photos or that sort of thing,' Grace said.

'But didn't you used to get Christmas cards from them? With the name "Hagen"?' asked Tina.

'We did,' said Grace, frowning. 'Although, now that I think about it, I never saw the envelope, which is where you might see a surname. Lawrence only ever showed me the cards themselves after he had already opened them at the office – or *said* he had.' She looked at Tina in shock. 'Do you think Lawrence wrote them himself? That would be crazy, surely. What sort of person "fakes" a Christmas card?'

'Nothing about that man shocks me anymore,' said Tina, though the tremor in her voice contradicted her words.

'I used to feel sorry for him that his family were so aloof. Now I feel so sorry for his mother. It sounds like they're just ordinary people. Probably quite nice.'

'Not good enough for Lawrence, apparently, so he invented a new family. Amazing that he got away with it for so long,' said Tina. 'If he is this Justin Odford, of course. What a bolt from the blue! What're you going to do?'

'It's hard to think straight; I feel quite shaky. I'm not sure if I want to open this can of worms.' Grace drew a deep breath. 'I'll answer her – I have to. But I won't get involved,' she said. 'I don't want to confront Lawrence with this until he and I are divorced. He'll have a fit if he finds out what I've uncovered.'

'Not to mention a whole new identity. Who knows what "Justin Odford" got up to before he moved to Australia and became "Lawrence Hagen"?' Tina said, sitting down next to Grace. 'Poor Daisy. Seems like he may have intended for her never to meet her other grandparents . . . So what if this lady writes again and wants to get involved with us?'

'I'll be firm and tell her Lawrence and I are divorcing. But I can't help being curious, and I feel I should get to the bottom of it for Daisy's sake. This could be her family, after all. I'll see what I can find out. Ammunition is always useful with Lawrence,' said Grace. 'I'll send her some photos and ask for some family history.'

'Well, good luck. Be careful that Lawrence doesn't find out,' said Tina.

Grace rose to get a drink from the kitchen. Sri and Putu had just gone to collect some produce from Nyoman. Tina had gone upstairs to her bedroom, and Daisy was in the garden putting out chunks of fruit for the colourful birds that usually darted around the flowers, although Grace couldn't see any birds there now when she looked out.

Then the windows started to rattle and Grace cocked her head as she heard a faint noise.

Suddenly Grace wobbled as the floor heaved a little beneath her, and she heard Tina give a sharp screech from her bedroom as everything else around them started moving, too.

'Mum, Daisy!' screamed Grace. 'Get under the big table!'

Daisy came running inside.

'Yay, is this an earthquake?' she shouted with glee. 'Come and see the pool. There are waves like at the beach!'

Grace grabbed her. 'No. Get under the dining table with me, quickly!'

'I want to see the volcano.'

'No.'

Tina, white-faced, had hurried in and was crouching under the table. Grace pulled Daisy under there too, ready to cover her with her body. There was a distant crash as something fell from a shelf.

Then there was silence.

'It's stopped,' said Tina.

They waited a moment or two, then they heard Putu and Sri coming through the side gate and calling to them.

Daisy scrambled out and ran to meet them, jumping up and down. 'We had an earthquake!'

'Yes. Just a baby one.' Sri smiled. 'Are you okay, Ibu Grace?'

'A bit shaky but fine.' She laughed. 'A baby one, eh? Will there be more?'

'No, all finished for now,' said Putu confidently as he put down the basket of fruit and vegetables for Sri. 'Maybe some small aftershocks a bit later. No need to worry.'

Daisy raced to Grace's laptop. 'I want to see some pictures of Mount Agung. How big was this one, Sri?'

'Maybe a five or six. Just a little shiver.'

Grace and her mother exchanged a look and the two women started to laugh.

'I'm still feeling wobbly,' said Tina. 'Like my equilibrium hasn't come back to normal.'

'I can't get over how I feel,' said Grace. 'It's like we are fleas on top of a massive animal that just shook itself gently. Reminding us how insignificant we are.'

Daisy was chewing her lip as she studied the computer. 'It's a six two,' she read.

'Six point two,' said Grace.

'Not so big,' Sri said and shrugged. 'Over seven is a big one.'

'This was big enough,' said Grace. 'Right, where were we?' She tried to keep her voice steady but she couldn't help thinking that the shock of the Facebook message was even bigger than the terror of the ground moving under her.

*

The gallery in Ubud was in a nondescript building, a simple space that, rather than drawing attention to itself, allowed its contents to shine. And indeed, as Grace walked into the room, the walls glowed.

Steve was there already and came over to her. 'Lives lived, places loved,' he said softly, staring around at the artwork. 'There are some amazing paintings here.'

'Sure are,' Grace said. 'This is even better than I'd expected.'

Rows of chairs faced a podium, and arrangements of flowers stood against one wall. Doors at the back of the room led to a patio, where tables were covered with trays of drinks and food. Two men, formally dressed, and a woman Grace figured was the gallery director, who was wearing severe glasses, were anxiously comparing notes.

Steve picked up one of the catalogues from a pile on a side table and raised his eyebrows. 'This is a serious collection. Wish I had the bucks.'

'I'm keen to see what Johnny chooses. Look, there's the Kamasan art over there.' Grace pointed to the opposite wall.

The gallery director came over to them. 'Welcome, thank you for coming to cover the auction.' She reached out and shook Grace's hand and then Steve's. 'I'm Simona Dryden. So, you're with Mr Pangisar?'

'Yes, we're here to film for him. This is Steve Boyd,' Grace said, 'and I'm Grace Hagen. We spoke on the phone. What are the regulations? I appreciate some people might not want to be filmed.'

'That's right. You'll need to let everyone know that you will be filming and get their permission before you begin.'

'No problem,' Steve said. 'And if we take shots of the bidders, it will be from the back of the room so they can't be identified,' he added.

When they'd covered a few more logistical issues, Simona gave them a quick tour around the gallery. 'We're very proud of this collection, it's quite significant,' she said. 'These works are for the specialist collectors – we have pieces by artists such as Ida Bagus Nyoman Rai, Miguel Covarrubias, Donald Friend. There's a lot of interest in the Walter Spies works as well. They fetch significant money. These days you'd pay around $10,000 for a pencil sketch alone.'

'Stunning, but out of my price range,' Grace said as she looked at an intricate work by Ida Bagus. 'While I'm in Bali, I want to find something that will always remind me of this trip, but I don't want to get just anything from the art shops and galleries in the tourist area,' she added.

Simona nodded. 'You have to know who's who, the artist, the dealer, the shop or gallery. It's occasionally possible to pick up a bargain. You have to know what's a fake or "in the style of",' she explained. She turned to Steve. 'Are you a connoisseur?'

'Not really, but I was very interested in Walter Spies's work when I did a documentary on him. There were so many famous artists working up here in the old days.' At that moment, Steve saw Henry and Mateo walk in and signal to him. 'Excuse me, I have to talk with my colleagues about the lighting.'

'Of course,' Simona said, and turned to Grace. 'Let me introduce you to the auctioneer, Kevin Chang. He's flown in from Singapore.'

After the introductions, Kevin said to Grace, 'It's unusual to have Mr Pangisar bidding here himself. Though I realise the family are collectors.'

'I know he was looking forward to coming along,' Grace said, not wanting to give Chang any ideas about Johnny's intentions to buy.

'Many of the Kamasan village artists receive commissions from all over Bali to produce large and dramatic panels on cloth,' said Simona, 'but these old ones are the most valuable.'

'Yes, it's wonderful to expose visitors to classical traditional art,' Grace said. 'It's the ideal way for them to appreciate its history and meaning, as opposed to the stuff that floods the tourist market.' It occurred to her that many visitors to the Kamasan Hotel might not realise they were looking at valuable originals. She had to hand it to Johnny. He never did anything by halves.

Kevin began to point out the order in which the paintings would go under the hammer and explain how the auction would be conducted with the bidders on phones as well as those in the room.

'Hey, Gracie.' Johnny's voice rang out. 'Pretty special work, eh? Got your eye on something?' He smiled as he came towards her, followed by an entourage that included

301

Madame Pearl, Rosie Chow and Mr Wija Angiman, the CFO from the Kamasan. No doubt he'd be watching to make sure Johnny didn't go nuts in the bidding, thought Grace. Kevin smiled and excused himself, moving away to prepare for the auction before Johnny reached her.

After they'd all greeted each other, Johnny turned to Rosie. 'I'll sit in the third row. I don't want to appear too keen,' he said, grinning.

'You're first here,' said Grace. 'That's keen.'

'I came early to decide which ones I'm buying and have a cocktail,' said Johnny. 'Excuse me while I take a look at the bidders' list.'

Grace glanced over a few minutes later and was surprised to see Johnny frowning. She was about to go and check if everything was all right when Steve tapped her on the shoulder to ask for her help with the filming run sheet.

Soon enough, people began to trickle in. Interesting crowd, thought Grace as she mingled, asking if they were agreeable to being filmed, and most were happy to oblige. Only one Chinese man vehemently objected, while another agreed to be filmed so long as the amount of any bid he made was not disclosed. Grace alerted Mateo to these special cases.

Then she headed out to the patio, which was now crowded, and spotted Johnny on his phone looking annoyed, his back to the crowd. She stood to one side watching him, and when he got off the phone, he turned and saw her, shrugged and came over.

'What's up?' asked Grace.

'Competition. Another bidder is here, and apparently he's after what I'm after.'

'How do you know that?'

Johnny winced and pointed to a man in the crowd. 'I know him from school. He'll just want to get what I want to stop me getting it. His family are stinking rich, to use an Aussie expression.' He smiled slightly. 'But neither of us will give in. It's going to be interesting for the auctioneer.'

Grace raised her eyebrows.

Simona was going around asking people to take their seats, so they walked inside. Grace spotted a late arrival, a Chinese-Balinese man, taking a seat a few rows behind Johnny, who did not seem to notice him.

She was fascinated by the crowd and the atmosphere that settled over the room. There were those who were really just spectators, enjoying the occasion; nervous newbies, who probably hoped they might score a bargain; the serious bidders; and the elite who obviously knew exactly what they wanted and what they'd pay, heavyweights like Johnny and possibly his school friend. Grace stood at the back watching the crew unobtrusively filming.

It didn't take long for her to understand how people could get carried away. The effusive auctioneer drummed up excitement about each piece, focusing on the sheer beauty and fascination of the art, and worked the competitive atmosphere between bidders to his advantage. Rosie Chow stood beside Steve, quietly filling him in on the big-name bidders and their strategies.

There was an intake of breath as the first big sale of the night, a work by internationally in-demand contemporary Indonesian artist Christine Ay Tjoe was knocked down to Madame Pearl.

Grace then saw Johnny straighten in his seat as the first of the Kamasan pieces was put on the easel next to Chang, who began his spiel about its impressive provenance.

The bidding was slow at first; nobody seemed to want

to go first. But then Johnny jumped a bid above the first offer and was swiftly followed by the man Johnny had said was his old school friend.

Then the bidding sped up to become a battle between the two of them, the price rising fast. But then a third bidder raised his arm, and as Kevin Chang thanked him by name, Johnny spun around.

A man standing next to Grace muttered to no one in particular, 'This is going to be interesting.'

She asked in a low voice, 'Why's that?'

'He's a rep for a large mining company who've just built new offices in Jakarta. Apparently the boardroom walls are empty. He has form, as they say in the art world. Mining people are not short of cash.'

Suddenly Johnny's old school friend raised the mining rep's bid. The auctioneer looked at Johnny.

Johnny glanced at his phone and shook his head, now looking disinterested. The school friend hesitated and seemed annoyed, and the mining rep leaped in to make the winning bid.

There was an expulsion of breath in the room. The excitement of seeing Johnny Pangisar bidding madly and throwing money around had dissipated.

The mining rep quickly snapped up several more Kamasans.

Johnny went quiet and soon, in the few moments between auction items, he disappeared with his entourage.

When the auction had ended, Grace walked over to the film crew. 'Johnny must be disappointed,' she said.

Steve shook his head. 'Something's not right. This is out of character for Johnny – the flamboyant showman.'

'I think he was texting someone during the auction, and then went cold on bidding.'

'Do you reckon he found out the artworks were fakes or something?' said Steve.

'Not sure. We'll find out tomorrow when we go to the hotel, I guess. Don't forget we're shooting some of the interiors they've just about finished.' Grace smiled at a couple of very pleased-looking bidders as they walked past her. 'Johnny was so excited about the Kamasan paintings. And they are stunning,' she added. 'They would have looked good in the hotel.'

Steve nodded. 'Yes, the perfect finishing touch to the foyer,' he said, looking around at the dispersing crowd. 'Look, I think we've finished here. Will we have a wrap-up drink then go to dinner?'

'Yes, please. And I really want to talk to you about K'tut's book, but we've been so busy I haven't had the chance.'

'Sure, I've been meaning to ask you about it too.'

They helped the crew pack up the gear and a small group of them went for a drink. There was a lot of discussion about the auction. Mateo was shaking his head at the numbers being thrown around.

'Remember, those were millions of rupiah, not dollars,' said Steve. 'Except for the big money on the Spies paintings and a couple of others.'

'Still, I can't see a picture being worth that much,' said Mateo.

Henry suggested they could order some tapas with their drinks, but Steve said, 'Grace and I are going to try out one of the restaurants here. Want to join us?'

The two men hesitated. 'We kind of wanted to get back,' Mateo said. 'By the time we unload and sort the gear and stuff . . .'

'We want to go for an early morning surf before we

shoot at the hotel tomorrow, so we should get an early night,' said Henry.

'That's okay,' Grace said. 'Putu is seeing some friends, but he'll be ready when we've finished dinner. Drive carefully, it's such a bad road.'

'Yeah, we noticed.' Mateo grinned.

'Thanks, guys,' said Steve, and Henry and Mateo finished their drinks and said their goodnights.

*

'No way! What an astounding place,' said Grace as they walked into the 1920s-style restaurant, with its dramatic black and white tiled floor, chandeliers and Art Deco décor. 'And Andy said that the food lives up to its setting.'

'Be criminal not to order a cocktail in a place like this,' said Steve, striding towards the bar.

They talked easily, and after their entrée plates had been taken away, Steve stretched then rested his arms on the table. 'So, K'tut's book, which part are you up to?'

Grace leaned forward, smiling. 'I've been reading it madly all week. I'm hooked! I'm at the bit where after being in prison she agrees to help the revolutionaries and becomes a guerilla fighter for Indonesian independence. I had no idea that she ended up becoming famous around the world as the pirate broadcaster "Surabaya Sue"! What was it they called her? "The Voice of Free Indonesia"? I just can't get my head around all the incredible and terrifying adventures she had – smuggling opium, running guns, and attempting to find her lost and beloved Prince. Well, that's as far as I've got, anyway.'

'I know, astonishing, isn't it? You just couldn't make this stuff up,' said Steve. 'Like you said the other day, it's got the guts of a movie script.'

'That's what I want to talk to you about, actually.' Grace reached across the table and took his arm. 'I've been thinking about it ever since that day at Uluwatu. Let's do it!'

Steve looked blank for a moment, and then understanding dawned in his eyes. 'What, a movie? Based around K'tut?' He paused for a minute, thinking, and then said, 'You mean, you and me? Together? Form a production company and make a film?'

She nodded. 'Yep. I always knew I was working towards something more than commercial TV and advertising media. I know I can handle this, raise the money, organise, coordinate. You have film experience and an amazing reputation. We know we work well together . . .' She let the idea hang between them.

'Bloody brilliant,' Steve said slowly, grinning.

'Maybe we could film in North Queensland. Get some funding from the Queensland Film Commission. Just do some necessary exteriors here.'

'Actually, from what I've learned, filming here is far cheaper than in Australia. And it'd be a shame not to do it all here. I sense K'tut would want us to promote the old Bali.' Steve smiled.

Grace nodded, her eyes sparkling. 'I can't stop thinking about it. Every time I read the book, I see it all unspooling on the page like a film. I can't wait to see how it ends.'

Steve grinned. 'Then I won't spoil it for you, except to say that K'tut Tantri lived into the 1990s. We can ask Professor Lindsey about her too. He said he'd be here for a few days. We'd better pin him down.'

'Yes, we should. I'd better read his book, too,' said Grace. 'I know you said he questions whether parts of

K'tut's story are true, but I don't think we should let that put us off. If we have to take some artistic licence here and there, then so be it.'

Steve went to speak, but stopped as the waiter brought their main course, placing the artfully presented dishes in front of them.

'How gorgeous,' said Grace.

'Art on a plate. Beautiful ingredients. *Bon appetit.*'

They ate slowly, savouring each mouthful, as the waiter poured the wine.

Smiling, Steve lifted his glass. 'To your friend K'tut!'

'*Our* friend.' Grace leaned forward. 'So, what do you think, Steve? I'll produce, you direct. First step will be getting investment. We need a really hot screenwriter to do a treatment to whet investors' appetites. I'll take your advice on key crew, and we can argue over who to cast. K'tut herself is such a fabulous role. At that time, when she was fighting for Indonesia, she was in her early thirties.'

Steve started to chuckle. 'You've really got the bug. I can see that being up here brings the story to life for you.'

'I was thinking we could get Indonesian investment, maybe even government funding. She's the forgotten heroine of Indonesia.'

'Hang on, you're forgetting a very important point.' Steve took a sip of his wine.

Grace finished her mouthful of Crab Papua and looked at him. 'I realise there's a lot to work on, but what were you thinking?'

'The rights to her book. She's dead. You'll have to chase her publisher, her agent, or her family. How're you going to do that? Didn't you or Andy say that the publishing company doesn't exist anymore? And from what I read about her, she didn't have children. We don't know where she saw out her days. Back on the Isle of Man? California? Here?'

'We'll have to ask the professor,' said Grace, unfazed. 'I'm sure we can jump all these hurdles. So when can we see him?'

'He said he'd call me. I'll send him a text tomorrow to jog his memory.'

'Now you're sounding keen.' Grace smiled. 'I just knew there was a reason I felt so attached to the Sound of the Sea.'

'Oh, that reminds me.' Steve put his cutlery together and pushed back his plate. He reached into his satchel hanging by its strap on the back of his chair.

'I found this and thought you might like it.' He handed her a small rolled-up canvas tied with twine.

Grace put down her glass and stared in surprise. 'What is it?'

He smiled. 'Have a look.'

Puzzled, she unrolled a painting and stared at the scene.

Quickly Steve said, 'This is not in Johnny's league. It's the idea of it . . . not the execution . . . that I thought you'd like.'

Grace stared at the oil-colour scene of a deserted beach at sunset. The curve of the beach and the leaning palms were familiar. She looked up at Steve, eyes shining. 'It's the Kamasan beach!'

'Oh good, you recognised it.'

'This is amazing, and you are wonderful to think of me! Thank you.'

Steve leaned over the table and tapped his finger on the painting. 'See the signature in the corner? It's not a famous Balinese artist . . . but –'

'Oh, that's incredible!' Grace gasped. '*Vannen Manx!* I don't believe it.' She stared at him. '"Manx", that was K'tut's nickname here. And "Vannen" . . . that rings a bell from her book. How on earth . . .?' She stood up and hugged him, then sat down quickly, feeling a little embarrassed. 'This is by K'tut. This is an omen . . .' Grace said softly.

'No. It's just a simple little painting, done by a woman who'd found her piece of paradise. Like I said, it's not a famous artist and she was a modest painter, but I thought there was significance enough in it for you to like it.'

Tears sprang to Grace's eyes. 'I'm so touched, Steve. It's very thoughtful.' She brushed her eyes, thinking of the showy presents Lawrence had given her that were measured by their dollar value. This little oil painting held much more meaning for her. It was such a special, considerate gift. She reached out and squeezed his hand. 'Thank you.'

He took her hand in his and held it tightly for a moment, then sat back.

Grace smiled. 'How on earth did you find it? And how did you know who Vannen Manx was?'

'Long story. The short version is, I asked Andy's mate who owns the bookshop if he knew of any of K'tut's paintings, and what had happened to them. He said he knew someone who had met her once and gave me that man's contact details. The guy's in his late eighties and told me he was happy to get rid of some things, including this painting, but he wanted it to go to someone who'd appreciate what it meant. I figured that'd be you.'

Seeing that Grace was too choked up to speak, Steve went on. 'She used aliases, apparently, to confuse people for various reasons. "Manx" was a nickname for her homeland, and she told him "Vannen" was a Nordic name for the Isle of Man, but she could just as easily have invented it.'

'Steve, I don't know what to say. I've never had a gift that's so . . . special. Although, maybe it's up there with some of Daisy's efforts,' she said, smiling at him with tears in her eyes.

'I'm glad.' He seemed to be moved by how much it had obviously touched her. 'We'll get it framed and hang it in our production office for the movie, eh?'

*

Putu pulled up out the front of Steve's villa and it seemed easy and natural when Steve leaned over and kissed Grace lightly.

She returned his kiss and smiled. 'Thank you for a wonderful dinner . . . and K'tut's painting . . . and agreeing to go on the mad journey of making a film with me,' said Grace.

'Slowly, slowly,' Steve said, giving her one last kiss and then getting out of the car.

At home, Grace thanked Putu and went inside. Daisy was sound asleep, a small smile curving her mouth. 'Sweet dreams,' whispered Grace.

Her mother's door was ajar and the light on. Grace wanted to show her the painting, so she quietly pushed the door open.

Tina was asleep, her glasses and a book abandoned on the bedcover. Grace leaned over and gazed at her mother's serene face, weathered with faint wrinkles, her long, strong fingers free of jewellery, her nails and the shape of her hands suddenly so familiar.

These were the hands that had smoothed her hair, tickled her toes, hugged her and occasionally smacked her.

Hands that had cooked and cleaned and tenderly helped her hold a pencil, braided her hair. This was the woman who had held her close at the death of a pet, had always been there through the laughter, tears and triumphs of teenage years, and later showed her how to guide a nipple to her newborn baby's mouth. She was guiding Grace still, through the choppy waters of recent times.

How does one ever repay the selflessness of a mother's love? Grace thought. Would Daisy feel the same love and gratitude for her? she wondered. She knew she would give her life for her daughter. Her mother was strong and independent, but entering into a new stage of her life. And Grace saw their roles shifting. She wanted Tina to have freedom and opportunity to do whatever mad and crazy things came to her mind. Grace suddenly saw how it was to let go . . . when a child starts school, leaves home, gets married.

Suddenly Grace felt a positive strength, knowing there was a different path ahead of her. Where it led, she didn't know, but the choices about when to stop or go, turn left or right, were hers and hers alone. She knew it was more important than ever that she disentangle herself from the only thing that had been holding her back the last few years: Lawrence. There was much to do – she needed to sort out custody of Daisy, and the legal hassles with the trust document and the insurance money – but she resolved to sort it out as soon as she could. She would find her way.

Gently she clicked off the bedside lamp and softly closed the door on her sleeping mother.

*

With light streaming into her room, Grace pushed the

plantation shutter doors wide and walked out to see her mother and Daisy sitting at the table by the pool eating breakfast.

'You slept in, Mum!' Daisy ran to give her a hug. 'I made an omelette, by myself. Well, Kamsi helped a little bit.'

'Hi, sweetie, what time is it? We have to get ready so I can take you to school.'

'It's okay. I still have ages,' Daisy said. 'I was there on time yesterday, remember.'

'Yes, well, but today we need to arrive before the bell goes at eight.' Grace rubbed her eyes, knotted her sarong more firmly and smiled as Kamsi came outside with juice and fruit.

'Thank you, Kamsi.' She sat down and peeled a tiny banana. 'How was your dinner with Daddy, honey?'

'I had a mocktail! It was yummy.'

'How was your night?' asked Tina.

'Amazing. The food was fabulous.'

'Nice, but I meant the art auction.'

'Oh. Yes.' Grace chuckled and shook her head. 'I'm not awake yet. Actually, it was disappointing. Odd, in a way.'

'Really, why was that? The art didn't live up to the hype? Or was it out of Johnny's price range? Though I can't imagine that, especially if he wanted it so badly.'

'Yes, that was it. He seemed to know one of the other bidders and after he missed out on a few items he dropped out altogether. However, I came home with a fabulous painting.' Grace smiled.

Tina put down her cup. 'Good grief! You bought a painting at that auction?'

'What's an ock-shun, Mum?' Daisy interrupted.

'Well, it's when a group of people get together in a special place to buy things, and whoever says they'll pay the most for something – that's called bidding – is the one who gets to buy the item.'

'Did you . . . bid . . . a lot of money?'

'Gosh no, honey, those pictures were really expensive. The one I got was a gift from Steve. Let me get it and show you.'

Grace unrolled the painting and took it outside, pausing to look at it in daylight. She handed it to her mother as Daisy squeezed in to look too.

'It's our beach! I can do a painting like that.'

'It's by a lady called K'tut Tantri, Daisy,' Grace said, then turned to her mother. 'She fancied herself as an artist and sold some of her work to tourists here.'

'Really?' Tina leaned over and studied it. 'The woman who wrote the book you're reading? The amazing one? This could be valuable.'

'Not in the art world. But as a memento of an extraordinary woman, I think it's fantastic.'

'That was very thoughtful of Steve.'

Grace took back the painting and stared at it. 'Yes. Very thoughtful. He knew it would mean something to me,' she said. 'Anyway, what did you do last night, Mum?'

Daisy jumped in and shouted gleefully, 'We played cards, when Dad brought me home. And I beat Andy!'

'Andy was here?'

'Yep,' Daisy said, then ran inside, calling out to Sri on the way.

'He just stopped by,' Tina explained. 'Kamsi served dinner early, so Andy stayed and when Lawrence dropped Daisy back the three of us played cards. Just for fun. After Daisy went to bed, Andy and I had a drink and talked.'

'Really? What did you talk about?' asked Grace, glancing at her mother with a smile.

'Oh, the old days. The changes here. His late wife. He still misses her, as you would, I guess.'

'It's been a long time since she died, I think. He has plenty of friends here, though.'

'I know. But he can't chat to them about the old days on the northern beaches, talk about how his mother is getting on and he feels he should be there with her, and he's worried about his son. Young girlfriends don't want to know about that stuff.'

'Why is he worried about his son?'

'Works too hard, Andy says, and seems to be in a social set Andy has no time for.'

'It must have been nice for Andy to unload all that on you,' said Grace, grinning. 'I hope you didn't go on about me and my problems with Lawrence.'

'Oh, he seems to know all about that. He had dinner with Lawrence that night, remember . . . so he has Lawrence's number. So does Johnny, he said.'

'Really?' Grace frowned. 'What's that mean?'

'I think that's why Andy dropped in to see you,' said Tina. 'Anyway, he said he'd find you round and about.'

Kamsi put a pot of tea and some toast in front of Grace, along with her favourite marmalade and the jar of Vegemite she'd bought at an exorbitant price in the local supermarket.

'Thank you so much, Kamsi.' Grace poured her tea. 'I'm thinking Lawrence is up to something.'

'I would put nothing past that man,' Tina said quietly.

They ate in companionable silence for a while, enjoying the sunshine, until Daisy came skipping back out to them, now wearing her neat school uniform.

'Nana, can you do me up, please?'

'Of course, darling. Are you all ready for school?'

'Yep. I just have to pack my schoolbag,' Daisy replied.

'Okay, I'll get dressed and we can go,' Grace said, finishing her toast and standing up.

*

The crew was already at the hotel, filming its grand entrance. Steve was directing some 'guests' as Grace arrived.

'Hi. Sorry, am I late?'

'No, the boys got here a little while ago. They've been for a surf. It's going to be hard to drag Henry back home to Sydney.'

'Thank you for dinner last night. I was happy to go Dutch with you. So it's my treat next time.' She gave him a quick hug. 'I love the painting.'

'Like you said, it seems a bit of an omen. By the way, we're meeting Professor Lindsey the day after tomorrow, if that suits you?'

'Sure. I can't wait to hear some of his stories. So, where are you up to here?'

'We'll just get some footage of this couple stepping out of the limo and then we'll do the interior reception area. They've gone mad with the flowers, apparently.'

'Let me see what they've done and check out the couple. They have to look like they can afford to stay here, but not snooty,' Grace said, then walked out to meet the models.

After two takes, Steve called, 'Cut,' and Grace came over to him. 'It all looks good to me,' he said. 'Let's go check out the lobby.'

'I was thinking that beautiful, curving staircase to the mezzanine would be a good spot to shoot the interior . . .' Grace's words tailed off as they entered the building.

On the delicate pale green walls of the foyer hung six magnificent Kamasan paintings.

'What the . . .? Aren't they the ones from last night?' she said.

Slowly they walked over to the elegant paintings of old Bali village life, where the stories from Hindu classics and Balinese ceremonies were described in fine brushstrokes.

'Unbelievable! They look fantastic. As if they were made to be there,' Steve said. 'Johnny's got an eye, that's for sure.'

'But they were sold to that other guy,' said Grace, shaking her head.

'Did Johnny go back and make a counter-offer?' said Steve.

'Aha. No, not necessary,' said Johnny cheerfully as he strolled out of the boardroom and came over to join them. 'You should see what's in there.' He indicated the plush boardroom. 'My father is rather chuffed, as those Pommies say,' he said, chuckling.

'Okay, tell us how you pulled this off,' said Grace.

Johnny tapped his head. 'Up here for thinking, down there for dancing.' He pointed at his toes.

'C'mon, spill the beans. You never left your seat. And you started a massive bidding match,' said Steve.

Johnny shrugged. 'Ah, as I think I mentioned, I knew one of the guys from my student days in Australia. An old school chum. Super rich. I had my father on the phone listening. As soon as I heard that mining rep's name I knew who he was. I hung up and Dad texted the mining guy, because we know the family. I stopped bidding and my old school friend panicked, assuming there was something wrong with the paintings, so he dropped out. Dad had sent a quick text to his mining friend, who then bought the lot uncontested for relatively low prices.' He smiled and continued, 'Later we came to an arrangement. And here is the result. For quite a modest sum.' Johnny waved at the magnificent collection of rare Balinese art.

'Jeez, Johnny, you're like a rat with a gold tooth,' said Steve, laughing.

'Make it all look good in the promotion,' he said as he walked away.

Grace hurried after him. 'Excuse me, Johnny, do you have time for a quick chat?'

'Sure, Grace, what's up?'

'This may be out of line professionally, but may I ask you if my soon-to-be ex-husband has been in touch with you?'

'Ah, yes. He tried to spin a deal to me over dinner the other night at the Sundara, after you'd been to the monkey dance. I agreed to meet him. He had an offer for an investment for us. Nothing I was interested in, and I don't deal with guys like that. No offence to you, Grace.'

She gave a dismissive wave. 'Been there, done that. I just want to make sure you and your family don't get sucked in to something because of me. Lawrence has tried to use my friends and family before, I'm sorry to say.'

'I get that. But you know, his idea is not so silly. Cybersecurity, which he was talking about, is a hot and competitive field and you have to move fast. Technology dates easily these days. Start-ups in any field either work or go bust pretty damn fast. Make your money, sell it, and move on as soon as you can. That'd be Lawrence's motto, I assume.'

'Do you mind telling me more about what he's pitching this time?'

'It's not original, but it's an advanced version of a drone used for cybersecurity. It's a powerful motorised camera that runs on fixed wires. They started using them for sports, to run alongside the athletes at the Olympics, the Super Bowl, and in big movie special effects. But for security it can span large areas, with a powerful zoom and face recognition. The feed goes live to a base and is HD quality and records everything to digital files. And it doesn't require an expert to operate it.'

'Where would you use this?'

'At open-cut mines, inside and outside airports, down city streets, inside hotel foyers, around a property like hotels, businesses, in gardens and around the perimeters of a property. Unlike with normal drones, weather doesn't affect it, it's super secure and safe, and won't drop out of the sky to hurt people or damage property. Most of the time no one knows it's there. It's also silent and doesn't need special clearances. Lawrence thought we might need it at the Kamasan, but he was really after us buying in and selling it worldwide.'

'Sounds a bit "Big Brother",' said Grace. 'But exactly the sort of toy Lawrence would like. How'd he find this, I wonder?'

'Some bright young hotshot at a new start-up company in Singapore, I believe.'

'What did you say to him, if I may ask?'

'It's up to my father, ultimately. I made the introduction. As I said, I didn't want to be involved. But I doubt my father will support anyone who causes you trouble, Grace,' Johnny said gently.

'Thank you, Johnny.'

*

At their lunch break, Steve and the crew went off to meet Andy, who wanted them to try Chef Gede's Indonesian degustation. Grace stayed behind and found a quiet corner of the hotel where she opened her laptop and began researching motorised cybersecurity products. She had to hand it to Lawrence, he was always onto a trend the second it started.

Then, in preparation for her meeting with Professor Lindsey, she searched the title of his book and read the synopsis. She was looking forward to meeting the professor. She felt confident that tackling a film about K'tut was exactly what she'd been working towards. She had just needed the right project to come along, she felt. And no matter what anyone might say about her lack of film-producing experience, the story of this woman had slowly etched itself into her soul and had become a passion.

When the boys returned, Steve found Grace and sat down next to her. 'Bit of news from Andy.'

'Oh?'

'Seems there was some action and arrests during a drug bust last night. A few big names have been taken into custody, part of a drug ring in the high end of town. It looks like the demise of Chef Emile was used as an example of what happens when a customer doesn't pay their cocaine bills. But it was a mistake to bump off a foreigner connected to important people like the Pangisars.'

'Wow, that is news. Will it have an impact on the hotel?'

'They're playing it down in the media. Bad for tourism. I'm sure it's nothing Rosie can't handle.' Steve rolled his shoulders. 'It's insidious. High rollers or homeless kids, a drug habit only takes you in one direction.'

Grace nodded. 'Do you think Johnny had anything to do with the raid?'

'The gist of the opinions in the kitchen is: don't mess with the Pangisars. They don't like their staff being knocked off.'

'Johnny and his family have influence, that's for sure,' said Grace. 'Is it because they're rich, or because they have connections, or they have a long history here?'

'Possibly all of that,' said Steve. 'Seems a bit far removed from Lavender Bay and Bilgola, doesn't it?' He smiled.

'I wouldn't be so sure. Mum and Andy were reminiscing about some notorious bouncer down at the Newport Arms pub in the old days. He was pretty tough too, by the sound of it.'

Grace's phone pinged.

'Back to work,' she said with a grin.

But it was a message from Lawrence. Grace went still as she read it.

I have important business in Singapore. I will call in to say goodbye to Daisy (for the moment) at 4 pm. I have instructed my solicitor that I want full custody of Daisy and that means bringing her to London when I go.

10

It was that laid-back siesta time, between late lunch and the first cocktail, as Johnny described it. Even the air and the breeze seemed to be dozing – the leaves and the palm fronds were still.

Grace walked through the quiet gardens to the place she'd come to regard as her special time-out spot – a fallen stone pillar close to the site of K'tut's hotel. She could sit there, unobserved, in the solitude of the old garden. She needed some time to herself following Lawrence's visit the previous afternoon.

Lawrence had had a driver waiting to take him to the airport and he'd dashed in to say goodbye to Daisy, who'd just come home from school. Grace and Tina had greeted him civilly and then left the two of them alone at the chairs beside the pool.

But after only a short while, Daisy had run inside, followed by Lawrence, who stopped at the door and announced, 'I've told Daisy she will be staying with me as soon as I am settled. You can make arrangements through your lawyer to visit.'

'*What?* Don't you think it would have been prudent to discuss this with me before informing our daughter, Lawrence?' Grace said through gritted teeth. She couldn't believe what she was hearing. 'One quick text and you think it's a done deal? And just *where* will you be settling? London, Singapore?'

A sudden flush of pure rage raced through her. It was too much. Lawrence thought he could waltz in anytime, anywhere, and do exactly as he pleased, with no thought to the consequences for anyone else. Well, she'd had enough. Without waiting for a reply, she stood up, slamming her fists on the table. 'You'll have to rethink your plans, Lawrence. When my work project is finished, Daisy and I will be returning to Australia.'

Daisy was clinging to Tina, her small face pinched with worry. Grace disliked that this scene was playing out in front of her, but something had to give. She lowered her voice and hissed at Lawrence, 'Your crazy schemes, your unstable lifestyle, your lack of support, financially and otherwise, your lack of parental parameters make you an unsuitable primary parent. You're the flaky, sometimes-fun, part-time father.'

Lawrence's expression was inscrutable. He said very quietly, 'I will be settling down to a very stable life, Grace. Speak to your lawyer.' He turned on his heel and left.

Grace reached out and clasped Tina's hand, tears springing to her eyes. 'I just can't *bear* the way he behaves!'

'I know, honey.' Tina stroked her daughter's hand and then Daisy turned to hug her mother.

'It's all right, Mumma. I don't want to go and live with Daddy and Alicia.'

Grace and Tina looked at each other.

'Who the hell is Alicia?' said Grace.

At that moment, Putu walked in to give Tina a bag she'd left in the car.

'Your friend, he works for Kamasan too?' Putu asked, pointing out the front door as he handed Tina her bag.

'Lawrence? Daisy's father? No. He does not,' said Grace firmly.

Putu looked surprised. 'Oh, I saw him just now with my friend, who drives limos for Kamasan staff.'

'What the hell is Lawrence up to *now*?' Grace said to her mother. 'What's the time? I'm calling Mr Judd.'

But Mr Judd had been tied up in court all day and would be the next, too, so Grace had made an appointment for a phone meeting as soon as he was available. Even though she was soothed by the beautiful garden around her, she still felt anxious. As far as she was concerned, getting herself free of Lawrence couldn't come soon enough.

*

The next day, at exactly the appointed time, Mr Judd called. The solicitor was calm but frank.

'Mr Hagen is pushing your buttons. It's not the first time he's made this threat. I doubt he would be awarded sole custody of your daughter, especially if he were to move overseas,' Mr Judd explained. 'I think this would be the case even if he tries to paint a picture showing you as hostile to him having contact with his daughter, or say that you're seeking to alienate her from her father, telling her stories to turn her against him, et cetera.'

'Now that is totally crazy,' said Grace. 'How would he be able to get away with such lies?'

'You'd be surprised. There are some lawyers who do a great job of pathologising women's behaviour and who would try to present your behaviour as you endangering your child, with your "unnecessary travel" and a time-consuming job and delusions about insurance fraud, and so on,' said Judd dryly.

Grace was stunned. 'What? Make me out as some kind of nutter? You're joking.'

'These issues can be addressed, Grace. Just keep calm and carry on, as they say. Let's see what his next move is.'

'My daughter mentioned a woman. Does it make any difference if he suddenly has someone in his life?'

'It depends. It could possibly work in his favour if he has a stable relationship, steady income and an appropriate home. It will show he has all the means necessary to take care of his daughter. But as far as I can ascertain from you, he has not been a hands-on father; although, that is hard to prove. It's all a matter of interpretation.'

'Thank you, Mr Judd,' she said, but she didn't feel especially convinced or calm.

Grace gathered up her bag and phone as she heard Steve pull up out the front to pick her up for their meeting with Professor Lindsey.

She'd been looking forward to this meeting, but after talking to Mr Judd she felt sick to her stomach. Lawrence always twisted things, making her feel she was going nuts, and he would be sure to do so again when it suited him.

As she got in the car Steve looked at her. 'What's up?'

'Oh. Is it that obvious? I'm a bit shaken really.

I've just had a conversation with my lawyer about Lawrence and I'm angry and I feel like an idiot.'

'You're no idiot. Do you want to stop somewhere and have a quick coffee, talk it through? I'm sure the professor will understand if we're ten minutes late,' he said kindly.

'Thanks. I'll be okay. I wonder why I never saw what he was doing to me. I just accepted it.'

'That's the art of manipulation; it can be so subtle, you start to mistrust yourself. Deep breaths, Grace. You have a whole new life opening up before you. Don't give him an inch. You've got a great big dream here, let's see you tackle it.'

'Okay,' Grace smiled. 'Thanks Steve, I keep reminding myself how strong K'tut was.'

They easily found the Revolver Café in Seminyak, where Professor Lindsey had suggested they meet.

'Man, this looks great.' Steve studied the menu.

'The coffee smells good.' Grace looked up to see a tall man walk in and greet the young guys behind the counter in Indonesian. There was no mistaking his Australian twang.

Grace waved when he looked across at them. 'Professor Lindsey?'

He strode over with a big smile and an outstretched hand. 'Hi. I'm Tim.'

Warm and attractive summed him up, she thought. He was tanned and casually dressed, with a friendly, open face. Grace and Steve introduced themselves and they all shook hands and settled at their table.

'This place has the best coffee on the island, I reckon. Have you ordered?' said Tim.

'Just about to,' said Steve.

They took Tim's recommendation for food and also ordered coffee and fruit juice. Then Grace jumped right in. 'I can see why you were captivated by K'tut Tantri's book. It's like an adventure novel. Steve has read your book, but I haven't got to it yet.'

'How did you get such personal insights into her life?' asked Steve. 'Though I notice there are some questions left unanswered.'

Tim gave a shrug and a slight smile. 'You might say it was a bit like a duel. This was no forgotten heroine anxious to have her story told and go down in history. K'tut felt she'd done that already, so she saw no need to explain herself any further.'

'Feisty, eh?' said Grace.

'To put it mildly.'

'But she agreed to let you base your PhD thesis on her life,' said Steve. 'She must have wanted some glory.'

'God no,' said Tim. 'She had become a recluse – refused to see me, actually, or anyone else, for that matter. I discovered by accident that she was living in Hyde Park Plaza in the centre of Sydney. So I sent her a letter saying my thesis was based on her autobiography. I told her I had been going to Bali for years and specialised in Indonesian history and politics, so her story had captured my imagination. But I didn't say that I had plenty of questions about the veracity of parts of it.' He stopped while the waiter placed their drinks in front of them. 'Actually, that's what got me interested – sifting out what was romantic hyperbole and how much was true. I mean, the basis was true, there's no disputing that, but her rather colourful descriptions had me wondering where the line between truth and fiction really was.'

'So she agreed?' said Grace.

Tim gave a short laugh. 'No way. Once I found out where she was staying, I tried calling, but she'd given the hotel instructions not to put calls though. In fact, the receptionist wouldn't even admit K'tut was staying there and the letters I sent were returned.'

They paused again while their food was served, and then Steve asked eagerly, 'What did you do?'

'Kept calling every month or so,' Tim replied. 'Then I got lucky one day when there was a temporary operator on the switch, who let slip her room number, telling me Ms Tantri wouldn't take the call. So I went up to Sydney to the hotel.'

'Wow, that was lucky,' said Grace.

'Sort of. She refused to answer the door.'

'Oh no.' Grace gasped.

Tim put down his coffee. 'I sat in the hallway outside her door, hoping she'd come out or someone would go in. No luck. At one stage a waiter came and knocked on her door, carrying a tray with a can of beer on it and a bowl of rice pudding, of all things. She opened the door but kept the chain on and made him hand it to her through the narrow slit. Just a hand came out and grabbed the things. The waiter said they normally just left the tray outside the door. They called her the Hyde Park Howard Hughes, as she never left her room.'

Grace laughed and sat forward, pushing aside her plate. 'What happened then?' she asked.

'I stayed there the whole weekend, but I had to get back to Melbourne so I slipped a note under her door saying I wanted to talk to her about her wonderful book and life,' Tim said.

'Did she reply?'

'She scribbled a note on the bottom that said, "Why?

Anyway, no one is interested." "Yes they are," I replied. Back came a note with "What sort of questions?"'

'Not the easiest person to deal with!' Steve grinned. 'She was, what, in her seventies?'

'Eighties. She told me to come back in three weeks. So over the next couple of months I went up and down to Sydney from Melbourne and we sent scribbled notes back and forth under her door. I was a penniless student so it was bloody expensive. But finally, one day she opened the door a crack, left the chain on, and this one eye peered out at me through huge owl-like glasses.'

'Great opening shot.' Grace grinned.

'It took more cajoling and talk but finally she let me in,' said Tim. 'The room was a shambles; stuff everywhere. She didn't let the housekeeping staff in often, it seemed. The floor was covered with papers, books, boxes and bags, with her sitting in the middle, huddled under a blanket in a huge armchair. She was tiny, but fierce.'

'I can picture it,' said Grace, shaking her head.

'It was still a duel, she still didn't trust me, but by now her ego was piqued. I'd talked to her about her legacy, about what she'd done since the revolution ended and President Sukarno finally won control of the country. She said she had helped write some of his speeches during the revolution and did what she called some "special missions" for him, gun-running and opium smuggling and so on, so she was a favoured guest at the palace. But once Sukarno was ousted by Suharto, things changed and she wanted to get out. She said she'd done a lot in Australia for Indonesia during the revolution in the forties. One of these "special missions" was to Australia, so, although by now she had travelled the world, she thought she'd give Sydney another try.'

'Was she welcomed there back then?' asked Grace.

'No way! Australia was on the Dutch side when the revolution began. When she first arrived in Australia in 1947, the police warned her not to cause trouble. But that didn't stop her. She started making speeches, going to meetings where she spoke to the waterside workers, revving them up to keep blockading the Dutch navy in Australian ports, to prevent ships sailing to Indonesia. She made wild speeches to get support for Indonesia's independence and stop the Dutch moving back in. She even helped start a riot at Sydney Uni. The mounted police had to be brought in to stop it.'

Steve chuckled. 'Incredible. She must have been so determined.'

'She was,' Tim said. 'In the end, our government chucked her out, but by then she had helped reverse Australia's position completely: Australia was backing the Indonesian revolutionaries, not the Dutch, and we ended up being the leading supporter of the new Republic in the UN. K'tut Tantri's CIB file from that time is, ah, very interesting. And you should see her FBI and CIA files!' He took a sip of coffee.

'If I remember correctly, her book ends with her finally getting a passport and returning to America, if rather reluctantly,' said Steve.

'Did she ever go back to live in Bali with her friends? What happened to the Prince and young Pito?' asked Grace.

Tim shrugged. 'The Prince died, but I don't know if he was really her lover, which is what you might think. A lot of people say the man she portrays in the book was not actually the real-life prince, but a distant relative, who wasn't glamorous enough, so K'tut upgraded her lover to local royalty in her book. I did try to trace Pito, but I don't think he ever existed – or more likely, he was a composite of lots of kids.'

'Really?' said Grace. 'I loved that part of her book. Oh well, Pito made for a good story.'

'Sure did. Anyway, she wrote her autobiography when she was back in the USA and it was published in 1960. It was a huge success for a while, translated into God knows how many languages – including Indonesian, of course.'

'What happened next? After the book?' Grace asked, keen to hear every detail.

Tim smiled. 'That's when the movie chase started. Went on for twenty years or more, with big-time movie producers from all over the world chasing her for the rights to film it. Even Michael Curtiz, who'd made *Casablanca* with Humphrey Bogart and Ingrid Bergman, signed her up.'

'Why wasn't it made?' asked Steve.

'Well, it's not hard to imagine that she wanted things done her way or not at all.' Tim rolled his eyes. 'The movie people wanted some romance in her story . . .'

'Between K'tut and the Prince,' said Grace.

'Exactly. In all the months of interviews I did with her, she told me again and again that she refused point blank to have their relationship portrayed as romantic or sexual. No kissing, she said! Denied it all.'

Steve looked at Tim and raised his eyebrows. 'What do you think?'

'Hard to say, and I never got it out of her. Maybe because it was really someone else, not the Prince, who was her lover, so she wasn't keen on the fictional version hitting the screen. Or maybe she just really didn't want to be a romantic heroine. A bit of both, perhaps. In the book, it's a deep and passionate closeness – sister or lover – but of course, every film producer will want the romance angle.'

'Of course,' said Steve, 'that's what would sell the movie.'

'K'tut wanted full control of the script, done her way, or she wouldn't sign over the rights.'

'Strong woman,' said Grace.

'Difficult when she wanted to be, and very clever, too. She spent the best part of thirty years living off producers' courtships.' Tim shook his head, looking bemused. 'In the early 1980s, an Aussie production company made a big fuss, announcing they had the rights and were producing the movie of the book. K'tut went along with it, at first.'

'Then what happened?' asked Steve. 'Same old thing?'

'Yes, sadly. When we talked about it, she shrugged and said she'd told them her ground rules.'

'But they thought they could change her mind, I suppose,' said Grace. 'The lady's not for turning, obviously. So what did you end up writing for your thesis?'

Tim finished his mouthful. 'This was no quick Q and A. It took a long time. Dragged on for years, actually,' he said, then paused. 'At the same time,' he went on, 'my life had its own ups and downs – personally as well as with the thesis – and I was working as a barrister by the time I finished it.' He leaned back in his chair. 'K'tut was a bit of a puppet master. I'd turn up for a working session and she'd announce out of the blue that she wanted to go out, even though she hardly ever left the hotel. This involved disguising herself with a towel and sneaking out the back way via the trades exit. Of course, she wouldn't have fooled a single staff member in the hotel, but it made her happy.'

'Where'd you go?' asked Steve, exchanging a grin with Grace.

'There was a pub she liked. She'd order a drink then chat up a bunch of blokes, who'd humour this old lady.

Then she'd start to gamble with them, and before they knew it she'd have cleaned them out. I did get a few stories out of her after several beers, which she always drank through a straw.' Tim paused. 'It was sad, really. She was married, you know. A Scandinavian-American called Pearson. And while I never got a straight story or the facts, it seems it wasn't a happy marriage; maybe it was an escape. And there's the unanswered question about their child. A son.'

'Oh no! What happened to him?' asked Grace. 'I don't think she mentions him in her book.'

'I think he died. Maybe a car crash. We don't have all the details, but she told me that was the real reason she ran away from Hollywood. I always felt Pito, whoever he was, filled that role for her,' said Tim softly.

Steve looked down at his coffee and said quietly, 'For all her heroism, it sounds like she was a lonely woman.' He turned to Tim. 'You were, what, in your twenties when you met her? Do you think she ever saw you as a son figure in her life?'

'I sometimes wondered,' admitted Tim. 'We had a . . . well . . . "challenging" relationship. She was difficult, obstreperous, arrogant, tricky and feisty. She made me work for every answer. It was a constant war of words. I'd ask a question, and she'd give a wicked, impish grin and say, "Ah, that's for me to know and you to find out, sonny boy". It was her favourite saying.'

Grace shook her head. 'How frustrating.'

'She once said to me, "The Japs tortured me for months and I didn't tell them a thing. What makes you think I'll tell you?"'

Steve and Grace burst out laughing.

'What a character. How did you ever find anything out?' Grace asked.

'Well, the deal was that she wouldn't acknowledge or admit anything unless I put irrefutable evidence down in front of her.' Tim smiled. 'I was running all over the place – to archives and libraries, lodging FOI requests, digging through people's memories in Bali, Jakarta, America . . . Then I'd present it to her and she'd kind of wink and give a grudging smile and say, "Well, ya got me there, sonny boy". I saw the discrepancies between her novel and what I was learning from her, and what I was hauling out of the archives.'

'And this went on for years?' asked Steve.

'Yes, and I had a life happening as well, of course. But I have to confess there was a fondness growing between us. I did eventually finish my thesis. And got my doctorate and realised that with all the material I had there was a book in it. Also, she was getting frailer, so I had to work quickly to ask her more questions.'

Steve changed tack. 'How did she pay her bills? A hotel in the centre of Sydney wouldn't be cheap.'

'You're right; it wasn't. She was a bit evasive at first but then rather airily announced she sent the bills to the Indonesian government. They owed her, she said, "After all, I saved their country."'

Steve and Grace had to laugh.

'She sounds so gutsy. Got to love her,' said Grace.

'Oh, she had her enemies, plenty, in fact, and some of the expats in Indonesia couldn't stand her. The Dutch still absolutely loathe her!'

'Did she have anyone else in her life,' Grace asked, 'apart from you? Was she able to look after herself?'

'Good question,' Tim said, looking at Grace. 'Sandra, her lovely lawyer, visited her and found the place in such disarray that she told K'tut she had to move somewhere she'd have more help. Also, the hotel had run out of patience with K'tut long before.'

'Perhaps not surprising,' Steve said, leaning back in his chair.

Tim nodded. 'I helped tidy and pack up the rabbit warren of stuff in that hotel room. I found suitcases under her bed filled with valuable documents and files and all manner of things she'd kept. K'tut told me to toss them, but of course I didn't,' he said. 'Most of it is in safekeeping with Sandra's husband since, sadly, Sandra died some years back. Some of it should be in a museum or archive, really. I kept a few things K'tut gave me.'

'Like?' prompted Grace.

'The deck of palm-leaf cards she made when she was a prisoner of the Japanese. They're very moving, actually. You would have read about them in her book – the cards kept her alive through solitary imprisonment and torture.'

'Yes, I remember that,' said Grace. 'She scratched faces and numbers onto the leaves that blew into her cell, so they became her deck of cards.'

'That's right,' Tim said. 'Then she played Patience to stay sane.'

'What happened about your book? Did she ever read it?' asked Steve.

'No. I was away for a couple of months and when I came back she was in a nursing home in Redfern,' said Tim. 'Reduced circumstances, as they say. Sandra and her husband Michael used to walk their dog up to visit her every Sunday, and they were even able to persuade K'tut to join them at their home for champagne to celebrate her ninety-fourth birthday. But she was very frail by then and it was a major exercise. I think it was her last outing.'

'And what about your book?' Grace prompted.

Tim looked a bit sheepish. 'I had, as you now know, a pretty intense relationship with her over a decade or more.'

The waiter came to clear away their plates and Tim sat back and stared into space for a moment. 'Even in her nineties she was still pretty determined,' he went on. 'But she wasn't strong physically. She was bedridden by then, and the hard life she'd led as a rebel, prisoner and a revolutionary was finally catching up with her. So I decided I'd wait till she'd died or it could no longer hurt her to publish my book.'

'That was incredibly thoughtful of you. Sentimental too, perhaps?' said Grace, as Tim glanced away and gave a faint shrug.

Steve leaned forward. 'Tim, Grace is thinking of producing a film – at last – of K'tut's life.'

'Fantastic.' Tim sat up straight and turned to her. 'It's an incredible story – almost unbelievable. Such a complex, colourful character. There's history, romance, exotic locations, the birth of Bali tourism – for better or worse – and Hollywood. And, of course, above it all, the poignancy of a brave and significant woman who is now a forgotten shadow in Indonesia's history, even though Sukarno once described her as "the only foreigner to come openly to our side, more Indonesian than American". But maybe she wasn't entirely forgotten. Soon after she died the Indonesian government awarded her their medal of honour.'

'Did she have any family still alive?'

'No one. There was just Sandra and Michael in Sydney, and me. I wrote about her and there were obituaries but no long-lost relative ever emerged.' He looked into the dregs at the bottom of his coffee mug. 'At her funeral there were just a few of her Australian support team, and an official from the Indonesian government. Her coffin was draped with the Indonesian flag.'

'No Pito?' asked Grace.

Tim shook his head. 'No one knew how to find him, I guess, if he did exist. Many decades had passed and in her last years here, Bali changed so much, not always for the best, and she lost touch. I'm glad she didn't see it, actually.'

'Where is she buried?' asked Steve gently.

Tim gave a soft smile. 'Sandra and Michael took her ashes back to Bali soon after she died and scattered them in the ocean, in front of where her hotel had been. Kuta Beach had changed so much.' He gave a slight shrug. 'There was just one piece of untouched land left there. Maybe the locals think she haunts the place. No idea what's there now.'

Grace and Steve exchanged a glance. 'We know. That's where the new hotel has been built, the Kamasan. Steve and I are filming all the promotional material for its opening campaign,' said Grace. 'That's what led me to her.'

'It's all been – what's the right word? – serendipitous.' Steve grinned.

'Splendid. And tell me, are you going to make a romance with the Prince, or take K'tut's version of their relationship? Just curious,' asked Tim.

Steve turned to Grace. 'You're the boss. How're you going to handle that?'

'I think we'll have to decide that down the track when we have a scriptwriter on board. I know audiences love a romance. It seems she loved her Prince, or whoever he was, like a brother, according to her book. But another thought occurs to me,' said Grace. 'Yes, we could make an adventure–romance from her story. I mean, there's enough there to work with. But . . . equally, we could portray the duel between you both to get to the heart of K'tut's story, the years of psychological interplay, the unearthing of what was true or not. There's great richness in that part of the story, too – you can't hide the fact you felt real fondness for her despite her temper and her naughtiness. We could have the lead actress play the thirty-something K'tut and later the older K'tut . . . someone like Cate Blanchett could pull off both roles. Or we have a second actress play the older K'tut.' Grace smiled at the two men, and added, 'Someone like Guy Pearce could play you, Tim.'

Tim laughed and lifted his arms. 'K'tut Tantri was the most frustrating, fascinating, beguiling, cunning, annoying, outrageous, noble, brave, loyal, heroic and fun woman I've ever known. If you could capture even a tiny bit of all that on the screen, you'll have a winner.'

'So do you think you might be willing to let us have the film rights to your book?'

He nodded. 'Absolutely. If you can pull it off, you'll have done what countless big-time movie producers never could.' He leaned his arms on the table and said, 'Until you came along, Grace, no one has had much interest in K'tut Tantri since the early 1980s.'

'The next challenge is hunting down the film rights to *her* book,' Grace said. 'The publisher is long gone.'

'Good luck with that,' said Tim. 'She was very secretive and sneaky about her business dealings. And there're no files or paperwork that I know of.'

They ordered more coffees and kept talking until Grace realised they were taking up a lot of Tim's time. 'We can't thank you enough for sharing all this,' she said.

'Anything else I can do to help, just ask. Keep in touch.' He smiled. 'More than anything, K'tut wanted to see her own story on the silver screen. It was what she was really living for all those long years after her book was published.'

They stood up and said their goodbyes, then Tim dashed off to his next appointment.

'Look, I better run, too,' Steve said. 'I didn't realise we'd been here so long.'

'That's the power of a good story, I suppose.' Grace put her notebook in her bag and they walked down the street together.

'I'll head home and catch you later,' she said. 'Thank you so much for tracking Tim down, Steve. He's great.'

'No worries,' he said, though he seemed a bit distracted. 'See you.' And, after giving her a quick smile, he strode off.

*

Grace worked at her computer until she heard her mother return from the markets with Sri and Putu.

'Hi! How was the shopping trip?' Grace called.

'Excellent. Guess what we're having for dinner?' Tina smiled at Grace. 'Goat curry – don't tell Daisy what meat it is – and spinach in coconut milk, sweet potato rice, some mild sambals.'

'Yum. Daisy will love it if we don't mention the poor goat! She's getting used to eating spicy food. I think it's because she watches Sri and Kamsi making it all from scratch.'

'Speaking of food, I saw Steve having coffee at that Zippy café next to the market,' said Tina.

Grace looked up. 'Oh? We had a lunch meeting and he rushed off when it finished. Why would he go down there, I wonder?'

'Looked like a coffee date, with none other than our resident goddess – Rosie Chow.'

'She does get around,' said Grace tersely. 'Probably business. We have a lot of media due in soon.'

Tina gave her a quizzical look. 'I can see when a woman is flirting and reeling a bloke in, hook, line and sinker.'

'Rubbish!' Grace was tempted to say that she thought Rosie and Andy had something going together. But she decided not to as her mother seemed to have made a good friend in Andy. Instead, she said in a neutral voice, 'Did it look like Steve was flirting back?'

'I'm not sure,' admitted Tina. 'He wasn't giving much away. But they're both attractive young people, working in the same business, here in a romantic, tropical wonderland.'

'They're not in the same business,' said Grace. 'She's in public relations and he's a film director. And I'm going to be working with him on a big project. We've decided.'

'Well, perhaps Rosie can promote your film when it's done,' said Tina with a grin. Then, seeing Grace's unamused face, she added, 'I'm sorry, honey. Is anything wrong?'

'No. I don't like the idea of mixing business and romance, that's all.'

Tina laughed. 'Oh, come on. Listen, my girl, you have been deeply wounded and I understand how unhappy you've been, for years, really. Even though it's still messy, you've made your decision to move on, so it's time to get out there and live a little. You're attractive, you're fun, but you are also very efficient and smart and good at what you do,' Tina said, putting her arm around her daughter's shoulders. 'I think you've forgotten how to be carefree and let your hair down on occasions, and that can come across as a bit intimidating.'

Grace knew there was a kernel of truth in this, though it was hard to hear. She swallowed and said nothing.

Tina walked around the table and sat down opposite her daughter. 'Yes, you have responsibilities, especially Daisy, but a person like Steve doesn't walk into your life every day. I've seen how easily you get on with each other. And it's clear you have a lot in common.'

Grace sighed. 'Mum, it's a fine line. I really like Steve.' She paused, then said softly, 'I don't want to get involved and have it fall apart, and then still have to work closely with him. Film units are pretty tight and shoots can be very intense. But I take your point.' She straightened up and smiled. 'Anyway, it's a great way to get to know someone well. All the pressure involved in making a movie can bring a team together.'

Tina reached over and took Grace's hand. 'I just want you to be happy. That's what every mum wants.'

Grace pushed back her chair and stood up. 'I know. I get it. I'm so loving seeing Daisy happy here, learning new things, being immersed in a different language, absorbing a new culture, meeting different people. I think it's already broadened her horizons, young as she is.'

Tina smiled at her daughter. 'I'm so proud of you, honey. But don't let your principles about not mixing work and love get in the way of something that could be great. Steve is a gentleman and a professional, he won't overstep a line if you rule it in the sand. Just keep the door ajar, okay?'

Grace went over and gave Tina a hug. 'Thanks, Mum.'

*

They were gathered around the boardroom table, where an exquisite Walter Spies painting, an old Kamasan artwork and a contemporary I Nyoman Masriadi hung on the walls. The morning sun was gently filtering through a delicate bamboo blind. Johnny was looking very pleased with himself, Grace thought. He was dressed in a pink open-necked shirt with a long silk scarf knotted at his throat.

Grace pointed at the scarf. 'Stunning! Where's that from?'

He unknotted it and opened it out, revealing exotic dark jungle, flowers and mystical figures of a Balinese painting reminiscent of a classic Spies painting.

'New idea, what do you think?'

'Love it! I'd like a silk sarong with that print!'

'I'll work on it,' he promised.

Grace was sitting next to Harold Pangisar, and also present were Wija Angiman, Farrouk Eljoffrey, Andy, Rosie Chow and a Balinese man she didn't know.

After he'd called the meeting to order, Johnny introduced the visitor.

'I am proud to introduce Professor Johannes Sastro, a close friend of our family for many years and professor of Indonesian and Javanese language and culture at a leading university in the Netherlands.'

The professor smiled and nodded to everyone. A small, wizened man, he had a slightly bemused smile and alert brown eyes and was probably close to eighty years old.

'Professor Sastro is home in Bali for a couple of weeks and when he came to visit my aunt yesterday, I invited him back this morning so I could show him around our hotel,' Johnny said, sounding far more formal than usual. 'After our little tour, he asked if he could join our meeting now to say a few words.'

'Thank you, Johnny.' The professor smiled slightly as he spoke in a cultured Indonesian-Dutch accent. 'Ladies, gentlemen, thank you for having me today. I must say I am very impressed after having had a tour of the Kamasan. It is not what I have come to expect from the usual up-market resorts appealing to international visitors, even those of a certain financial standing. Its design shows a deep respect for our land and culture.

'Over the decades, as the appeal of our local culture in Bali was replaced by holiday and resort tourism, catering to visitors' needs as opposed to our own, it has evolved that visitors rarely see or truly experience genuine Balinese culture. At best, they see it on a superficial or commercial level.

'Our lifestyle has adapted to western sensibilities. We have gone from commercialising and promoting our culture to the development of our land for resort holiday tourism, and that is now the mainstay of our economic existence here. Lifestyle residential opportunities, no matter what present regulations might say, have segregated the visitor from what appealed to them in the first place: the village life of Bali.' He looked around the table. 'I am not saying that we need to preserve Balinese culture as if it were frozen in time, for as we know, it is alive and well. It is adaptable and continues to flourish away from the gaze of the tourist eye most of the time. Our cultural origins are strong.'

He paused and took his glasses off to wipe them.

'My concern, which I raise with you today, is that the natural environment must be allowed to remain and flower, as well as the spiritual and intellectual aspects of Balinese life. Our land, which is threatened, needs to be protected. If the core of our country, our land, is sold for short-term interests, then we have sold our soul.

'So on behalf of the community I'd like to acknowledge to you today the service the Pangisar family and their associates do for Bali. Over the years your philanthropic Pangisar Foundation has supported, among other things, a push to improve children's nutrition,' the old man said, looking around at everyone.

'In South East Asia, poor nutrition leads to thirty-eight per cent of our children under five years old having stunted growth – that's close to sixty-five million children being affected. What you have done to improve nutrition standards in this area should be applauded. Also, your hotel shows where Bali must look to the future. I hope it will serve as an example of how tourism can be done. Congratulations. Thank you.'

Johnny thanked the professor as everyone at the table gave him a round of applause. Harold rose and shook his hand warmly, then his assistant came in to escort the professor outside while they continued the meeting.

Grace looked at Andy. 'That's a horrible statistic about so many kids being malnourished. I had no idea.'

'Madame Pearl heads the foundation,' said Andy. 'Johnny's mother started it before she became too ill to carry on. She's an invalid these days.'

'The family are modest about their philanthropy,' said Grace quietly.

Johnny resumed his seat, and looked around the table. 'As you know, we like to keep a friendly eye on development on our island, so following on from what the professor had to say, there is another matter I just thought I'd mention, which is that later this year the Trump Organization plans to open a mega resort, with a signature eighteen-hole golf course, beach club, and luxury residences. It is a controversial project as it's on a clifftop above one of our important temples, Tanah Lot. Many people are particularly concerned about the development's impact on Bali's rice terraces and irrigation systems. Overdevelopment on the island in recent years has caused saltwater to leak into groundwater and damage local farms.' He looked at Rosie. 'What's that report say?'

Rosie glanced down at her notes and read, 'Tourism uses up half of our groundwater supply. That's partly due to poorly designed hotels that don't consider the water needs of the locals,' she said, looking up. 'Many of our rivers are running dry or they are heavily polluted, the water table is so low it is being drawn on faster than it is being replenished, and we have issues with water salinity. These are critical concerns for residents and for Bali's tourism industry and economy.'

'And let's not forget the great mass of water needed to keep golf courses green,' Andy added.

Johnny nodded. 'So what we are doing here at the Kamasan is an example of the future if Bali is to survive, and it shows how we can share our way of life and culture with visitors. Our desalination and cutting-edge environmental designs and practices are as important as the aesthetics. Remember that.'

He straightened up and grinned.

'So that was the serious news. But before you throw yourselves off the cliffs at Uluwatu –' He glanced around at each of them with a glint in his eyes. 'I am delighted to announce that our opening-night, guest-star performer is . . . Bruno Mars!'

There was a ripple of excitement around the table. Grace stared at Johnny in amazement. 'He's the biggest recording star since Michael Jackson,' she said.

'I'm staggered! Wow, well done, Johnny,' said Andy in admiration.

Johnny seemed pleased with the effect his announcement had made, but Harold leaned forward and asked, 'Who is this man?'

'He's a global superstar! Think Presley, Prince, Michael Jackson, Ed Sheeran,' Johnny said. 'Singer, dancer, composer, instrumentalist. His dance routines are fantastic – like James Brown and The Splits. He's a brilliant performer and he brings a big show with him – dancers, his band – The Hooligans – plus pyrotechnics and incredible laser lighting.'

'And where do we hold this extravaganza?' asked Harold.

'Got it sorted. Bruno and the support acts will play on an elaborate stage built in the grounds for the night. I tapped into a local company that does the logistics for all the big shows here on Bali. For the support acts I've got our local superstars, Judika and Agnes Monica. They have a massive following.'

'Do we sell tickets?' asked Farrouk Eljoffrey.

Johnny shook his head. 'Invitation only; 1500 guests. The bluest of the blue-chip crowd from Singapore, Jakarta, Sydney, Melbourne, Perth, Hong Kong. The word is out there already.' He grinned at Rosie. 'Private jets – many. Helicopters – many. Drivers and support teams – many. Paparazzi and media – many. You'll be busy.'

Rosie chuckled. 'Do you want to tell your father about the accommodation plans?' she asked.

'About 250 guests are wealthy locals, both Balinese and expats, so they have their own accommodation. The Kamasan can handle 400 guests in 200 rooms and villas, plus the two presidential suites for the stars. And the Mulia Hotel and the Kempinski will take any other guests that can't fit in here.' Johnny smiled broadly. 'From now on, international visitors will know that the Kamasan is the true heart of Bali.'

'What's on the menu?' Harold asked, and everyone laughed.

Andy looked at his notes. 'Chef says he'll be preparing the highest quality modern Indo cuisine. As well, there'll be a whole-animal open-air roast as a happening event, with pork, beef and lamb all roasting away over red-hot coals.'

Harold nodded in appreciation, and then Johnny picked up the thread again. 'This event has been a year in the planning. I've had a team working on it alone. There'll be a massive monkey dance performance before the biggest fireworks display ever seen on the island. I've organised the pyro team that do Sydney Harbour New Year's Eve to run it.'

'You've been busy spending,' said his father dryly.

'The promotion and publicity, not to mention word of mouth and social media focus, will eclipse anything done here in Bali before,' said Johnny confidently.

'It's going to be sensational, Johnny,' said Grace, adding with a smile, 'Steve and I will start recruiting extra crew to cover it all.'

'Me too,' added Rosie. 'I've hired some more assistants. There will be a media frenzy.'

'There certainly will be, and it's only a month away.' Johnny looked around the table. 'Thank you for all your work on this extravaganza, and for fitting in with the events team. And most of all, for keeping their plans and your own preparations confidential. So far, so good – no one outside of our group knows what's about to hit them.'

Following Johnny's big announcement, the rest of the meeting's business was wrapped up quickly.

Grace couldn't wait to break the news to Steve about the star act, and was about to leave when Mr Pangisar walked over and took her aside.

'Grace, I had a meeting with Mr Hagen,' he began.

Grace winced. 'Oh, dear. I hope not just because of me.'

'I understand your situation,' he said gently. 'The product is excellent, fantastic. A step up from the first version on the market. I agreed to meet with Mr Hagen and host him at a friend's hotel and I loaned him a driver from here.'

'That was generous of you. Had I known I would have warned you not to do anything for him. Especially if you felt you had to do it because of me,' said Grace.

'We are always cautious, Grace. Johnny made a few enquiries. And indeed, it was a good thing he did, because when we contacted the company in Singapore that took this product to the next level, they had never heard of Lawrence Hagen or had any dealings with him. They think he might have gone directly to the young inventor and persuaded him to let Mr Hagen have certain rights to which he is not entitled. So we declined Mr Hagen's offer.'

'Oh dear,' Grace groaned. 'I was afraid something like this would happen. I'm relieved you didn't get involved.' She took a breath. 'He told me he was going to Singapore. I guess his dealings were not with this company you mention after all, though.'

Mr Pangisar looked at her piercingly. 'Was this a sudden decision of his? It is not easy to establish oneself in business in Singapore . . . unless you have connections. And money.'

'I have no idea,' said Grace, shaking her head. 'I am so sorry my personal life has crossed over into my working life and affected you, Pak Harold.'

'I understand. We like you very much, Grace. You work hard and you think like we do. You are now part of the Kamasan family,' Harold said kindly.

Grace had to turn away as tears came to her eyes. Fortunately, Andy was suddenly beside her.

'Grace, can I check some details with you about the filming of the banquet?'

'Of course.' She clasped Harold's hand as she thanked him and then left with Andy, who was enthusing over Johnny's plans. But outside the boardroom, Andy stopped.

'What's up? You looked a bit upset in there and I thought you might need some fresh air.' He smiled at her.

'Oh, I'm so embarrassed and angry. Lawrence tried to spin a deal to the Pangisars, of all people! He used me to get to them, but now it looks like he tried to hoodwink the inventor of the cybersecurity product he's peddling, who must have thought Lawrence was working with the company that actually owns the rights.'

Andy nodded slowly. 'Right. So Lawrence on-sells the rights, takes his money and moves on, leaving them to fight it out.'

'I guess that was his idea. Something like that. I never followed how all his deals and his businesses worked. I only know that he either has a lot of money or none at all.'

'Be careful, Grace,' Andy said as they walked across the garden at the front of the hotel. 'It sounds to me like he was trying to cash in on your goodwill with the family here, and he might be feeling desperate if this latest ploy didn't work out. But as we know, you don't mess with the Pangisars.'

Grace shrugged. 'I've realised that Lawrence isn't a good judge of whether or not people can see through him and his plans. I don't think he reads people well.'

'I think you're right.' Andy gave her shoulder a comforting squeeze. 'Let me know how things go, okay? Come on, you and I have a lot of work to do.

*

There was a certain energy and buzz around the place as word spread of Johnny's coup in booking Bruno Mars for the grand opening. Steve, Henry, Mateo and the production boys were already in the bar area when Grace and Andy walked over.

Grace noticed that Rosie was sitting beside Steve, showing him something on her phone. In a minute everyone was clustered around her, watching a video clip of Bruno Mars singing and dancing to 'Uptown Funk'.

Steve turned and saw Grace and made room for her to sit down, but she shook her head.

'It's okay. I can see from here,' she said, her voice flat, and she realised that Steve must have noticed because he stood up straight away.

'What's worrying you?' he asked quietly, standing next to her.

She shrugged. 'Do I look worried? Apart from this big job getting bigger?' Even to her own ears she sounded petulant. What was wrong with her?

'Yes. You gave me such a cool look just then. Is it to do with Lawrence? Is he butting into your life again? Don't let him put you off us blokes.'

Grace suddenly felt limp. 'That's part of it, yes. He's been trying to pull the Pangisars into a shady deal of some kind. I'm just fed up.'

'Bad move. Oh Grace, I'm sorry you're having such a hard time.'

'It's more than that. He says he's going to find

somewhere to live – possibly in Singapore, maybe even London; he never says anything concrete – and he wants Daisy to live with him.'

'That'd be laughable if it wasn't so transparent. He's stirring you up.' Steve dropped his arm around her shoulders. 'It's incredibly complicated to get permits and visas to live and work in Asia. And you need a fat bank balance, which I guess he doesn't have.'

'Who knows? I don't know him anymore. Never did, I realise now. Somewhere along the line he changed his name, divorcing himself from his family in England. Re-invented himself. Why? I hate to think,' she said. 'I don't know how I never saw this side to him. Maybe I didn't want to.'

Steve gave a low whistle. 'A teller of tales, a spin doctor, a deceiver. You saw what you wanted to see,' he said gently. 'Don't beat yourself up.'

'I try not to. I feel badly enough. What I can't seem to escape is the feeling that he'll never let me go.' She saw Andy wave at her and gave herself a little shake. 'Anyway. It's my problem. The last thing I want is for it to interfere with my working life, all this.'

Andy had ordered champagne and the group gathered around him to celebrate Johnny's announcement.

'Johnny is a networker,' said Andy. 'He put the word out to agents in LA and London a year ago, and as it happened the dates for the opening suited Bruno, who is doing a concert tour in Singapore, KL and Manila, and visiting family as well. I'd say Johnny offered up a shitload of US dollars, private jet, choppers and a good time . . . easy peasy . . . Bruno booked.'

'I feel like saying to Johnny, "Enough already!" I'm on overload.' Grace laughed.

Steve chuckled. 'He only operates at one speed – full on! I'm thinking we might need body cameras on some extra cameramen, to walk around into the action and film it like virtual reality.'

'So long as they don't film any of the performers,' Grace said. 'Record companies usually don't allow their major artists' performances at private parties to be professionally recorded. We need to see people dancing, enjoying themselves, the atmosphere, food and drinks, that sort of thing, so the viewer feels they're there.'

'Righto, boss,' said Steve affably. Then he leaned in and said more quietly, 'Say, want to find somewhere quieter and have a coffee?'

Grace nodded.

They walked to a nearby café that had become their favourite and sat down under the shade of a colourful, wide umbrella.

'By the way,' Grace said after they'd ordered their drinks. 'I have some news about K'tut's book rights. Well, nothing too productive, unfortunately.'

'No luck, huh?' Steve asked.

'The mystery deepens. After we met with Tim yesterday I found the Aussie producer who bought the rights to her autobiography and announced they were making a movie of it in the eighties. I tracked him down in Sydney and rang him. He's retired from the business now . . .'

'That might help our cause. What'd he have to say?'

'To quote him directly, he said, "Don't speak to me about that woman! She took me to the cleaners!" So the conversation didn't go too far.'

Steve gave a half smile. 'She was really something by the sounds of it. What now?'

'Well, I did push a bit more, but all he said was that

he later re-couped a bit of money on-selling the rights to a producer in Hollywood. A French guy. He couldn't remember the name exactly, gave me a couple of similar-sounding sorts of names, and then he hung up.'

'So that was in the early to mid-1980s. A dead end?'

'Maybe. I'm still thinking. Haven't had time to search the internet or make calls.'

'You're not exactly sitting on your hands. You have a lot going on,' Steve said, smiling at the waiter when their coffees arrived. 'Let me know if I can help with the search.'

'Thanks. Of course, we have a job to do here first.'

'Sure do, and it's getting bigger and more exciting by the day. Thanks for bringing me on this ride, Grace.' Steve reached out and took her hand.

*

Wrapped in a damp sarong after an afternoon swim, Grace lost track of time as she worked her way through a maze on the internet trying to find the French Hollywood producer. She made one international call – it was a dead end. When she resumed searching online, the most prom-ising lead came up as deceased.

'Grace, honey, shall I go get Daisy from her friend's place?' called Tina, seeing her so deeply engrossed.

'Oh, yes please, Mum. That would be great. Then I can keep working.' She knew her mum had made friends with some of the other parents and grandparents at the school, and enjoyed the time with them at school drop-off and pick-up, and on playdates.

Grace was pretty sure she had the correct name of the producer now, as there were lots of references to him and his work, but he was long dead and the trail was cold. There was only one other person whose name matched the one the Aussie producer said he had sold the rights to, but it was a French-Canadian businessman who had nothing to do with the film industry and the link seemed tenuous at best. Scrolling through his references she saw he had addressed a business conference in Montreal. His speech had something to do with new synthetics. She clicked on the link and saw that it was in the early 1990s and sounded stultifyingly dull. Nothing to do with films.

Another dead end. Grace sighed. She had nowhere to go from here. Her mind switched gears. She had to think of some way of adapting Tim's story that he'd told them at lunch, working a fictionalised framework around it, perhaps. K'tut's life was a dazzling drama. But without the imprimatur of it being a true-life story, she knew it didn't have the same punch.

She was about to close the web page but her eye caught on something in the Canadian man's speech, which had been reproduced in full. The man had talked about synthetics, about the art of selling and packaging a product, and Grace nodded. 'Yeah, tell me about it,' she said aloud. Then she read on . . . *Look for that extra something that puts your name in front of your audience so they remember you, and no other competitor. Believe me, enabling the vision is the key to success. My father was a film producer and in every film he sold a vision: the story, the whole package. He knew how to seduce an audience.*

Grace sat bolt upright. 'Whoa!' she shouted. His father was a film producer in Hollywood!

She found the man's contact details on the company website and sent him an email.

*

Tina, Grace and Daisy had a quiet night playing a board game after dinner, then Grace sat in bed reading Daisy a story.

As she cuddled her little girl, gave her a kiss and tucked her in, Daisy reached for her hand.

'I'm always going to live with you, Mum. I can *visit* Dad, but you will always be with me, won't you?' she said, looking earnestly at Grace.

Grace wrapped her arms around her daughter, and held her tight, trying to swallow the lump that had formed instantly in her throat. 'Of course. No matter what, you are always my girl, and Nana's girl. And you have to remember that I'll always be here with you, my darling.'

Daisy gripped Grace tightly and then curled on her side, snuggling down beneath the coverlet and, reassured, closed her eyes.

*

In the balmy tropical air, Grace sat outside looking up at the stars. Her phone pinged and she saw she had a message.

She smiled, thinking it might be Mel. But no, she realised, with the time difference it was too late.

It was from Lawrence's sister, Beatrice; Grace had given Beatrice her mobile number when she'd responded to Beatrice's Facebook message.

Thank you so much for sending the photo of your daughter. She looks sweet. My mother was thrilled. I hope we can meet one day. We'll leave that up to you. I imagine life with my brother hasn't been easy for you. Sarah and Jamie have made their way on their own. Jamie is a lovely boy. It makes us sad he doesn't know his father at all, but Sarah feels things are for the best. I hope they work out for you too. Sadly I never married or had children. My role has been to care for my parents. If you can, do mention to my brother that our father is very frail. Blessings, Bea.

Grace sat frozen for a moment. What the hell? she thought. Who were Sarah and Jamie? Was Lawrence's sister inferring that Lawrence had had a wife called Sarah who had a son called Jamie . . .?

'What else haven't you told me, Lawrence!' she hissed, clenching her fists and looking angrily up at the night sky.

11

GRACE WAS GLAD THAT the next few days would be crammed full of work. There was a general feeling of things cranking up and moving faster, and an air of excited expectation seemed to pervade everyone and everything. Even though, as Tina and Grace had noticed, Balinese people never seemed to actually hurry, there was nonetheless a sense of efficiency and moving smoothly, of the hotel staff knowing exactly what to do. Scheduling, lists, plans, bookings and the constant checking and re-checking of every detail, from bedsheets and fresh flowers to kitchen stocks and rubbish disposal, filled their days as the opening date for the hotel approached. Johnny continually threatened that if it wasn't ready, it wouldn't happen.

Grace had to admire Rosie, who had turned into the

equivalent of a military commander, leading troops of media about, rounding up talent and story ideas, supervising photographers and TV crews to make sure they got what they needed. They were all obviously blown away with the experience of the Kamasan, from what Grace could tell.

Andy ruled his domain with cheerful humour and his seemingly casual style, while actually keeping a forensic eye on every move his staff were making and every drink and dish that was tested for the final menu.

Advance staff working for the high-profile guests and the show talent were already checking things out for their bosses as the countdown continued. Steve and Henry were briefing the extra crew Grace had hired, as she kept refining their schedules to fit in with fluctuating scenarios.

Suddenly, three weeks on from the meeting when Johnny had told them about Bruno Mars, Grace had some breathing space. There was always something to do, but with a week to go all her preparations for the opening were on track, and without Lawrence around to distract her, she had been able to really knuckle down and add the finishing touches to the campaign.

'I'm heading home for a bit, to hang out with Daisy. It's been so hectic I haven't spent much time with her lately,' Grace told Steve as they walked through the hotel grounds after lunch.

He glanced at his phone. 'Sure. Relax while you can.'

'Maybe meet later for a quiet drink?'

'Love to,' he said, not looking up. 'No news from Lawrence?' he added.

She shrugged. 'Nope. I haven't heard from him for a few days. Judging by what he's said on the phone to Daisy, he's left Singapore and now he's swanning around

Kuala Lumpur with his new girlfriend and her jetset family. Still can't get over the news that he had another family that he's just ignored. I can't stop thinking of the boy Jamie, his son.'

'I'd say he's been better off without having Lawrence in his life,' said Steve.

Besides her mother and Mel, Grace had only shared this bombshell about Lawrence with Steve. They'd developed a kind of divided friendship, keeping business and personal matters in separate boxes as much as possible. Steve was always calm, never probed too deeply, but he was supportive and sympathetic when needed. So far neither had made any romantic overtures apart from Steve's gentle kiss the night he'd given her K'tut's painting, and Grace was happy to take things slowly. She didn't want to damage their friendship or their compatible working relationship.

As she waved goodbye and headed across the hotel lawns, Steve immediately started making a call on his phone. Grace wondered what the urgency was, but then again, everyone seemed busy all the time at the moment.

After walking the short distance to her villa, Grace went inside, dropped her bag on the table and called out, 'Daisy.'

'Out here, out here, c'mon, Mum!' She sounded excited.

Daisy and Tina were sitting by the pool, talking to a third person – Grace gasped, speechless for a moment, as Melanie stood up, arms lifted jubilantly above her.

'Surprise!'

'Mel!'

The two women raced to each other, hugging, jumping up and down, laughing and exclaiming as Daisy clapped and danced around them, and Tina smiled smugly.

'How . . .? Mum! You knew about this!'

'Of course she did,' Mel said, laughing. 'You didn't think I'd miss the party of the year, did you?'

'But you said you were busy doing some lectures somewhere . . .' Grace said in a rush.

'I did say that, didn't I? Well, here I am. You should thank your mum really, for pulling it all together.'

Grace looked fondly at her mother. 'You knew this would cheer me up, didn't you?'

'Mums always know the right medicine.' She smiled as Daisy hugged Grace.

'Surprise, Mum! Are you surprised?' the little girl said. 'Really?'

'You bet I am. And it's the best surprise ever.'

On cue, Sri and Kamsi came out with a tray of champagne glasses, a decanter of fresh orange juice and canapes.

'Perfect timing,' said Grace. 'Thank you.'

'Yep. Steve alerted us,' said Tina. 'He just rang.'

'He's in on this too?'

'Well, I had to make sure you wouldn't have to work this afternoon if it wasn't totally necessary,' said Tina. 'So I asked Steve for his help. He's popping over for a celebratory drink with us.'

The girls and Tina lifted their glasses of mimosa as Sri poured orange juice into Daisy's glass.

'To good friends,' said Tina.

'I'll drink to that,' said Mel.

Grace couldn't speak for the moment. With tears in her eyes, she looked at her dearest friend, managing only to say, 'Thanks, Mel . . .'

'Oh, just drink your drink,' said Melanie gruffly.

*

Grace and Mel spent a hilarious evening at the Kamasan, having dinner with Steve and the crew, Tina and Andy, while Daisy went to dinner at a school-friend's house. Early the next morning, refreshed from a swim, they sat by the pool with their coffees.

'What a night, such fun people. And this is heaven.' Mel sighed. 'How can you ever go home?'

'It was a great night. Though it was unusual. With the upcoming opening, it kind of felt like a last hurrah. I don't think things will ever be that laid-back again once the place is functioning with paying customers,' said Grace. 'I feel so lucky to have been part of all this.'

'Everyone raves about what a fabulous job you're doing, and how lovely you are. They're right, of course.'

'Tell that to Spencer the jerk.' Grace sniffed.

'Oops, I nearly forgot. I ran into Allison from Carson's last week.'

'Really? Oh, she lives near you, doesn't she?'

'Yep, we go to the same bakery on Saturday mornings,' Mel said. 'She asked how you were going. I think she was worried about you after the way things ended.' Mel looked at Grace and smiled. 'Anyway, she's quit.'

Grace laughed. 'Well, good on her. None of the good people will hang around there.'

'It sounds like Spencer has wrought havoc.' Mel sipped her coffee, then said, 'Alli asked if I'd let you know she's looking for a job.'

'Oh, of course. If I can get this film up, I'll hire her in heartbeat,' Grace said. 'I'll text her and let her know.'

'So you think this film has legs?' Mel raised a quizzical eyebrow.

'It's moving in the right direction. I got a message from the French-Canadian guy whose father seems to have been the last one to hold the film rights. When we first spoke he told me his dad died a few years ago and he didn't know anything about it. He messaged me today to say he's since checked the contract and it appears the rights reverted to K'tut's estate on his dad's death.'

'You really are keen on this,' said Mel quietly.

'You don't think I can do it?'

'Grace, I *know* you can do it. You don't realise how talented and capable you are. Lawrence put you down for so many years; it broke my bloody heart. I just love to see you kicking ass up here!'

'I do no such thing. Balinese people are very proper and polite. I've learned a lot,' said Grace.

'Hey. I hear you.' Mel threw up her arms. 'I'm just thrilled to see my old friend find her feet again, remember who she is, and not be crushed by a narcissistic dickhead.'

'Don't hold back, Mel, tell me what you really think,' Grace said, and they both burst out laughing.

'But seriously, what are you going to do about him?' asked Mel. 'I worry about you. Every time you stood up, he bowled you over. You can't let him do that again.'

Grace was thoughtful. Then said slowly, 'I kind of ran away by taking this job. It was a huge step, and I needed the money. But I didn't know whether I could do this – take on this big campaign and make it work. It was a risky thing to do just when I'd separated from Lawrence. He's such a control freak. It was like I broke my leash and bolted under the fence.'

'And look where you are. Movies! Men! Millionaires! And, my dear friend, the gate is open. Go where you want.' She leaned over and squeezed Grace's hand.

'We'll see, we'll see. But what about you? C'mon, what's your current deep dark secret?'

Mel spread her arms. 'Numbers always add up. You can never change that two and two equals four.'

'What does that mean?' said Grace, shaking her head in confusion.

'Buggered if I know. Just thought it sounded like the sort of thing a maths whiz would say.' Melanie grinned.

Grace laughed. 'You're such a frustrating friend. You get me to spill my guts and you don't tell me anything about your life.'

'I'll tell you one thing for free . . . as my dad always said to me. I wouldn't let that Steve stray too far. He's nuts about you, even if he doesn't know it yet.'

Grace paused. 'Only you, Mel. You're the only one who shoots straight from the hip.' Another reason she loved her, Grace thought.

'I know what you're saying, Mel,' she said, more serious now. 'Lawrence has screwed me around, and I'm nervous about starting anything new. Mum sees it too. Also, I don't want to complicate what is a great working relationship. Steve and I have to work together. I want him to stay in my life in some capacity. I really like him. I don't want to frighten him off.' Grace sat up straight and looked at Mel. 'Oh, I've so missed our deep and meaning-fuls. Thank you.' She bounced up and smiled. 'Let's go. I have the morning off.'

They took Daisy to school and waved till she was inside. Then Grace smiled at Mel and felt almost light-headed. The two of them together could do anything. It was a sensation she'd forgotten; that feeling of being carefree. With her friend beside her, Grace was starting to look at the world differently.

Then her phone rang, and when she saw who the caller was, it was as if a black cloud had suddenly descended.

Mel was talking to one of the school mothers, so Grace walked quickly out of earshot.

'Hello, Grace, sorry to disturb you,' said Mr Judd. 'I thought it easier to ring you.'

'Oh, no, Mr Judd. What's he done now?' Grace sighed. 'Sorry. Thank you for calling, but I'm assuming this is not good news.'

'Well, it depends. Lawrence's lawyer has contacted me to say his client will fully cooperate with the divorce process. He has no alternative, actually, but this is better than if he tried to throw obstacles in our way, which can happen.'

Grace stopped still. What was this? It sounded positive, but she couldn't quite bring herself to believe that Lawrence was interested in cooperating. 'So . . . that's good news, I suppose,' she said.

'It's a good start, yes,' replied Mr Judd. 'There's more, though: we have just received a date for the mediation, which is in two weeks. I'll send through the details. Lawrence's lawyer was on to it very quickly, and he's informed me of the line they'll be taking: Lawrence wants custody of Daisy, and there are some other matters. He made it clear Lawrence is not willing to negotiate his terms. I should also let you know that he now has a slick lawyer working for him as well as the man I've been dealing with.'

Grace was almost speechless. Lawrence's threats had mostly been a lot of hot air to this point, but it now looked like he was playing hard ball. She managed to ask, 'What are the other matters?'

Mr Judd sighed. 'As well as custody, he wants you to pay child support.'

'*What?* He wants *me* to pay *him*, when he hasn't paid me a single cent for Daisy's upkeep ever since we separated!' Grace felt rage throbbing through her. She took a long breath and tried hard to calm down.

'I suspect he's after money and you're the easiest target,' Mr Judd said. 'Worst case scenario is that if he were given custody of Daisy, and you were earning money while he was not, you might be required to pay some child support.'

'Does he have any chance of getting full custody?' said Grace, suddenly close to tears. 'I can't believe he'd try this! I very much doubt he even wants custody of Daisy. I just don't understand.'

'As we've discussed, it's unlikely he'd get sole custody. But if you can't agree at mediation, which seems likely now, the next step is to proceed to court. Even if you were to win in court – and I think you'd have a strong case – it would be emotionally draining as well as expensive.' He paused, then continued. 'I know this is a lot to take in, Grace, but unfortunately there's something else as well. I don't know if you've had a chance to check your messages today, but your solicitor Mr Jamison has emailed you, and he copied me in as the matter also concerns Lawrence.'

'Oh no – what?' said Grace, dreading his reply.

'Lawrence has relisted the Paddington apartment for sale.'

'Of course he has,' said Grace in a flat tone. What more could possibly happen? she wondered. She felt like she was hanging on by a thread, which was probably exactly what Lawrence wanted. She steeled herself. No. She would not let him get to her. 'Okay, Mr Judd,' she said as calmly as she could, 'what should we do about all this?'

'All right, let's just take things step by step,' said Mr Judd. 'From what I can gather from his lawyer, Lawrence seems anxious to move on with this new woman of his, Alicia Feng. As I've explained before, if he can show he's in a stable relationship with her, it may help his case. I know she's a businesswoman and is part of an influential Chinese family from Singapore, who are keen to establish permanent Australian connections. There could be a trade-off. You must consider your bargaining chips,' he said carefully. 'Think through all you have learned about him: what information he would not want made public, for example. Do your research about the Feng family. That's all the advice I can offer, and it's all unofficial. But I'm here for you when you are ready to make a legal move, and of course, we should speak again next week to discuss the mediation.'

Grace thanked Mr Judd and ended the call, but she stood still for a few more moments, stunned, sifting through the lawyer's conversation and reading between the lines of his advice. Things had come to a head, she realised. What he was telling her was that the ball was in her court for match point. If she didn't hit it back, hard, as a winning shot, she might lose more than just the game.

Think through all you have learned . . . She'd learned a lot, that was for sure. Not just all the ins and outs of Lawrence's complicated life, so much of it a mystery to her, so much he'd kept secret, but about herself, too. She had to be ready for this fight.

Would Grace-before-the-fire ever have dreamed of standing up to Lawrence, supposedly a big successful CEO, even though he only ever worked alone? A man who told lies and didn't face reality? She knew the answer was no, but she was ready to take him on now.

'Mel,' she said when her friend come over to her. 'A change of plans. We have to go back to the villa; we have work to do!'

*

Tina brought them coffee as the two women made notes, scrolling through their phones finding old emails and messages. Grace wiped her eyes, and occasionally banged on the table, cursing Lawrence. Mel searched the internet for information about Alicia, her parents and the extended Feng family. They assembled facts, collated figures and events, and began to put together a clear picture of the manipulations and misdemeanours of a marriage.

Grace sent off emails to both Mr Judd and Mr Jamison, asking for advice and filling them in on all the information she and Mel were collecting, and what she was planning to do with it.

'Now don't forget, you have notarised photocopies of the stuff we found in his office safe,' Mel said. 'You have the copy of his old passport, the jewellery Lawrence moved to the safe, other documents –'

'Like what?' asked Grace. 'There really wasn't much in the safe.'

'But he doesn't know what you've seen or not seen,' said Melanie. 'What about Beatrice, his sister? Can you ask for more info about this Sarah and the son Jamie? Did Sarah actually marry Lawrence? Where are they? Does he support them?'

Grace looked dubious. 'I doubt he's ever given them a cent, unless he paid her to disappear from his life. It must have been about fifteen years ago. And I doubt she'd want to get involved with anything to do with him. Steve was right: not having Lawrence in their lives is probably a blessing. They're not going to want to tangle with him now.'

'Well, at least ask Beatrice where they are,' Mel said. 'You can make it clear that you don't want to bother them. Information is going to be the best ammunition we have.'

'Okay. I guess then I'll have more facts to put to him.'

Tina sat down and stared at the laptops, phones and notepads covering the table. 'May I ask what you're planning, exactly?' she asked quietly.

'The showdown to end all showdowns,' said Mel. 'Grace is going to call Lawrence's bluff.'

Tina looked shocked. 'How? You never know with Lawrence . . . he can bluff better than anyone and spout what sounds like ridiculous bulldust only to damn well pull something off.'

'Or he just gets lucky. You never know with liars, cheats and conmen,' said Mel.

Grace was reading the email from Mr Judd in which he'd forwarded the details of the mediation date, and tapped her finger thoughtfully on the table. 'What I can't work out is why Lawrence is suddenly okay with the idea of a divorce, but desperate to have Daisy and not willing to negotiate about anything else. What's he up to?'

Mel's eyes widened 'What's more romantic and stable than a loving single father? I bet he's just going to use Daisy as a prop, so he can present a squeaky clean image to help woo this Alicia!'

Grace sat up straight. 'Now there's a thought. Alicia Feng . . . Mr Judd said she's a businesswoman from an influential family.'

'She sure is. Listen to this.' Mel flipped to an internet page on her laptop. 'To paraphrase this article, the Fengs are old money, highly regarded, and they have been running major businesses in Singapore for generations.' She read on further to herself then said, 'Have connections in Malaysia. Recently invested in a tech enterprise in KL and Australia is next in their sights. Seems they want to do something in the Australian education and training sector for students from Singapore. That's a big part of the student body at my uni,' Mel said. 'It's certainly still a money-spinning growth area.'

'I'll bet Lawrence wants some money to splash around and impress Alicia and her family, and a neat divorce so he can tie the knot with her quick smart.'

Mel grinned. 'We need to leverage this, Grace. The Fengs would want to be squeaky clean. They couldn't tarnish their reputation by anything Lawrence did or has done in the past, because word would spread among other wealthy families who are considering sending their kids to Australia.' She sat back and smiled. 'It can work to your advantage if he wants the divorce to go through smoothly and quietly just as much as you do, Gracie.'

'But what about the flat?' Tina sounded worried.

'I won't let the sale happen, Mum. I'll text Lawrence now to arrange a meeting. I want this sorted before it gets any messier or, god forbid, gets to court.'

'He's in Kuala Lumpur,' said Tina. 'Are you going there?'

'I will if I have to. I'm not waiting about.'

'I'll come with you,' said Mel.

Grace shot a smile at her friend. 'Thanks. But you can't be at the meeting, so I'd rather you stayed here, if that's okay. This is between Lawrence and me. I appreciate the offer, though,' Grace added, more firmly than she felt.

'Atta girl,' said Mel.

'Do you think Lawrence will agree to this meeting?' asked Tina dubiously.

'He'll probably try stalling, but I'll say we should have one last attempt at coming to an agreement before the mediation. He can hardly say no to that without looking unreasonable.' Grace finished typing the text, sent it, then put her phone down. 'Done.'

'Good one, Grace. Now we wait. And in the meantime, let's get back to work.'

*

Later that afternoon, Lawrence replied. Mel grimaced as she read the text over Grace's shoulder. 'Typical Lawrence,' she said.

'What is it?' asked Tina.

'He's deliberately asking for the meeting on the afternoon of the grand opening of the Kamasan. He knows damn well Grace has to be here for it,' Mel said.

'It will be okay. This is more important,' said Grace. 'Of course I'd like to be there, but I can get Steve and the crew to cover my role if I have to. The preparations are all in place, anyway. I'll check with Johnny, of course, but I'm sure he'll be fine with it, and even if I miss some of the lead-up, I should be able to get there for the main event.'

'Lawrence knows how important that night is, and that you'd want to be there, which is why he's trying to ruin it for you,' said Mel angrily.

'This seems such a gamble.' Tina sighed. 'What if he just says no, he's going ahead with his plans?'

'Well, he might, but nothing ventured, nothing gained. He doesn't know what we know,' said Mel.

'And if he is pinning his hopes on this woman and her influential family in some way, he won't want details from his past to be aired in front of them, and he won't want any delays in the divorce,' said Grace. 'Lawrence always said timing is everything. I reckon this is my time. I have to get to him fast, before he can start to spin his wild tales to his girlfriend and her family.'

They went back to their work, and Tina headed out to the pool to 'calm down and stop thinking about what I'd like to do to that bloody man', as she told the girls.

'Forty-eight hours to go,' said Mel, standing up and stretching. 'Do you want me to book your flight?'

'When Andy called earlier, I told him what was going on. He said to let him know where I was at, and he'd arrange my travel through the Kamasan office.'

Mel smiled at her. 'He's a great mate, isn't he? I think he's taken you on as his new daughter.'

'Ha, you might be right.' Grace smiled gently, then stood up. 'I'd better start making plans with Steve, in case I won't be here when they film the opening.'

*

The time had gone quickly, but the more preparation she did, the more convinced Grace became that she was doing the right thing.

Steve and Mel stood by the car talking to Grace as Putu waited.

Tina had taken Daisy out, because she didn't want to get upset in front her as Grace left for the airport. Grace had told Daisy that she was going on a quick trip for work.

'But it's the big party, Mum,' Daisy had cried. 'Are you buying a new dress?'

'Well, that's a good idea.' Grace had tried to smile.

Putu glanced at his watch. 'Must go, Ibu Grace.'

'Okay, I'm as ready as I'll ever be.'

Mel gave her a quick hug. 'Now, let's run through this again – make sure you have your ammunition ready in your head; you can't look at notes and you can't forget anything. And you've got your lawyers' support, remember that, and mine and Steve's, and your mum's,' she said firmly.

'Don't cry, don't get upset. Be cool and calm. You *know* you're right. It's *your* bloody turn, Grace.' Mel was close to tears. 'You deserve it. Sometimes the good guys have to damn well win.'

Steve touched Mel's arm, reassuring her, as Mel let go of Grace. He gave Grace a warm hug, then, holding her shoulders, he looked into her eyes. 'We'll manage everything here. You've set it all up beautifully, and the crew know what they're doing. Just get back when you can. Don't let him bully you anymore. Those days are gone, Grace.' He smiled, locking her eyes with his. 'I'll be here waiting when you get back. Okay?'

'That makes me feel better. Thanks, Steve.'

He kissed her softly on the lips. 'We have a lot to look forward to, Grace. Go do what you have to.'

'Yeah, go get him!' cried Mel as Putu opened the car door.

As they drove away, Grace saw Steve put his arm around Mel to comfort her. She could never remember seeing Melanie cry before.

*

The airport hummed with cars and people as they drew up.

'I'll just jump out, Putu, don't bother parking.'

He nodded. '*Semoga berhasil. Salamat jalan*, Ibu Grace.'

Grace smiled over her shoulder as she pushed the door open. She'd need more than luck. '*Salamat tinggal*, Putu.'

She hardly registered the journey to Kuala Lumpur as she read through her notes of all she and Mel had learned and deduced, pared down to the facts, and she remembered Mel's advice to avoid any emotion.

Easier said than done, she thought wistfully. Her whole body thrummed with nervous tension.

At Lawrence's suggestion they'd agreed to meet at the Whisky Lounge bar at Marini's on the fifty-seventh floor of the Petronas Towers. It sounded masculine and intimidating, but his rationale had been that she could catch the fast train from the airport directly to the Petronas Towers. This was the place for a power suit, which she didn't have in Bali. So she'd chosen a simple white linen fitted dress and the Walter Spies scarf Johnny had given her slung across her shoulders.

She arrived early and found a couple of lounge chairs and a low table as far away from the bar as possible. She hated being a woman alone in a place like this. At least the lunch crush had dissipated. There was an older man reading a magazine nearby but the tables around her were empty. She turned her back to the room, ordered a coffee and looked at her phone, re-reading her notes.

'Good afternoon, Grace.' Lawrence suddenly loomed above her. He pulled out the chair opposite as a waiter hurried over.

'Good afternoon, Mr Hagen. What can I get you?' The waiter glanced at Grace with a polite but cool expression. 'Madam?'

'Another coffee. Thank you,' she said.

'An espresso and sparkling mineral water.' Lawrence sat down, putting his briefcase beside him and unbuttoning his jacket.

Grace recognised that smile; she'd seen him use it on people he had no time for, but whom he needed or was humouring. For a moment she stared at him, seeing him as perhaps others saw him, and realised with a shock that he was a stranger. Had she ever really known him?

Had she been just another in a line of people he'd used, to meet a need or complete a picture? He'd wanted to present himself as a successful businessman and family man, and that was where she and Daisy had fitted in.

Was this the man she had given up her career goals for, the man she'd wanted to start a family with? The man she'd thought she'd loved, with whom she'd had sex, a child, and with whom she'd been prepared to spend the rest of her life?

He smiled easily. 'You're looking very well, Grace. Classy, successful, always an attractive woman. Asia agrees with you.'

She ignored this. She wasn't going to give his artificial flattery any more oxygen. Instead, she launched straight in. 'Lawrence, it sounds to me like we are now on the same page about a divorce. I'd like nothing more than for it to go through smoothly and as soon as possible. And I think we would both like to settle our other issues out of court. Do you agree?'

'Perhaps,' said Lawrence coolly.

'Well then, there are only two things I want. First, I want to dissolve the family trust to ensure that ownership of my Paddington flat will go to Daisy when she comes of age. And second, I want custody of Daisy. She will live with me and I will remain her primary parent. I have documents prepared to finalise both these matters.'

Lawrence threw his head back and laughed. 'No way in hell, Grace. Didn't my lawyer tell yours that I won't negotiate on either of those points? It's laughable that you'd even try.'

'If you'll hear me out, Lawrence,' said Grace mildly, 'I think you might have a change of heart.'

'Don't be a fool, Grace,' said Lawrence coldly.

Grace pretended to change the subject. 'Tell me, just what are your plans with this poor woman you've romanced?'

Lawrence blinked. 'Poor is not a word I would use to describe Alicia or her family. She is an exceedingly smart businesswoman.'

'Then what's she doing with you, Lawrence?'

His smiling mask dropped instantly and she saw the Lawrence she recognised.

'You don't have to be vulgar, Grace.'

Grace leaned forward. 'Just what do you want, Lawrence? You know I would never willingly give up custody of Daisy. So why are you pushing so hard on this point? To come out looking like a good guy? You know damn well I have no money from our life together, even though I was the one earning a regular salary when I squeezed a job in between being a mother and a house-wife, and making you look good.'

'Rah-rah for you, Grace. That's what wives do. Support their husbands. And you seem to be raking it in now, with your cushy job.'

'I have no interest in supporting someone whose modus operandi is lying, cheating in business, and hiding his family history. I don't think anyone would be keen on that.'

His eyes narrowed. 'What's that mean?'

'Well, I just think there are a lot of things Alicia might like to know about you, things I suspect you might not have told her.'

'Don't be ridiculous,' Lawrence said, though Grace could see the tension in his jaw.

Grace pressed on, again catching Lawrence off guard. 'Why did you choose the name Lawrence Hagen? What was wrong with Justin Kenneth Odford?'

Lawrence couldn't hide the flash of shock that registered on his face, but he controlled it in an instant. 'I don't know what you're talking about.' His answer was too quick.

Looking at him, she felt a small glimmer of elation. At last she had an advantage over him, had managed to score a point in spite of his arrogant, conniving ways.

She lowered her voice. 'I know it all, Lawrence. You don't have a posh, rich family in Sussex, you have a working-class family in the fishing industry in Grimsby, who no doubt sacrificed lots to send you to a half-decent school . . . but certainly not Oxford or Cambridge. Your sister Bea seems perfectly lovely to me. Yet you have abandoned them.'

'Just stop right there, Grace.' He sat up straight and hissed at her. 'This has nothing to do with you and me. What happened with my family is my business –'

'No, it's not. Daisy is part of that family too, don't forget. Were you ever going to let her meet them? And, which family are we talking about? What about Sarah and Jamie in California?'

Lawrence's eyes flickered and his hand, resting on the table, tightened convulsively on his napkin. Grace pressed on.

'Bea has told me all about them. Does your new girl-friend and her family know any of this? I assume not.'

Lawrence drew a short breath. 'They have nothing to do with any issues between us, Grace.'

She almost laughed. 'How can you say that?' She shrugged. 'But whatever.'

He looked taken aback that she'd seemed to drop the subject.

'There are other things, though, you know,' she said conversationally. 'For example, selling my Paddington apartment. Which you know is meant for Daisy. It's not the best look, you'll agree – selling your daughter's apartment out from under her.'

'I have responsibility for it, as *you* well know, because I have the legal rights to manage our assets.' His face was turning red but Grace could tell he was trying to stay calm. 'All our valuables are covered in the family trust. You are the co-signatory and I manage it.' He spoke as if to a child.

'Yes. Because you gave me the documents to sign when I was pregnant and told me you were setting things up for our child's future. How did I know what I was signing?' Grace raised an eyebrow. 'I remember you smiled at me and said there was no need to read it – and I trusted you, as a person should be able to trust her spouse.'

He shrugged. 'You should have asked a few questions.'

'I should have, but I shouldn't have needed to. You conned me; you conned your own wife. As no doubt you conned the insurance company over the house fire. But then you had help. What's his name? Oh yes, Tony Freeman.'

There it was again: that twitch of the eye and hand that showed she was finding chinks in his armour. Grace continued in a low, insistent voice. 'Did you know the insurance company's legal team is looking into allegations against a certain insurance investigator, Tony Freeman, who has been accused of taking bribes to falsify insurance claims? For instance, that certain fires were "accidentally" caused by some technical fault, when in reality they were deliberately lit by a professional hired to do the job?' Grace sat back and sipped her coffee, watching Lawrence carefully. 'Perhaps this man, Freeman, had plans to split the proceeds with the crooked owners who were in on the arrangement with him.'

Putting her cup down, she watched the effect of her words sink in.

Lawrence spluttered, 'Are you suggesting what I think you're suggesting? Grace, this is preposterous rubbish. Pure speculation. You have no proof of any of this. You're just angry that you lost valuable things in the fire. But you were never entitled to anything from that place. I paid for all of it.'

'So you keep reminding me. I tried, but I never liked that house. It's typical that you bulldozed over what anyone else thinks, Lawrence. You never considered what I thought or liked or wanted.'

She could see his mind was whirring.

'You were responsible for that house too,' he shot back. 'It was in the family trust. You also have to be responsible for its loss.'

'But it won't be my name that comes up when the insurance investigator goes to jail for fraud and reveals the identities of everyone who came in for a cut on his tacky deals,' said Grace. 'The lawyers from the insurance company have asked to speak to me about the fire.' This wasn't strictly true, but Grace knew it would spook Lawrence even further.

And it was working: a vein had popped out on his forehead as he ground his jaw. 'You don't know anything about it, no one does. You can't prove a single thing.'

This was what Grace had been waiting for. 'Maybe not,' she said quietly, 'but there are a few things I'm sure the lawyers – and the police – would be interested to hear. Let's start with the cars. For some reason, you took your fancy car to drive a few blocks to the Robinsons' house on the night of the fire, not my old station wagon as we usually did. You always kept your precious car locked in

378

the garage. Second, just before we left that evening I stuck my head in the door of your study to hurry you up. You were putting documents in your precious briefcase – the one I gave you – that you always kept locked on the floor next to your desk.' She saw him shift slightly in his seat. 'Yet, oddly, you drove your car, with your briefcase in it, to a casual dinner. So when the fire broke out, both of those things were miraculously safe. That's the briefcase. Still can't part with it, eh?' Grace pointed to the mono-grammed briefcase she'd given him and knew so well, which was resting on the seat beside him. She went on. 'And how strange that you had suddenly "decorated" your office with your most precious possessions, those pieces of antique silverware? And, according to Jenny, your PA, you did it only a couple of weeks before the fire.'

Grace took a breath. She could see fury, and something else – could it be fear? – bubbling below the surface of Lawrence's still stony expression. She continued, 'You must be pleased that certain other items escaped the house fire, too. What luck that you moved all my jewellery, without telling me, to your office safe. You can return that to me at your leisure, Lawrence. I did wonder why you would bother keeping an out-of-date passport, though.'

'This is all purely circumstantial. Wouldn't hold up in court for a second,' Lawrence snapped. 'It proves nothing.'

Grace went in for the kill. 'Maybe not. But then again, if I were to pass on the details and raise the alarm, so to speak, maybe it would be enough to start an inves-tigation. Do you really want your name – and through you, the good name of the Fengs, too – associated with a scandal like that?'

She saw his inner turmoil as he struggled against shouting or hitting her. He looked like he was trying to find a quick answer. She noticed that the bartender was watching them. Lawrence must have seen him too as, with what seemed a monumental effort, he chose to try charm instead.

'Grace, I came here to reach an arrangement with you, as we are both after the same thing. It's very simple. I want custody of my daughter and you have to pay for her support. You can give me that and cooperate, or I could force you into bankrupting your mother to pay your legal fees and compromise your job. I always plan every detail, you know that. That's my insurance policy.' He gave a thin smile and seemed to relax as he changed tack. 'You know, two can play the game you're playing. Stuff can get out there on the internet – lots of stuff – very, very cleverly photoshopped.'

'Like what, Lawrence? I've never done anything to be ashamed of.'

'These guys are good. You'd have to work *really* hard to convince the world it's not *really* you.'

She hesitated but straightened up. 'You'd try that hard?'

It was a stand-off for a second or two. Then out of the blue something came back to Grace. Whenever they'd watched a quiz show on TV, Lawrence had always tried to answer the questions, to show off what he knew whenever he could. If they were going to meet anyone with a high-profile job, Lawrence would swot like crazy about them and their field so he could challenge and debate them to show them how smart he was. Even at a friendly dinner party he always had to come out on top. It was a weakness of his, and she aimed straight for it now.

'I don't have to convince anyone of anything, I've earned my stripes,' she said smoothly, adding, 'I don't have to get honours degrees forged and a whole fake academic career mocked up so I can hang fraudulent certificates on the wall.' Grace had no idea if he'd done this, but she now recalled glimpsing framed certificates of some kind on her last visit to his office that she'd never seen before.

This time Lawrence didn't bother to hide the grimace that crossed his face. 'Rubbish. What bullshit. I can destroy you and your fragile reputation.'

'Well, go ahead and test me then.' She folded her arms. 'Nobody who knows me well would ever believe anything you say or do, especially if I let them know that's what you're planning. And you don't have to resort to gutter language.'

Grace knew his mind must be spinning as he looked for another bluff or threat, so she ploughed on before he could settle on one.

'So, Lawrence, I'm asking you to reconsider. I want a new start. My lawyers have prepared documents: one dissolving the family trust, and another in which we jointly agree that I will be Daisy's primary parent.' She took the papers from her bag and put them on the table in front of him. 'As you know, if we submit reasonable, signed parenting consent orders, there is no need for us to go to court. But if you'd rather go to court, really, it's fine by me – because when they hear that you abandoned a son for fifteen years or more, it'll be pretty clear you don't really care about your kids. They're just weapons to you, pawns in your great scheme of making yourself number one.' She leaned back, suddenly feeling drained.

Lawrence was not one to cave in. 'Don't fight me, Grace. I always win,' he said smoothly. 'I am sure we can come to a compromise.'

Grace's flagging mood lifted. Although she wasn't across the line yet, this was a concession. He hadn't walked off arrogantly as he normally did. He was trying to negotiate. She felt a flush of triumph that, finally, she'd hit a nerve. She took aim at another one.

'By the way, Lawrence, speaking of your former family, Beatrice said to tell you that your father is very frail. She knows you've had your differences, but she was wondering if you were man enough to reach out before he dies.' Seeing this stab home, Grace looked away. 'Just passing on a message.'

'Enough of this. What do you want, Grace?' he asked calmly, if coldly.

Grace looked Lawrence straight in the eyes. 'I want to be left alone. I'm not asking for money. And I won't unfairly prevent Daisy from seeing you, but you cannot have full custody of her. You drop your threat of taking her from me, and I will not pursue you. We will come to an arrangement where you will help me financially with her support, and I will not be unreasonable.' Grace paused and breathed in. 'I will not tell anyone about your name change or the son you left behind. As you say, that is your business, not mine . . . although it might not look good to your friend Alicia Feng and her family. I probably won't say anything to the insurance people either.' She stopped and looked at him.

'That's it?'

'Unlike you, I don't like playing games, Lawrence. Take it or leave it. I have to go back to work.' She paused for a beat. 'With the Pangisars. One of the most influential families in Indonesia. As you well know. Shame about your aborted deal with the cybersecurity cameras. The Pangisars are very good to me.' She took another stab in the dark. 'They are a well-connected family, as you may know. And of course, they are socially and financially connected to Alicia's family here in Malaysia.' She lowered her voice. 'Whatever you're trying to pull off with them, through Alicia, could be jeopardised very quickly by my boss, should I mention it.'

Lawrence shot her a furious look which Grace could instantly read as, *Since when do you call the shots, bitch?*

She stared directly at him, so he could read the silent challenge written on her face. *Since right now. Final offer, Lawrence. Or whoever you are.* She pulled a pen out of her bag and put it on the table in front of him. 'I am willing to go to court if I have to. As you can see, I have a lot of information to share – more than you know. Or we can settle this right now. It's up to you. Sign these, and then keep your word for once, Lawrence.'

There was an agonising silence. Lawrence stared at her with cold hard eyes as if she were a stranger and there had never been a kind or loving moment between them. Then he snatched the two documents and skimmed them.

Even though this was what she had hoped for, Grace found she was astonished it was actually happening. Suddenly it hit her. There might have been others out there – women and perhaps children who had been in his life. He didn't know who she might have found, what she might know, and he couldn't take a chance.

Lawrence finished reading and looked up. 'Don't look smug, Grace,' he said in a grating voice. 'But, all right. I agree.'

He scrawled his signature on the bottom of each page and shoved the papers back across the table. Grace signed her name next to Lawrence's on each document while he drummed his fingers angrily on the table-top. Then she signalled the sniffy waiter for her bill, dropping the cash on his tray.

After the waiter had gone, Grace put the signed documents carefully into her handbag and put it on her lap. 'I'm glad we could come to an agreement. I'll let the lawyers deal with it from here. You know something, Lawrence? I had a lot of help with this, from other women. What's the saying? "A woman scorned . . ."? I hadn't realised I wasn't alone. At the end of the day, women will come together and support each other. We know that what you did to one of us could happen to all of us. When it comes to our survival and our kids, women will stick together. There are too many men like you out there, Lawrence. I wish I'd known that before I met you and got sucked in by your spin.'

Lawrence said nothing as he roughly handed her the pen, as if making a point. But there was no point to make, because Grace knew she had won.

'Thank you. Goodbye, Lawrence.'

He didn't answer, and she walked away, past the man at the nearby table, who was closing his magazine and counting out money to pay for his drink.

She concentrated on putting one step in front of the other, expecting Lawrence to call her back, to have changed his mind, to have the last word. But then suddenly she straightened her spine, stuck out her chin and strode forward with confidence. Then she was out the door and in the lift, swooping downwards, and suddenly she felt shaky, light-headed and dizzy, her breath coming in shallow gasps. She thought she was going to be sick. She doubled over for a minute and rested her hands on her knees, then straightened up.

Going outside to take a breath of air, she looked at the two Petronas Towers above her, which caught and reflected the sunlight. They were strong, impressive and almost otherworldly. She would bring Daisy here one day and they could explore this city together, she thought. Now, she realised, she could make plans for their life – for her and Daisy – without Lawrence's threats always over-shadowing her.

Sitting down in the train carriage, Grace realised she was still trembling, but the nausea had passed, replaced by a deep sense of relief and a sudden wild streak of joy. She had fought for Daisy, and for herself, and she had succeeded.

As the blur of scenery flashed past her window, Grace tried to rewind all that had transpired. Lawrence had signed the documents – she could barely believe it. She had been hopeful but realistic; she had thought he would fight her as he always had before.

When she called Tina and then Mel from the train, she could barely recall what she'd said to Lawrence, even though it was less than an hour ago. She had never stood up to him in all the time she'd known him, had never felt she'd had the upper hand, ever. She'd always disintegrated in tears and frustration. But this time Mel had pushed her, her mother and friends had supported her, the lawyers had worked quickly, and she'd been prepared. In standing up to Lawrence, she now realised, she had rattled him.

But most of all, she now knew there'd been another voice in her corner – and that was the voice of a woman alone, who'd been brave and strong, and gutsy, despite everything that had happened to her. Although Grace's own problems might pale in comparison to hers, Grace suddenly smiled – you never knew what you could do until you were tested, or where life might take you.

'I owe you one, K'tut!' She blew a kiss to the sky outside the train speeding her forward.

*

The sun had set by the time Putu reached the Kamasan entrance, which was packed with limousines and staff ushering guests into the magnificent lobby while flashes from cameras sparked like fireflies. The press were now banned from the grounds and hotel complex as they'd had their red-carpet moments, opening photos and sound grabs earlier. The mega names present were not to be photographed by the paparazzi as they let their hair down and enjoyed themselves in the protection and privacy of the Kamasan.

Grace hurried through the staff entrance, talking to Rosie on her phone. 'I'm in the kitchen behind the main bar. Where are you?'

'On the mezzanine with the Pangisars. Take the stairs up from the bar and I'll meet you there.'

Grace raced up the quieter set of stairs, where the guests wouldn't see her. She didn't want to join the party in her day clothes.

'How's it going?' she panted when she reached Rosie.

Rosie smiled at her. 'All systems go. C'mon, there's a small bedroom here where you can get ready.'

'Thanks, Rosie. Do you know if my friend Mel dropped off my bag?' Grace hadn't had time to buy anything new but had packed a dress and shoes in a hurry and asked Mel to bring them to the hotel.

'Mmm, I'm not sure,' said Rosie distractedly. 'Here we are.' She pushed a door open. Standing on a table was a bucket of iced champagne and a small vase of flowers.

'This is for you from Johnny.' Rosie poured her a glass. 'I only just opened it.'

Grace looked around but couldn't see her overnight bag.

'We'll celebrate properly afterwards,' Rosie said. 'But for now, Johnny and your friend Melanie have a little surprise for you. Check the dressing room.'

Puzzled, Grace took a sip of the icy Taittinger, the bubbles sparkling as she drank. 'Okay.'

She opened the door to the dressing room to see a length of champagne-coloured silk draped on a hanger like a river of shimmering light, sparkling with small crystals.

She gasped. 'I don't believe it! That is so beautiful!'

Rosie stuck her head around the door. 'Johnny thought it was very you. Melanie helped him choose it. It's by one of our top designers. Get dressed – there's make-up, perfume, hair things all there on the vanity in the ensuite. Johnny was hoping you'd be in time for the opening speeches. Half an hour, okay?'

'Where's my crew?'

'Busy.' She smiled. 'All good. See you later.'

'This is crazy. Thank you, Rosie.'

Grace stripped off and lifted the hanger, finding silky matching underwear. 'Mel, you've thought of everything,' she murmured, and smiled with delight.

The dress slithered over her lightly tanned frame, feeling like a second skin. It clung in the right places but swung as she moved, reflecting different shades of warm gold and silver. It was the most beautiful dress she'd ever worn. There were shoes that matched, casual slides with a low heel, simple but elegant. She knew all this would have cost a ridiculous amount of money. She touched up her make-up, pinned up part of hair, leaving a few blonde tendrils loose, tucked the fresh gardenia from the vase into her hair, then saw a small box and a card with her name on it sitting on a side table. She slid out the card.

You have Grace-d our Kamasan with your dedication, hard work and beautiful smile. You are part of our success. Please always think of this as your second home. A small memento.
Johnny and Harold P.

Inside the box was a pair of exquisite diamond earrings. Shakily, she put them on, trying not to cry and ruin her make-up.

And then the madness began.

After a knock on the door, Mel danced in, dressed in a short, sparkling, emerald-green dress that was dazzling yet casually showed off her long brown legs and back. Her red-auburn hair was artfully styled, and her drop earrings captured the light. They'd spoken on the phone a second time while Grace was waiting for her flight, and Mel had made Grace repeat verbatim, as best she could, every moment of The Showdown.

'Hey, champ!' They raced to hug each other. 'I'm so proud of you! I can't believe it!' Mel squealed.

'Neither can I, but it's done. It's over.' Grace laughed with relief and happiness.

'And this is the perfect way to celebrate,' said Mel. 'Wait till you see the boys! They're all spivved up. Steve insisted. C'mon, let's go, they're doing the speeches in a minute.'

'Where did you get that dress? What there is of it,' asked Grace, admiring Mel.

'Johnny and I went shopping. I paid for mine. But we

had a lot of fun. He's a crazy guy. Pretends to be so tough,' she added.

'You got him in one,' said Grace.

Then they were swallowed up in a swirl of action, as events rolled on exactly as Johnny had planned.

Suddenly Henry was at her side. 'Hi. Wow, you look hot, Grace! We're over there. Steve has set up the three cameras, follow me.'

'You look pretty darn good too,' she said, noticing Henry's new shirt and trousers, which replaced his usual t-shirt and old jeans.

The opening ceremony was short but filled with heart-felt speeches and thank yous, delivered at the top of the sweeping staircase in the massive foyer of the Kamasan. One of the revered artists spoke on behalf of Kamasan village, thanking the Pangisar family for their support and the beautiful showcasing of the important pieces of art hanging above them.

Then in a surprise twist that had the crowd laughing one minute, then dabbing at their eyes the next, Johnny and his father spoke of their shared dream for this place. Johnny was first.

'I'd like to welcome and thank all our foreign friends – you *bule*! Our long-time friend Andy over there, who truly is a great mate. As many of you know, Andy wears the mantle of *bule* proudly and we love him for that, as we Indonesians also tend to call a spade a spade. As you might also know, I was educated among the *bule* in Australia. At first, I thought it lived up to its repu-tation as being outrageously racist . . . until I realised many people were simply having a joke. Australians do that a lot. Anyway, what I am trying to say is thank you to all my Aussie *bule* mates for teaching me not to take life too seriously, to always appreciate your family, and to hang on to good friends. Now, here is my father . . .'

Johnny handed the microphone to Harold and draped an arm about his shoulders as Harold spoke.

'The Kamasan represents not just a hotel, but a place for visitors to briefly share what makes us Balinese – it is filled with blessings of love, beauty, hospitality and generosity. We invite you to share our respect for our land, our culture and our past, and to pass on a future to our children where everyone may share a little in all these things that the Kamasan represents. Welcome to our family.'

The speeches ended and the applause thundered.

Amid the sounds of laughing guests, the smell of flowers and roasting food, the gongs rang out. The traditional dances were about to begin on the garden stage, lit by flame torches and stunning subtle lighting effects, which were studded around the grounds as if conjured by a magic wand.

Grace felt a hand gently take her arm.

'Hey, fairy princess!' said Steve softly.

'Hey, look at you.' She smiled. He was wearing a signature Johnny silk shirt tucked into crisp linen trousers. 'Everything under control?'

'You bet. They're an excellent crew. It's all going to look stunning when we edit it together.' He was still holding her arm. 'You okay? Sounds like you did great.'

'I think I did. And I think Lawrence will keep his word this time.'

'I'm sure he will. Johnny and old Harold will make sure of it, I reckon. Apparently they had a fellow watching on the whole time in the Whisky Lounge, in case Lawrence caused you any trouble. They think the world of you. So do I.'

'Is that your professional opinion?' She smiled, tilting her head.

'You're flirting!' He laughed and wrapped his arms around her. 'I think you're gorgeous and clever, and we're going to be an amazing team.' He pulled her to him and kissed her long and lovingly. Grace felt herself shiver and start to melt as some inner barrier gave way, and warmth took its place.

'I should get to work,' Grace said, smiling and pulling away from him. 'I can't come in late and then just swan around.'

'It's fine. I'll go and check on the crew but I know Mateo and Henry will have everything in order.' He took her hands. 'You go and find your mum. She's been worried about you, but she was trying hard not to let anyone know.'

'Okay, I will. Thanks for looking after her.' She reached up and kissed him.

She found Andy and Tina dancing with Daisy, who wore a new dress, the coloured batik print flowers outlined in tiny beads and little crystals that sparkled. A tiara of flowers was securely anchored around her head. When she saw her mother, Daisy ran over, squealing, and threw herself at Grace, who held her darling child as if she'd never let her go. And now, she hoped, she would never have to.

'Gracie,' Tina called, coming over to join them. 'Honey, I am so proud of you.'

Grace reached out and took her mother's hand. 'I have lots more to tell you, but it can wait.'

A drifting parade of staff and friends stopped by to chat with Andy and Grace, compliment Daisy on her dress and meet Tina. Andy opened a bottle of champagne and an ever-growing group joined them to celebrate the huge achievement that was the opening of the Kamasan, and Grace felt perfectly content for the first time in months.

*

It would soon be dawn. They were a small group sitting at the comfortable and now quiet bar pool area. Tina and Daisy had gone home long before; Grace, Steve, Mel, Johnny and Andy were lingering over their drinks. The crew had gone off on their own to party, and Rosie had a date.

Andy was in an expansive mood, knowing what a success his bars and eateries had been, as had every moment of the night.

'This won't be topped for a long, long time, mate,' he said to Johnny. 'Bruno and the band were bloody amazing.'

'One of the best nights ever,' said Mel.

'Grace, I have to tell you about the blessing ceremony,' Andy said. 'The leaders of the local *banjar* from the council precinct the Kamasan is in did the ceremony earlier this afternoon. Only the family and some of the team were invited,' he said. 'Everyone was dressed in ceremonial garb including Harold and Johnny. It was very special.'

'I'm so sorry I missed it.'

'Don't worry,' Steve put in. 'I was allowed to film it, so you'll see it when we start editing.' He smiled and stretched back in his chair.

'It's been a special day all round.' Grace sighed. 'You must be so proud, Johnny. All the work you did for so long behind the scenes paid off tonight.'

'Thank you, Grace, and thanks for inviting your friend Melanie.'

'Johnny's given me a job.' Mel laughed.

'What is it?' said Grace, looking from Mel to Johnny.

'I will head up the Kamasan Numeracy Program. We just cooked it up.' She lifted her glass. 'We're going to grow children's minds as well as their bodies, right, Johnny?'

'Exactly, Mel.' Johnny smiled affably.

'I'll still be working at the uni in Sydney, but overseeing this program and visiting when I can.'

'I'm amazed but not surprised,' Grace said. 'Bring two dynamic people together and watch out!' She laughed.

'Dawn is breaking, time for bed,' said Andy. He rose and hugged Grace and Mel goodnight, slapping Johnny on the back. 'G'night, old mate.'

'Want to see the sun rise?' said Steve to Grace.

'Sure. Let's walk along the beach,' she said, pulling off her shoes.

Mel and Johnny looked at each other. She held out her glass and he poured champagne.

'We'll hold the fort,' said Johnny.

'See you guys at breakfast,' called Mel, and she sipped her drink and smiled.

Holding hands, Grace and Steve walked through the soft grass and damp fallen flowers towards the beach where dreams were born and the tide washed away fears and worries.

As they passed the grove where K'tut's hotel had been, Grace took the flower from her hair and gently placed it on the cornerstone of the remains of the gateway to where a woman's dream still survived.

Epilogue

Twelve months later . . .

In the grounds of the Kamasan, the small replica of part of K'tut's hotel is finally finished, with the garden flowering, the shell paths shining, and on the terrace, several of 1930s Hollywood's elite stars, including Noël Coward, sit drinking G & Ts and champagne while playing cards. Smiling staff await their every command. And front and centre, in her loose batik Mother Hubbard dress, her dark hair tied back with a flower tucked in it, owl glasses almost dwarfing her face, strides the hotelier and hostess, the woman known on this magical island as K'tut Tantri.

'Cut.'

The actors relaxed and everyone else immediately stopped what they were doing.

From under the shade of the coconut palms, a woman's voice said, 'Tell Noël Coward to learn how to shuffle cards properly, for goodness' sake. Get him to practise!'

Steve chuckled. 'Well spotted. Are you a card shark, Gracie? That's one thing I didn't know about you.' He glanced at his watch and called out, 'Take a break, folks. Fifteen minutes.'

The drinks man, hired from the village, hurried forward with his trolley filled with ice and cold drinks, the make-up artist's tissues keeping cool near the ice. The cast flopped in chairs as the crew checked equipment, re-set furniture and props, and huddled with the assistant director. The continuity editor snapped photos and Alli, who was now an essential part of the team, looked at her schedule.

Steve sat in the director's chair beside Grace, who was checking their shooting script.

'You okay?' He leaned over and squeezed her shoulder.

'Yep.' She turned to him. 'Hard to believe we're a third of the way through the script already. It's all actually happening.'

'Wouldn't have without you. You're determined, aren't you? Another reason why I love you.'

Grace smiled. 'Some of it was luck and a lot of it was thanks to you. Through your detective work I met Tim, who led me to Michael, who became the executor of K'tut's estate after Sandra passed away. And that was where the brown suitcases stashed under beds came in.'

'What do you mean?'

'That's where Michael had it all stored. Didn't I tell you?' Grace turned and looked at Steve. 'He'd sort of forgotten about K'tut's papers till I asked, and then he rummaged under a bed in his apartment and found them in a couple of old suitcases. He's such a lovely man.'

'As is our mate Tim. I hope he approves of our film.'

Grace glanced around. 'The Pangisars have done such a fabulous job with this garden and the recreation of the front rooms of the hotel. I think K'tut would have loved it.'

'Johnny said he'd turn it into guest accommodation after we've finished filming.'

'I'd stay in it,' Grace said, her gaze still soaking up the beautiful grounds. 'He's convinced our film is going to be a hit.'

'Hope so! Well, I'm off,' Steve said, standing up. 'I have a meeting with the location manager then I can do school duty. See you later.'

She leaned forward and took his hand. 'Thanks for collecting Daisy. She'll be excited to see you – her favourite person in Bali! Is anyone coming back for dinner?'

The villa they now shared as a couple had become a popular drop-in hub for their many friends linked to the Kamasan, the crew, and their lead actors.

'Nope. Just us tonight.'

'Okay. I told Mum I'd call. She's having Andy over for dinner. He wants to hear how things are going with us over here.'

'How's his mother?'

'Doing okay. She likes having him around. So does my mum! Andy does miss Bali, though. He said he might come over next month to check on things. Johnny has made him a kind of visiting specialist here.'

'Pierre does a great job running F & B. But he doesn't have Andy's pizzazz,' said Steve.

'True. I've noticed lots of changes in the time we were away. Even Johnny seems less "out there", but in a nice way.'

'Do you think Mel has calmed him down?' Steve said.

'Don't say that to Mel. She'd think it makes her sound too safe and staid!' Grace laughed. 'She loves coming up here. Did I tell you they're rolling out the numeracy program through the whole country now, not just in Bali?'

'Really? That's fantastic,' said Steve, and he pulled Grace up next to him. He pressed his lips to hers and their kiss lingered.

Grace hadn't told Steve all her news today as yet. She would tonight. Johnny had swung by earlier to tell her the latest gossip.

'I hear mutterings about Lawrence and Alicia down under,' he'd said. 'Her family put him up as the front man of one of their companies, and it looks like Lawrence was set up to take the fall if anything went wrong. Which seems to have happened.'

'I'm not surprised and I'm not sympathetic.' Grace had shaken her head. 'No matter what happens to him, where he goes, I'll never feel free of him, because of Daisy. But at least now I feel liberated and proud of myself that I stood up to him.' She'd looked at Johnny and said, 'It just worries me that there are so many women – bright, confident, clever women – who are under the control of men like Lawrence. I was lucky I had my mum's support and such good friends, and found myself in a place like this.'

'Don't underestimate what you did, Grace. I'm proud of you too,' Johnny had said. 'And . . . you're a free woman now.'

'I am and it feels amazing,' she'd said with a laugh.

'I still can't quite believe the divorce went through as smoothly as it did. But it gives me confidence that Lawrence will remain cooperative from now on. I hope so.'

Johnny had grinned. 'And what next for you?'

Grace had thought about Steve, such a gentle, talented and caring man, and now the centre of her life, along with Daisy. 'Well, it feels like the world is my oyster! Now that this film is under way, Steve and I will find another project. Never fear, Johnny, I have a few ideas.'

She and Steve weren't rushing anything, just working together, growing together with Daisy, and loving each other. Sometimes the gods did smile on you.

As everyone returned to the set to pick up the scene, Grace paused to glance over at the wonderful actress playing K'tut, who was listening closely as the assistant director led her through what he wanted in the next take. Mateo was hunched behind the camera and Henry was watching on, making notes for Steve. They were a tight-knit crew, and Grace felt they were pulling together a significant and special movie.

Yes, it was 'based on a true story', but she hoped it was a story that would more than entertain; that it would tell the tale of an extraordinary woman, in extraordinary times, in a place that captured your heart.

Di Morrissey
Arcadia

A breathtaking Tasmanian tale of ancient forests; of art and science; of love and, above all, of friendship.

In the 1930s, in an isolated and beautiful corner of southern Tasmania, a new young wife arrives at her husband's secluded property – Arcadia. Stella, an artist, falls in love with Arcadia's wild, ancient forest. And when an unknown predator strikes, she is saved by an unusual protector . . .

Two generations later, Stella's granddaughter, Sally, and her best friend, Jessica, stumble over Stella's secret life in the forest and find themselves threatened in turn.

What starts as a girls' adventurous road trip becomes a hunt for the story of the past, to solve the present, and save their future . . .

Praise *for Arcadia*

'There's no denying the beauty and opulence of Morrissey's rendering of place . . . She is a master of the genre.'
Weekend Australian

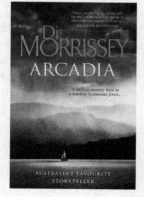

Di Morrissey
A Distant Journey

**Di Morrissey's A Distant Journey is a tribute to the real
Australia she knows so well.**

In 1962 Cindy drops out of college to impulsively marry
Australian grazier Murray Parnell, moving from the glamorous
world of Palm Springs, California, to an isolated sheep station
on the sweeping plains of the Riverina in New South Wales.

Cindy is flung into a challenging world at Kingsley Downs
station. While facing natural disasters and the caprices of
the wool industry, Cindy battles to find her place in her new
family and continues to feel like an outsider. As she adjusts to
her new life, Cindy realises that the Parnells are haunted by a
mystery that has never been solved. When she finally uncovers
the shocking truth, her discovery leads to tragedy and Cindy
finds herself fighting to save the land that she has grown to
love as her own.

Praise for *A Distant Journey*

'One of Morrissey's best tales yet.'
Australian Women's Weekly

'A sense of place . . . the sweep of
history, the winds of change which
blow through the towns and cities,
the forests and farms, the cold
mountain ranges and the hot,
dry deserts . . . fill her books.'
West Australian

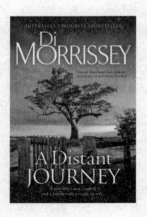

Di Morrissey
Tears of the Moon

**Tears of the Moon is the bestselling first book in
Di Morrissey's spellbinding Broome trilogy.**

Two inspiring journeys. Two unforgettable women. One
amazing story.

Broome, Australia, 1893: It's the wild and passionate heyday
of the pearling industry, and when young English bride Olivia
Hennessy meets dashing pearling master Captain Tyndall,
their lives are destined to be linked by the mysterious power
of the pearl.

Sydney, Australia, 1995: Lily Barton embarks on a search for
her family roots which leads her to Broome. But her quest
for identity reveals more than she could have ever imagined.

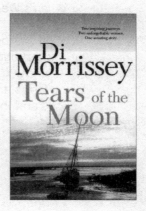

Di Morrissey
Kimberley Sun

The second book in the captivating Broome trilogy: a story about modern relationships and the unbreakable ties we all have to the past.

Lily Barton is beautiful, adventurous and 50-something. She is looking for a complete life change. Sami, her daughter, is 30, driving alone through the outback and finally, reluctantly, confronting her family roots. Together they are swept into a world where legends, myths and reality start to converge.

Those who come into their orbit bring stories that change each of them. From Farouz, the old Afghan camel driver, to Bobby, the Chinese/Aboriginal man who is tangled in the murder of a German tourist, to Biddy, the survivor from Captain Tyndall and Olivia's era . . . and who is the mysterious artist hiding in the desert? All have a secret and all have a story to tell until each finds their place under the Kimberley sun.

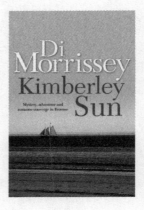

Di Morrissey
The Red Coast

**In the third and final book of the breathtaking Broome
trilogy, Di Morrissey returns to the red earth of the
Kimberley with a passionate story of resistance and
resilience under its soaring blue skies.**

After the upheaval which separated Jacqui Bouchard from
her beloved son, she has finally settled in Broome, a magical
remote town on the northwest coast of Australia.

But when a proposed mining development is unveiled, the
town begins to tear itself apart. Rifts run deep, as friends,
families and lovers are faced with a battle that could change
their lives irrevocably.

As everyone takes sides, Jacqui confronts her own dilemma:
to stay or leave? Who to trust . . . Who to love?

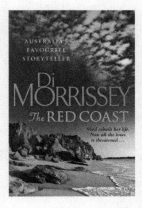

Di Morrissey
Heart of the Dreaming

**The book that launched Di Morrissey as Australia's most
popular female novelist.**

At twenty-one, Queenie Hanlon has the world at her feet and
the love of handsome bushman TR Hamilton.

Beautiful, wealthy and intelligent, she is the only daughter of
Tingulla Station, the famed outback property in the wilds of
western Queensland.

At twenty-two, her life lies in ruins. A series of disasters has
robbed her of everything she ever loved. Everything except
Tingulla – her ancestral home and her spirit's Dreaming place.
And now she is about to lose that too.

An extraordinary story of thwarted love and heroic struggle,
Heart of the Dreaming is the tale of one woman's courage and
her determination to take on the world and win.

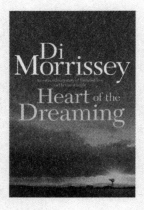